Coming Day

LITTLE DOZEN PRESS

Coming Day

Published by Little Dozen Press
Stevensville, Ontario, Canada
www.littledozen.com

Cover artwork by Deborah Thomson, copyright 2011
Cover design by Mercy Hope, copyright 2015

ISBN: 978-0-9739591-8-5

Coming Day

The Seventh World Trilogy
Book Three

Rachel Starr Thomson

Table of Contents

Prologue

The boy had wandered out of the mountains north of Angslie. He was small, blond, perhaps seven or eight years old. Where he could have come from was anyone's guess. His feet were not the tough goat-feet of a mountain child. They were bare, cut and bruised from walking, and soft like the skin of a newborn baby, though he blithely ignored any pain in favour of cheerfully investigating his surroundings.

Roland MacTavish was not sure what to do with him.

Roland had left his father's inn the night before, abandoning his responsibilities because, from his room over the tavern, he could hear the MacTavish and his comrades drinking up a wave that would last for days and break over Roland's head if he stuck around long enough. The MacTavish would be angry when he found his son missing, but by the time he had sobered, pride would prevent him from inquiring too much into where Roland had been while he was blindly, stupidly drunk.

Roland had lowered a rope from his window, left the village, and headed for the hills. He was fifteen years old, and he reveled in the night's freedom.

True dawn was a long time in coming. It sent out hints and lightened the sky while Roland followed little-known paths through the glens. He was looking north at the white rock formations that ran down the side of a mountain, and when he turned his face to the east, the sun all at once blazed in his eyes. He squinted and shaded his eyes to rid himself of the sun-puddles obscuring his sight, and as he did he became aware of a figure standing only ten feet in front of him.

His first impression was of a tall man, but as the sun cleared from his eyes he saw only a boy, small, with a white face and large eyes, clothes tattered and bare feet soft. The boy was wreathed in the light of the rising sun. Wind moved in the edges of his clothing and blew in his hair, the golden strands shining in the dawn light.

Competing instincts wrestled in Roland. One deep instinct yearned after mystery. The other instinct was for solid ground, somewhere to put a foot down and not feel the earth slipping away from beneath him.

He put his foot down. "Are ye lost?" he asked. His voice shattered the spell completely.

"No," the boy said.

Roland raised an eyebrow. "Where do ye live?"

The boy looked confused, then gestured vaguely to the hills. Roland began to grow impatient. "What do ye do with yourself?" he asked.

The boy looked at him and did not answer.

"Not terribly quick, are you?" Roland muttered. "Will anyone be missing ye?"

"No," the boy said.

"Well," Roland said, smiling in spite of himself, "come along then, Stray. Ye'll bide with me a few days."

A few days passed, and the child learned eagerly from

Roland and helped him fish, build a fire, and roam the hills. At night Stray tucked himself under Roland's arm and slept there. When the time had come to return home, Roland kicked dirt over his fire, rolled up his bundle of belongings, and sighed at the sight of the child playing in the dirt.

What could he tell his father? The MacTavish did not even like stray dogs or cats.

Perhaps he could convince one of the old women in the village to take the child in. But his mouth turned down of its own volition at the idea. There were two old women in the village, one toothless and nearly senseless, the other a drinker almost as bad as the MacTavish. One of the village families, then? But they had their own cares, their own children, their own needs to look after. The MacTavish, with a good livelihood and plenty of room in the inn, was the most likely candidate to be saddled with a foundling if the villagers decided it was their duty to take him in.

Besides, there was the money the MacTavish paid his son —just a small sum, laid away under Roland's straw mattress for the day he'd be a man. He could delay that day a little, use some of the money to make sure Stray was taken care of.

Roland hoisted his small pack over his shoulder. "Come along," he said.

* * *

"What do ye take me for, a fool?" the MacTavish snarled. Stray was playing in the yard behind the kitchen when Roland confronted his father. Hanging onions and root vegetables framed the MacTavish's head.

"But I'll pay for his keep myself," Roland protested.

"No ye won't," the MacTavish said. "I pay ye that money, and I say not a penny of it goes to the urchin. Ye'll keep it in your own pockets where it belongs!"

Roland's face burned, but he forced back the words he wanted to say. "He's got no one else. We were in the hills three days together; no one came looking for him."

"Then no one wants him," the MacTavish said. "And I'll trust they've good reason for it."

Roland turned away. He could still smell alcohol on the MacTavish's breath. Why should the money he helped earn pay for drink instead of helping Stray?

"I'll go to the magistrate," Roland said. "The village will judge what's right. They'll make us take him in; there's no one else so well suited."

"Well suited," the MacTavish repeated, disdain dripping from every syllable. "You think because we've a roof and an honest livin' that we ought to throw it all away."

"I think we ought to share it with one boy," Roland retorted.

"And I told you, I'll have none of it. You go to the magistrate. See what he says. I'll wager he'll not take your side any more than I do."

Roland stalked out of the kitchen and grabbed Stray's hand as he passed. The child tried to pull away, but Roland held the grubby fingers tightly.

"Where are we going?" Stray asked.

"To see the magistrate," Roland said. "We're goin' to find ye a home."

"But I'm staying with you," Stray said.

"Ye can't," Roland snapped. He stopped and looked down at the blue eyes that goggled up at his. "I'm sorry," he said. "My father says you'll not stay with us. So I've got to find ye another home. I'll come to see ye every day—I'll make sure you're taken care of. But we've got to find ye a willing roof first."

Stray looked away, obviously unconvinced of the worth of Roland's plan.

The inn was on the road just outside the village of Angslie, and soon they were in the town proper, passing the black-smith's shop and the collier's and the weaver's. At the end of the main street was a tall, gabled house covered in ivy: the home of the magistrate, the man who oversaw the affairs of the town under the lordship of Lord Robert Sinclair, Laird of Angslie.

The laird, of course, had been gone more than two years—he'd disappeared with Virginia Ramsey, leaving two dead soldiers behind. The laird's house had fallen into ruin; the villagers thought it a haunted and evil place. But the magistrate had not abandoned his post.

Curious onlookers watched the boys pass, and a small crowd of village lads gathered after them, whispering and poking each other. Roland ignored them. He climbed the steps to the magistrate's house, squared his shoulders, and rapped the knocker as loudly as he could.

After a few minutes the door swung open, and a tall man with a ponderous head and a wrinkled neck looked down on him. "Well?" he asked.

"Please, magistrate," Roland said. "I've found this stray. I want the village to take him in."

"Take him to your father," the magistrate said, peering

shrewdly at Stray.

"I tried that, sir," Roland said. "He won't take him in unless he's got orders to do it."

"Well," the magistrate said. "So you want me to give the orders, do ye, son?"

"To him or to another," Roland said. "It would be a shame to leave a child out in the hills alone."

"The hills?" the magistrate said. "And that is where you found him?"

"Yes, sir," Roland said.

The magistrate cleared his throat, and the loose flap of skin under his chin jiggled. "Ring the bell, boy. We shall call the village together and discuss the matter."

Roland nodded and hoisted himself up the ivy, over the window frame, and onto the roof where he grabbed the pull of a brass bell high over the front door. The yard was already filling with townspeople who'd seen him go past. He rang the bell as hard as he could and jumped down, sitting on the steps by the door and motioning for Stray to sit down beside him.

When the villagers—twenty or so men, including the MacTavish, and a collection of wives and children—had gathered in the dirt around the house, the magistrate cleared his throat again. "Hark ye all," he said. "Roland MacTavish has brought this child out of the hills and wishes us to take him in."

The announcement met with a slight clamour, and Roland looked across the crowd and met the eyes of Wee Cameron, the blacksmith, his oldest and best friend among the villagers. Cam inclined his head, but said nothing.

"He's small and scrawny," one woman offered. "He won't eat much."

"Looks like to work hard enough, if you push him to it," said the collier. "And young enough to train well."

"He's an outlander," spoke the MacTavish from the back of the crowd. "He's not one of us, and I want no part of him."

"He's a child!" Wee Cam said, giving the MacTavish a glare that could have moved boulders. A couple of the women chimed in.

With one finger stuck out like a schoolmaster's pointer, the weaver came forward and stopped just short of Stray. "He's from the hills," he said. "Came from near the House of Angslie, didn't he?"

Roland didn't answer, but shifted in discomfort. A murmur picked up again. The weaver waited for it to die down and said, "All is not right with the child. Ye can sense it—ye can smell it. He's got the cursed ways on him." The weaver's words seemed to affect the whole crowd at once. The magistrate took a step backward. And the cowardly action brought Roland's blood to a boil.

"He's a child!" he said, jumping to his feet. "Are ye afraid of a child? The laird would have taken him in!"

At those words, the crowd burst out in shouts and accusations. The weaver cut through all the voices, glaring at Roland. "Aye, he would have! Just as he protected Virginia Ramsey, she that saw into our souls and brought the High Police upon us! Just as he brought the woman in black here, and the outlanders all those years before! The Council for Exploration Into Worlds Unseen—have any of us forgotten them? Is that what we want? To go back to entertaining accursed strangers? How do we even know this boy is human?"

"Are ye human, child?" asked the magistrate just as the

collier shouted out, "Are ye somethin' else?"

"Yes," Stray answered, his voice trembling just a little.

"Well," the magistrate said, "which is it? Are ye human or are ye something else?"

"Yes," Stray said again.

"You hear him!" the weaver shouted. "The boy is trouble, magistrate, mark my words. We should not keep him here."

"What then?" Roland asked, frustration stinging his eyes. "What then, send him back to the hills?"

"Yes," said a strong voice from the back of the crowd, voicing what every face was silently saying. The voice was Wee Cam's. Roland felt as though someone had punched him in the gut.

"Yes," the blacksmith repeated. "Send him back to the hills. This village is no place for the child."

The eyes of the crowd turned on Cam with the surprise Roland felt, but they voiced their agreement. The magistrate nodded, his jowls punctuating the movement. "That's the decision," he said. "You'll take him back yourself, boy."

Roland nodded dumbly. Anger was still building up in him, but he knew better than to let it off here—he'd done enough damage. He should have known better than to invoke the laird. He should have remembered the village's hatred of Virginia. Of course they would not welcome a child who looked as though the sea and its wildness was contained in his eyes.

The truth hit Roland as he stood. From the moment he'd seen the child, he'd been trying to convince himself that Stray was normal. Now he knew that he only cared so much to keep the boy and help him because he knew he was not. Stray *was* like Virginia. Human—and something else. He shot the small boy an incriminating glare. But then, he was only a small boy —whatever else he might be.

"Come on," he said to Stray, who followed him gladly.

As they passed the blacksmith's shop, a gruff voice called out Roland's name. He hesitated, then ducked inside, Stray at his heels.

"Why did you do that?" Roland demanded of Wee Cameron, who was bent over a piece of glowing hot iron. "I count on you to be friend to me, and to what's right."

"And so I am," Cam said. "I spoke true. This village is no safe place for that child. You can see as well as I that they were right—he's not like the rest of us. He's like Virginia."

"And so you'd throw him friendless back to the hills?" Roland said.

"No," Cam said, looking up and calmly meeting Roland's eyes. "I'd send him back to the hills with you." He nodded to a long sack on the floor, lumpy with its contents. "There's provisions in there and a good start to surviving—flints and knives, a lantern, a bow, and money. Take it. Go make your home in some dry cave until it becomes clear to you what to do next."

Roland found himself suddenly groping for words. "I . . ."

"I don't know what will come next," Cam said. "But that boy needs a friend and protector, and this village will not be any safer for him than it was for Virginia. Or have you forgotten who it was that told the High Police how to find her?"

Roland shook his head. His father's betrayal of the blind girl had been the greatest shame and horror of his life. He had never forgotten it. Or shaken the guilt he felt, even though he had done everything he could to warn her in time.

"Thank you," he told Cam.

"No need," Wee Cameron said, striking the hot iron so that sparks flew. "Be on your way. If you need my help, you know where to find me."

Part 1: Portent

1

Survivors

THE ROAD WAS WET FROM SPRING RAIN, but gravel and mountain rock kept the wagon wheels from miring. Sitting on the back with her legs dangling off, Maggie Sheffield held the rails as the cart bounced and rumbled down a steep mountain slope toward the outcrop-strewn village of Morvo. Beside her, Virginia Ramsey rode with her usual placid expression, holding a plaid woolen cloak of grey and green around her shoulders.

They leaned on the tarp-swathed cargo behind them: housewares and tools from the nearly abandoned city of Pravik and a few well-protected precious stones from the Darkworld. The Ploughman hoped to earn enough food from the jewels to feed his people for the summer.

But it all depended, as Maggie well knew, on how they were received.

The road stretched back up the slope behind them, the earth dark with rain, bright green trees bending over it, rock erupting along its borders. Maggie hummed to herself as the wagon strained down the slope, a song picked up from the mountain air and the budding trees, woven into sound by her own peculiar Gift. Virginia smiled.

"A cheerful melody," she said.

"Spring songs are," Maggie answered. "At least, so it has seemed to me since I began singing."

"And what have you learned of the other seasons?" Virginia asked.

Maggie considered. It had been two and a half years since her Gift of song first manifested itself, restoring a burning room and driving away the power of the Blackness. It had never shown so dramatically again. But she had been learning the Gift, slowly, honing her skill month by month. "That winter is expectant," Maggie said, "summer drowsy. And fall melancholy."

"Protesting winter?" Virginia asked.

"Perhaps," Maggie said. "But needlessly, I think. Winter doesn't wallow in itself. It looks ahead to spring."

The wagon drove over a deep pothole in the road, and Maggie laughed as she grabbed more firmly hold of the rails. Virginia seemed unshaken. It wasn't easy to jar the blind Seer of Pravik.

"When did you first know you were Gifted?" Maggie asked.

A shade of trouble passed over Virginia's face. "I was a child," she said. "My visions began to come not long after I lost the last of my eyesight."

Maggie regarded her companion curiously. "I thought you were born blind."

"Nearly," Virginia said. "I lived in a world of shadows and shapes for a time. I could see the sun, and the openness of sky. But the world faded away. I was seven when it all went dark for the last time."

"So young," Maggie said. "And then you began to see?"

Virginia nodded. "Some things." She smiled wryly. "It did not make people love me."

A masculine voice called from the front of the wagon, "Nearly there!"

"I thought as much," Virginia said. "There has been smoke lingering in the air for some way now."

Maggie shook her head at Virginia's sharp perceptions. She held the rail tightly as she stood in the rattling wagon and looked over the pile of cargo to the village below. Morvo was one of the larger towns in the mountains of Slojzca, sitting in the bottom of a small valley, its houses and craftsmen's shops built of stone and shingled with slate. Outcroppings of rock were scattered through the village, and the human habitations were built all around them.

"There it lies," said the Ploughman. "Our best hope for trade in these parts, I think."

The Ploughman rode at the front of the wagon, head and shoulders taller than the driver, his hood thrown back from a handsome face and thick dark hair. He wore his usual dark cloak, and Maggie knew he carried a sword beneath it. But he would not show the sword, only his staff and his wares, as the man who led the only free city in the Empire came to trade with his neighbours like a common peddler.

It was the Ploughman's willingness to sell housewares as readily as lead an army that made him beloved among the few hundred rebels who now lived in the city of Pravik. After five hundred years under the rule of a tyrannical dynasty, the Seventh World needed a ruler like him.

Until the King comes, Maggie thought. She hadn't missed the strain in the Ploughman's voice. The battles in Pravik and Athrom two years before, won at least in part because of the manifestation of the Ploughman's warrior Gift, had freed Pravik from the Empire's rule and transformed the former militia leader and landlord into a folk hero, a legend, and the administrator of a city that was now only barely surviving. Hopes had been high after the battles: the impossible wins had given everyone hope. But hope was wearing thin now, as the realities of hostile neighbours, little food, and their tenuous position under the Empire set in and dragged on. Two years was a long time to hang onto hopes that were not now, despite Maggie's songs and Virginia's sight, bearing themselves out.

As the road leveled out, Maggie heard cows lowing, voices, the rattle of trade and craft and hooves on gravel. The smells of smoke, manure, and beer filled the air. She glanced down at Virginia, still sitting calmly with one hand holding the rails, and then looked ahead to the greeting that might await them.

The wagon splashed through a puddle. A knot was forming in her stomach. Morvo was their best hope for trade—and perhaps their last. Five other villages and towns had refused to trade with them in as many journeys. None wanted to risk the emperor's enmity. It seemed that all who cared enough about freedom in the Seventh World to support Pravik had already come to the Ploughman—and now they all had to be fed.

The wagon rolled past the outskirts and into the town. Heads turned to watch them come; eyes followed them. Here and there a craftsman left his work and followed the wagon toward the town square.

They creaked to a stop. The Ploughman jumped down and

swept the gathering spectators with his eyes before turning and offering his hand to Virginia, then to Maggie. The street was soft and dappled with puddles of water. The air smelled strongly of stables nearby.

"Good people!" the Ploughman said. "We bring greetings from Pravik—and wares to trade." He took hold of one of the grey tarps, cut the ropes that bound it, and pulled it back with a flourish. Brass lamps glinted dully amidst wooden furniture, iron tools, rolls of cloth. Libuse and her team of women had spent days going through the spoils left in the city by those who had fled after the Battle of Pravik two and a half years earlier, cleaning, polishing, and setting aside what looked to be the best of it all. A crate of books peeked out from beneath a raft of shirts tied with twine, taken from the old university of Pravik to tempt scholars among the townspeople. Not, Maggie thought, that they were likely to find many.

A broad-shouldered man stepped out from the shadow of the blacksmith's shop and spat in the mud. "We want nothing of your devilry here," he said.

The Ploughman plucked a solid hammer out of the wagon and held it out to the man. "Hardly devilry," he said. "A fine piece of work, likely to be of use to you. We ask only fair price —in food, nothing more."

"Winter's hardly past," the broad-shouldered man said, but he took a step forward to look at the hammer despite himself. "What food do you think we have?"

"Enough to trade with a hungry neighbour," the Ploughman said. His voice sounded weary in Maggie's ears. She wanted to smile encouragement at him but found she could not. He turned. "Maggie, if you would—the bundles of wool.

Take them to the weaver. And the clothing to the dress shop, if you can find one."

"She'll find one," the belligerent man said, suddenly snatching the hammer from the Ploughman's outstretched hands and testing its weight in the air. "Morvo is no backwater hamlet."

Maggie followed the man's short nod to the likely end of the street with her eyes, then pulled two carefully wrapped bundles of wool, each the size of a barrel, from the wagon. She handed them to Virginia, who slung one over her back expertly and held the other before her. Maggie drew the the bundle of shirts and another of dresses away from the book crate, and with a sigh, she left the Ploughman to reason or haggle with the men over tools.

After the battle, inhabitants of Pravik who did not side with the Ploughman had left the city. They had taken food with them, but little else. The Ploughman's people had left the ghostly households alone for nearly two and a half years. But things were becoming desperate now. The second victory, in Athrom, had cast the fear of the Ploughman into the world, but men do not trade with those they fear. The forested slopes and rocky crags around Pravik could not be planted, and the Ploughman feared attack if his people were scattered too far from the city to plough and sow and reap. The stores of food they had brought with them had run out; they were surviving on the little they could scrape together from the river and the forests now.

Maggie knew for herself how bad things were getting. She could feel it in the ache of her stomach, in the inches she had removed from the waistlines of her skirts. She could see it in the gaunt faces of the others. The dream of Pravik had survived betrayal, battle, and burial. But it could not survive starvation.

With her arms full, she trusted Virginia to listen to her steps and follow by her own sharp senses without touch to guide her. Maggie stepped around puddles and warned Virginia when one was coming up. People moved out their way.

Maggie scanned the street for the dress shop. The thud of wooden shutters slamming against stone walls drew her attention, and forgetting momentarily about Virginia, she clutched her bundles more tightly and ran across the street where the dressmaker was just closing up the last window of her shop.

"No, please," Maggie panted, holding out her bundles of cloth. "It's good cloth, and good workmanship. Please, just look."

The woman turned such a scowl on Maggie that she took an involuntary step backward. "We don't buy from troublemakers," she snapped. "Least of all them which turn the world upside down and steal from good people. My daughter lived happy and pretty in Pravik until you came along!"

Maggie looked about for help and noticed Virginia slowly crossing the street. "Here," she called, and Virginia picked up her pace. "I don't blame you for being angry," Maggie said. "But we didn't force anyone to leave Pravik. It was the emperor who declared it a battleground, and all that time, we had to hide too —and we left everything alone until now, in case anyone wanted to come back for it."

Virginia's soft voice joined Maggie's. "The cloth might have rotted had we left it longer," she said. "It seemed a shame to waste what good merchants such as yourself could put to use. And we are hungry. We come appealing to you as women —to your business sense, and to your mercy."

Maggie simply nodded. The woman kept scowling, but something in her face softened as she looked at Virginia, who, with her pretty face, unfocused eyes, plaid cloak, and bundles of wool, looked every inch a hard-working, hard-done-by peasant. To a woman who had probably raised daughters with a mind to protecting them from begging and hunger, Virginia's appeal could not be easy to deny. The woman released the cord she was pulling and let the wooden cover spring back up, opening the main shop window.

Maggie chuckled inside herself. If this woman had any idea that she was speaking to the fabled Seer of Pravik, whose visions had launched the battle in Athrom and mysteriously affected the earlier one in Pravik, she would likely have closed the window and barred herself up inside the shop. As it was, the scowling dressmaker looked both ways, glared at a few of the townspeople watching her, and motioned for Maggie and Virginia to come inside.

Inside damp stone walls, the dress shop was a riot of colours, thread, and cloth. The air was close, almost fuzzy from the motes of thread drifting in it. A cutting table lay along one end of the shop, and the scowling dressmaker led them to it.

"Now then," she told Maggie. "Lay out your wares and let's have a look. But I'm not promising anything, do you hear?"

Maggie smiled in response. She laid the bundles down and untied the twine from around the dresses, spreading them out on the table. The dressmaker looked them over quickly and fingered a few of the finer garments. She grunted. "Not entirely without worth," she said. "You'd not get silver for them."

"We only ask bread," Virginia said.

The dressmaker looked Virginia over again, and her eyes narrowed. "Where are you selling that wool?"

"We thought it might interest the weaver," Maggie said.

"It interests me," the woman snapped.

Scenting competition, Maggie smiled. "It's good wool. But perhaps the weaver would have more to pay for it?"

"Don't get smart with me, girl," the dressmaker said. "You're lucky I even let you in." Her voice lowered dramatically. "If our magistrate wasn't out on a hunt, you'd be run out—or hung in the square. If you're smart you'll not be coming back here."

"The King protects us," Virginia said.

The woman shot her another sharp look. Virginia didn't react, her eyes unfocused as usual.

"It's talk like that makes you the enemy," the dressmaker said. "The King, the Blackness, ancient covenants . . . we were all better off before you came with your hateful stories."

"What happened in Pravik and Athrom was real," Virginia said. Maggie could hear the strain in the blind girl's voice—the pain that still lingered in her memories. The others had fought for their cause, but Virginia more than anyone had suffered for it. "The Blackness is no mere story. Nor is the King."

The woman's lip jutted a little as she pulled a floor-length silver gown off the table and held it up.

"Leave me the wool and this gown," the woman said. "Take back the rest."

"All of it?" Maggie said. "But surely these—"

"Do you think I don't know quality in my own profession?" the woman snapped. "I said leave me the wool and this gown. I don't want the rest of it."

Maggie bit back further protest as she started to gather the dresses up again. Virginia had set down one bundle of wool and was unslinging the other from her back when a shout in the street drew all their attention. The shout sounded again. This time Maggie recognized her name.

Her heart sank. *Not again.*

The door banged open, and the Ploughman appeared in it. He gestured with his head. "We go," he said.

"But—"

"We go," he repeated. "Now." Once again Maggie heard the weariness in his voice. "We haven't much time." Maggie reached for the bundle of dresses, but the Ploughman shook his head. "Leave it," he said.

Maggie took Virginia's hand and led her to the door. The dressmaker crowded after them. The streets were full now—men, mostly. At the head of the street stood a man in hunting garments whom Maggie took, with a further sinking of her heart, to be the newly returned magistrate of Morvo.

The driver was already waiting at the wagon—empty but for a few scraps of wood and cloth. The Ploughman's face forbade questions. He helped Maggie and Virginia into the back, then climbed up next to the driver. The crowds did not move as the driver started the horse, and they wheeled around and began to drive back the way they had come. The Ploughman's hand was on the hilt of his sword.

He did not draw it. They rode past the silent crowds, through the outskirts of the town, and back onto the road before he relaxed.

"What happened?" Maggie asked.

"They took everything," the Ploughman said. "I am grateful we escaped with our lives."

"But why?" Maggie burst out.

"They've had troubles," the Ploughman said. "Not two months ago the magistrate's son was killed by something in the forest. They blame us."

"The Blackness," Virginia said.

"Other villages have spoken of monsters newly dwelling in the woods," the Ploughman said. "But this is the first I've heard of a death."

Maggie closed her eyes. She could still recall the images of the Blackness that had chased and haunted her when she first began to seek the truth about her world: the terrible death-hound, the giant raven, the hordes of creatures and terrifying warriors unleashed at the Battle of Pravik. Suddenly the stony faces of the townspeople made more sense. They were grieving. And afraid.

"But all our wares . . ." she said.

"There is more in the city," the Ploughman said. "I only hope word does not get out to the towns that we are so easy to rob."

The driver snorted, but they ignored him. After a moment he spoke up. "As if they don't have enough. Lean winter, they said. They were well fed, and they've stores yet. Mark my words."

The road began to slope steeply uphill, and the horse strained at the wagon. Maggie took hold of the side slats again to hold herself steady. Virginia did likewise with one hand.

The driver cleared his throat. "Forgive me, my lord, but they're not the only ones who can wield swords and make threats. There's a good lot of food in that town. We could take it by force."

The Ploughman turned his head to stare at his driver. "Raid the village? Like bandits?"

The driver grimaced. "We raided the High Police often enough. We *were* bandits then, and we weren't hungry."

"We ate from our own farms, whatever the emperor hadn't taxed away from us," the Ploughman said. "We took weapons and supplies from the High Police to stop them destroying us. Those townspeople aren't our oppressors."

"They've left us with nothing but an empty wagon," the driver argued, but he knew he had lost the fight.

"Not quite empty." Virginia's voice rose from behind them, and both men turned in surprise.

"The dressmaker," she said. "She paid for the wool. Five loaves of bread and a bottle of wine."

Maggie smiled as Virginia pulled out a bottle from her cloak and held it up beside a golden loaf.

It was so little.

But somehow, in these circumstances, it meant much.

* * *

A mile from Pravik, the Ploughman bade his driver pull off the road by a stream. Maggie watched as the tall warrior knelt and washed his face and hair. He knelt by the water for a time, then wandered upstream. He pulled his boots off by a great boulder and began to wash them. She couldn't help watching, as much as she knew she was intruding.

There was to be a celebration in Pravik tonight. They had

hoped to bring back something special for it—Virginia's wine and bread would have to do. Added to the meager feast Mrs. Cook was even now preparing, it would serve as a benediction on the announcement of the Ploughman's engagement to Libuse, the lady of Pravik.

Virginia's quiet question cut into her thoughts. "Is he preparing for tonight?" she asked.

"Yes," Maggie said.

"Maggie . . ." Virginia paused. "Take the bread and wine to the celebration."

"Aren't you coming?" Maggie asked.

Virginia shook her head. "I want to be alone. I feel that sight may come."

"Surely you could wait till later?" Maggie said, aware of the tone of her voice but unable to change it. Pravik's survival depended so much on the loyalty and unity of its people, especially its leaders. It didn't seem right for Virginia to go off on one of her solitary rambles when the others were all gathered together to show their love and support for the Ploughman and Libuse.

Virginia didn't answer. She was looking with her hands for the bottle of wine, which she'd laid in the straw on the bottom of the cart. It was obvious from her expression that she was troubled. Maggie sighed in frustration.

Virginia's abandonment of the celebration was just one more bad turn in a day that had not gone well.

* * *

Maggie saw the Ploughman relax as they passed through

the gates and entered the familiar narrow streets of Pravik. The entrance would widen until it became the thoroughfare that crossed the Guardian Bridge over the Vltava River and led to Pravik Castle, high on the plateau across the river.

Unhailed, they drove through empty, silent streets and dark houses. Beyond the bridge were lights and voices. The people who now lived in Pravik were clustered around the castle. Maggie felt the tension and unhappiness of the day leaving her as they rumbled past the statues on the Guardian Bridge and approached the warmth of home. The wagon pulled to a stop in the courtyard of the castle, and Virginia pressed the bottle of wine into Maggie's hand before slipping away.

Maggie sighed again. She tucked the bottle into her own brown cloak, packed the loaves of bread beside it, and jumped as a loud, cheerful voice hailed her from behind. "Maggie!" Patricia Black called, her voice a slap on the back. "It's about time. We were about to start the Ploughman's engagement party without the Ploughman."

She took the last of the loaves from Maggie with a grin. "This is nice. Were you successful then?"

Maggie's silence and a glance at the empty wagon—empty of wares but also of food in trade for them—answered the question. "Oh," Pat said. "Never mind. I refuse to be brought down by it. You should too. Tonight we celebrate."

"As best we can, Pat," Maggie said. She smiled at her old friend and foster sister, whose short dark hair contrasted oddly with the purple dress she had chosen to wear for the party.

"You look lovely," Maggie said.

Pat snorted. "I feel like a girl."

"You *are* a girl," Maggie said. "Even if you carry a sword

more naturally than you keep house. You look like you're planning to attack me with that loaf of bread."

Pat looked at the loaf in her hand and laughed. "You? No. You're no threat. But if the High Police should arrive—" She thrust the loaf forward like a blade.

Maggie grinned and held out her arm. Pat looped arms with her, and they laughed.

Together they left the castle courtyard, where the driver was looking after the horse and wagon, and walked into the street. Cheerful evening voices sprinkled the air. Carriage wheels and horse hooves rattled on the cobblestones; somewhere in the distance the river rushed with melted snow from high in the Eastern Mountains. Cool air, full of spring, had fallen over the city of Pravik and filled it with hope that refused to die, even now, even at the end of a day like this.

They wound their way past old farmers and rebels who tipped their hats and greeted them by name, up a small flight of steps to an old brick townhouse where the smell of meat wafted tantalizingly through the air. "Mrs. Cook has been at it for three days now," Pat said. "Where she's found the ingredients is a mystery—well, other than the birds I caught her. I suspect she'll be serving us shoe leather tonight. But making a good show of it, I don't doubt."

Pat thumped the heavy front door and pushed her way in without waiting for an answer. The inside air was warm and close; there was a fire burning in the hearth and people gathered around—every face welcome and familiar, representing the comfort and strength of friendship. The door closed behind them and shut out the mountain air with its wildness.

"Something smells delectable," Pat announced. "Bless the

one who brought our dear Mrs. Cook such a harvest of fowl for her pots."

Jarin Huss, standing by the fire with his reddish-grey beard lit by its glow, answered her dryly. "Is it quite right to bless oneself so loudly?" he asked, and general laughter followed the comment.

Maggie smiled warmly at the professor as she settled close enough to the hearth to feel the plumes of heat flowing from the fire. His eyes crinkled as he smiled back. Huss had been Maggie's first real friend in Pravik, the one who had opened her eyes to the truth of the worlds unseen and led her to believe in the King. His apprentice, Jerome, had just managed to capture Maggie's heart when he died. Now, she had come to view Huss as something of a father—at least, he was the closest thing she had ever known to one.

A high-backed chair waited next to Huss, and in it a woman whose face still moved Maggie with its beauty and royal dignity. Libuse, last of a long line of eastern kings. She wore blue, as she usually did, and her long brown hair was loose and curled. A ring on her finger sparkled in the light of the fire. The Ploughman himself had taken it from a mineral deposit deep in the Darkworld, and with the help of a jeweler among his followers, had carved it to bring out its facets of purple and green and clear crystal.

Libuse remained seated as she greeted the men who came into the house, old farmers who had long fought by the Ploughman's side. She took their weathered hands, looked into their eyes, and inspired their devotion by her graciousness and warmth. A few of the farmers stopped as they passed through the room to lay their big hands on Maggie's shoulder and say hello. She was grateful for every one.

Voices hummed. Mrs. Cook giving orders from the kitchen. The Ploughman's men rumbling in conversation with Jarin Huss. Pat announcing things, making people laugh, sailing in and out, everywhere at once. The smells of roasted fowl, mulled cider, and hot bread mingled with the voices and made the atmosphere warm even as they made Maggie's stomach ache. She knew the scents indicated more food than there truly was, but even so, Mrs. Cook was a miracle worker to come up with such a feast at such a time. Some of the men had recently begun digging up the city streets in an attempt to plant them, but the soil was poor and the work slow.

Wind pushed at the door, and new feet glided over the threshold. The swish of long robes, the padding of bare feet, and courtly greetings accompanied the arrival of the Darkworld priests and their prince.

"Hail the Darkworld," Maggie said softly. She turned to watch them enter: Prince Harutek, his head shaven but for a single lock, his small, hard stature and large eyes distinctive. He wore fish-scale armour and ornate robes embroidered with human hair, as was the custom of the Darkworld nobles. The priests who followed were also small, but their hair was long and flowing, and they wore grey robes that covered their bare feet and hands.

"Welcome, Harutek," a deep voice from the other side of the room said, and the Ploughman stepped out of the shadows. Maggie smiled to see him. He strode forward and clasped elbows with the Darkworld prince.

"Deepest blessings to you both," Harutek said, his voice warm and strangely accented. Maggie waited for Harutek to bring greetings from his father, the Majesty of the Darkworld, but he did not.

Maggie felt a small hand on her shoulder, and a thick curtain of tiny braids brushed against her skin. A young woman's voice spoke softly in her ear. "And our blessings upon you, Singer of the Sunworld."

Maggie smiled as she turned and grasped Rehtse's hand. The youngest of Divad's priests, Rehtse was striking with her ankle-length, tightly braided hair and luminous eyes. Although she was bound to the service of the Majesty and the people of the Darkworld, Rehtse interacted often enough with the people of Pravik to show herself for what she was: a deeply faithful believer in the King, full of enthusiasm for the new world represented by Pravik, someone to whom the wind seemed to cling and few setbacks could dampen.

The Ploughman took Libuse's hands and pulled her to her feet as the priests of the Darkworld fanned out and blessed them in their formal, archaic ways. The warrior and his lady looked deeply into one another's eyes, and for a moment it seemed that everyone else in the room retreated into shadow before the firelit brightness of their love. A ruby ring, Libuse's long-ago promise to love the Ploughman, glimmered on his finger. When the blessing was finished, he turned to face the others who filled the room and crowded the doorways.

"My friends," he said. "My family. You are all so much more than followers, as the villagers would call you. You have taken us into your hearts, and so you care to hear me say what I say tonight: that I will take the princess Libuse to wife a fortnight hence."

He smiled as the old soldiers and farmers voiced their

approval, and Maggie kept back a chuckle as she thought of how hard Pat was working to hold back an unladylike whoop.

"I thank you all for who you are," the Ploughman said. "Pravik needs you. I fear I have less happy news to give you also. Our hope of establishing trade with the villages is . . ."

He could not finish. Some sort of commotion was taking place in the street. Those closest to the window moved toward it, and Maggie stood and tried to peer past their shoulders. Pat dashed through the crowd and looked out into the darkness.

"Strangers," she said.

The farmers at the window moved aside to make room for the Ploughman, Libuse, and Harutek. Three men with an unmistakably military air were riding up the street on horseback. The street lamps, lit by a faithful few who had appointed themselves to the task, illuminated their faces.

"Do you know them?" Harutek asked.

"I have never seen them before," the Ploughman answered.

"They are not peasants," Libuse said as she peered into the street striped by torches and the darkness of the impending night. "They ride like lords."

"Worse," Pat said, her voice sharp. "They ride like High Police."

2

Visions of Ash

Virginia watched the strangers ride toward the castle.

She stood on a rope bridge, high in the cliffs where spectators could look down over the city and the fifteen great bridges that spanned the black river and connected the halves of Pravik. She had heard the disapproval in Maggie's voice when she declared her intention to be alone, but alone she needed to be.

She was not surprised when sight stirred in her and they were there.

Their leader turned toward her, though she was too far away and it was too dark for him to see her. And yet, as he looked up at the cliffs where Virginia was, fear darted through his expression.

As the strangers rode by, Virginia watched their hoofprints burning. In her sight every step was aflame, and they left burning places in the cobblestones that turned to black ash and began to crumble away, opening a chasm beneath the streets of Pravik. Still they rode, step by step, flame by flame, crumbling by crumbling, and the holes became a fissure that ran the whole length of the street until the city began to collapse into it, swallowed by the darkness below.

Virginia stayed on the bridge as her sight faded away. A cold breeze blew against her cheek, and she pulled her woolen cloak tighter. The night heightened her senses; her heart beat more alive beneath the warmth of her cloak.

For a bare moment, the wind leaped and swirled and blew Virginia's hair.

"Llycharath . . ." she breathed.

No answer met her ears. Yet the wind was more than wind tonight. There was an urgency in it that hastened her steps as she turned and made her way from the bridge down the paths in the cliffs that she had memorized by scent and touch and sound. She made it down and felt cobblestones under her feet again, then the furrows where the Ploughman's men had been digging up the streets for sowing. The shape of streets and paths laid themselves out in her mind, and she began to run, until a pair of arms grabbed her in mid-flight.

She struggled, but a friendly voice broke into her struggles. It was one of the Ploughman's farmers. "Seer!" he said. "Seer, what's wrong?"

She fought to catch her breath. "I must see the Ploughman," she said.

"He's in council, my lady," the old farmer said. "We were gathered to celebrate his engagement to the princess, but strangers . . ."

"I know," Virginia said, "I saw them. You understand that —what it means that I saw them? I must talk with him now." She was struggling against tears. The old man's voice, gruff and gentle, reminded her of her grandfather. It made her want to crumple like a little girl.

"I'll take you to him," the man said.

* * *

Virginia knew as soon as she entered the ancient throne room, where thrones had long been displaced by the council tables of the overseers and then by the Ploughman's rule, that the strangers were already gone. She breathed sharply in fear.

"Virginia," the Ploughman greeted her. She heard him crossing the stone floor, but he stopped short of touching her. "You're trembling," he said.

"The strangers," Virginia said. "Did they come here?"

"They did," the Ploughman said. She heard the guardedness in his voice and silently cursed it.

"They have brought danger," she said.

"No . . ." the Ploughman said. "Perhaps not, Virginia. This time they may have brought hope."

"Tell me," she said.

A chair scraped across the floor as someone pushed away from the council table, and Virginia heard the rustle of a skirt. "They were emissaries from the emperor," Libuse said. "They have offered us alliance."

Virginia was momentarily speechless. "With the Empire?" she asked. The blackened streets of her vision, falling away into ash, suddenly seemed very real.

"Allied with the emperor, we would be free to trade and expand our borders into farmland," the Ploughman said. "Two years ago I would not have considered it, but now . . . I know this is not easy for you to hear. It's not what we pictured when we began this journey. We have not yet given them an answer."

"But we cannot turn away the chance without even considering it," Libuse said. "We never dreamed the emperor would recognize us as anything but rebels—but as rebels, we may not survive. We need him to recognize us. And it seems he is willing."

"What did you tell the strangers?" Virginia asked.

"That we would take three days to make up our minds," the Ploughman said. "And if we decide to explore the matter further, we will send an entourage to Athrom to discuss the matter with the emperor."

"You would go back into that den of dragons?" Virginia asked.

"If we must," the Ploughman said. "I do not trust the emperor, Virginia—I know that he has his own purposes in this. But maybe his purposes can work to our advantage, at least for a while. I will lead the entourage myself. If there is danger, my warrior Gift will be enough to break us out. I have fought in the heart of Athrom before." He hesitated. "If we go, I want you to come with us."

Virginia sought words that she couldn't find. Libuse's softer voice spoke again. "We are not naïve enough to think there is no danger in this," she said. "It might be a trick. But with your sight and the Ploughman's strength, we can anticipate and defeat tricks."

"Then hear what I've seen already," Virginia said. "I saw the men enter the city, and destruction followed in their steps. Every step lit a flame that became ash and swallowed Pravik in darkness. You must not go with them. You must not consider this offer."

Silence met her words. Then the Ploughman spoke again. His voice was heavy, but determined. "We have little choice," he said. "We can take your vision as confirmation of what we already suspect—that the emperor's motives are not entirely pure. But we must take advantage of his offer nonetheless. Virginia, our people are starving. *My* people. I gathered them here; they came to my banner because I promised them something better. And now it falls to me to provide for them."

"But the King . . ."

" . . . is not here," the Ploughman said. "If he still fights for us, maybe this is how he's doing it. By opening a door for us in Athrom. Perhaps, face-to-face, we can persuade Lucien Morel of the justice of our cause."

Virginia shook her head in frustration. Tears were pricking at her eyes, making her impatient with herself. "Persuade a man of justice who tried to wipe out the Gypsies at a blow? Persuade a man whose family has covenanted with the Blackness and supported the Order of the Spider in their sorcery for five hundred years? Persuade the sworn enemy of the King?"

"Virginia," the Ploughman said gently, "his forefathers may have sworn against him, but whether Lucien Morel even believes in the King is doubtful."

Virginia was quiet a moment. "As is your own belief," she finally said.

Again, silence met her words. Libuse answered. "He is not here," she said. "We have seen—things. Signs. But no final fulfillment of those signs. It has been two years. We have Gifts, but no proof of where they come from. We have to live here,

Virginia, here in this world, and our people will starve if something does not change."

"Yes," Virginia said. "I know."

She turned away. The Ploughman took her arm. She stiffened, though his touch was not forceful.

"We need your sight," he said. "We need you to help us."

She turned slowly and faced him, her memories fusing with this moment in a way that made her ache. "You are not the first man to say that," she said. "The last betrayed me— betrayed the King, betrayed all of us. Ploughman, our Gifts are something greater than ourselves. They aren't meant to be used to fulfill our own pleasure."

"This is hardly pleasure," the Ploughman said. "I may have no choice. The decision is not yet made—but if in three days we leave this city for Athrom, then on your love for this place, Virginia, I ask you to come."

Virginia did not answer. She turned and left the throne room, stumbling against the door frame as she went out. She knew their eyes were following her, but she didn't care.

She had seen, and they had not listened.

The wind blew softly through her hair as she stepped back into the street, and a voice said, *All shall be well.*

"How can it be, Llycharath?" she whispered to the Wind-Spirit. "They are turning against the King."

But you are not.

She sat down on the stone steps of the castle, listening to the voices and carriage wheels in this city where the King had once shown his power. On a hillside not far away, a burned patch of earth was all that remained of the unholy fire that had called the Blackness into the battle—with her own unwilling help. She could still feel the power of the Order of the Spider as they turned her Gift of sight against her and against the people of the King. She could still feel the pain as they tore her spirit apart.

"The King is all I have left to hope in," she said. "Not this madness of men."

Footsteps on the stairs silenced her, and she tensed as a booted figure drew near, his sword belt jingling. His shadow fell over her. A sense of being hunted washed over her so strongly that she nearly choked.

The voice that spoke was foreign—Southern. One of the strangers.

"Virginia Ramsey," he said. "The Seer of Pravik—or am I mistaken?"

"And who are you?" she asked.

She heard the creak of his leather armour as he bowed. "General Merlyn Cratus," he said. "Leader of the High Police."

"Lord of ashes," she said.

An edge came into his voice. "Pardon?"

She stood a little uncertainly and took her skirt in hand as she began her descent to the street. "You are not mistaken," she said. "And neither am I."

* * *

Far below the streets of Pravik, another city—another world—lay hidden. Ancient, steeped in tradition, and long hidden from the world above, the Darkworld had maintained its underground colony for nearly five hundred years, ruled by a line of kings, tempered by a priesthood devoted to the King of legend.

Their history was tumultuous. Traitors to the King in the Great War, they had stopped just short of swearing allegiance to the Morel Empire and gone underground instead. They vowed to wait until the King returned, planning to beg his forgiveness and offer their long dark years as penance.

But life without the sun was not life as men were meant to live it. Waves of a mysterious disease they called sun-sickness swept their numbers, killing hundreds. The priesthood faithfully tended the wounded, singing to them and telling them stories of the King. They learned to fish from the underground rivers and make bread from roots gathered near the surface. They burned fish-oil lanterns and made clothing of human hair. They grew pale-skinned, large-eyed, small of stature. Sun-sickness and other diseases decimated their numbers over the decades, until at last, the Majesty Nahtano, son of Tebazil, Sire of Seventeen Sons and Guardian of the Holy Priesthood, ruled only a tiny tribe of survivors in the dark.

But rule them he did, and jealously.

Fish-oil lanterns flickered with sickly blue flame in the hall outside the throne room as the doors burst open, and the council, dismissed, flooded out. Soldiers and nobles talked animatedly as they passed through the hall. The priests were quieter, more thoughtful, hands clasped with long sleeves falling over them. One, the young priestess Rehtse, lingered.

Harutek, the Majesty's son, was the last to leave the throne room. He saw Rehtse waiting and appraised her with a stormy expression.

"Well?" he asked.

"Are you all right?" she asked.

"How should I be?" he snapped. "My father is a fool."

"Hush, Harutek," Rehtse said. "Don't talk treason."

"No one else has a right to," the prince said.

"It may be your right," Rehtse said. "But it does not become you. Honour your father, my prince."

He looked her over and smiled sardonically. "You are not any happier with me than he is."

She hesitated. "For different reasons."

"Always honest, aren't you?"

"I'm a priestess," Rehtse said.

Harutek snorted. "That does not make you honest. I have seen enough of the priesthood's lies."

Rehtse felt her blood growing warmer, but she forced back her retort. In Harutek she could still see the playmate of her youth—just as, in the Majesty, she could still see the man who had been a grandfather to her while she played with his sons. Her family had sent her into the priesthood, and thus into the circle of royalty, as a little girl. The royal family and the priesthood had been her world. She knew perfectly well that her world was dividing now. But it hurt, and she was determined to do what she could to hold it together—if only by reaching out to this hard-headed prince with love.

Still, she couldn't entirely keep the rebuke out of her voice. "What we teach is not lies," she said. "It is our whole purpose for existing. You should be leading the Darkworld in waiting for the King, Harutek." She was quiet for a moment. "You should not have brought those men here."

"Look at me, Rehtse," Harutek said. She hadn't realized she wasn't—she had turned her eyes to the floor. She looked back up at him now. His face was so much like Caasi's. It was just a little older, a little harder, and his eyes were brown where Caasi's had been grey. But they were just as passionate.

"I know I am not my brother," Harutek said. "I know it is hard for you to believe that I will do right. But I will do what is best for our people—now, and when I take the throne. You have to trust me."

She didn't answer that. He brushed past her and descended the steps into the caverns of the Darkworld. She watched him go, lingering still on the steps, and quietly prayed the ancient blessing over the royal family.

"May they stand faithful in thy stead, care for thy people as fathers, guard them as warriors." Tears pricked at her eyes, and she began to repeat it, just for good measure. "May they stand faithful . . ."

"Rehtse!"

She turned her head toward the throne room. The Majesty's tone was belligerent, and she sighed inwardly before lifting her chin and answering the summons. The throne room was a work of art, its limestone walls and ceiling carved with stylized symbols of the past—suns, moons, stars, and a seven-starred crown. Animals featured there too, winged birds and running deer, curved fish and clawed bears. After council, the room was eerily empty and quiet.

In the center, the Majesty sat on a carved white throne. Flames flickered from lantern poles and candlesticks on the dais, casting light over his snowy white lock of hair, his wrinkled face, and his sharp eyes. The dais around the throne was empty of its usual company of priests.

Rehtse crossed the smooth floor to a small table beside the

dais, where she poured warm water from a stone pitcher into a basin. A flame beneath the pitcher kept the water warm. She draped a cloth over her arm and carried the basin to the Majesty.

Without a word, she knelt before him with the bowl raised, allowing him to reach in and wash his hands. The ritual was old—a cleansing from all that had been said, from all argument, from all animosity council might incur. Rehtse hoped that the Majesty was engaging in the tradition with his heart as well as his hands.

But she knew better.

When he had finished, she set the basin down and handed the Majesty the cloth to dry his hands. He did it wordlessly, then gave the cloth back to her. Ignoring the uncomfortable stone beneath her knees, she set to washing his feet.

"What did you say to Harutek?" he asked. His voice startled her, but she kept her hands steady.

Pouring water from her palm over his feet, she said, "I told him that he should not have brought those men here."

"As if your opinions matter," the Majesty said. He was silent a moment longer. "I heard him out there, cursing me."

"Not . . . *cursing,* your highness. He differs with you on what is best for the Darkworld."

"Everyone differs with me," the Majesty said. "My son does, Divad does, even you do." He nodded in mock approval. "Yes, it's good that you keep your tongue and avoid my eyes. I know what you think. You show it every time you go above, fraternizing with the wreckers of our world."

Rehtse swallowed her reply. Instead, she said, "Harutek is wrong to seek allegiance with the Empire."

"You would rather he do what Caasi did," the Majesty said. "Go off and fight the Empire and die. You're a cold-hearted wench. You should weep for Caasi and hate the cause that killed him, not idolize it. You should weep for yourself."

I have, Rehtse thought. Caasi had been her playmate, then her best friend, then the one to embrace the old ways with her —the one to believe in the King with all his heart. Given a few more months, he would have been the one to marry her, and together they would have helped renew the Darkworld's faith in the King.

Yes, she had wept when he did not come back from Athrom.

"Fight them or embrace them, it does not matter," the Majesty said. "When I die, this world goes with me. That is the curse of a man whose sons care nothing for him or the world he has preserved."

Rehtse dried the Majesty's feet and stood, grateful for the opportunity to turn away. She could feel the Majesty's eyes scrutinizing her, and she winced. Rehtse's soul bore twin wounds, and the Majesty was deliberately picking at both. The loss of Caasi, whom she had loved, and the royal family's slow apostasy from all that she believed so ardently.

So she fought back. The washing of the Majesty's feet was always followed by a blessing. It was tradition. It was expected of her. She replaced the basin on its stand, climbed the dais again slowly, and with her head bowed and her palms turned to the Majesty, she recited a blessing she did not think he would want to hear.

"May you be blessed in your reign," she said. "May the King keep you as his emissary and regent until he returns, and may he in whose grace the Darkworld hopes and has being find you faithful to the end."

She smiled serenely. He glared up at her.

"Get out," he said.

She obeyed.

* * *

Libuse stood in the midst of upturned ground at the end of the second day since the strangers had come, heaps of cobblestones forming mounds all around her. An evening breeze blew back her hair. Ahead of her, the Ploughman was picking his way carefully through the newly ploughed ruts. He wore a dark cloak and a sword. Rain spattered his hair and shoulders.

He looked back at her, his face torn.

She said nothing. She felt what he did. They had both struggled with a decision they felt was inevitable. For hours, over the ruts in the ground, under the spitting clouds, they had argued alternatives, possibilities, ways to keep existing, feed their people, and defend themselves against the Empire *without* alliance. They had debated ways to take Virginia's advice without destroying themselves. But they had arrived at no new answers.

They had wanted more than anything to form a new world on their own. But it was not going to work.

"My lord, my lady." The voice belonged to Rivan, one of the Ploughman's farmer-guards. They turned to face him, and the Ploughman strode forward so they could talk without raising their voices.

"What of the strangers?" the Ploughman asked.

"They disappeared for a few hours last night," Rivan said, holding his hand up to stall the Ploughman's reaction. "But we found them. They were below, meeting with Harutek and the Majesty."

The Ploughman frowned. "What?"

"My lord, whether or not you accept Cratus's invitation, it seems Harutek has already done so," Rivan said.

The light spring rain was dissipating, yet Libuse drew her cloak closer around her as though it was picking up. She said nothing. Nothing needed to be said. Their relationship with the Darkworld was already a sensitive one. The priesthood had embraced them. The Majesty hated them. Harutek, who was perhaps more truly influential than the Majesty, viewed them as a means to some end they had not entirely identified yet. But they did not rule out the possibility of his becoming an enemy.

If the Darkworld and the Empire joined hands, Pravik would have no choice.

"Thank you, Rivan," the Ploughman said. "Tell no one yet —I don't want rumours spreading."

Rivan bowed and left them. The rain continued to spatter.

"We have one more day to give Cratus our decision," the Ploughman said.

"We do not need it," Libuse asked. "Harutek has made our decision for us."

The Ploughman's hand had been clenched in a fist. Now he released his fingers, and clumped soil fell out onto the ground. The street smelled of wet stone and earth. A few labourers were still digging up the ground, hoods pulled over their heads against the damp and the cold mountain air.

"What if Huss is right and the King does come back?" the Ploughman asked.

"He will have to understand," Libuse said. "There is no other decision to be made." Tears pricked at her eyes. "I do not want you to go. You were to be my husband in a fortnight."

"I will be yet," the Ploughman said. He took her hand and laid it over his heart. "Athrom is five days' hard riding. We can go and meet with him and be back here in time."

Libuse blinked away tears. "Then do not make Cratus wait any longer," she said. She touched his face. "Go, and hurry back to me."

"And Virginia's vision?" the Ploughman asked.

"Use it," Libuse said. "Use it to keep you on your guard, and turn the emperor's plans against him where you can. You are wise, my warrior. Take good counselors. You can do this."

He smiled. "I will do as you say," he said. "And I will hurry back, to the city where my heart lies and to the woman who keeps it for me."

She smiled in return, despite the tears. Libuse was a daughter of kings, and her line had been displaced by the Empire for centuries.

She knew how to wait.

* * *

Hours passed as Virginia sat alone, back on the high rope bridge, feeling the day pass from morning into afternoon, feeling the passage of shadows. No more visions came.

The bridge creaked beneath her as someone else stepped

onto it. She did not turn her head, but waited for him to reach her.

"This is not an easy climb for an old man," Jarin Huss panted.

Virginia smiled. "I am sorry."

"How does a blind woman climb it?" he asked.

"I know the way," she said.

"You saw something last night," he said.

"The Ploughman told you?" she said.

"Yes. When he told me that he will be leaving for Athrom tomorrow. He feels it is useless to wait any longer."

Virginia kept staring out into the darkness. "He wants me to go with him."

"You must not," Huss said.

She turned her head in surprise. "You would have me abandon him now? It is a foolish decision he makes—I fear it will destroy us. But what else can he do? He is right—the people will starve."

Huss grunted. "You see the problem. It's unthinkable that we should join hands with our enemies. But there is no other choice. So they say."

"There *is* a choice," Virginia said.

She heard the gentle smile in Huss's voice, and the weariness in it also. "You see that too. We cannot exist in this world of great powers without a greater power to uphold us, not even with the Ploughman's Golden Warriors at our call. For all we know the Empire has far greater forces at its behest, and we have succeeded in the past only because of luck. We need the King, Virginia."

She nodded, swallowing back the longing that rose in her

at the mention of the King's name. "But the Ploughman is not willing to wait for him. He has never believed fully, not as we do."

The old man was silent for a moment. "You have seen the King, Virginia," he said. "Maggie has touched something of his nature, I think; she continues to touch it in song. But Libuse and the Ploughman—they cannot act on what you have seen and what Maggie has touched."

"But the Ploughman is also Gifted," Virginia said. "And his Gift comes from the King. It is the King's power that works in him."

"That is true for all the Gifted," Huss said, "but that does not necessarily mean all the Gifted recognize it. Your Gift feels a part of you, does it not?"

She nodded.

"You and the Ploughman both gained your Gifts at a young age. So he struggles to believe that it comes from outside him. Don't be too hard on him, Virginia. It is difficult to wait for something you believe in. It is much harder to wait for something you only hope is true. And even I do not know *when* the King will return, only that it must be soon—the time of the Veil is over. Morning Star will be upon us."

Virginia thought again of the mountainside where the Blackness had used her, and she shuddered. "So tell me," she said. "Why should I not go with the Ploughman? Perhaps he is right and I can help him."

"I want you to go back to the Highlands," Huss said. "I want you to seek out the King there."

Virginia was silent. The bridge swayed in a gust of wind, wild with the scent of pines and mountain streams. She tried to deny the feeling of being suddenly suspended over a world that might drop away from beneath her.

"What makes you think he will be there?" she asked.

"My own search for the truth began in Angslie," Professor Huss said. "The Council for Exploration Into Worlds Unseen began there, and though things ended badly for us, we walked for a while on the edge of this reality—we were close to the truth. And you have seen the King there. You once told me that he spoke to you—that he prophesied that he would wake the world through you. Virginia, my deepest hope is that if you return to Angslie where you saw him before, he will come to you. You will bring him into the world."

Virginia let her protests die as Huss continued, his voice gentle and urgent. "When you traveled here with Lord Robert, the Earth Brethren awakened to you. It was your prophecy that led to victory in Athrom. You are at the heart of everything, Virginia, you and Angslie itself. Yes, I want you to go."

Her voice was terse. "Have you forgotten that it was I who betrayed you all in the Battle of Pravik?"

Huss was silent for a moment. "You were not the betrayer," he said at last.

There were tears on Virginia's face, but she turned her unseeing eyes toward the west and let the wind dry them. "Does the Ploughman know what you are asking of me?"

"No. He would not be pleased with me if he did. You should leave the city without his knowledge. He would not force you to accompany him, of course, but he might talk you into it. I would advise you to go this very night—before he gathers his entourage to leave in the morning."

"I will go," Virginia said. "Of course I will go. But

Professor, I cannot go alone." She smiled, almost apologetically. "If you have forgotten, I am blind."

A gnarled hand touched her cheek. "I have not forgotten," he said.

Wind played around them. "Go tonight," Huss said. "Hide yourself in the mountains so the Ploughman cannot find you. I will see what I can do to bring you eyes."

3

Leave-taking

In the courtyard of Pravik Castle an hour before dawn, the Ploughman's entourage made ready for their journey, packing and inspecting horses and two wagons. Harutek and six of his Darkworld warriors had joined them from below. Their interaction with the Ploughman's men was cordial, yet tense. With Cratus's two, the entourage totaled twenty-one men, plus Jarin Huss, Maggie, and Pat.

Pat was coming because she insisted on it. Maggie was coming because of her songs.

"You are Gifted, Maggie," Professor Huss had said when she protested, in the quiet of his study high in the castle. "As such you are a link to the King and a special strength to the Ploughman. He needs you."

"But I don't even know how to use this Gift," Maggie said. "I'm not like Virginia. I've never seen the King—I don't see how I can be of any help."

"You don't want to leave the city?"

Maggie had looked out the window at the narrow streets below, winding down the plateau to the bridges that crossed the Vltava. She remembered entering the city for the first time on horseback, its bridges and streets lit with lamps and torches, the sounds of a riot at the castle gates reaching her ears. She had been with Nicolas Fisher then, carrying an ancient scroll in search of Huss, and entirely unaware of how her life would change.

But it had changed. She had become someone else, someone who loved a man who had died since, someone who sang supernatural songs and saw supernatural beings in the skies. And now she clung to Pravik as the only place the changed Maggie really knew. The rest of the Seventh World was part of some other life. And it threatened her.

"I don't know," she said. "I'm afraid of what might happen."

"Because of all that *has* happened," Huss said. "But think, Maggie—would you really change any of it?"

She had shaken her head. "No."

Maggie went through her things one last time, spare though they were—two changes of clothes, a bone flute from the Darkworld that she was learning to play. Mrs. Cook had added quite a few things to Maggie's load: a kettle and tea, three woolen blankets, stockings.

"You're going to freeze to death on the road, child, and I won't have that on my head."

"It's spring," Maggie had answered. "Late spring, and we're going south."

Pat snorted. "And you expect her to trust the weather?"

Pat had managed to pack exactly what she wanted without Mrs. Cook adding a single item, which meant that her saddlebags were considerably smaller and lighter. Maggie felt guilty every time she looked at her horse.

She patted the animal's brown neck with a comforting word and turned to survey the rest of the band. Huss was seated on a stool in the middle of the courtyard, leaning forward on a gnarled staff, watching. Pat and Mrs. Cook were laughing about something, Pat determined to keep her foster mother from crying and Mrs. Cook determined to cry through her laughter anyway. Her girls were leaving her again, after all.

Virginia was conspicuously absent, as Maggie had somehow known she would be. When Professor Huss had pressed her to come and be their link to the King, she had known the Seer would be staying behind—knew it though she didn't understand it. But she didn't tell anyone else what she knew.

The Ploughman held a long staff in his hand such as he had always carried in the old days when he was a country landlord leading a secret militia. He looked, Maggie thought, like a ballad. Strength and romance and uncertainty in a single man: a prince who didn't know he wasn't really a pauper. Libuse had hardly left his side.

Rivan and two other men entered the courtyard and bowed to the Ploughman.

"Still nothing?" the Ploughman asked.

"Nay, my lord," one of the men said. "There's not a trace of her anywhere."

Maggie's stomach knotted. She felt a pang of anxiety for Virginia and hoped, despite herself, that the Seer wouldn't be found. If she wasn't coming, she had a reason for it—and surely she had been hunted enough.

Rumour said Virginia had refused to go and had faced off

against the Ploughman like some kind of traitor. Others speculated on why. Maggie heard soldiers talking about it in low voices and shook her head. If Virginia had spoken to the Ploughman, it had been only yesterday. It was incredible how quickly rumours could spring up. She remembered, with a little guilt, her own annoyance when Virginia had chosen not to come to the Ploughman's engagement celebration.

The arrival of General Cratus and his men broke the camaraderie in the courtyard. The general strode in as though he was looking over troops of his own, holding a torch high in the cold, dark morning air.

Huss remained seated in Cratus's presence. The general stopped in front of him.

"Are you sure you're strong enough to make this journey, old man?" he asked.

"That is hardly any of your concern," Huss said.

"I would hate to come late before the emperor because we were slowed by one who should have stayed home," Cratus answered.

"We will not go without him," the Ploughman said, stepping to Huss's side. "He has strength we would sorely miss."

"Does he now?" the general asked.

"Indeed," Huss said, looking up past the staff in his hands. "I have the strength, for example, to remain sitting when other men would stand—invaluable, I think, in the presence of bullies. Do you not agree, general?"

"And that is what you expect in Athrom?" Cratus asked. "Bullies?"

"The emperor has never been anything but," Huss said.

Cratus laughed. "You may find," he said, "that the emperor is not at all what you expect."

Maggie shivered. There was too much in this whole business that felt like being fed to the lions. *Although*, she thought as she watched the Ploughman give orders, *the lions may be surprised to find they are more than evenly matched.*

She knew the plan. They would keep together in Athrom, allowing nothing to separate them for long. If the emperor's purposes were treacherous, the Ploughman's Gift—the battle-heat that came on him and the Golden Warriors who were there whenever he needed them most—would be enough to help them fight their way out. Even to do great damage on their way. The Ploughman's Gift might not be enough to keep the concentrated forces of the Empire at bay in a protracted war, but in the fire of an unexpected battle it would be enough to rescue them.

At least, Maggie sincerely hoped it would.

Pat's hand on her left shoulder and Mrs. Cook's prodigious presence at her right brought sudden comfort and strength, even in silence. Together they watched as Cratus finished his unofficial inspection, made a displeased comment about the Seer's absence, and left the band alone again, almost chased out by the force of their combined loyalty and fierce hope. They were Pravik, the city that existed against all odds, and they would face Athrom together.

Two hours later, with the sun still shining golden and new over the horizon, they rode out of Pravik. The people of the city, early out of their beds but unwilling to miss saying good-bye, lined the street from the castle down the plateau and across the Guardian Bridge. Beyond that the city was as ghostly as ever.

Maggie stored up images as she rode: the empty streets, the patches of upturned earth where the farmers had pulled up cobblestones and tried to plough, the silent houses, the sun on Pravik's eastern spires. Images she might try to sing later. General Merlyn Cratus and his three men, dressed now in the black and green uniforms of the High Police, rode slightly ahead of them.

"It's hard going, this," Pat said under her breath as she drew up alongside Maggie. "Every time I see those colours I want to fight."

Maggie laughed. "Self-control is a virtue, Pat."

"As I well know," Pat answered. "But then so is loyalty. Wisdom, too. This seems all wrong."

"It isn't disloyal to try to secure a future for ourselves," Maggie said. "For all of us."

The thought of the King came to her, and she shifted uncomfortably. He had not forbidden this. And he had not come to show them another way. She wondered where Virginia was and hoped that her disappearance had something to do with the King. At least *someone* among their number was still seeking him.

The western gate of Pravik was just ahead, and Maggie looked up at the wall's ancient stones and felt the smile leaving her face. This place had been their protection, their world within a world they were sure was at enmity with them, for more than two years now. Two years they had somehow expected would last a lifetime.

The horses' hooves beat placidly on the cobblestone road as they neared the gate. The Ploughman gave a command to the few men who watched it. The gate lifted, exposing green forested mountains glimmering like a jewel in the early morning sun beyond, and in a moment they were through.

"Thus changeth the world," Pat said, and Maggie felt that somehow she was right.

* * *

The Darkworld child looked up, wide eyes dilated in a pale face. Rehtse touched the shaven head gently as she lifted a cup of water to the little boy's lips. His skin was hot with fever. He lay in the limestone infirmary, where the cool air did little to bring down his temperature. The floor had been carved away around raised beds, which were thickly padded with braided hair and covered with tightly woven, thin sheets of the same material. The beds lay in rows twenty long and six across. At times they were all filled.

Thankfully, most were empty now.

The low ceiling was carved with a stylized sun nearly the size of the entire infirmary. Hanging candles around its perimeter and all down its rays lit it up like a giant chandelier.

Rehtse left the boy and wandered down the rows, delivering water to more sufferers. She sang softly as she went, an old song praising the glories of the sunlit world and of the sun itself—a giver of life and health, whose light was dimmed only by that of the King himself. Sun-sickness, the Darkworld's age-old affliction, was thought to be an illness of the soul as well as of the body. So songs, stories, and the giant sun carving were all part of its treatment. The priesthood had been using them all in this same infirmary for hundreds of years.

"Rehtse." The voice that beckoned her was Annan's. She looked up to see him standing in the doorway. "Divad wants to see you," he said.

The young priest crossed the floor and held out his hands for the water jug she carried. "I'll take over for you," he said.

She nodded and headed out of the infirmary, down the torchlit corridors to the high priest's chambers. The doors were open, and she passed through the curtains without announcing herself. Divad was seated at a low table, fingertips touching and elbows resting on the table. She recognized the position. He was deep in thought.

For a moment she thought he'd missed her entrance, and she opened her mouth to speak. He beat her to it.

"Sit down, Rehtse," he said.

She crossed the floor and sat at the low table with her legs tucked to one side. She waited.

"Harutek has gone," Divad said. She bowed her head and swallowed. Divad had embraced the Ploughman and his people and struck a close friendship with the scholar called Jarin Huss. But she knew he did not approve of the emissaries from Athrom, or of Harutek's decision to go with them, any more than she did.

"It has been five hundred years," Divad said. "Do you know what that means?"

She looked up and met his striking blue eyes. The intensity in his gaze matched that in her soul. She answered, "If the legends have it right, it means the King will soon return."

"Or Morning Star will," Divad said. "The Blackness will be unleashed and destroy the world above. And Harutek is making us a part of that world."

A smile quirked at her mouth. "You sound like the Majesty."

"The Majesty is wrong to doubt the King and reject the Ploughman," Divad said. "But he is right to disagree with his son. I wish with all my heart that Caasi had lived."

Rehtse looked away.

"I am sorry," Divad said, his voice gentler. "I would have rejoiced to see you and Caasi wed, Rehtse. From the day you came to us, I sensed that you had a special purpose among the priests."

She looked back at him, and there were tears in her eyes.

He continued. "Do you know what Hazrit dreamed the first night you were here?"

Rehtse shook her head, puzzled. This conversation was not going as she had expected it to.

"Hazrit was a young woman then," Divad said. "She tucked you into bed and dried your tears as you cried for your mother. Then she came to me and told me that we should send you back. No child had ever been given to us so young."

"I—" Rehtse looked for words, then gave up. Better to keep listening.

"I said that was not ours to decide," Divad said. "Your parents had offered you, and the Majesty had accepted you. I suspected him of ulterior motives. You were a beautiful child, even then, and the priesthood lacked likely wives for his sons. Though I think he meant you for Harutek."

Rehtse looked down at the table. She cleared her throat. She loved Harutek—she always had, as an older brother who teased, bullied, and frustrated her. But nothing on earth could ever have enticed her to marry him, and she was quite sure the feeling was mutual. Caasi, on the other hand . . .

"Hazrit came to me again early, before morning prayer," Divad said. "She said she had dreamed of you, and she knew now that we could not send you back. She had seen you beneath the stars, on a mountaintop with wind in your hair. The stars had gathered in a circle around you, and voices came from them. Hazrit could not remember what they said. But she knew you were destined to be one of us."

"I didn't know," Rehtse said.

"Hazrit's dream told me something quite different," Divad said. "That you were to be one of us, yes. But also that you were to leave us."

The words hit Rehtse like a shock. "What?" she asked.

He looked into her eyes once more, and this time he spread out his hands, as though his thinking was done and now he had only to explain a settled decision. Firelight flickered blue off the carved stone walls. "You are to leave us," he said. "Now, in fact."

"I cannot leave," Rehtse said. "What about my duties here? The children—"

"Hazrit and Annan can handle their care," Divad said. "The sickness is not bad for the time being."

"—and prayers," Rehtse continued, "and the Majesty. I am his attendant. And you know that no priest is free to leave his service. We are bound to him."

Divad's eyes flicked away from her face. He looked—unsettled? Guilty? "I do not know what to do about that," he admitted. He picked up something that had been lying on the table, bringing it to Rehtse's attention for the first time. It was a letter.

"Professor Huss has gone to Athrom, but he sent this," Divad said. "A request that one of my priests might accompany Virginia Ramsey on a journey to the Highlands where she came from. She needs eyes, he says. To help her find the King."

Rehtse fought to breathe as the implications sank in.

"You, Rehtse," Divad said. "She is waiting for you."

Rehtse shook her head. To go into the Sunworld—to seek the King—to serve one of his Gifted—all her heart desired it. But she had vows to keep. She could not simply leave the Majesty.

"You know the penalty if I leave the Majesty's service," she said.

"Death will not find you," Divad said. "The Majesty will not send soldiers into the mountains to track you down."

The stone table beneath her palms felt warm. "And what will I tell the King when I find him?" she asked. "That I am a vow-breaker like our forefathers? A traitor, faithless? That one loved me like a daughter and I abandoned him?"

She pushed herself up and stood slowly. "I cannot do this thing, Divad, though with all my heart I desire to go. Faithlessness is the curse of the Darkworld." Her eyes went to the door behind Divad, and she set her jaw. "No, I cannot go—not unless he gives me leave."

"You're not going to ask him?" Divad said. The alarm in his voice surprised her. It was not a common reaction for the high priest. "Rehtse, I know you love him—more than any of my priests, you care for the royal family. And at times he has loved you. But he is volatile, and angry. He might—"

"He will not make a martyr of me," Rehtse said. "Not this time." She held out her hand. "May I?"

Divad handed over Huss's letter without a word. Rehtse rolled it up and tucked it into the fine red braided belt she wore. She left Divad's presence with her heart pounding.

* * *

The first day's ride brought the Ploughman's entourage down to the foothills of the mountains, just above the thick forests of Galce. Maggie sat with Pat and Professor Huss by a new-lit fire in the camp, carefully hanging Mrs. Cook's teakettle on a stick over the flames. Its copper sides, black and smudged along the bottom rim, glinted cheerfully in the evening light that fell through the new leaves and buds on the trees around the clearing.

Maggie worked her fingers over the holes on her bone flute. Hazrit, the elder of the Darkworld priestesses, had given it to her. She blew into it experimentally, enjoying its melancholy tones.

"Not a cheerful sound, is it?" Pat asked.

"The Darkworld is not a cheerful place," Huss said.

Maggie smiled. "Not cheerful, but beautiful, I think."

"I'd rather hear you sing," the professor said.

Maggie laughed. "Professor, I love to sing. But I can't escape the feeling that I'm meddling with powers too great for me when I do. Now and again I want to make music without any great significance."

He chuckled in response, and Maggie blew a few notes, a melody that sounded strangely familiar though she wasn't sure why. Pat watched her from across the fire with her chin in her hand. Maggie closed her eyes and let the song shape itself, drifting up with the tendrils of smoke, giving notes to the feel of the spring air. She stopped abruptly. She knew this song—Mary Grant had sung it. It was a lament for the old world and a prayer for the King's return.

So much for making music without significance.

She opened her eyes, and the professor nodded. His expression was sympathetic. He understood what had just happened.

Soldiers passed the little campfire, carrying supplies and talking in low voices. One of them stopped. Maggie looked up and recognized Harutek.

"An instrument of home," he said, gesturing to the flute. "Though I do not recognize the song."

"It is one of ours," Huss answered. "Will you have a seat, prince?"

Maggie expected Harutek to deny the request, but instead, he laid his cloak on the ground and sat cross-legged upon it. His fish-scale armour gleamed in the firelight, as did his shaven head. Harutek was muscular, handsome, and dignified, every inch a warrior and a prince.

"I hope you will play often," Harutek said. "It will alleviate the hardship of riding. The Ploughman says it is four more days to Athrom."

"Are you eager to get there?" Pat asked. Maggie shot her a look, but Pat didn't acknowledge it.

"Of course," Harutek said. His tone was quiet—humbler, perhaps, than Maggie had expected. She'd been angry with him for forcing Pravik's hand. But it was hard to be angry with what she heard in his voice. Hope.

He looked her directly in the eyes as he spoke. "The

Darkworld has been cut off from mankind for five hundred years," he said. "Our people have lived and died without the sun. We have been decimated by sickness, weakened by lack of light. We should have come above ground long ago."

"But you had a reason to stay hidden," Huss said.

"Yes," Harutek said, and here his voice took on a note of bitterness. "The priests told us it was our duty to stay loyal to the King. Loyalty—that's what they call our hiding like rats in the darkness, giving ourselves over to die."

"And how does loyalty figure into what you're doing now?" Huss asked.

"My loyalty is to our people," Harutek said. He sat a little straighter, and this time looked Huss straight in the eye. "To our future. Not to a being who, if he exists, has shown little love or care for us in centuries."

Maggie blew into the flute once more. The note was mournful.

By late evening, darkness rolled over the camp, felt more than seen. The horses twitched their ears and looked nervously around them, and the soldiers hushed them and stroked their necks, watching the trees just as keenly.

Still sitting by the fire, Maggie let her eyes rove the treetops. In her hands, she clutched a tin cup, tea warming her palms and calming her increasingly edgy spirit. The trees were rustling, but no wind could be felt. The camp was hemmed in on one side by sheer rock, a last remnant of the mountains before the foothills would give way to flatlands, and on the other by the woods—and the aura coming from the woods was unfriendly. Maggie cleared her throat and strained to hear music, a song in the air to give her strength, but she could hear little.

The camp was silent.

Nearby, Rivan stalked from the horses to the Ploughman, who was standing in the midst of the camp. His rough voice echoed off the rock face. "Something is wrong, my lord. Horses don't like it, and neither do we."

"I feel it too," the Ploughman answered. "What would you have us do?"

Rivan opened his mouth to answer, but Cratus, seated at a fire a few feet away, cut him off. "There is nothing *to* do. I would not have thought you Easterners would be so easily spooked by your own forests."

"There is something here," the Ploughman said quietly, "that is not a part of our forests."

"Nonsense," Cratus said, but his voice faltered as a heavy rotting stench filled the air, and from the shadows of the trees two pale blue lights suddenly shone.

Cratus drew his sword. The Ploughman did likewise. The blue lights—eyes, they could now see, pale and pupiless—rose in a wolf-like head from a pool of darkness.

"Great stars," Rivan said. "'Tis a serpent."

What had seemed simply a deep place in the ground, merely a mass of shadows, could be seen now to be the coiled body of an enormous snake. Maggie stood slowly and backed away from the fire as it raised its head, rising until its eyes were level with the horses and then even higher, looking down on the frozen band from a towering height. A snake it undoubtedly was, but not like any serpent they had ever seen. Its was a blind wolf's head, with a wolf's great ears and teeth. And from its mouth came the smell of rot, of death and decay.

Maggie dropped her tin cup and reached for the knife she wore at her side. She had seen such creatures before.

It was Blackness.

The serpent's tongue, forked and blue, flicked. Cratus was the first to act. He shouted a battle cry, running straight at the snake with his sword raised. The serpent's head shot forward. It caught Cratus by the leg and slammed him against the rock face. Maggie heard a crunch and tried not to be sick. Knife in hand, she moved backwards, away from the snake, giving the warriors room. The Ploughman bellowed a cry of his own, and Harutek's warriors let fly their two-pronged spears. The points bounced off the creature's scales. The Ploughman ducked a lash of the creature's long body. Maggie lost sight of him as the horses broke in a panic, pulling their stakes from the ground and shrieking with fear as men tried to get control and fight.

Shadows seemed to attend the creature. The clearing grew darker by the moment. The farmers grabbed at the horses, trying to calm them and get them out of the way. The professor's hands took Maggie's shoulders. He was trembling, though only a little. She turned to look at him. "It will be all right," she said.

Another battle cry sounded, and Maggie turned her head back to the rock face to see Pat leaping onto the serpent's back and trying to drive her sword into it. Pat began to slip as soon she touched its slimy skin, her blade glancing off, momentum making it impossible to finish her attack. She hit the ground, palms first, and the serpent's side undulated toward her as though it would crush her. She rolled out of the way, toward Maggie. Pat's eyes widened as the slime began to eat into the sword, hissing as it did. The metal corroded so fast she was forced to throw her sword aside.

"Ploughman!" Pat shouted. "Aim for its head!"

"Pat!" Maggie screamed. The snake's head was lunging straight for her. As Maggie watched, Harutek appeared seemingly out of nowhere, grabbing Pat and bearing her out of range of the snake's strike. The prince turned and slashed at the creature's head, bellowing as the long fangs hooked into his arm. The serpent jerked him into the air and threw him aside.

"Here!" a loud voice cried. "Creature of darkness, look to me!"

With the words, golden light exploded from the ground beneath the snake's head. The creature dropped the professor's body and recoiled from the force of the light.

The Ploughman's Gift.

The Ploughman stood before the serpent, sword in one hand and staff in the other, his eyes ablaze with golden light and the air whirling with power around him. With a cry, he plunged his sword into the serpent's underbelly. It wailed and shuddered, pulling back, but somehow the Ploughman got his footing on the creature's back and leaped to its head, driving his sword in. The long body shuddered and began to shrink, its wet sides shriveling before their eyes. In minutes all that was left was a long, stinking carcass, and the Ploughman was watching his sword dissolve, steaming and hissing. He dropped it, but the serpent would move no more.

Its black body was streaked with gold dust, as though light had taken form and settled over it.

Cratus still lay groaning on the ground. "Come, Maggie," Professor Huss said. She followed him without question, and he knelt by the Southern commander. The man's leg was soaked with blood where the serpent's fangs had pierced and shaken him, and he clutched a dislocated shoulder.

"Sing, Maggie," Huss said tersely.

Cratus glared at them, but he submitted as Huss tore aside the ripped clothing to examine the wound. The sight and smell made Maggie's stomach lurch. Harutek appeared at her side and knelt by the wounded man as well. His own arm appeared to have been protected by his armour and the cloth of his sleeve, which was torn by the serpent's fangs. "I have some training," he told Huss.

Huss nodded. He looked back at Maggie. "Sing," he said.

She closed her eyes and sought for a song. Strains were rising from the forest, and she took them and wove them into a melody. She wasn't sure what words she was singing or where the melody was coming from, but she sang with one shaking hand on Huss's shoulder. At first she could hear Cratus swearing and protesting, but in a few minutes, he had fallen silent. Everything had.

She wasn't sure how much time had passed when she stopped singing and opened her eyes again. Cratus was sitting up, leaning against the rock face. Huss had finished dressing his leg with Harutek's help. The shoulder was no longer dislocated.

Maggie frowned. She cleared her throat.

"It healed itself," Harutek said quietly. He patted her on the shoulder. "Well done, Maggie."

The old man stood and wiped his hands clean on a rag one of the farmers offered him. The Ploughman was watching the proceedings with his arms folded.

Cratus looked up at him.

"What was all that?" Cratus demanded.

"A serpent," the Ploughman answered. "A creature of the Blackness."

"Not that," Cratus said. "The song. And you. The light. The way the air moved around you—the way *you* moved, like a warrior not of earth. What was all that?"

The Ploughman looked down at Cratus, his expression inscrutable. "Some call them Gifts," he said.

Harutek remained by Cratus as the others moved away.

4

People of the King

IT WAS THREE HOURS AFTER MIDNIGHT when three cloaked and hooded figures proceeded on foot through the streets of Pravik toward the gates and the mountains beyond. They walked slowly, deliberately. None saw them, as was their intent.

They passed through the gates together and followed the road into the mountain forests until they had passed beyond sight of the walls. There they halted.

The tallest of them removed his hood, revealing long, dark hair tied back with a leather strap. The others followed suit, and Divad, Hazrit, and Rehtse regarded each other in silence.

"Kneel, Rehtse," Divad said.

She obeyed. Hazrit and Divad each laid a hand on the young woman's head.

"We speak the words of denouncing," Divad said slowly. "We proclaim you traitor and heretic by the word of the Majesty and release you from his service."

Rehtse closed her eyes and let the words sink in. She had never imagined this ceremony would be used against her— much less that she would ever deliberately provoke the Majesty into denouncing her.

Of course, had they been following protocol properly, one of the Majesty's more muscular sons would finish the ceremony by raising an axe and taking Rehtse's head to seal the denunciation. They were not. Hazrit moved her hand so her palm rested against Rehtse's cheek. Rehtse leaned into the motherly gesture.

"So it has been decreed," Divad said. "So it is done." His voice leveled out a little. "Stay kneeling, Rehtse."

Rehtse heard the smile in Hazrit's voice as she spoke the words of another, very different, ceremony, one that had first been enacted in her life when she was only a small child. "By the will of the King we accept you into the service of the priesthood of the Darkworld," she said. "From this day forth you are his servant. Yours it is to pray and worship, to carry the knowledge of the past forward that our people may be found faithful, to heal and tend their needs. And to serve the Majesty as a daughter serves her father. Will you swear to all these things in the King's name?"

"I will," Rehtse said.

She stood, and Hazrit embraced her. Rehtse clung tightly to the woman who had been the closest thing to a mother to her. Divad waited his turn, and when Hazrit reluctantly let go, he also embraced Rehtse. He laid one hand on her head and said, "Bless you, child. The King be in all your ways."

Rehtse blinked back more tears. Excitement was leaping in her for the journey ahead, but the somberness of denunciation threatened to pull it back down.

"There," Divad said as he stepped away. "You are the first priest in the history of our people to take that vow twice."

"I am the first to survive denunciation," Rehtse said. Her

smile faltered a little. Only two priests in all the last five hundred years had ever *been* denounced—one for plotting to murder the Majesty and one for teaching the people to go aside after Morning Star. She was not especially happy to be in their company. But she turned her face to the shadowed mountains and pulled the letter out of her belt. She had memorized the directions to the cabin where Virginia was waiting.

The cabin where they would begin their journey to find the King.

* * *

Virginia lay in an abandoned shack in the mountains outside Pravik, listening to the sounds of the night. She fingered a pouch full of seeds lying next to her on the musty old cot.

It was her second night in the cabin. She was still waiting for Huss's promised gift of eyes. As she waited, she let the last two and a half years play themselves out in her mind as though she was watching them from some close vantage point. One memory, made all the stronger by the pouch of seeds, was that of awakening the Earth Brethren. Tyrentyllith, the Forest Lord, had given her the seeds. They were life. New life, not yet realized.

She'd fallen asleep in her memories and awakened to a song.

Its notes were sweet, its melody peaceful. A song of healing and triumph. A song of hope. As Virginia listened to it, she saw light battling darkness, a serpent and a golden man. Images and music died away together.

She smiled in the darkness.

An instant later, she was startled by the sound of cloth rustling against the door frame. She sat bolt upright, snatching up the bag of seeds and tucking it inside her cloak. "Who's there?" she asked.

The voice was familiar, but she hadn't placed it before the newcomer answered the question. "Peace," she said. "Professor Huss sent me. I am Rehtse of the Darkworld." Virginia could hear a smile in her voice. "I have come to be your eyes."

* * *

When morning came, Virginia awoke to the smell of something cooking outside the cabin—fish? She stood carefully, feeling her way to the door. The air outside was perfumed with the scent of flowers blooming. Virginia breathed it in as she crossed the damp earth to the fire where Rehtse was cooking breakfast. Her head swam. She was hungrier than she wanted to admit.

Rehtse helped her find a seat on a fallen log and then got busy serving breakfast. Virginia sorted out questions in her mind, wondering where to start. But before she could ask, Rehtse was praying aloud. She chanted softly in a sing-song blessing Virginia couldn't understand. The words were in a lost tongue, one of the languages of the world before the Empire. Then she repeated it in the common tongue.

"We thank thee, O King, for the gift of fish and water," she said. "The life of the Darkworld is in the river thy hand hath created."

Rehtse pushed a small bowl into Virginia's hands. It was

warm.

"Hazrit sent it," Rehtse said. "The soup, I mean. After this I will have to say a new blessing."

Virginia smiled. "Thank you," she said.

Rehtse did not answer—Virginia suspected she had nodded. "Has there been any word of the entourage to Pravik?" Virginia asked.

"Did you expect word?" Rehtse asked. "This is only the second day of their journey."

"No," Virginia said. "Of course not. Forgive my asking—when I am alone, time gets away from me."

Rehtse settled onto the ground next to Virginia, and a moment later began to pray again. "May thy great presence guard their way," she said. "Blind them to the deceiver's ways; deafen them to the deceiver's tongue. Bind them close to thy great heart, King of Heaven, Heart of the World."

Silently, Virginia added her own agreement. She hoped that the King could hear. But even if he could not, it felt right to pray. How better to begin this journey?

The soup was good—salty and oily, but nourishing. When they had finished, Rehtse took Virginia's bowl, clanked around with some equipment, and finally offered her hand.

"To the Highlands?" she said.

* * *

The entourage to Athrom went on in the morning, more sober and watchful after the serpent's attack. Cratus and the Ploughman rode at the head of the column, both men bandaged and stiff. Harutek kept command of his own warriors.

Maggie rode with Professor Huss in a wagon just behind Harutek's warriors. She sang throughout the day, sometimes wordless songs, sometimes stories or poetry in music. Now and again she played with the flute. She knew Harutek was listening, so she sang especially for him. It seemed to her that he needed it. As the miles fell away, so did her unhappiness with this journey. She was still not at all certain they should be doing this—but they had already defeated the Blackness once, their Gifts were strong, they were together. Some among them were even hopeful.

* * *

Virginia and Rehtse walked throughout the day, following a common road, until dusk began to fall on their way. They didn't stop. Rehtse's eyes were sharp, and to Virginia, loss of light made little difference. Birds called back and forth in the woods, their cries loud and lonely. They talked little, both lost in thought and concentrating on their steps. But as the road leveled out for a while, Virginia finally asked the question that had been on her heart since Rehtse's arrival.

"How is it that you are here?" she asked.

"You were in need of eyes," Rehtse said. "The King saw your need and sent me."

It was a good answer, a faithful one. And one that purposefully left out a great deal. Virginia stumbled a little over a rough patch in the path. "I know a little of you," she said. "I know you lost one you loved in the battle in Athrom."

There was silence. Then, slowly, Rehtse answered, "Caasi

would have been glad of this—of where we are going. He truly believed in the King, as I fear his father and brother do not."

"The Majesty is called the father of seventeen sons," Virginia asked. "How is it that I've only heard of two?"

"The others are insignificant," Rehtse said. "Because they are not really his sons—the young men who stand up with him at feasts are surrogates, there for ceremony. His real sons died in childhood."

Virginia gasped. "Fifteen of them?"

"Sun-sickness," Rehtse said. "Many who are born to the Darkworld do not live to full age. That is the curse of living in darkness. We priests do the best we can to help. But we also live without the sun. We cannot do all we would."

"None of us can," Virginia said. She fell quiet a few minutes more, letting bird calls fill the silence between them. "Caasi was one of the first to answer the call when I shared my vision about the Gypsies and urged the men to Athrom to rescue them. I have always felt . . . responsible for his death."

The words were a reaching out. Virginia held her breath as she waited for Rehtse's response. All her life her Gift had made her enemies and driven even her friends from her. With this young woman from another world, she hoped it might be different somehow.

"Then you are responsible for making Caasi more than a man," Rehtse answered quietly. "His death was earned gloriously in obedience to the King, in defense of the innocent. He was all that the Darkworld is supposed to be—all that he wanted to be in his most beautiful ideals. For that I thank you."

"And yet you were wounded by it," Virginia said.

"I do not deny the wound hurts," Rehtse said. "I have been

accused of not feeling it, but that is only because I do not weep in the presence of those who do not honour him and his death as they should."

"Rehtse," Virginia asked again, softly, "how is it that you come to be here?"

This time the pause was sighing, and Rehtse did not give the same answer. "The Majesty does not believe in the King any longer. I opposed him to his face—deliberately provoked him. So he released me from his service."

Virginia heard the pain in Rehtse's voice, the depth she was not sharing.

"I am sorry," she said.

Leaves rustled overhead. Rehtse's voice shook a little, but she was no less sincere. "He has only sent me where my heart longs to go—in search of the one I truly wish to serve." She tightened her guiding grip on Virginia's arm. "I am glad to be going with you. It is not easy to serve the King when others do not believe."

Virginia smiled and laid her free hand over Rehtse's. "I could not ask for a better guide," she said.

* * *

The wagon rumbled over the road, bumping and jolting. Evening was falling on another day, and the road through the mountains was strangely hushed but for the sounds of the horses and wheels. Pat, on horseback, pulled alongside the wagon to check on Maggie and Huss before cantering ahead to the front of the line. They had opted to ride in the wagon for awhile, giving relief to both the horses and their own bodies.

Maggie looked out over the side at the flatlands of Galce stretching below them, crowned by a setting sun that turned the sky gold, orange, and faint purple. Athrom was still three days away.

Another shadow fell across the wagon: Merlyn Cratus, riding back through the column. He paused and looked keenly down at them. Maggie kept her face composed as she met his eyes.

"Good evening," she said.

He nodded curtly. "And to you."

She cleared her throat. "You are well?" she asked.

He smiled, but there was no joy in the smile. "Healing very quickly," he said. "My wounds are minor. By some miracle. I know what they were before you sang."

"You might try thanking her," Huss said.

Maggie shook her head, flushing. "There's nothing to thank me for," she said, giving Huss a look that pleaded with him not to push the issue. "You are simply a strong man who's healing well."

"By some miracle," Cratus repeated. "Perhaps the same miracle that is eating the rust and restoring the metal on these wagon wheels."

Maggie frowned, unsure of how to respond. Was he joking? Before she could say anything, the general nodded again, said, "Good evening to you," and rode ahead.

They stopped for the night not half an hour later, the men at the head of the column already making camp in a hollow by the time Maggie and the wagon reached it. As the men unloaded the tent and a few other necessities, she rounded the cart and stared at the wheels. The metal was shining in patches.

It looked as though new metal was bursting out through the rust. She frowned. Had it always been like that?

Fireflies began to flicker around the wagon, lighting up through the spokes of the wheels, and she stood and brushed herself off. Tents rose and pots clanked: the comforting sounds and sights of camp. The smell of woodsmoke reached her as a fire was started, and she realized how dark it was quickly getting. The men around the fire were reduced to silhouettes in the deepening shadows.

Overhead, stars were beginning to come out.

When the tent was erected, Maggie sat in the opening and hugged her knees to her chest. Huss wandered over and stood near her.

"I wish you wouldn't call attention to my singing," Maggie said. "It makes me uneasy. And I don't like Cratus watching me."

In the darkness she imagined she could see his eyes, somber as he spoke. "There is power in your songs," he said. "Like there was in Mary's songs. For all of us. You have truly inherited her Gift, Maggie."

Maggie just sighed. She knew she was Gifted—that somehow she had inherited the Gift born and then killed in Mary Grant, her former guardian and member of the Council for Exploration Into Worlds Unseen. But she was not sure she liked it.

Crickets were singing in the woods around them, the chirps punctuated by cracks from the fire as the farmers stoked the pile of wood. The night was full of songs. Maggie could feel them all there, waiting for her to hear them and weave other music from their strains.

"What does it mean?" she asked.

Huss was silent. "The Gifts are a sign of the King's coming," he said. "I think in some way they manifest his power through you."

She shook her head again. "That doesn't help me. How are we are supposed to use them? What are we for, Professor?"

A dark shadow approached. It was Harutek. "If you'll allow me," he said. "The priesthood taught us that among the Gifted, six would be chosen for a special task. They would usher the King back into the world. That is why our priests have so embraced some of you. The Six are named by their Gifts—the Warrior, the Seer." He smiled in the darkness. "The Singer."

"And yet you don't believe it?" Maggie asked.

Harutek sighed. "I am not sure what I believe," he said. "I only know that our beliefs in this King have hurt us more than they've helped. I am not faithless as the priests would paint me. But I cannot cling to a faith that is killing us and keeping us in darkness when light beckons. I do not believe your King would want me to."

"In a world like this one," Huss rumbled, "it is not always easy to know the difference between darkness and light."

Harutek bowed. "Perhaps. But this is not why I came. I came to say thank you. I hear your songs, and they lift my spirits. I think you mean them to."

"I do," Maggie said, smiling.

Harutek bowed again, more deeply this time, and withdrew. Something else was drawing his attention near the edge of the camp. He walked into hushed conversation with a few of the guards.

The Ploughman approached, his eyes on Harutek and the

guards. "What is it?" Huss asked.

"Harutek believes something is following us," the Ploughman said.

"Another serpent?" Maggie asked.

"Perhaps. His men have been hearing and seeing things in the dark. No one else has sensed anything amiss. Cratus thinks it is nothing."

"But you have great respect for Harutek's ability to see in the dark," Maggie said.

"Precisely."

"What do you think it is?" Maggie asked.

"I don't know," the Ploughman said. "But I will be happier when we get out of these woods and onto the plains where we can see what's around us."

"Then we will not be far from Athrom," Maggie said.

"I confess I will be happier when that is the case too," the Ploughman said. "The closer we are to Athrom, the closer we are to leaving it again." He fell silent. Maggie listened to the balladry playing in his cloak and hair like a wind.

Harutek appeared before them suddenly again. "We should not camp," he said, his arms folded in what Maggie was coming to recognize as a stubborn stance.

The Ploughman frowned. "The men need rest."

"They are soldiers," Harutek said. "They can do without."

The Ploughman glanced at Maggie and Huss. "We are not all soldiers."

"Regardless," Harutek said. "Here there is danger."

Another voice intruded—Cratus's, near enough to make Maggie jump. She hadn't realized he was there. "It is nonsense," he said. "My men have heard and seen nothing."

Harutek's eyes bored into the general. "It is your men the presence follows," he said. "Something in the forest is angry with you. Just because your eyes and ears are not sharp enough to sense it does not mean it is not here."

Cratus's eyes narrowed. "Are you insult—"

A sudden call, lonely, eerie, rose over the forest. The encampment hushed and held silent under its spell until at last it died away, mournful as the cry of a wolf but far less earthly.

"Look there!" someone shouted, and Maggie turned to see, through the jumping silhouettes of the men, a tree where a human shape stood, holding to a branch high above. The form was slender as a boy and unmoving. It seemed almost to be part of the tree. One of Cratus's men let fly an arrow, but it missed. In the next instant the shape had disappeared. Only the trees could be seen in the darkness.

"Gather weapons; go after him!" Cratus declared. The Ploughman reached out and stopped him.

"No," he said. "It was only a boy."

"A scout," Cratus countered. "He will bring back others."

"We do not know that he is an enemy," the Ploughman said. "I will not be responsible for the life of one who was merely curious."

"My lord," Harutek said. "My suggestion has not changed. We ought not to encamp here tonight. There is danger in the woods, and none of us wishes another battle. If our presence here offends the forest, then why do we not keep moving?"

Cratus scoffed. "Offends the forest, man? Do you think it a living thing?"

Harutek's eyes bored into him again, an unnerving stare that made the general shift uncomfortably. "I have spent all my life buried beneath unliving rock," Harutek said. "That"—he waved toward the trees, swaying gently in a summer wind, their creaks and the rustling of leaves mingled with the chorus of crickets and the noises of other creatures stirring—"that is alive. And it does not want us to be here."

The Ploughman nodded. "I will tell the men to break camp. Maggie, you and Professor Huss can continue to ride in the wagon. We'll erect a cover for it. Try to get some sleep."

A moment later the leaders broke up to gather their men, and within minutes the process of tearing down had begun. Maggie blinked at the speed with which things could change. She looked back up at the tree, hoping for another glimpse of the shape that had looked down on them from the branches.

This is alive, Harutek had said. Maggie recalled Virginia's story of awakening the Earth Brethren, spirits of trees and beasts and wind.

But though her heart pounded with anticipation as she lifted her eyes, nothing was there.

"They are wise to leave the forest," Professor Huss said.

"I don't—" Maggie searched for the right words. "I don't feel danger here."

"Not for you." Huss smiled. "The power here is not angry with you."

"Professor," Maggie blurted, aware that the clamour of packing up camp kept her words from any who would overhear, "where is Virginia? Do you know?"

The old man smiled and looked away, but Maggie stood and leaned close to him. "You had something to do with her disappearance. Tell me."

Huss gestured vaguely to the darkness. "She might be . . .

out there," he said. "She is going to Bryllan to find the King."

Maggie's heart skipped a beat. "Alone?" she asked.

Huss shook his head. "Not for long," he said. "I have asked Divad to send one of the Darkworld priests with her, and I believe he will do it." Huss was quiet a moment. "I do not trust the prince, Maggie. He is turning against the King."

Maggie winced. But she didn't defend Harutek. She was too busy processing what Huss had told her. "We're on this journey," she said slowly, "because the Ploughman doesn't really believe the King will come soon. Because we're all afraid we have to do without him. Do you really think Virginia will find him?"

"I think we need him," Huss said. "More than ever. That is all I know."

Thirty minutes later, they loaded into the wagon. Huss's words had troubled her—had undone some of the confidence she'd been gaining on the journey. She sang softly, songs more sad and confused than she wanted to admit. Perhaps she was drawing them from somewhere inside herself. The songs offered up by the earth around her were still there, still to be woven into music, but there was in them anger and mystery and power so deep it frightened her. So she left the forest's songs alone, and the entourage rumbled down the road in the dark toward the flatlands of southern Galce—and beyond them, Italya and the capital city, Athrom.

* * *

In the morning, Rehtse and Virginia followed a little-used road southwest. They spent the day mostly in silence, as Rehtse tried to navigate territory that was utterly unfamiliar to her and Virginia concentrated on keeping her steps steady beneath her. But the silence was good and companionable, punctuated by Rehtse's prayers and strengthened by the sense of oneness both felt. When the sun was again setting over the dusty road and evening birds were singing in the thick trees, they stopped to make camp.

"In the Darkworld we burn fish oil," Rehtse said. "I used all I had to warm up that soup of Hazrit's. Forgive my ignorance. Tell me how to make a fire?"

Virginia laughed and began to give instructions, relying on her memories of sleeping in the hills with her grandfather. She felt around for a stick and found one, breaking it easily. "You need them dry, not wet or green. You might have the best luck if you gather branches that have fallen into the road."

Rehtse went off. The falling light bathed Virginia's face as she sat facing west, toward the thick forests of northern Galce and the open sea, the Isle of Bryllan and the Highland slopes of home. Rehtse was singing to herself as she worked. The song was in a minor key, haunting and ancient, yet Virginia heard the joy in it, the unquenchable hope.

She let the sounds of the woods come over her, the evening fragrance of trees and flowers, the texture of dry earth and rock beneath her fingers, the wiry length of creeping plants encroaching upon the road. She knew they were still in the Eastern Mountains—not far from Pravik, really, despite the ground they had covered. She wondered if Rehtse knew a prayer that could give a blind woman swiftness in her steps.

Rehtse's footsteps were light as she approached. She lowered an armload of branches to the ground at Virginia's feet.

"Will these do?" she asked.

Virginia reached down and started to order the pile, laying kindling, her fingers feeling out the wood. She tilted her head up and smiled.

"Very well," she said. She held up a bigger branch. "Can you find more of these?"

Rehtse was off again without a word—Virginia thought she had nodded in response—but she was soon singing again. As she listened, Virginia became aware that the song was another prayer, an evening chant. She wondered what it would have been like to grow up in a world that believed in the King and honoured his memory in its traditions. She frowned. Chants and prayers had not kept the Majesty and his son from forgetting. Just as exposure to the world beyond the Veil had not kept Lord Robert from siding with the Blackness and betraying Virginia nearly to her death. Was this mankind's doom—to forget and betray the One who was the life in their veins?

When Rehtse came back, it didn't take her long to light the fire, and they sat together listening to it crackle and spark. In the silence and the listening was companionship. Both felt it, and both were as warmed by its presence as by the fire.

* * *

Rehtse awoke as soon as the sun began to rise and sat marveling at the world as it moved from green to green, from deep depths to brilliance. Virginia was asleep, her face resting on her arm, her grey cloak covering all but her feet and head.

Even she changed in the light of the rising sun. Rehtse had never known that the air could be so alive with light that everything within it could be transformed.

There had been lights in the Darkworld, the lights of fish-oil torches. But they moved the air only from shadow to shadow. That light had been sleep. To be in the sun was waking.

Rehtse breathed the living air and tried to feel it flowing all through her, from her head to her fingertips to her feet. She closed her eyes for a moment just to feel the sun falling on her face, the breeze blowing through her hair, the openness all around. She had always known the Darkworld lacked light and space, but never in all her dreams had she imagined how much that meant. Only sometimes at night, when she had lain awake thinking of the King and worshiping in her deepest heart, she had felt something like brushes of light and air and open places, and then she had experienced longing.

Once she had dared express this to Divad. "All worship now is longing," he had told her. "Only when the King returns will worship cease to hurt."

Those words rang in her head now as she lifted her hands in the sunlight and swallowed back a lump in her throat, quietly murmuring the words of the ancient morning prayer, thanking the King, the Heart of the World, in an ache that was newly strong here where she was surrounded by beauty and by light.

Movement behind her caused her to turn. Virginia was sitting up, pushing her cloak aside. Rehtse found herself smiling with an unexpected burst of affection for her companion. It was, it seemed to her, another part of her worship.

"Good morning," Rehtse said. To her relief, her voice did not break the spell of the sunrise.

Virginia's smile was soft. She covered her knees with her cloak and let her hands rest in her lap, idly wiping away drops of dew. The fire next to her was black, still smoking just a little.

"Do you want me to bring more firewood?" Rehtse asked, poking the smoking sticks and flaking ash away.

"Do we want to build a fire?" Virginia asked in return. "We have nothing to cook on it." She sighed. "It may well be a hungry, difficult road to Bryllan."

Rehtse smiled as she uncovered a few glowing embers at the bottom of the fire, golden in the morning light. "I am a priestess," she said. "My whole life has been a difficult road." She held out her hands and soaked up the warmth, then took Virginia's hands and moved them over it as well. "I have learned to make the best of it," she said.

The island of Bryllan lay to the west. When the road forked and plunged more deeply down the mountain, Rehtse waited at the fork for a few moments, lifted her hands, and murmured something. Then she took the left path, and they journeyed on. They talked a little. After several hours Virginia asked, "Do you know where we're going?"

"West," Rehtse said.

"How does one born in darkness tell direction?" Virginia asked.

Rehtse smiled. "A strange question for you to ask."

Virginia smiled. "I have to trust others."

"As do I," Rehtse said. "In the Darkworld we made markers on the cavern walls, and some made a life's study of the paths underground. They became guides to lead us."

"And now?" Virginia asked. "Who leads us now?"

"I am trusting to the King to direct our paths," Rehtse said. "He wants us to find him. So he will guide me aright."

"And how do you know that he's guiding you?" Virginia asked.

"I am believing," Rehtse said, "that he will guide where I put my feet."

"Rehtse," Virginia said, hesitating a little, "that sounds an awful lot like trusting to luck."

"I am a priestess," Rehtse said. She grinned. "I don't believe in luck."

An hour later, they came across markings on the trees showing the points of the compass. The path was indeed heading west. Rehtse announced as much to Virginia, who shook her head and smiled as the priestess formally lifted her hands and gave thanks. The markers also indicated that they were still much closer to Pravik than Virginia wanted to be, but she swallowed her frustration. They could only move as quickly as they could move.

Night fell once again. Their stomachs and feet ached, but still they walked.

Virginia heard a sound and stopped Rehtse with a touch.

"What is it?" the priestess asked.

"Come off the path," Virginia said quietly. She let Rehtse lead her off the road into the underbrush, branches pulling at her skirt as they ducked into the shelter of the trees. Rehtse did not ask again, but she was tense with unknowing.

Virginia said nothing. She listened.

She heard it again. Male voices, somewhere close by.

"Men," she said, her voice even quieter than before. Rehtse pressed Virginia's hand and sucked in her breath as the voices became suddenly loud enough to indicate that the men were on the road just before them—probably within sight, Virginia thought. Their voices had been muffled by the trees; their footsteps unheard on the damp earth.

". . . nothing out here anyway," one of them finished. The other grunted in reply. One man—a third?—coughed.

Virginia could hear the clink of weaponry and chain mail. Rehtse was still tense, and Virginia tried to crouch even lower in the brush.

"Back to camp," the first man announced. "Patrols are a waste of time. Those cowards never even leave their city."

"Wait," said another man, and Virginia's heart stopped. "What's that?"

They were quiet for a moment, swords clanking as they bent down. Rehtse's hand closed around Virginia's. She was poised to run. Virginia didn't have to ask what the men had seen. She knew. Footprints in the damp earth, probably leading straight toward them.

And though they were close to Pravik, Virginia knew from Rehtse's reaction and the way her own hair stood up on the back of her neck that these men were not friends. Their leader's words also betrayed them. His accent was Southern. The other speaker's words bore the tinge of some other region, perhaps of the far north. They were almost certainly High Police.

But why were High Police patrolling the forest?

Rehtse shifted as though she would reveal herself. Virginia gripped her hand more tightly. The brush before them was moving, branches clearing away.

"Well, well, well," the Northern voice said. "What do we have here?"

Rehtse stood suddenly and brushed off her long skirt. Virginia stayed where she was, crouched in the underbrush. Rehtse's voice, tinged with its own strange accent, greeted the men in the name of the King. She was utterly calm.

"The King, is it?" the Northerner said. "And who might you be—both of you?"

"I am Rehtse, a priestess of the Darkworld," Rehtse answered. "My friend and I are traveling through these lands."

"Alone," the Northerner said, "and unprotected." Virginia's skin crawled. The third man cut in. "Don't be a fool," he whispered. "She might be—"

"She isn't," the Northerner hissed back. "These two are no threat." Virginia could hear the leer in his voice. "Just two women alone in the woods."

"You are mistaken," Rehtse said. "We are not unprotected."

Twigs crunched as the man took a menacing step forward. His voice was low. "And who protects you, woman?"

"The King himself," Rehtse calmly answered. "And all the world in his service."

A smile pulled at Virginia's mouth. Rehtse was incredibly foolhardy. But after all, hadn't Virginia known the protection of the King before this?

She stood slowly, staying close to Rehtse so the men couldn't suddenly step in and separate them. "Rehtse is right," she said. "We are not unprotected. But *you* are on unfriendly ground. What are the High Police doing so far from home?"

"The whole world is under our rule," the Southerner said,

his tone surly but lacking the leering undertones of his companion.

"Not this corner of it," Virginia replied.

"That is our business," the Southerner said. "As are you. You'll come with us, no trouble given." To his companions, he said, "We take them back to camp and turn them over to the commander. They are under my protection for now, understand?"

Virginia smiled at the grudging grunts that replied. A hand took her arm—Rehtse's hand, firm but gentle. The men didn't touch them as they stepped out of the brush and began to follow the police up the road. Soon, Virginia could smell campfire smoke on the wind and hear more voices, along with the sounds of horses and wagons. This was more than a small scouting party.

Great King, she sent up, *if you can hear me, protect us. We are coming to seek you if only you will grant us freedom.*

A light wind rustled the branches over their heads.

They stepped out from the tree cover into some kind of clearing. Rehtse's voice sounded low in her ear, remarkably unafraid. "It is an encampment," she said. "They fly flags of green and black. I see thirty men, maybe more."

Virginia nodded. From the sounds and smells she would have guessed as much. But the question remained: why were they here, so close to Pravik?

The men halted, and Rehtse and Virginia stood waiting while the leader entered a tent. Virginia could hear his muffled voice drifting out through the cloth, reporting to someone who answered gruffly. A moment later the women were ushered inside.

The smell in the tent was overwhelming, a mix of meat, unwashed flesh, and smoke. Virginia nearly gagged on it. The gruff voice addressed them quickly. "Well? Who are you? What are you doing skulking in our woods?"

"I am Rehtse, a priestess of the Darkworld and servant of the true King," Rehtse said. "We are journeying west to Galce. All this we have already told your men."

"And who is she?" the voice asked. Virginia remained silent and cautioned Rehtse with her fingertips. The priestess did not disappoint her. "My sister. It is my privilege to speak for her, for as you can see, she is blind."

The gruff man snorted. "That hardly affects her mouth."

"It is not easy to speak to someone you cannot even see," Rehtse said.

"While you seem to have no trouble speaking," the man said. There was a sound as though he was pushing a stool back and standing. "And what can you tell me of the other woman in the woods?"

Virginia frowned. Who were they talking about?

"It cannot be a coincidence that you are wandering these forests around our camp just as that black-cloaked witch has declared war on us," the voice said. "You are working with her."

The words escaped Virginia almost without her bidding them to. "We are not," she said.

"Oh, so you can speak!" the commander said. "And with feeling."

"The woman of whom you speak," Virginia said. "She is one of the Order of the Spider?"

"She's a witch, yes," the commander said. "Gone rogue,

they say. Rumour has it she no longer pays allegiance to the emperor. Rumour has it she's killing off her Order and using their power to grow her own. But you would already know that, wouldn't you?"

Virginia's hands trembled. "If you believe us in nothing else, my lord, believe that we have nothing to do with the woman Evelyn and her designs, whatever they may be. We did not even know she was here."

"She's here all right," the commander said. "Panicking our animals and poisoning our food. That pestilence is here."

"Why do you not simply take her captive?" Rehtse asked.

The commander ignored her. "If you're not one of hers, whose are you? Everyone has a side in this world, for all we're supposed to be one single blighted empire."

"We told you," Rehtse said. "We are servants of the true King."

The man snorted again. "So you believe in fairy tales. Very good. That still doesn't tell me what I want to know. Do you come from Pravik?"

"My home is in the Darkworld," Rehtse said.

"And mine in Bryllan," Virginia said.

The commander laughed. "I'll believe that. Your accents betray you—if you are sisters, you were divided at birth. So tell me—"

Suddenly he tore Virginia away from Rehtse, shoving her against a post in the tent and holding a blade to her throat. "Who are you?"

She was silent, and he continued. "These woods are full of rumours. I've heard tell of a blind woman the Order wants. That witch will pay a handsome price if you might just happen to be her."

"My lord . . ." one of the men said nervously.

"Shut up!" the commander snapped back. He didn't release the pressure on Virginia's throat, and the cold steel began to sting. "Tell me," he said, "blind Seer of Pravik, how well can you see?"

Virginia did not answer. Finally the man pulled his knife away, and she swallowed convulsively. She wondered what was happening to Rehtse.

"Your silence betrays you," the man said.

Virginia swallowed once more. "What would the witch want with me?" she asked.

"I suggest you ask her that when you see her," the commander answered. Virginia heard something behind her, and Rehtse cried out.

Then everything went black.

5

Enemies and Friends

THE LIGHTS OF THE CITY glowing into the darkness were the first glimpse of Athrom the entourage saw. They had been passing through Italya's flatlands with hardly a pause, and now the land dipped down as though the course of the world was rushing toward the imperial city.

Athrom, City of Dragons, City of Lights.

Maggie left the covered wagon to stretch her legs and breathe fresh air just as they crested a ridge and saw the city beneath the stars. The Ploughman rode at the head of the line, wrapped in his dark cloak, a warm wind blowing around him. He reined in his horse at the sight and sat motionless, looking toward it.

What was passing through his mind was anyone's guess. Maggie thought of Libuse in Pravik and wished her well.

A silhouette appeared from below: Cratus, riding back after scouting ahead. He said something to Harutek and the Ploughman, and the men exchanged murmurs. Maggie shivered in the warm breeze and turned back to the wagon. Cratus had been watching her, and it unnerved her. But the rust on the wagon wheels had cleared completely. A lame-footed horse walking by the sick cart while she sang cantered beautifully now. And her songs continued to come, wanting to be sung more than she wanted to sing them.

Prince Harutek rode up beside the wagon. "Shall we draw back the cover?" he asked. "So that you may see the city as we enter it? It is a great wonder, they say—whatever else it may be."

Maggie nodded. She wanted to see the others as they rode, and the sky overhead, and the city itself. She wanted to feel the warm wind. Harutek set to work pulling the cover back.

And so Maggie sat in the open air, holding Huss's hand, as they entered the city. The gates soared overhead, golden, ivory, carved and glorious. They were there not for protection—Athrom was not a walled city and had no enemies—but for ceremony. Maggie kept silent as they passed through, straining her neck to their carved heights. The walls of a great coliseum were visible in the distance. Maggie saw Harutek's grim face as he looked at it. It was in defending the Gypsies there that his brother Caasi had died.

Maggie's throat tightened, and she thought of Virginia whose vision had sent the Ploughman, Harutek and Caasi, and many other brave men to the Gypsies' rescue. They had gone, recognizing their enmity with the Empire and all it stood for. They had gone because they could not allow a race of people to die, and with them, the hope they stood for—the hope of freedom and of the King.

So why were they here now?

Horse hooves beside the cart drew her attention, and she met the eyes of the Ploughman. He too felt the strangeness of being here, of the very idea of alliance with those who had always been their enemies. Her heart went out to him. Cratus was near, so Maggie dropped her voice to keep him from hearing.

"You have seen supernatural deliverance in Pravik and here in Athrom. Even on the road as you battled the serpent. The powers that served you then have not abandoned you now."

He tried to smile, but was not triumphant. "This is not a battle," he said.

She looked at him, equally unsmiling. "Isn't it?"

"There!" Cratus cut in, pointing toward a shining ivory palace on the crest of a hill, rising from the very center of the great city. He rode up alongside the Ploughman and cast a glance at Maggie, who turned her eyes to the palace. "That is the Jewel of Athrom," Cratus said. "The palace of Lucien Morel, the man who rules the world. You are facing your destiny, friend. The emperor will see you tomorrow."

The Ploughman nodded, but still he seemed troubled.

* * *

The main street of Athrom was a wide thoroughfare passing through rich boroughs, with darkened shops and gardens on all sides. The scent of orchids and orange blossoms drifted through the night air, and glowing lamps flickered as the cart rolled over a smooth marble road.

It was beautiful, Maggie thought. Truly, peacefully, awe-inspiringly beautiful.

At the end of the thoroughfare, the palace itself glowed

like an ivory moon setting on the horizon. Guards came out to meet them as they reached the low walls that surrounded the palace, wearing the black and green of the hated High Police. But they came courteously, opening the gates and allowing them quick entrance.

The wagon rocked as Pat jumped inside. She hunkered down next to Maggie with her arms folded. She stayed silent, aware of the listening ears on all sides, but Maggie saw the words written in Pat's eyes.

I don't like this.

For a moment Maggie closed her own eyes and tried to listen to the song of the city, but she could hear nothing. The silence was not like a breathing thing in waiting, but like a great absence—she had felt and heard such silence just before the serpent attacked. Suddenly the grandeur and beauty of the city felt hollow.

"Come," one of Cratus's men said, holding out a hand to her. Reluctantly, she released Huss's hand, exchanged a quick glance with Pat, and accepted the man's assistance. Pat jumped down before anyone could offer to help her. All around, the men were dismounting, unloading, brushing themselves off. In the courtyard of the ruler of the world, the men of Pravik were suddenly very small, very dusty, very gruff and quiet.

A palace servant—one who carried himself with some authority—offered his hand to Maggie. "This way, miss," he said. "You will stay in the west quarters for the night."

Alarm filled her at the thought of being separated from the others. "But—Ploughman!" she called, relieved that he was quick to hear her and approach. "I do not wish to be separated from you," she said.

He frowned at the servant. "We did not plan to separate," he said. "General?"

Cratus approached. "Yes?"

"We do not wish to be separated," the Ploughman said. "Is there nowhere we can stay all together?"

Cratus cleared his throat. "I had you all stationed for the night in rooms that would befit each one's status."

The Ploughman shook his head. "One room," he said. "We do not care much for status. Surely somewhere in this palace you have a room big enough for all of us? My men, and the women, and the professor and me. Harutek and his warriors too, if they will stay with us. If you cannot accommodate that request, we will happily stay in a stable. Forgive us, general, and write us off as shameful rustics. But we would stay together."

Maggie's heart nearly burst with gratitude, even as Cratus gave the Ploughman a grudging acquiescence and some of the guards sneered. Let others think them ridiculous. Here in this place, they were a family. And they needed each other desperately.

"I will keep my own men with me," Harutek said quietly. "But we need not stay with the Ploughman."

"Come then," Cratus said, scanning the yard to see if all were ready. They were. He turned and led them up a flight of marble stairs. Grand doors opened for them, and they passed into a great hall adorned with fountains and paintings and crystal lights. Guards lined it. They watched the newcomers wordlessly.

A man in long blue robes met them and bowed. "Your journey has been long, General Cratus," he said.

"Indeed it has, steward," Cratus answered. He fell to discussing the travelers' peculiar requests for sleeping arrangements. The guards in the hall watched, every eye on the people of Pravik and every mouth utterly silent.

"Curse their quiet," Pat muttered suddenly.

With Pat's words, Maggie knew why the men's silence was so unnerving.

Unlike the absence of song underlying the city, this was a waiting silence, and she did not know what they were all waiting for.

* * *

The Ploughman stood at the door, staff in hand, as his farmers filed in one by one. The room was large and ornate, a banqueting room. To Cratus's credit, he had not put them out in a stable. The Ploughman had waved away the suggestion that Cratus rouse servants to prepare beds. A few of the men brought their traveling things in, and they laid out their bedrolls, this time under chandeliers and a muted mural instead of under the stars.

Maggie sat on the floor, and the Ploughman came and sat beside her. Huss settled on her other side. No one was sleeping. Every eye was on the Ploughman now.

He cleared his throat. "We have come a long way," he said. "If all goes well, we will make the journey home in a few days' time. I know you are anxious to be gone from here. You are not more anxious than I."

Some of the men answered that with chuckles and cracks about the Ploughman's waiting lady. The Ploughman ignored them and continued. "I know that some of you have questioned my decision to come here. Perhaps you have feared that I was giving up on our dream. I am not—I have not. I never will. We are here to see if, as Pravik, we can find a way to coexist with the Empire. But we will not give up who we are. Pravik remains a bastion of freedom, and always will—because of you. Because you are committed to that freedom, and you are willing to give your lives for it."

The Ploughman hesitated. "On the road here we faced a creature of the Blackness," he said. "We defeated it. I believe it is a sign of what is to come for us. There may be a battle of some kind ahead. But we will fight it, and we will prevail."

He turned to Maggie, catching her off guard. "Will you sing?" he asked.

Maggie nodded, seeking for words. She closed her eyes and tried her hardest to listen past the city's terrible silence. Her songs always began with hearing: she did not create them. It had been the same way for Mary Grant before she was murdered by the Order of the Spider.

But she could hear nothing.

She tried hard to lose awareness of her surroundings, of the clearing of voices and the expectant faces. She tried to will away the consciousness of Pat's presence, even of Huss and the Ploughman. Just to hear.

Still nothing.

Her mouth was dry. She had not always heard songs, of course. But since the first song had come to her in Pravik, the songs had been ever present, *always* there if she listened hard enough.

Where were they now?

"Maggie?" Pat asked. "What is it?"

Opening her eyes, she blinked away tears. "I can't hear anything," she said. "No songs—nothing."

"Make your own," Pat urged. "Can't you?"

"I—" Maggie frowned. "I can't sew without thread. I can't hear anything." She swallowed hard. "It's this city." she said. "There's no song here—nothing, only a silence I don't understand." She didn't say the words that were shouting through her now, feeling traitorous after the Ploughman's comforting speech. *We should never have come here.*

Pat cleared her throat. "Do you remember the silver thread?" she asked. "The Huntsman you saw in the Eastern Lands? The story about the King you heard in the Gypsy camp?"

Maggie nodded. Pat was naming things close to her heart, small things that had stirred her hope in the King more than the great battles fought by the Ploughman and his Golden Warriors. Pat had shared none of these experiences, but Maggie had told her of them, and now Pat told them back.

"Well," Pat said. "Can you listen beyond the city?"

For a moment they looked at each other. Then Maggie felt a smile tugging at her lips, and she closed her eyes and bowed her head. Her mind ranged beyond the painted ceiling and the crystal chandeliers, beyond the city, up into the stars where the Huntsman was on the ride.

Somewhere impossibly far off, she thought she heard a horn sounding. And then a song.

Hear the call of the Huntsman's horn,
The stars all sing when the chase is on.

Over the sky fields and 'cross the moon
The darkness meets its downfall soon.

The song rose warm and alive in her throat, a song that had never before sung itself through human instrument. Its strains were burning, distant, far, and cold, an otherworldly chant of adoration, of highest praises, of dreams.

And then, though her eyes were still closed and she could not see it, the mural overhead came to life.

It began as rays of light falling through the darkness of the room like starlight, sparkling, forming celestial patterns on the floor. The eyes of the travelers were drawn up in wonder to see the colours of the mural swirling and rearranging themselves, pictures of the Empire swallowed up in far older images. They saw the River-Daughter in crystalline beauty, Tyrentyllith of the Woods in verdant splendour, Gwyrion of the Wild Things attended by his winged and four-footed attendants. They saw a great hunter riding across the sky with stars in his cloak. They saw the Sea-Father in regions of ice and fire, and they saw the dancing colours of the ancient Shearim.

Falling rays of light lit upon each one who watched, eyes wide, and in the gentle touch of light they heard the wind blowing, Llycharath, Spirit in the Wind, echoing the sweet, strange strains that Maggie's voice still sang.

And then, for an instant, all the colours gathered themselves together and became a pure white light like the heart of the purest star, and in the light everyone in the room thought he could see a man. Maggie opened her eyes. The light illuminated her face and her eyes, and she opened her mouth to speak and smiled, reaching up as though she could touch him.

The light vanished.

The vision, and the man at the center of it, was gone.

* * *

Virginia awoke to the gentle playing of the wind through her hair. Her head was throbbing, and moving it sent pain all through her neck and shoulders. A voice was calling her.

"Little sister . . ."

"Llycharath," she whispered back. Her hands were bound in front of her, as were her feet. She was leaning on something warm—Rehtse's back, she realized.

"You are not alone," the voice of the wind whispered in her ear. The cool breeze, bearing the scent of flowers with it, felt good around her aching head.

"Can you help us?" Virginia asked.

A boot nudged the side of her leg.

"Who do ye think you're talking to?" a rough voice asked. "Your companion ain't even awake."

Virginia fell silent and listened for the wind to answer her. But though the breeze continued to stir the tent and her hair, Llycharath's voice did not come again. Rehtse turned her head not long after, indicating she was awake. Aware of their surly guard, neither said anything.

Besides, there was plenty to listen to without making conversation. They were still in the commander's tent, and into his presence in the next several hours came reports from other camps and scouting parties, until the size of the High Police contingent hiding in the mountains had grown in Virginia's mind to five or six hundred. The reports chilled her. A report that the entourage under General Cratus had safely traveled through the mountains. A report on the activities of the people inside the city walls—on the slow going in the streets where they were trying to dig up the cobblestones to make way for crops, on the movements of Darkworld people in and out of the castle, on small groups that left the city only to return.

How long had Pravik been so closely watched? And how had they known nothing of it?

One report, brought later in the night, mentioned a Gypsy caravan on the move through the mountains just to the north.

Another, causing chills to go down Virginia's spine, reported that the woman Evelyn had "disappeared again" but was not thought to have left the mountains. Was the man still with her? the commander asked. Yes.

Virginia closed her eyes. The memories were still so sharp —the pain of being used by the Blackness, the burning sensation of the covenant fire on her skin, and the hurt of being betrayed by one she had trusted.

From the sound of the report, Lord Robert still accompanied Evelyn.

The commander sat in his tent and smoked a cigar all through the reports, the smell within the canvas growing worse by the hour. Virginia slowly twisted the ropes around her hands, but they held tight. In vain she wracked her mind for some plan of escape. If only she could speak with Rehtse. But the priestess followed the same instincts and was as silent as she.

Night grew long. The reports ceased. The commander slept, snoring loudly. The deep breathing of the guard filled the air beside them. Virginia did not know if she also slept—she thought so. But suddenly her ankles were free, and fingers were working swiftly at the knots around her wrists. Rehtse took her hands and pulled her to her feet. Neither said a word. Carefully, Rehtse led Virginia into the open air. The fresh smell of the night was potent relief.

Rehtse continued to lead, and so Virginia followed, still saying nothing as her heart beat hard. With every step she expected the crack of a stick or an unfortunate trip to give them away, but their footfalls were remarkably muffled. Perhaps Rehtse's unusual eyesight in the dark, developed in her Darkworld people over centuries in caves, was serving them better than Virginia knew.

No voices called out to stop them. Soon Virginia knew the camp was far behind. They made a little more noise now, though only a little, as they journeyed through the forest, the trees sparse amid the rocks.

"Virginia," Rehtse said suddenly and quietly. "How do we find north?"

Virginia paused. "Does moss grow on the trees?" she asked.

"Yes," Rehtse answered.

Virginia nodded. "It will grow most heavily on the north side."

"It is good," Rehtse said. "We travel aright."

"Where are we going?" Virginia hardly needed to express her bewilderment. She still wasn't sure how they had so easily escaped.

"To join the Gypsy caravan the reports spoke of," Rehtse said. "Alone, the scouts will catch us again, but if we can seem to be part of a Gypsy band, they will let us pass."

"Rehtse—" Virginia stopped walking and released Rehtse's hand. "What happened back there?"

Rehtse sounded puzzled. "We escaped."

"I know that," Virginia said. "But how?"

"My bonds were loose," Rehtse said. "I waited until the guard slept and then released us both."

"But—they heard nothing, saw nothing. And why would they leave your ropes loose?"

"The King watches over us," Rehtse said.

"Yes," Virginia said. She shook her head, wanting almost to laugh. "In the Highlands, where I come from, they say that some people are born favoured—lucky. Might you be one of them?"

Rehtse's voice was solemn. "I have lost too much that I value to be considered lucky," she said. "But I do believe the King favours us. Did you not hear the voice in the wind?"

Virginia smiled. "I thought I was alone in hearing it. That was Llycharath, the Wind-Spirit. He rescued me once before."

Rehtse was quiet, waiting.

"The woman they spoke of—Evelyn—is truly a witch. She is one of the Order of the Spider. She once took me captive and . . . and did what she could to turn my sight against the people of the King. She is as great a threat as the High Police, if not greater. I cannot imagine what she is doing here." Urgency suddenly gripped Virginia. "But Rehtse, how can we continue on? Libuse must be told that she is sitting in the midst of a trap."

"I have thought of that," Rehtse said. "My people also are threatened. But we cannot go back to the city. The commander desires you now. The police see everything that comes in and out of Pravik; they will see us and capture us again, and we will do Libuse no good."

Virginia nodded. It was true, of course. But still—how could they continue on their journey without sending word to Libuse of Cratus's treachery?

"We must go to the Gypsies," Rehtse said. "The High Police will let them pass; we heard them say as much. Perhaps they will help us send word to the city. But that is not all. Virginia—I feel that this is meant to turn us off course, and we cannot allow it to do so. We must not leave off seeking the King. The emperor has deceived the Ploughman and my prince Harutek, for these outlying camps are no forerunners of peace. We know now that Cratus meant no good. The King alone can help us all."

"The Ploughman and Harutek," Virginia repeated. "And the others with them—who will warn them? They also are going into a trap."

She could hear the concern in Rehtse's voice. "It is too late to send them word now. We must leave them to the King's care."

* * *

After they left the commander's camp, two hours of wandering in the dark brought Virginia and Rehtse back into the proximity of voices. They could hear low murmurs, the sound of footsteps on gravel, the crackle of a fire. Virginia could smell horses and smoke.

"Wait here," Rehtse said, and she ducked away into the night while Virginia stood in her constant darkness, wondering where "here" might be and hoping Rehtse would not be long.

Something in the woods unnerved her. Something hung in the air—a rank scent; a heaviness. She wished to sense the presence of Llycharath, but the night was deathly still.

Not far away, Rehtse peered through the trees at the single fire that burned in the midst of the Gypsy encampment, shining on the painted sides of the wagons. The wagons had been drawn close in a small clearing. Shadows on the other side of the camp betrayed the presence of watchmen. Satisfied that these were friends, Rehtse straightened and walked forward.

"Stop there," a voice called. She stood still. Two young Gypsies emerged from the trees, arrows pointed at her throat. Rehtse smiled and bowed, knees to the earth. "My lords," she said.

The foremost of the watchmen could not have been more than seventeen. He cleared his throat. "Rise," he said. "Look, who are you? What are you doing here?"

"I am a friend," Rehtse said, "of Pravik and of the Gypsies —a priestess of the Darkworld. I come seeking asylum from the soldiers in these mountains and safe passage to a western road."

"How do we know you're telling the truth?" the second boy demanded. "How do we know you're not really the w—"

The first boy cut his companion off. "Peace, she's not the witch. She's a Darkworlder. I know the look of them."

The boys lowered their arrows. Rehtse arose and dusted off her skirt. "Better come with us," the first boy said. His forehead was creased with care. His face was young, but his eyes were haunted—he had seen trouble in his young life. Rehtse's heart moved with compassion for him, and for a moment she regretted bringing him still more trouble.

But the path of the King had to be followed, no matter how it led.

The young man held out his arm for Rehtse, a courtly gesture. She smiled and took it, then cocked her head. "Have I seen you before?" she asked.

"Could be," the lad answered. "I'm called Darne. I lived in Pravik before the men went to Athrom. I helped dig into the caverns when they found the Darkworld. I'd know your kind anywhere."

As Darne led Rehtse into the center of the camp, he let out a signal that was a cross between a whistle and a bird call. A wagon directly across from the fire burst open, and the lithe figure of a young man jumped out and stood in the firelight with his arms crossed.

Rehtse caught her breath at the sight of him. There was something in him that stirred her spirit. Only as she drew near and knelt once more did she realize that his eyes were the colour of fire.

"Who is this?" the Gypsy asked.

"I am Rehtse of the Darkworld," she said. "I come seeking shelter from the High Police, for myself and a companion."

The boys exchanged looks. They hadn't know there was anyone else with her.

"Why should we shelter you?" the young man demanded.

"In the name of justice," Rehtse said, "for it was my people who rescued yours in Athrom, and at the behest of my companion. And in the name of the King."

She felt the young man's hand on hers, and he pulled her to her feet. His fiery eyes took her in with piercing rapidity, and then he bowed from the waist, firelight glinting from a ring of gold in his ear.

"I am Nicolas Fisher," he said. "Leader of this band. And we are all at your service, priestess." He straightened. "Darne, Rolto, bring this woman's companion here. Bring her with honour. If we were saved at her behest, then she is the Seer of Pravik."

Rehtse told them where to find Virginia. As the boys melted into the shadows, Rehtse and Nicolas were joined at the fire by a beautiful young woman with a tiny babe in her arms. The woman took Rehtse in with the same piercing gaze possessed by her husband.

"My wife," said Nicolas, "Marja. And our daughter."

Rehtse smiled at the sight of the baby nestled against her mother. Marja nodded in greeting but said nothing, querying Nicolas with a gaze he didn't answer. Instead, he looked beyond the fire, searching the darkness until Virginia appeared. When she did, he rushed to take her hand. "Seer," he said. "We are honoured."

"What are you doing here?" Marja asked, directing the question at both the newcomers.

Virginia answered. "We are seeking the King," she said. "But soldiers waylaid us, and we have escaped. The High Police fill these woods. They have surrounded Pravik."

Marja frowned. "How can this be? We have seen nothing of them."

"But we have not been looking," Nicolas said. "Are you sure of this?"

"Your own movements were reported to their commander earlier this night," Virginia said. "That is how we knew how to find you. They seem inclined to let you pass without troubling you. But they are watching everything that happens in the city."

Nicolas and Marja exchanged a troubled glance. Marja spoke, her voice bitter. "So it begins again."

"Nothing has begun yet, so far as we can tell," Virginia said. "Only watching. But there is more. The soldiers reported that a great evil lurks in these woods."

"That we do know," Marja said. "The witch Evelyn. She met and cursed us on the road three days ago."

Virginia started. "Cursed you?"

"Indeed," Marja said with a sarcastic smile. "It is a miracle all our wheels have not fallen off and our hair still remains in our heads."

Rehtse smiled. "More luck?" she said softly. Virginia didn't respond. Instead, she asked Nicolas and Marja, "Did she have a man with her?"

"She did," Nicolas said. "A tall fellow. Her slave, from the look of him."

Virginia nodded. Rehtse could see the pain etched across her face—the pain of memory, and perhaps of regret. "Why is Evelyn here?" Virginia asked. The question seemed directed at herself as much as anyone else.

"For no good purpose," Marja said. "She curses us in vain, for we are protected by my husband." She laid a slender hand on Nicolas's shoulder. "He is blessed of the King, and so no curse clings to us. But do not think we underestimate her." Her voice lowered a little, and she addressed Virginia. "We know, Seer of Pravik, something of what you have suffered."

"But soldiers too," Nicolas said. "Is it too much to think they have been working together?"

"Not they," Rehtse said. "The commander who took us captive said Evelyn had declared war on them."

Another voice, behind them, snorted. "Good. Let them all bash their brains out against each other. The witch versus the High Police. A fine match. May the contestants all equally fall."

"Amen," Marja muttered. Amusement gleamed in Nicolas's eyes. "Hiding in the shadows, Major? Come out and greet our guests."

From behind one of the wagons, the tall, broad-shouldered Gypsy leader called the Major peeled himself out the shadows. A dark form waited behind him—a great animal, Rehtse realized, black and powerful. The animal came snuffing out of the shadows and nosed Marja's hand. She pushed it away impatiently.

The Major took Virginia's hand and kissed it. He nodded to Rehtse. "You are welcome, the both of you," he said, "to the camp of Nicolas Fisher, for I no longer lead this ragged band. But your news is ill."

"I wish that it was otherwise, Major," Virginia said.

"As do we all," Nicolas finished. "But enough regrets. We have a problem now. Advise me, friends, what shall we do?" He caught the worried look on Rehtse's face and hastened to assure her. "Don't be afraid—we will of course give you safe escort through the mountains. That is, some of us will. But we can't just pass out of the mountains without sending word to Pravik."

"That is not all," Virginia said softly. "A contingent has left Pravik for Athrom. They will be there already—I wish with all my heart we could have warned them first."

Darkness passed over Nicolas's face. "For Athrom? Why?"

"The High Police came to the city five days ago," Virginia said, "led by General Merlyn Cratus. They invited the Ploughman to Athrom to speak with the emperor about forming a peaceful alliance. He felt he had no choice but to go."

Marja burst out with a sound of mingled horror and outrage. "Ay," she said, "have they lost their minds?"

"I should have been with them," Virginia said, "but Professor Huss sent me away to seek the King—unknown to the others."

"And the professor himself?" Nicolas asked.

"Gone to Athrom," Virginia said. "With the Ploughman, and Maggie and Pat . . . and several of his men, of course. Now I fear they've been betrayed."

"Did they truly expect anything less?" Marja spat. "They walk into a den of dragons and expect a gentle welcome?"

"Peace, Marja," Nicolas said.

The Major took a pipe from his mouth and blew out a puff of smoke. "Are you sure you two weren't seen?" he said.

"As sure as we can be," Rehtse answered. "They sounded no alarm at our escape, and the High Police cannot see in the dark."

"We won't arouse their suspicions by setting out now," Nicolas said. "Much as I'd like to be out of these mountains. Marja, will you take our guests and find them a safe place to sleep? New clothes, too. Especially the priestess. Those robes look like nothing anyone else in these mountains would wear."

Marja nodded, handed her baby to the Major, and linked her elbows through Virginia's and Rehtse's. Nicolas looked into the forests beyond them.

"Then come back to me," he said. "We've got plans to

make, and I need your quick head."

Marja's eyes sparkled, but she said nothing in reply—only turned her guests toward a garish purple wagon and led them quickly into hiding.

6

City of Dragons

When morning came, Pat crouched in front of Maggie and cocked an eyebrow, holding up a bar of soap. "Are you going to ready yourself to meet the emperor?" she asked.

Maggie looked down at her travel clothes, dusty from the road. "I am ready."

"Cratus will not be pleased if you don't at least try to make yourself presentable," Pat said.

"I am not concerned about pleasing Cratus," Maggie countered. "But for my leader, I'll put myself to the necessary pains. Ploughman?"

He smiled. "If Libuse was here, she would say we should all look our best. We are the heralds of a new world, are we not?"

"The new world is more often dusty than not," Maggie said. "But you are right."

Obediently, Maggie and Pat took themselves to a washing room in the same wing of the palace, pulling rumpled dresses from their sacks—Pat's dark purple, Maggie's light green—washing their faces, and combing their hair. They did not,

Maggie thought, look much better.

Pat made a face at herself in the mirror. "Shabby excuses for ladies of the court," she said. "But at least we tried."

Maggie smoothed out her dress. She thought of Libuse for a moment and wondered if the princess of Pravik was thinking of them.

Her mouth twisted in a wry smile. The Ploughman was here. Of *course* Libuse's thoughts were with them. Besides, they were here to decide the future of Libuse's ancient city and people.

Surely, nothing transpiring in the Eastern Lands was more pressing than that.

A knock came at the door, and Pat took Maggie's hand as she had so often when they were small girls and Maggie was too afraid to go into some mad exploration on her own. Pat had always been the confident one, the adventurer.

"Ready, little friend?" Pat asked softly.

Maggie smiled. She squeezed Pat's hand. "As ready as you are," she answered.

They stepped into the hall where the men were gathering. The Ploughman wore a deep green cloak, and she recognized the skillful touches of Libuse's embroidery in its gilt edging. A single silver thread woven into the lining by his throat glimmered, and for an instant Maggie thought she heard the strains of the night before once again.

The air around the Ploughman seemed to shift with golden energy. They all felt it. Golden Warriors in waiting, their unseen presence pulsing around their human leader. Professor Huss, too, looked straight and regal. His red-grey beard was neatly combed, and he wore the long crimson robes of a teacher.

Rivan bowed as he approached their leaders and held out a slender sword. "Professor," he said. "Will you bear arms with us?"

Jarin Huss chuckled as his fingers closed around the hilt and he gingerly lifted the sword. "I would hardly know how to use it."

"For ceremony," Rivan said.

"For ceremony," Huss repeated, but the look on his face was grave as he buckled the sword onto his belt.

Footsteps in the marble hall announced the approach of Harutek and his warriors, dressed in ceremonial armour—ceremonial like Huss's sword, but still useful in a fight. Cratus's men were nowhere to be seen; servants lingered at a distance.

"We will keep together," the Ploughman said, meeting Harutek's eyes and then those of his men. "If anything goes amiss, gather round me. The High Police are only men; I can protect us, and we can break free from an attack, but only if we act as one."

"We hope for better things," Harutek said.

"Of course," the Ploughman said. "There will be no attack. All will be well. We hope for that."

The Ploughman smiled and offered his arm to Pat. With a bow, Harutek held out his hand to Maggie. The farmers formed a loose line behind them. Cratus would have said they should stay behind. Who brought peasants into the presence of an emperor?

We do, Maggie thought, her heart smiling. *We of Pravik do.*

They passed down a long, polished hall, its marble floor

and white pillars gleaming. The walls and ceiling were painted with ornate murals. Vases and statues sat in lit hollows in the walls. Ahead of them, two enormous, polished golden doors awaited.

As they drew near, four servants took hold of rings in the doors and drew them open.

Maggie caught her breath as the opulence of the throne room opened before her eyes. The sun streamed in through windows of translucent stone. Six massive marble pillars held up the high ceiling, so high that Maggie didn't bother tipping her head to see it all. Chandeliers hung to half the room's height, crystal suspended in gold frames. Paintings as high and narrow as the golden doors hung all around the room, depicting Bryllan, the Eastern Lands, Italyan vineyards, Fjordland in the North Country, the Green Isle, Galce, the distant islands, spacescapes, the wonders of the natural world.

Ranks of High Police stood between the paintings, ringing the room like a second, living wall.

On a dais at the focal point of the room, a high throne carved of ivory and adorned with gold sat empty.

Before it, on the steps leading to the throne, hunched a man in soiled clothes of linen and gold.

His hair was long and thick, curls an unruly mass around his head. His beard had grown untrimmed for some time, a second mass of curls around his face. He was too thin for his clothes, and his eyes darted back and forth with the air of a cornered animal.

As they drew closer, Maggie could see the hunched man's little fingers twitching, rapidly, with such violence that they shook his hands and threatened to put his entire body into tremours. He looked up suddenly, and Maggie caught her breath at the madness in his eyes.

She looked past him to the empty throne as dread seized her. A familiar figure stepped out from behind it.

Merlyn Cratus smiled down at them, but there was no friendliness in his eyes.

"Cratus," the Ploughman said, his voice low, "what is this?"

"Did I not tell you," Cratus said, "that much would be revealed in the presence of the emperor?"

The madman shook at Cratus's words. "Bow!" he shrieked. "Bow before me, the lord of the earth!"

Maggie's mouth dropped as she turned incredulous eyes away from the Ploughman and looked again at the madman.

"It can't be," she said.

"What can't?" Cratus asked. "Is it the emperor's madness you doubt? Or that a soldier could rule in his place? Or perhaps it is your own foolishness that you find hard to grasp?"

"You have brought us here on false pretenses, general," the Ploughman said. The air around him was beginning to shift, to glitter as though full of gold dust. Pat let go of his arm, and Maggie saw her reaching for a dagger she had tucked into her sash. She took a step closer to them, her senses heightening as she recalled the Ploughman's words. *Keep close together. We can escape, if only—*

She stopped when she felt a sharp point in her back, and with a gasp she stood a little straighter.

"Keep quiet," Harutek murmured. "I am trying to help you."

"I suggest you calm yourself, Ploughman," Cratus said. "You place great confidence in yourself, but think. More than one of your people will die if you attempt to use your . . . Gift . . . here."

Maggie cried out as the knife point dug into her back, and suddenly Harutek was dragging her forward, away from the others—away from the safety of the Ploughman's protection. *Great King, help me,* she prayed.

"Harutek!" the Ploughman roared, and in the same instant Professor Huss lurched forward with his sword in his gnarled hands, his eyes wild with fear for Maggie. Clumsy and uncertain, he attacked.

"Stay back!" Maggie cried, but it was too late—wrenching her arm behind her back, Harutek defended himself by driving his knife into Professor Huss.

The old man cried out and fell to the floor, blood seeping through his crimson robes. His eyes were fixed on Maggie's face. She fought back a wild sob. Harutek pulled her closer and held his knife at her throat. He was breathing hard, his voice shaking.

"Do not try to escape," he said. "They will only kill us all."

The Ploughman's eyes were glowing with rage, yet he stood unmoving. The others had gathered close to him, all but Harutek's men.

"Fight your way free if that's what you want," Cratus said. "But the professor and the Singer will die if you do. You cannot save them all. You might get yourself out—but do you really think all ten of your men would make it? You are surrounded by fifty of my finest soldiers, and there are many more outside. And your lover is likewise surrounded. The mountains of Pravik are full of High Police. An entire army, in fact. Waiting for me to give orders. You could leave here, Ploughman. But you would not find any home by the time you got back."

The Ploughman glared at him. Still, he did not move.

Harutek pushed Maggie to her knees and held his knife against the back of her neck. She swallowed and looked across the floor at Professor Huss. He was still alive, though his eyes were clouding over from the pain. *Go,* she silently urged the Ploughman. *Get out of here.*

"This is for all of our best," Harutek whispered.

Cratus strode across the dais, obviously enjoying the view. He gestured, and his police began to close in.

"This is your chance," he said. "Take your stand now. Fight."

The Ploughman dropped his sword. It clattered on the marble floor, and Maggie shut her eyes. She heard the echo as the others released their weapons also, and then the sounds as the police moved in and began to bind their hands. Harutek's knife was still at the back of her neck.

"A wise choice," Cratus said. "The Darkworld prince said you would not fight if it meant sacrificing any one of your people. Perhaps especially the Singer?"

"Alliance is clearly not why you brought us here," the Ploughman said, ignoring the soldier who was chaining his hands. "Tell me what you do have in mind."

"Originally?" Cratus said. "I meant to bring you here and kill you, thereby destroying Pravik, the one black spot in an otherwise wonderful Empire. Well, of course, there are still the Gypsies—but without your city to rally round, even they would not be so well off. But that was before I saw you fight." His eyes went to Maggie. "And before I saw songs heal wounds, reverse rust. Before our friend Harutek apprised me of things I did not know—about the Gifted."

He descended a step, scaring the emperor away. "Now that I know more of what you are, I've decided to keep you alive. You see, I do have one more problem in this Empire of mine. The Order of the Spider. You know them. They served the Morels well, but in recent years have grown . . . independent. I had planned to go on as the emperors did, bribing and bowing and making do with a bad alliance. But Harutek tells me my options are not so limited. And my own eyes tell me the same thing."

He descended two more steps and stood eye to eye with the Ploughman, whose rigid control showed in every line of his stance.

"There is power in you," Cratus said. "I want it. So I cannot do as I planned to do—I cannot just kill you. I need you both. And I need the rest of you too."

"The rest?" Maggie asked, and Harutek dug the knife in a little deeper. She yelped and glared over her shoulder at him.

"I paid attention to the priests when they raised me," Harutek said. "They and their talk of the King's coming again, of prophecies and stars—and the Six. Two more are well known to us all: the Seer, and the Gypsy who hears."

Maggie closed her eyes. Virginia and Nicolas.

"I have already sent word back," Cratus said. "My men are looking for them. As for the final two, they are a mystery still —but they will not be impossible to find."

"You are a coward," the Ploughman said. "Hiding behind a madman—stealing the power of others. Are you supposed to inspire our awe?"

"No," Cratus said. "Because I am not a Morel. I do not care

to inspire feelings. I am a practical man. I only want power."

He turned and looked at Maggie. "Where is the Seer?" he demanded.

"I don't know," Maggie said. She was glad—deeply glad—that she spoke the truth. *She has gone to Bryllan to seek the King*, she could have said—but where exactly Virginia was she had no idea. And Cratus did not need to know even that much.

Cratus smiled as he turned back to the Ploughman. "No battle?" he asked. "No desperate, heroic attempts to break free?"

A soldier behind the Ploughman clubbed him in the head, and the tall warrior fell.

Cratus looked past them all to the rows of High Police.

"Take them away," he said. "Put the old man with the girl. No doctors. It's time we see just how much power there is in song."

* * *

Early that morning, Virginia dreamed.

She stood in a grey haze, looking at a barren path that stretched out before her. She stared down it, afraid to move, but something at the end was calling to her. Through the haze a blue light began to shine, but its light was not light—it was hungry, consuming. A man stood within it, and his features slowly became visible.

Lord Robert, her once-guardian and betrayer.

He opened his mouth and said, "Help me." His eyes pleaded out of emptiness and pain.

Behind him dark clouds gathered, swirling, sweeping

down over the road like smoke. The light that was not light played among the clouds, drawing shapes and faces. The clouds swallowed Lord Robert in their darkness, and then they swept up around Virginia also. She was not on the road anymore, but back on the hilltop.

She stood where the Order of the Spider had taken her and twisted her, leaving inside her a pain too deep to touch for fear it would destroy her, while the laird looked on and allowed it.

All around, the black clouds swallowed the earth. From the hilltop she could see the world spread out before her and the Blackness destroying everything. The clouds swallowed Bryllan and the hillside where she had grown up. They took Pravik down into a deep black place and scorched the life from the woods and the ocean, from mankind, from the Earth Brethren.

She reached out in the roiling blackness, where faces leered and claws grabbed at her, reached out with all her spirit for the King.

He appeared before her. She saw him as a man, a young man whose whole being was life. He smiled at her. But as she watched, the clouds reached up around him like clawed hands and dragged him into darkness too.

A voice spoke out of the death on every side.

The voice said, "And thus it must be."

Virginia woke, and she was not dead, and the world was not dead. Her heart was pounding.

The door at the back of the wagon stood open, and the early morning air outside was alive. Insects were singing ancient songs of their own. A few birds were calling. The trees around the Gypsy camp moved in a gentle breeze. Virginia shivered; she was cool with sleep and clammy with the dream. She gathered a scratchy wool blanket tighter around herself and sat up.

She knew if she closed her senses she would be able to recall the nightmare in every detail. The voice and its prophecy hung in her heart like a heavy iron bell she was afraid to ring.

Someone in the doorway moved, cloth rustling against the frame. Virginia thought it was Rehtse, but when a voice spoke quietly, it was Marja's.

"We were in the coliseum in Athrom, Nicolas and I," Marja said. "We married there. If you had not sent the soldiers from Pravik to save us from death, perhaps we would not be here to save you. Strange how life turns, isn't it?"

"Why are you here?" Virginia asked.

"I couldn't sleep," Marja said. She sounded a little embarrassed, but defiantly so—a personality trait Virginia suspected marked her. "And I wanted to come and look at you. I am sorry if that unnerves you."

Virginia shook her head, smiling a little. She had often wished she could look at others, could really see them for any length of time. "Why me?"

"Because I know when I'm looking at a legend," Marja said. "Your visions have already changed the world. And my life. I thank you for that."

Fingers gripped Virginia's as Marja knelt beside the bunk. She had moved so lightly from her place in the door that Virginia hadn't heard her. Her grip was tight, her voice earnest.

"I didn't mean to wake you, but now that you are awake— let me say it again. Thank you. What you did saved our lives."

Virginia shook her head. "I did so little," she said. "Only

saw—and told others what I had seen."

Marja hesitated to reply. "You are troubled?" she said.

"I have seen again," Virginia said. She hadn't meant to tell anyone about the dream. Especially not a near-stranger, no matter how compelling that stranger's presence might be.

"And what you have seen disturbs you," Marja said.

Virginia didn't answer. Marja stood and released Virginia's hands, moving back to the door again. "Among our people, I am a storyteller," the Gypsy woman went on. "And I have learned something about stories. They always grow dark near the end. Sometimes so dark that it seems there is no way out."

Virginia bent her head toward Marja's voice, letting her words sink in.

"But that darkness is never truly the end," Marja said. "What you have seen—it may not be the whole story."

"Virginia?" a voice called. Rehtse—coming from somewhere outside. "Are you all right?"

"Perfectly all right," Virginia called back.

"It's wrong of me to keep you awake," Marja said. "The whole camp will be rousing in an hour or so. Sleep a little more while you can." The wagon creaked as Marja turned to jump down.

"Wait—" Virginia said. Marja paused. "You married in the coliseum?" Virginia asked softly. "Under the sentence of death?"

"Yes," Marja answered.

"Some would call you foolish," Virginia said.

"What do you call me?" Marja asked.

Virginia smiled and shook her head. "Remarkable," she said.

Marja departed.

In her wake, the dream had lost some of its power.

* * *

The prison was damp and cold, despite the warm air outside. Maggie's voice shook as she sang a lullaby. Her fingers stroked Huss's beard almost convulsively, wiping away blood-flecked spittle near his mouth. Her throat was raw, but she couldn't afford to stop. He clung to her other hand and kept his eyes fixed on her face.

On the other side of the cell, the Ploughman groaned.

Maggie raised her eyes to look at him, and her song devolved into a hum. The Ploughman should have awakened before now. The soldiers had forced something down his throat when they brought him here. A drug, she suspected.

Footsteps outside the cell announced the presence of Merlyn Cratus, and Maggie abruptly stopped singing. She tightened her hold on Huss's hand and waited.

The general stepped into view and looked down on them. He was silent.

"Well?" Maggie said. "What are you hoping to see?"

"The old man is still alive," Cratus said. It was a question, though he did not phrase it as one.

"No thanks to you," Maggie said. "He needs a doctor."

Another voice came from the shadows beyond Cratus, and Maggie stiffened. Harutek.

"One of the Six is a healer," he said. "But she isn't the one. You can't keep her singing forever."

Cratus sniffed. "And he doesn't have to live forever. I'm no fool. When I collect power, I keep it under control. This is easier than drugging her too." His mouth crooked in a smile. "And far more interesting."

Harutek met Maggie's eyes, and she looked away quickly. His expression was too hard to face. She wanted to be angry with him—but she saw compassion there, and real concern. When he spoke, his voice was heavy.

"Men should not meddle with powers that are beyond them," he said quietly. "We have learned that much in the Darkworld. We would have been better off without stories of the Gifted . . . of the King."

"No, Harutek," Maggie said. Her voice barely held out, and she cleared her throat, wincing against its rawness. "Look around you. This dungeon—this cell. This is what life without the King looks like."

Professor Huss groaned, and Maggie closed her eyes and sang again, ignoring the visitors.

Harutek was right. She was no healer. But her songs with their reconstructive power could help a little to stave off death. She refused to look back up as she sang to her dying friend. Into the song she tried to weave something of her love, and of her concern for the others—for Pat, and for Rivan and the rest of the Ploughman's men, and for Libuse and the people in the city.

It struck her, as she thought of them, how far she had come. How far they all had come. She had been raised to believe that the present world, like a prison cell, was all that existed. That the Empire was supreme, that people lived and died without reference to any greater power, any greater song. Through happenstance—or perhaps providence—she had come to see another side of reality, and to believe in the King. To hope in him.

Now, in this place, he was the only real reality, and she clung to him.

Into her song's strains another prayer came. She thought the words even as she sang.

Go, Virginia. Find the King. We need you now.

* * *

Virginia did not sleep again, but lay awhile in thought. She drew Tyrentyllith's seeds from an inner pocket and fingered the rough bag. After an hour, Rehtse reentered the wagon and moved to Virginia's side, crouching down near her elbow and waiting.

"Didn't you sleep?" Virginia asked. "You've been gone most of the night."

"You are perceptive for one who cannot see," Rehtse answered.

"Yes, well," Virginia said, "one learns to pay attention. Where were you?"

"Outside," Rehtse said. "Sitting atop the wagon."

Virginia sat up and drew the blanket around her bare feet. "We have far to go," she said. "You should rest when you can."

"I am accustomed to little sleep," Rehtse said. "In the Darkworld we held long prayer vigils at night. Divad hoped they might speed the King's return."

"He felt that it needed speeding?" Virginia asked.

"He saw dark times coming," Rehtse answered.

"And what did you do up there?" Virginia asked, tipping

her chin to gesture at the ceiling.

Rehtse sighed. "I intended to pray," she said, "but I could not cease looking at the stars. How do you ever sleep when the stars are shining?"

Virginia smiled, and Rehtse caught herself quickly. "Not you," she said. "Everyone else. Those who *can* see the stars but do not—surely they do not, or they would never close their eyes."

Rehtse's voice grew distant for a moment as memories of the nightmare came back to Virginia. The bell was still hanging there, black and ominous. She refused to ring it. So she said, "I have never seen the stars. As a child I could see a little, but never that far. Describe them to me?"

There was quiet for a moment. "A million lights," Rehtse said. "Lights in a sky that isn't black, it's blue—deep blue."

"Is there colour to the lights?" Virginia asked.

"They're white like the heart of fire," Rehtse said.

They were quiet again. "A million million fires burning in deep blue," Rehtse repeated. "And if you know how to look for them, there are stories in the star patterns. Our fathers carved some of them in the caverns, hundreds of years ago, and they're still there in the sky."

"Did your fathers tell you the stories too?" Virginia said.

"Pieces," Rehtse answered. "We only know pieces. The stories are all about the King. They praise and adore him, and they say he will return to us."

"Do they say—" Virginia paused. "What?" Rehtse asked.

"Do they say how he will come?" Virginia asked. "Or if he will come in triumph?"

"Of course he will triumph," Rehtse said. "You are not

afraid that the Blackness is too strong for him?"

"The Blackness is very strong, Rehtse," Virginia said.

"Not stronger than the King."

Virginia nodded.

"Are you well?" Rehtse asked.

She nodded again. "I dreamed. But I do not understand what I saw. Perhaps it was only a nightmare." Her voice lost some of its strength. "I am sure it was."

A third voice intruded—Marja once again. "Nicolas and the Major think it best that you remain inside the wagons today. We will pull up camp in a few hours and continue through the mountains. Do not come out."

"And our news?" Virginia asked. "Will you take word of the soldiers to Libuse?"

"Fear not," Marja said. "The Gypsies carry the word now. We will make sure it reaches all who need to hear it."

She crossed the wagon floor with her characteristically light steps and pressed something into Virginia's hand—smooth, polished wood inlaid with carved designs. The pattern was stylized, but Virginia thought it was in the shape of a bird.

"I want you to take this with you," Marja said. "It is the treasure of my clan. When you find the King, and the time is right to reveal him, sound it—so that some who have long waited for him may know he has come."

"A whistle?" Rehtse asked.

Marja gave a low whistle of her own, trilling at the end in a bird call. "It is not only Gypsies and Darkworlders who wait for the King," she said. "Promise me you will do as I ask?"

Virginia nodded. "If it is in my power to sound it, I will," she said. "When the time is right." She tucked the whistle in beside her seed pouch, then reached up and touched Marja's face, taking in its youth and beauty lined with suffering and the maturity of motherhood and martyrdom.

The young Gypsy woman nodded, satisfied. "I only wish we could go with you," she said. "But the King will watch over your steps, and send those you need to help you along your way."

She stood as the creaking of the wagon announced that its wheels were beginning to roll.

The Gypsy caravan was on the move. It was time to escape the mountains of Pravik.

7

Attack

Nicolas Fisher rode at the head of the caravan, standing on the seat of a brilliant red and gold wagon. His son, whom he called Little Bear, played with a leather train beside him. The child's hands and eyes were enraptured by the worn object, and Nicolas smiled as he watched him play. But he could not watch long. He turned his fire-coloured eyes back to the road before them, looked down the sloping mountain path as it rolled beneath their wheels, and listened carefully.

A drab mare carrying a brown-haired Gypsy with a pipe in his mouth trotted to the side of the wagon. The Gypsy nodded up at Nicolas.

"Keep a sharp eye out, Peter," Nicolas said. The pipe-smoker kicked his mare's heels and cantered up the road ahead of the wagons. Other Gypsies were walking and riding on all sides of the caravan, eyes and ears alert for trouble. They had not been so guarded since the days before the battle in Athrom, when the High Police had hunted Gypsies. Nicolas and Marja had turned the tables then, hunting High Police and rescuing their people until they were captured and taken to Athrom,

135

where they would have died had it not been for the soldiers sent by Virginia, the releasing of the River-Daughter, and the intervention of the King himself.

Only Nicolas knew what he had seen and heard in the desolate land beyond the Veil. The Fire-Song encountered there had changed him forever.

He looked at his son again. Yes, things had changed.

He turned to survey the caravan of Gypsies under his command. The Major had led them for years, but they had put themselves under Nicolas's control when it became evident that he was touched by the supernatural. They believed his fire-eyes and unusual Gift of hearing protected them from evil. Perhaps they did.

"You are blessed of the King," Marja had said stubbornly when Nicolas protested that he didn't want leadership. "Who else should lead us?"

The caravan was fifteen wagons strong, a traveling home to several families with small children, a few elders, and many young and strong Gypsies who were proud to travel with the Fisher and his fiery, beautiful wife. In Nicolas and Marja they had found something legendary, something that made them feel as though the ancient days had taken flesh. Even Nicolas could see that. Even he could feel his blood quickening at the thought of reentering the battle to bring the Seventh World into the truth—into the realities that he could hear, that Virginia could see, and that Marja remembered in story.

The young and strong now rode in front of the wagons. A few jogged alongside. A black bear, Nicolas's old companion, shuffled alongside the horses, who ignored it.

Nicolas grinned. Bear had terrorized horses in the days of

the persecution, but the Gypsy horses didn't seem to know or care.

A disturbance up the path drew Nicolas's attention, and he pulled the long leather reins and signaled for the caravan to slow. From around a tree-thick bend in the road, Peter's riderless mare came galloping.

Nicolas jumped down, his sword drawn. He held up his hand again, stopping the caravan.

He listened.

Marja appeared wordlessly from within the wagon and drew Little Bear up in her arms. She paused to watch Nicolas, but he was motionless. After a moment, she ducked back inside to safety.

Peter's mare reached Nicolas, who stopped her with a hand on her bridle. He was still listening. Suddenly, he turned.

"Break up the wagons!" he shouted. "Scatter the people! They're coming for us!"

Hooves on the stone road punctuated his words even as Nicolas's people sprang into action, cutting loose their horses as Gypsies poured from the wagons and began to flee into the woods. Around the bend soldiers on horseback came, rank upon rank, weapons drawn and banners flying.

Black and green. The High Police were attacking.

Nicolas looked wildly around. Young men were gathering at his side, their swords drawn. The Major was suddenly beside him with an axe in hand.

"Up, lad!" the Major said.

Nicolas looked up and saw the low-hanging branch. He jumped onto the mare's back, stood on her backbone, and caught the branch, swinging himself up. All around him, the other young men followed him into the tree branches. He had no time to look for Marja or their children, but as the soldiers came closer, he prayed for their safety and that Marja would have the sense to run. For once in her life.

The soldiers reached them. Nicolas dropped from the tree and knocked one of the first off his horse. His boys dropped into the ranks, howling their war cries. He grabbed the reins of the warhorse and wheeled it around to face the onslaught, ducking as a sword swept over his head. He snatched up a spear from the saddle and rammed the butt end into his attacker's middle, knocking the wind out of him. As the man gasped for breath, Nicolas locked swords with him, disarming him in a flash of steel.

The High Police were well trained, but the Gypsies were fast and unconventional. Bear ran into the horses, spooking and scattering them as their riders shouted and struggled to gain control. Nicolas stood on the back of his horse and threw himself at another soldier from behind, taking him down to the ground. He finished the soldier off and looked up just in time to see the Major go down.

"Major!" he shouted, lurching forward to help his old friend. Sudden tears blinded his eyes. Music seemed to be playing through the fight, a wild lament, and the sound clouded Nicolas's other senses. Someone grabbed his arm and twisted it until he dropped his sword. A mail-clad fist delivered a blow to his temple, and he fell into the dirt.

"Major . . ." he called again.

Choking as the dust of the road filled his lungs and eyes, Nicolas reached his hand toward the place where the Major lay dead on the ground.

The fight was over. High Police were searching the wagons.

If only Marja and the children had escaped.

If only Virginia and Rehtse had gotten away.

Nicolas was pulled to his knees, but victory sustained him as he realized that both wagons had been searched and found empty. All around him, the High Police had forced his fighting boys to their knees. A commander walked through them, yanking each one's head back.

He reached Nicolas, grabbed his hair, and pulled his head back. He looked into his eyes.

"This is him," he said.

A soldier approached. "There's no sign of the Seer, my lord," he said.

The commander grimaced. "Search the woods. We'll find her yet. And if not, she'll go back to Pravik and take shelter there—so we'll have her soon enough either way. Cratus will just have to wait a few more days." He peered down at Nicolas with narrowed eyes. "At least we caught one."

* * *

At a run, Rehtse pulled Virginia over a thick carpet of pine needles where she hoped their footprints would be less likely to show. Pine branches snagged in their cloaks, and they pulled free and pressed on, ignoring even those branches that scratched at their faces. Rehtse kept her eyes fixed on the forest ahead and led Virginia without slowing.

Behind them, Rehtse could hear steel crashing and young voices crying. *Keep them, Great King, in the palm of your hand.* Virginia ran with one hand shielding her face, the other hand holding to Rehtse's sleeve. Horses neighing; a child screaming. A flash of fire-coloured eyes. *Be their shield and protector, Lord Avenger, great and merciful one.*

A thousand times Rehtse had prayed the prayer: it was liturgy, tradition. But now it meant something terrifying and real. The sounds died away, replaced by the whipping of branches through air and the thudding of their own feet on the ground. A stream turned white and tumbled beside them, and when the road grew steep it cascaded into a waterfall and wet their faces, their hair, and their clothes.

They slowed now out of necessity, Rehtse helping Virginia down, step by step, trying not to slip in the wet dirt or lose footing on the mossy stones. The path evened out in a shadowy glen where the waterfall poured into a deep pool.

Rehtse looked back up the glistening path alongside the waterfall. Only shadows and sunlight met her eyes. She could hear no sounds of pursuit—but then, the waterfall would drown out all but the loudest sounds.

"Are we alone?" Virginia asked.

Rehtse nodded, then caught herself. She struggled to catch her breath. The air was rich and pungent. "Yes," she said. "Yes, I believe we are."

High, grey-lichened rocks surrounded the pool. Rehtse helped Virginia to the top of one, then, with a profound sigh of relief, sat and immersed her aching legs in the cool water. They sat in silence and listened to the sound of falling water and the underlying calm of the glen. A single yellow bird flitted through the trees and from rock to rock, closer and closer until it lighted on Virginia's outstretched hand. It was beautiful, bright and trusting like a Gypsy child.

Rehtse blinked back tears at the thought of the Gypsies, and she said another prayer for them even as she watched, fascinated, as Virginia let the bird twitch and jump from finger to finger, then settle down in the palm of her hand as though it would sleep there. It closed its eyes.

A moment of peace passed, two, and then the bird opened its eyes and flew away. Virginia turned her head slightly, her hand still outstretched, and said, "Did you hear that?"

Rehtse looked up the path along the waterfall and caught a glimpse of sunlight on chain mail. Four soldiers emerged from the shadows and began to climb down. She pulled her feet out of the water and drew them up under her, reaching for Virginia's hand with her eyes fixed on the slowly descending soldiers.

"They are coming for us," she said quietly. "We must run."

"Not that," Virginia said. She was rigid. Rehtse tore her eyes from the soldiers and looked at her companion. The look on Virginia's face shook her.

"That."

This time they both heard it.

A moan that rose almost to a whine and then died away again.

"Some beast?" Rehtse asked in a whisper.

"No beast I have ever heard," Virginia answered. Slowly, they rose together, hand in hand, balancing precariously on the rocks. Above them, one of the soldiers gave a shout, and the men came crashing down the path. Virginia turned her head toward them, and her eyes seemed to flare to life. They widened at the sight of the enemy, and she turned again to the pool and pointed to a shadowy place near the base of one of the rocks. "There!"

Rehtse paused just long enough to look. Even as she did, she became aware of a terrible smell—rot hanging in the air, too strong for the mist to wash away.

A long, serpentine body with a huge, wolfish head was moving slowly through the water along the rocks. Where the light dappled the water, it did not dapple the creature: its body seemed to suck the light into itself. It was a continuous line of black, and its eyes, enormous for the size of its head, were pupiless, blue, and unseeing.

"Be still," Virginia said. "A moment longer. It does not yet see us."

Rehtse stood with all her muscles straining, obeying Virginia's command while everything in her screamed at her to run. The soldiers had nearly reached the base of the waterfall.

And the wolfish head turned to face the men.

"Now go," Virginia said.

Virginia and Rehtse leaped from the rocks and ran for the woods. Their pursuers shouted once again, and an arrow whistled through the air and embedded itself in a tree inches from Rehtse's waist. The serpent's moan lifted in the air.

And now the men were shouting again, but with very different words.

The tangle cleared suddenly, and they plunged through ferns, weaving around the dark trunks of taller trees, slipping in moss. Behind them the whine sounded, a hungry, lonely whine, over the shouts of men that turned suddenly to screams.

Virginia passed Rehtse and angled away. As they ran, the wind began to blow, whipping the tops of the trees high above them, urging them on. On through ferns and trees and hollows, until suddenly Rehtse realized she was running down the mountainside, and it was steep and sloping before her. The ground was rock, pebbles tumbling all around from the impact of their feet, and they were slipping and sliding toward sunlight, the air silent and the wind suddenly calmed, nothing driving them now but their own momentum. They could not stop.

Virginia grabbed a slender white tree and held on while she lost her footing and slid around its base. She reached out just in time to grab Rehtse, who was sliding after her in a crouch. Rehtse let Virginia pull her toward the tree and caught hold of its trunk as soon as she was close enough. They sat panting and clinging in the sun. Rehtse looked down the slope to the cliff edge, green forests stretching out beyond it, and laughed with relief.

After her heart had ceased pounding, Rehtse tested her feet and found she could stand, if she leaned forward, and climb back up the slope—at least far enough to reach another little tree and pull herself farther up. It looked as though they could make it back to level ground.

She began to tell Virginia that, and stopped. "But you can see," she said. "You saw the tree—you grabbed me. You saw the creature in the glen, and the soldiers. You're not really blind."

Virginia, still holding the white trunk, looked up with unfocused green eyes, and Rehtse knew as certainly as she knew anything that Virginia could not see her. Not now. "Or you are," Rehtse finished. "But then how—"

"I cannot control my sight," Virginia said. She smiled.

"And I didn't see you, I heard you. Tumbling down the slope."

Rehtse drew herself up a little. "That was not tumbling," she said. "Tumbling involves head and heels. I was sliding, with considerably more grace." Virginia laughed even as Rehtse realized that her feet were on fire from sliding down the rocks. Pebbles were embedded in her calloused heels. She lifted a foot and grimaced, pulling a thorn out as she did. She glanced back up the slope.

"We can make it back up," she said. "If you just hold my hand, I can guide you. But is it safe to go back up there?"

Virginia was clinging to the tree, staring out toward the cliff edge and the expanse of blue sky as a breeze blew her dark hair. "The men will not come after us now," she said. "They will not have survived." After a moment more she stood and reached for Rehtse's hand, and they began the awkward process of scrambling back up, using small trees and getting their footing wherever they could.

Back in the shadow of the trees, Rehtse looked all around, searching for movement or sign of danger. There was nothing. Even the air felt different—clean, peaceful, almost sleepy. A few bird calls, high up and far away, were the only sounds.

"What was it?" Rehtse asked.

"Nothing of earth," Virginia said. "Blackness abroad in the world—that should not surprise me, not now." She was quiet a moment. "It is a foretaste. Morning Star will come soon, and show pity to none."

Rehtse nodded, and suddenly trembling, she said, "And yet, it was not Morning Star who aided us in escaping. The King has used even the Blackness to his own purposes." Slowly, she knelt and lifted her hands. "The Great King has saved us, blessed be he," she intoned. "He is our shield and protector, our way in dark places."

"Amen," Virginia finished.

Rehtse turned her head to look at her companion. Virginia was standing in a patch of ferns, light dappling through the trees and spotting her skirt with sun and shadow. She tilted her head up, listening, taking in her surroundings. Rehtse waited.

"Rehtse," Virginia said, "do you still believe the King will direct our paths?"

Rehtse stood and brushed twigs and leaves away from her clothes and out of her hair. She didn't answer immediately. Instead, she looked around again, searching for any sign of a path. The trees on three sides were thick, casting deep shadows. To one side was the open sky beyond the cliff, a blue expanse over forests that to Rehtse had no name. She closed her eyes and lifted her hands once more.

Virginia cleared her throat. "Rehtse? Are we lost?"

"Shh," Rehtse said. "I am waiting."

A moment later, Rehtse lowered her hands, gathered her skirt in one hand, and tucked her other hand into Virginia's elbow. "Come," she said.

"Do you know where we are?" Virginia asked.

"No," Rehtse answered.

"Did the King answer you?" Virginia asked.

Rehtse hesitated. "Not—that I could hear."

"Then where are we going?" Virginia asked.

Rehtse smiled. "All paths in this world belong to the King. If he can use the Blackness to deliver us from wicked men, then he can turn even wrong steps into right ones. We are seeking him, so we will trust the road to lead us to him. But he cannot guide us if we don't move."

"Rehtse—" Virginia paused. "My dream last night. I saw the King overwhelmed by darkness."

"Perhaps you only saw him *using* it," Rehtse said. "As he has done today."

Virginia smiled.

* * *

Libuse was hoeing in the streets, her long brown hair twisted at her neck and covered with a kerchief, her skirts hitched up above her calves, dirt under her fingernails and sweat pouring down her brow. Mrs. Cook was hacking up remaining chunks of cobblestone from the earth beside her. Other women were doing the same while men hauled the cobblestones away. In one place, they had started ploughing deep furrows in the street. Shadows from tall townhouses and the city walls fell over the makeshift fields. Nothing about this place was ideal. Yet they dared not go out from the walls and begin to plant in fields until the Ploughman had returned to assure them that they were free to do so.

She swallowed as she swung the hoe forward and yanked at a stubborn piece of rock. She knew better than to expect word from him so soon. She had thought, when he came to Pravik to join her in ruling the city, that the days of hiding and waiting and wishing she could be with him were over.

The rock broke in two rather than dislodging itself completely.

She sighed.

"My lady . . ." Mrs. Cook said. Her tone sank in, and Libuse jerked her head up, a strand of hair falling across her eyes.

Gypsies were coming through the streets toward them.

They were ragged, torn, some bloody.

"No," Libuse said. "Please no."

Surely it had not started again—the persecution that the Ploughman had nearly given everything to stop. She could not handle it without him.

Libuse recognized the woman who led the fugitives with a baby in her arms and a little boy clinging to her brown neck. Marja, Nicolas Fisher's wife. She carried herself like another sort of queen, leading her Gypsies, past the farmers who stopped to stare and whisper among themselves, straight up to Libuse.

Marja bowed her head. The little boy on her back stared wide-eyed at Libuse. "My lady," Marja said. "We bring evil tidings. And beg shelter."

"You have shelter," Libuse said. "And we must have your tidings."

Marja looked pointedly around, unwilling to speak in front of the men and women who now strained to hear everything she said. Libuse dropped her hoe. "Mrs. Cook," she said, "please take our guests to the castle where they can wash and dress their wounds, if need be. The rest of you, disperse, please. Ready yourselves for council in two hours' time." As the little boy on Marja's back squirmed out of her shawl to go after a beetle in the dirt, Mrs. Cook called out for the Gypsies to follow her. Marja stood her ground. The princess recognized the desperate look in the young woman's eyes.

Marja was stricken with fear for one she loved.

"What happened?" Libuse asked.

"Nicolas has been taken by High Police," Marja said. "They ambushed us as we were traveling through the mountains. They killed others—they killed the Major. I had to flee for the sake of the children."

Libuse laid her hand on the young woman's shoulder. "You did the right thing," she said. "But—High Police, here?"

"They are all through the mountains. They are watching everything you do," Marja said. "We were coming to tell you before they attacked us. They are armed; war camps everywhere."

Libuse tried to steel herself even as she thought through the implications. "But—the Ploughman—"

"I know of his mission." Marja swallowed as though she was keeping back other words it was more tactful not to say. "But it seems you have been betrayed. I thank you for sheltering us, my lady. But you had best prepare for battle."

"There is so little we can do."

"Fortify your gates. Make the most of these walls. If you leave you are doomed. And help me get Nicolas back."

The princess met the Gypsy's eyes in surprise. "Do what?"

"Help me rescue Nicolas," Marja said again, setting her jaw. "He is blessed of the King. He is Gifted. You will need him as much—" She choked on her words.

"No," Libuse said. "We could never need him as much as you do. But for our sakes, and for your sake, we'll do what we can to help you. Do you have a plan?"

Marja shook her dark head. "My plan was to reach you and see my children safe. Then to go out alone to find him if I had to."

Libuse shook her head. "In two hours all the men of the

city will gather for council. We will find someone to help you then. And make plans of our own." She grew quiet and looked down at the earth beneath her feet, a street in torn heaps and furrows. "I wish with all my heart that the Ploughman were here."

8

A Broken Song

Virginia and Rehtse made camp beneath a copse of birch trees. They did not light a fire. They had left their cloaks in the Gypsy wagons and shivered now in the night air, but they sat back to back and did what they could to share warmth. Rehtse's long braids fell around her face like a curtain as she slept, head on her knees.

Virginia did not know when she passed into the dream world, but soon the laird was there once more, older now and hollowed with horror, his eyes sunken and needy. He held out his hands. "Help me," he said.

She was again on the hilltop in the darkness, where hordes of demons laughed, and a great howling Blackness swept all around. In the center of it all she saw the laird holding a large, flat blue stone, and his eyes bored into her—intense, desperate, full of hatred and of fear and of terrible, terrible longing. Before her he became more than the laird, more than a single man. He was all men, he was every traitor, he was even herself. And he was without hope.

She wanted to weep for him.

She could hear singing, a man's voice, off key and far away.

The night air was cold against her cheek. She blinked and felt dew on her lashes.

She could still hear the voice singing snatches of words, a broken song sung to no one.

Virginia was stiff as she moved away from Rehtse. The priestess did not stir. Virginia rose and followed the voice. Water flowing mingled with its strains. She pushed branches aside with a light touch of her hand, moving cautiously toward the rushing brook.

The man's voice spoke—to himself or another, she did not know. No one answered. She stood still and let her senses tell her what lay before her: a last tangle of branches, a clearing, a stream. And a man standing in it with water flowing around him.

The man began to sing again, and startled, Virginia recognized the song. It was a low dirge, one of the old laments of Angslie that she knew from childhood. Mingling with the rush of water, it faded in and out, a dying song from a man whose connections to his old life were likewise tenuous.

She caught her breath. It was him. Here—and so Evelyn had to be near also. For a moment fear threatened to rise up and overcome her. But then she saw him again as she had seen him in the dream. She heard the words, "Help me."

And the other dream, the one in which the King had been pulled down by darkness, came to her memory again and said something new. She feared still that it meant he might be defeated—that he *could* be defeated. But the dream now told her that, like her, the King knew suffering in this battle. And that, for the sake of a world drowning in lies and darkness, he was willing to suffer.

Her heart moved in worship. And equally in compassion for the man before her. He had so long wanted to experience the true powers of the world. Evelyn had drawn him into torment and darkness. Could he now come away?

The laird hummed, stopped, and picked up the song again. One thing Virginia was certain of: if he was making music, he was alone.

She groped out her way, moving more branches aside, feeling herself step into clear air and onto the rocky ground around the brook. The night air was deepening all around her, still and cold, and she knew things were nearly as dark to others as they were to her. But there would be a moon, reflecting on water. He would see her if only he turned. She could make out the sounds of water splashing against something—he was washing clothes on a washboard perhaps, or a tool or something flat and hard. She could hear him moving against the current. His back was to her.

The humming grew louder as he turned, and then it faltered and died away. He did not move.

"Laird," she said, her voice as quiet and steady as she could make it. She was shaking, she realized, but she held out her hand and stepped forward, fighting to control herself.

"Go back," he said in a voice that was all low, graveled threat.

"I want to help you," she said.

"And why would I need your help?" he said. His voice raised, suddenly accusing. "You were never willing to help me before."

Memories assailed her at the sound of his voice. Before—in

Angslie, on the journey to Pravik, on the way to the defining horror of her life—*before*, he had always tried to wrench from her something she could not give. Meaning, understanding, contact with the supernatural world. And in the end he had simply tried to take it from her, giving her over to the Order of the Spider to use as they would.

Suddenly, in the forest darkness by the rushing stream, the pain of it was raw and real. And yet, he too was in need.

"I could not give you what you wanted," she said, swallowing hard. "I could not give you what you took from me. But now—"

"Nothing has changed," he said. "You cannot give me what I want now. So what help can you be to me? You should not be here. Be gone before the Blackness claims you again."

Virginia shook her head, hating her own feet for the way they stayed rooted to the ground, hating her mouth for all it could not say. "It is you who are in danger. I want to help you. I cannot offer you what you *want,* but perhaps I can offer you what you need. I am going to seek the King, laird. Come with me."

"You've heard of moths drawn to flame," Lord Robert said. "It seems you have no more wisdom than they. Evelyn is near; you must know that. She still wants you. Why do you linger?"

"Because I cannot leave you in the darkness," Virginia said. "I want to forgive you. Help me. Tell me you will live again if you're given the chance."

"Live again? Do you think him dead now?" a woman's voice said.

Virginia closed her eyes as the voice hit her like a blow from behind. "Do you call him living?" she returned.

"He stands with his feet in the shallows of power you cannot even imagine," Evelyn said. "And he will know its depths before we are through."

"Much good it may do him," Virginia said, "when the power is all darkness and death and ashes. What you offer is no life."

"You are a very fool to come here," Evelyn said. "Surely you know that."

Virginia smiled faintly. "There may be some wisdom in foolishness."

"Is there wisdom in suffering?" Evelyn asked, a cruel smile in her voice.

"Some things are worth suffering for," Virginia answered quietly.

As Lord Robert watched, Evelyn raised one hand, palm up, so her black sleeve fell away. Something black and writhing hovered above her hand. The blue stone began to glow. It was as though Evelyn had gathered the darkness out of the very air, and now it swirled in her palm. She spread out her fingers, and the darkness dripped from them and formed itself into tendrils in the air. They moved on a breeze that did not exist and began to play around Virginia, through her hair and over her skin, pricking her with pain that shot lightly over her skin. The blind girl shuddered.

"The Spider has had you before," Evelyn said. "And has been hungry ever since. Are you so eager to be possessed again that you come seeking the darkness out? And you speak of light!"

Virginia opened her eyes. Lord Robert started at the change: her green eyes were suddenly alive, burning with a deep fire. She turned her head to face Evelyn.

"Do you even remember light?" Virginia asked.

Evelyn took a step back. "Link," she snapped, and Lord Robert answered the name she had given him.

It only took a single blow to drop Virginia to the damp earth.

* * *

Night had fallen over the camp of the High Police, so the soldiers did not see the figures that moved like shadows through the trees—the first scouts of a rescue party, fleet-footed and silent Gypsies who took the lay of the camp and reported back to the waiting soldiers of Pravik who bore swords under Marja's command. She wore leather armour under a dark shirt and a long dark skirt, and tarnished silver bands gleamed on her arms. She carried a sword and wore silver earrings in her ears. Her long black hair was tied back in a purple scarf. She was beautiful and foreign and, thought the Eastern soldiers who waited admiringly for her to give the word, terrifying.

The reports confirmed what earlier scouts had already said: there were close to two hundred High Police in this camp. One daring young Gypsy had dressed himself as a servant and made his way through the tents and watch fires, discovering that Nicolas lay captive and senseless—drugged, he guessed—in a tent in the center of the camp.

There were not more than three hundred fighting men in all of Pravik, and they had nowhere near the arms or the experience of the High Police. In a battle they would certainly be defeated.

So this would not be a battle. It would be the swoop of a bird upon the unsuspecting—a beat of wings, a flash of claws, and a swift leave-taking. Twenty of Pravik's best and a handful of Gypsies against a full camp of High Police: a game of distraction and speed.

Marja looked to the treetops as she waited for the last scouts to return. An owl floated through layers of shadow. She prayed the blessing of the birds upon herself, the ancient blessing of her clan.

Footsteps were fast approaching. She turned, frowning. The scout was coming too fast, too loudly—didn't the fool know to be quiet?

His scream reached her in a moment, the sound of hooves hard behind it, and with it the knowledge that they had failed before the attack had even begun.

"Marja! We are known!"

The scout did not reach them. Marja heard the sound of a spear and the crash of his body in the underbrush. In the next moment the High Police burst through the trees. Marja sang out a war cry as her men leaped to meet the trained soldiers of Athrom. Two on horseback crashed through the trees and rode them down. Marja whirled to meet them and staggered to her knees against every effort to stay standing.

Kneeling in the dirt, she looked down at the blood darkening her shirt. A convulsion ripped through her and she dropped her sword, unwillingly, fighting for her voice, for clarity of mind, for a way to leap up again and press past the fight, past the soldiers, through the forest, and reach Nicolas.

Somehow, by some miracle, to reach Nicolas and bring

him out.

She fell forward with a low grunt. She thought she could feel it now—the blade in her ribs, the alien thing that had brought her down. Another convulsion ran through her, and her fingers tightened into fists.

How had they known?

The sounds of battle were faint in her ears; she could not see.

A boot wedged itself under her shoulder and pushed. She rolled onto her side, fingers still tight. She looked up at the man whose face she could just make out in the moonlight. The face of the enemy.

"She was lovely," he said. "Pity she's dead."

"She was a demon," said a voice from seemingly far off. "Have you never heard of the Gypsies who hunted our men? This is one of them. But yes, it's a pity she's dead—the emperor might have rewarded us for bringing her to him."

The first man was still looking at her. "I'm surprised that Gypsy scout found it in him to betray such a beauty."

"For enough gold," the second man said, his voice still very far, "men will do anything."

Marja heard nothing more.

* * *

Rehtse woke with a gasp, suddenly aware that Virginia was gone. She jumped to her feet.

"Virginia?" she called.

There was no answer.

After a few frantic moments of looking around the moonlit

copse, Rehtse fell to her knees and searched the darkness for footprints. She found a slight impression in the damp earth and followed it to another, crawling until the impressions disappeared in a thicket. But now there were a few snapped branches, things Rehtse noticed as though some power drew her attention to them, and she stumbled after the signs until she reached a brook.

No one was there. But there were more footprints here, and damper patches where someone wet had stood, and one bloody spot that made Rehtse's heart leap into her throat.

The ground was stony beyond the brook. She could find no more signs.

Hours later, Rehtse fell by a stream deep in the forest, letting the spray wash her scratched, smudged face. Her hands were bleeding from pushing through underbrush. She rolled onto her back and stared up at the sky, where dawn was just beginning to light.

She was sure that Virginia was not dead. She could not be dead, for if she was, all this journey had been meaningless. Rehtse's eyes were heavy, and she slept for a little while. When she awoke, her muscles were cramping from the night's hard searching, and new-birthed sunlight was sparkling on the water. It was beautiful, and empty. For a moment she wanted to cry. She had so long dreamed of this world—but never of being lost in it. She waded into the water beneath a green canopy. Around the stream, ferns and blue flowers grew in abundance. The water was cold as melted ice.

Birds stirred in the high treetops. She watched their flurries in distracted fascination. Unexpectedly, memories came to her of sitting at Divad's feet as a child. The pictures carved into the stone walls of the Darkworld had illustrated his stories of creatures and spirits in service to the King, and of the rebels against him. He had taught the young priests the whole history of the Great War and of man's betrayal, and of the Darkworld's desire to repent and serve the King again—of their determination to wait for his return. Rehtse had made that desire, that determination, entirely her own.

She left the water, the bottom of her skirt dripping and heavy, and kept pushing through the forest. She stepped into a circle of moss-covered, ancient trees, the tallest she had yet seen, silent sentinels around a still clearing where tiny purple flowers grew. Mist hung around their wide trunks and over the flower patches.

Her breath caught as the beauty of it broke over her. Suddenly, the world seemed a hundred times more alive than it had a moment ago. The earth beneath her lived; the moss was alive; she was *aware* of the flowers, of birds in the trees, of the lingering aftereffects of rain, of the very air. Her skin tingled with the secrets bursting all around her.

What had Divad taught them? That the world was once full of majestic and mysterious beings, that the woods were full of the King's creatures, that all creation served the King and abhorred the Blackness.

A wild idea was coming to her. Not that wild, she told herself. Not wild at all, if the stories were real, which they were.

Rehtse thought of Virginia, embraced the knowledge that she could not possibly find the Seer on her own, and cleared her throat.

"Powers of the Earth," she called, "come and help me!"

Her voice grew stronger, and she turned and scanned the edges of the clearing as she summoned all her faith. "Creatures who serve the King, come and help his servant!"

She heard movement nearby. Rustling; creaking branches. Her heart beat faster. A soft breeze made the branches high overhead dance.

Someone melted out of the trees. Dark hair and piercing blue eyes. Skin brown and vaguely patterned like bark, yet undeniably human. His bare feet left no print in the damp earth beneath him. He was young, perhaps fifteen. He stepped toward her with a barely discernible limp. Where his lame foot had been, green shoots made the shape of a footprint. He stretched out his fingers and touched a great tree, its trunk wrapped with slender vines, and as he did, new buds appeared on the vine and old buds unfolded into bright green leaves.

"Who are you?" he asked.

A priestess of the Darkworld, Rehtse thought, but she did not say the words. Suddenly she knew they were no longer true.

"I am Rehtse, a priestess of the King," she said.

"Then the woods welcome you," the young man said.

"Who are you?" Rehtse asked.

The young man looked at her for a long moment as though he was trying to remember. "My name is Kieran," he said slowly, with a slight frown. "I am the child of the woods."

He took a step forward. "You called in the King's name," he said. "Now you tell me, please . . . why have you called?"

"I need help," Rehtse said. "I am on a journey to seek the King. I have lost my companion, and I don't know how to find her on my own."

The young man bent his head. "There are many dangers in the woods these days. Who is your companion?"

"Her name is Virginia Ramsey," Rehtse said. "She is Gifted —the Seer of Pravik. A young woman, like myself."

Kieran knelt and buried his fingers in soft brown earth. Rehtse blinked hard. For a moment he looked like something rooted to the earth, a tree or a moss-covered rock, not human at all. She might have easily walked by without seeing him. A low sound reached her ears, almost too soft to hear. Once more the branches and leaves rustled. The ground beneath her felt suddenly like a living thing. An instant later the sensation was gone, and Kieran was standing.

"We have found her," he said.

Relief flooded Rehtse, drowning out even her sense of wonder. "How did you . . ."

"The roots go everywhere," he answered. He smiled. A shy smile.

"Where is she?" Rehtse asked.

Now a frown crossed his face. "The woman in black has her," he said. He saw Rehtse opening her mouth to reply and raised his hand as though to calm her urgency. "We cannot go to her now," he said. "Wait until nightfall. My father will help us."

"Your father?" Rehtse asked.

The shy smile reappeared. "He is called Tyrentyllith," Kieran said.

* * *

Lord Robert Sinclair sat by a fire, the blue stone chained to his arms and resting at his feet. He stared into it. Power stirred deep within like a monster far beneath the surface of water, casting only the faintest of ripples to the surface.

The stone had been Adhemar Skraetock's handiwork. A melding of spell and stone, strength both physical and spiritual, and very, very old. It was designed to overcome the limitations of the human members of the Order of Spider, who could enact the Rite of the Spider only far enough to take in as much power, as much life and energy and breath, as they could contain without killing themselves. A sad limitation indeed. But the stone could contain far more and never burst.

Lord Robert had asked himself, many times since Evelyn had entrusted the stone to his carrying, whether it was growing heavier as she enacted the Rite upon her fellows in the Order, murdering them in the process, upon the earth and its children, upon innocents and upon Gifted, and poured all she took into it. He could not tell.

In return for his faithful service, she gave him a taste of what she took. It flowed through him into the stone. She called him Link. He was the conduit through which she strengthened herself for her last rebellion. He was glad to serve her this way, for he was convinced that Evelyn alone had the power now to save the Seventh World from the enemy who was coming.

Lord Robert had told himself for some time that Evelyn was not evil; that she had simply opened doors into the world beyond the Veil, and because others didn't understand that reality, they labeled her a witch and a threat. He knew now that he had been wrong, that he had been lying to himself. Of course she was evil. As evil as the powers she drew upon. And there were assuredly other powers in the world that she did *not* possess, powers of good and of light. He had seen enough in the council days to tell him that.

But such powers were far from him now.

He was left with a stone, with the stirrings of power that frightened and drew him, with the conviction that even in her wickedness Evelyn was the world's only hope, and with the old resentment against Virginia that plagued him anew.

Why had she come to him? How had she even come to *be* here? Lord Robert knew well enough that the stone already contained shreds of her, power Skraetock had taken from her on the hilltop. Evelyn was still twisting that power for her own ends. And Evelyn had intended to take Virginia prisoner when they took Pravik, with the intent of using her again. But neither the laird nor Evelyn could have suspected that she would come to them first.

Why would she seek him out?

His hands shook as he peered deep into the swirling blue.

Virginia was sitting in the shadows just beyond the fire, cross-legged with her skirt drawn over her legs like she had always sat on the mountainside at home. But now her arms were bound to the tree behind her, the side of her face bruised from his blow, blood crusting around her eye. She had not changed much, except that her presence was more unnerving than ever—more otherworldly, but in a way that felt entirely foreign to him now that he had been so long with Evelyn. Her dark hair fell over slim shoulders; her green eyes looked into nothing.

He sat watching her for a time, and she shifted as though she knew his eyes were on her. After a while, she spoke.

"I have been angry with you," she said, her voice steady

and quiet. "I have been angry with you every day since the hilltop, and only when I sleep have I been able to escape that. Sometimes not even then. You will never know how deeply you have hurt me."

Lord Robert thought of the power stirring in the stone beneath his hands, power torn from her until it nearly killed her. He thought of how, sometimes, he could see her face in the stone's blue surface.

He knew more than she imagined. "And you tell me that to make me feel sorry?" he asked.

"I tell you that because I am willing to forgive you," Virginia said. "And if I am willing—I think the King will be also. I want to help you. Help me escape, and come with me. Turn from this darkness, laird—turn from all that has trapped you."

"What makes you think I want help?" he asked.

"I have seen it," she said.

His lip curled. Still seeing into people's souls. But he had no choice but to stand with Evelyn now. He had come too far. He regarded her coldly. "You think you have something better to offer me?"

"Light," she said.

"Little good your light is doing you now," he said.

"The story is not over," she said quietly.

The laird stood slowly and walked over to her. She tensed.

"Listen to me, Virginia," he said. "You know as well as we do that Morning Star will soon appear. The rule of the Morel family is already over—the emperor has gone mad. His general rules in his place even now, did you know that? Morning Star's power no longer upholds the Empire. More of the Blackness slips through the tattered Veil every day, and the rest are waiting for their ruler. The five hundred years are over. Of your King there is no sign."

He knelt suddenly before her. "And now, if you want to stand against Morning Star, you'll take sides with the only person on earth who can do it—with Evelyn."

His words caught her off guard—it was clear in her face. "I don't understand," Virginia said. "Evelyn is a servant of the Blackness."

"Better to say that the Blackness serves *her,*" Lord Robert said. "She is no friend of Morning Star. Did you think she would just turn the world over when the Usurper returns? She is human too. She has given her life to learning the secrets of the world unseen and collecting the powers of this one, and she will not relinquish all that to some tyrant. She has the power to stop him. To assert human independence. And she will."

"And then what?" Virginia asked. "Enslave us all? It's a foolish hope, laird—even if she *could* do it, we'd only be trading one devil for another. But she can't. No human can defeat Morning Star and the Blackness, much less by using evil!"

"Cling to that belief, then," Lord Robert said. "Cling to it until it destroys you. Come to your senses, Virginia. Evelyn needs your power. She'll have it one way or another. You're angry with me for giving you up to them the first time—well, I remember what they did to you. And now I'm warning you. Better that you side with her of your own free will."

"I will die first," Virginia said.

"You might," he said. His voice lowered. "She is coming."

A footfall, very close, startled Virginia. She pulled against the ropes that bound her to the tree.

"Must you always come to us unwillingly?" Evelyn asked. "Always bound and imprisoned?"

"It is you who chooses it," Virginia said. "Not I."

Cloth rustled; Evelyn was kneeling. She was very close. Virginia's skin prickled, and she wished she could pull away. But Evelyn did not touch her.

"Allow me to loose you," the woman said. "Give me reason to treat you as an ally and a friend. I can do so much for you— teach you to master your power. Help you fight what you hate most."

Virginia said nothing. She kept her head bowed and sat entirely still. Evelyn's voice took on an edge.

"Morning Star will come soon and unleash his hordes on this world. *You*—you and the other Gifted have the power to oppose him. But you are untrained and scattered. Let me train you. Let me bring you together—and you will destroy the Usurper when he comes."

"To make room for another?" Virginia said. "Is the thought of you ruling this world supposed to be better?"

"The thought of yourself in power, then," Evelyn said. "And your Ploughman, and the Singer. The thought of all six of you ruling as a council, with me at your head. The Council for Exploration Into Worlds Unseen—reborn, and so much more than it ever was."

"Six?" Virginia asked.

"You see?" Evelyn said. "You do not even know. Yes, there are six. Six specially Gifted, worth more even than others, each bearing a piece of the King's power. The King is not coming,

Virginia. *You* are. You and the rest of the Six are meant to save this world. But you cannot do it without me."

"I know my purpose," Virginia said. "The King himself spoke it to me. I am here to awaken the world to him, not to usurp his place. I would not rule on his throne. And I will not help you do it."

Fingers suddenly touched her face, crawling over her eyes. Pain and fear shot through her, twining together deep inside, old pain and new terror. But she said nothing.

"You will help me," Evelyn said. "You do remember the hilltop? How Skraetock used your power? Of course you do; you still feel it. I am more powerful now than Skraetock ever was. I have discovered the secret of using his stone to its fullest potential. I am mistress of the Spider, and I will use it to destroy you and take your power for myself. I am offering you a better way. This is your last chance to take it."

Evelyn stood suddenly. The folds of her cloak were a blur of Blackness that even Virginia could see. The air felt polluted, sooty.

"I will rule from Pravik," Evelyn said. "All who remain in the city will swear allegiance to me or forfeit their freedom and their lives. Come with me—reign beside me. If you plead for their lives, I will listen to you. But if you choose to remain in your pitiful place of weakness, I will leave you there—and your voice will avail nothing, for yourself or for anyone else. Do you understand me?"

Virginia's mind raced with thoughts of Pravik—Libuse's voice, Huss's learned questions, Maggie's touch, the formal ways of the Darkworlders, the hope and loyalty and strength of the Ploughman's farmers. She had kept herself apart from them in many ways, yet they had all captured her heart. She forced back tears. She could not be weak now.

She closed her eyes. Words came to her: one of Rehtse's prayers. Urgently she lifted them in spirit. *Great King, my shield and protector be. May I not give way to wrong. I want to remember you—to cling to you. To awaken the world to you.*

In quiet desperation, she prayed, *Great King, come!*

And in the depths of her spirit, something answered.

I am, it said.

She could not smile, but she found the strength to raise her head. "You are deceived, Evelyn," she said. "The King himself will come and take the throne from Morning Star—and from every usurper."

"This is your chosen way, then," Evelyn said. "Link! Bring me the stone."

Virginia closed her eyes and tried to fight despair. She whispered one last prayer as she heard a humming in the air and the low chanting of Evelyn's voice. *Watch over Rehtse. Let her find you. Please.*

Without warning, tendrils pierced Virginia's skin, and she cried out. They tightened and coiled and stabbed holes through her, hundreds of knife wounds, and she was bleeding to death, bleeding out her energy and life and power.

She screamed.

Evelyn smiled at the sound and the sight of the Spider draining Virginia of her power—limitless power, Evelyn suspected, unlike the unnatural abilities stolen from the other members of the Order, power that would not be fully taken until the girl was dead. Or perhaps she would not kill her.

Perhaps she would let her live to be used again.

There was a flash of light, and for the space of a blink, Evelyn thought she saw a man's form superimposed over Virginia's. The Spider's tendrils writhed and released, drawing back into Evelyn's hands. The witch gasped.

"What is it?" Link asked.

"Nothing," Evelyn said. "It is nothing. We will leave her for now."

"I don't understand," Link said.

"We have taken enough for now!" Evelyn snapped. She took one last look at Virginia, who was unconscious, held up by the ropes that bound her to the tree. She could see nothing —and no one—else.

But as she stalked back to the tent Link had erected for her, her hands were shaking.

9

Rescue

THE MOONLIGHT GREW IN STRENGTH as Rehtse crept through the forest at Kieran's side. A meadow stretched out before them, grey-green and glistening in the moonlight. On the other side the forest rose up again, blue and shrouded in mist.

Rehtse heard Kieran, but she did not think he spoke aloud. Somehow he communicated without voice. *She is there,* he said. Together they dropped to a crawl, Kieran nearly disappearing. The long grasses parted just in front of them, enough to create a barely visible line leading into the meadow. The grasses waved in the tiniest of breezes, brushing against Rehtse's skirts and wetting her face with dew.

And then, unexpectedly, Rehtse heard another voice. In its near-silent strains was the creaking of boughs and the rustle of leaves. It was Tyrentyllith himself who spoke. She knew his voice though she had never heard it before: this was the Forest Lord, the spirit of the woods who had served the King faithfully.

We will help you rescue the Seer, Tyrentyllith said. *But we beg a favour in return. Take Kieran with you to seek out the King. Before he came to us, he was crippled and ill. He needs healing that we cannot give him. He is human, but we have been giving him life to keep him alive, and it makes him too much like us. He needs to be free.*

Rehtse nodded, wishing she understood better what she was agreeing to—what mystery this boy represented. She glanced at Kieran to see if he had any response, but he gave no indication that he had heard. Somehow Tyrentyllith had cloaked his words so only Rehtse heard them.

The forest was whispering, sighing. This time they both heard the Forest Lord. *They are sleeping.*

Come, Kieran prodded.

They crawled forward together through the long grass. A nightjar burst out of the meadow before them, and Rehtse's heart pounded at the unexpected movement. She followed the bird with her eyes, moonlight silvery on its wings. *Fly away,* she thought.

She could feel the shadows in the forest on the other side of the meadow, far darker than mere shadows.

Nearly at the end of the meadow, Kieran stopped her with a light touch. She looked at him, and he smiled. Then he slipped away from her side. Beyond the meadow, Rehtse knew, the trees were silently growing leaves; branches were shifting; trunks were leaning closer together. The camp of the witch was being cast into utter darkness, as Kieran and Tyrentyllith had planned it. The boy had explained the plan to her before they set out. Their movements would be cloaked in shadows so deep even the witch would not able to see them.

Rehtse rose into a crouch and peered into the dark tunnel formed by the trees. She slipped into the shadows and waited near the edge for her eyes to adjust. They did, and quickly. She smiled faintly. Even for a Darkworlder, she had unusually good vision. She had never expected to make such use of it.

* * *

As Rehtse crept closer to the camp, Kieran slipped in from another angle. The boy did not move silently, but his movements did not sound like anything human—they sounded like the slightest rustle of leaves high above, or the soft creeping of some nocturnal creature through the trees. Unlike Rehtse, he did not see well in the dark. But he did not need to. He moved slowly, kneeling to touch his fingers in the earth every few feet, learning what the roots would tell him of the lay of the land and responding to what he learned.

The camp was a simple one. A single tent was set up before a fire, and a tall man was asleep in the embers' last glow. The witch slept within. Kieran smiled in the darkness. He could sense in the air the reason for the man's slumber when he should have been awake and watching. Some of the trees contained in their flowers and leaves toxins that would work as sleeping potions. Tyrentyllith had simply released them into the air.

Still, the slumber would be tenuous. Kieran crept forward until he was close enough to the man to touch him. He knelt and buried his fingers in the earth, coaxing the roots up, calling to nearby vines to stretch themselves and come to him. Slowly they grew over the man's feet and legs, coiling around him so stealthily that they would not wake him.

Satisfied that the man was bound well enough to prevent

any quick escape, Kieran crawled into the witch's tent.

It was darker within than it had been even in the clearing. But Kieran could feel the evil—evil so tangible that it turned the air wrong. He had felt its like before. He had even known its power to tempt and beckon, before he had cast himself into the forest and Tyrentyllith's saving mercy. He frowned. His memories of that life were few and faded, and they disturbed him. There were people he remembered . . . family . . . He shook his head to concentrate on the moment at hand.

He dug down with his fingers, unable to break through the tent canvas to the soil beneath. But he called to the roots nonetheless, and he tensed as they began to rip through, tearing the fabric.

They were too loud. He feared the witch would awake.

A wind began to blow, a sound at once so natural it would not wake Evelyn and so loud it covered the sound of the roots as they worked through the cloth.

* * *

Rehtse reached the tree where Virginia was bound. Above, Tyrentyllith's cover had just enough cracks in it to let down strategic light. Even in the shadows, Rehtse could see that the Seer was hurt. One side of her face was bruised and crusted with blood—but the hurt was deeper than that. The bonds that held her to the tree seemed to be holding her up.

For an instant Rehtse's blood froze with the fear that Virginia was dead. She beat the dread down. She was not too late. She could not be too late.

The tree was only feet from the sleeping man and the tent

where the witch undoubtedly lay. Did she dare speak to Virginia? But if she did not, would Virginia cry out when Rehtse began to unbind her? It was dark in the clearing, thanks to Tyrentyllith—but sound could still betray them.

Great King, she prayed, *grant your servant wisdom.*

A sudden gust of wind blew into Rehtse's face, pushing her dark braids back. Overhead, the thickly grown trees trembled in the wind, branches rustling and creaking. The man at the fire stirred, and Rehtse saw him look up—and then let his head droop again. The wind was making a great noise.

So great, Rehtse realized, that the man would not hear her if she spoke. The wind would blow her voice away.

Smiling with the wonder of it—that not only the forests, but now the wind was helping in the rescue—Rehtse rushed to Virginia's side and whispered her name into her ear. At first there was no response, and Rehtse again felt fear. But then Virginia stirred, and she turned her head slightly.

"Who is there?"

"It is Rehtse," Rehtse said. "You are rescued, as soon as I can untie these bonds."

"Quickly," Virginia whispered in reply. She said nothing more. Rehtse pulled a small knife from her dress and cut the ropes loose. Virginia nearly fell. Rehtse propped her up and helped her to her feet.

"Are you—"

"I am alive," Virginia whispered. "I will be all right. Take me away from here."

* * *

In the tent, Kieran worked with his eyes darting to the fabric sides that rose and fell with the force of the wind. He too was full of wonder. This was no work of Tyrentyllith's.

This part of his task had taken longer, for the woman slept on a cot, and the roots had to grow high enough to reach her. They held her feet and ankles now in a great tangle and coiled around her wrists. For good measure, Kieran had brought a thick root up and over the woman's waist, and another over her neck—enough to keep her from struggling hard. He laughed to himself at his own work, at the image of these two trying to escape. And he stood and turned to go.

The woman's eyes opened, and from them a terrible blue light shone into the tent.

The light caught Kieran and held him fast. He could not move.

He watched in terror as the woman slowly pushed aside her cloak and swung her legs over the edge of the cot. His handiwork snapped as though the roots had been made of thread. The roots shriveled away into black, twisted versions of themselves. His hands, which had so carefully coaxed and shaped them, began to tingle.

The tingle grew into pain.

The woman stood. She was beautiful—pale and black-haired, wearing a white shift, her hair long and flowing over her shoulders. The blue light illuminating the tent made her look ghostly and ethereal. She held one hand out, palm up, and in it something was turning, a black light like a knot of tendrils and smoke . . .

Something in Kieran jarred itself awake. The pain went searing up his arms, and he fell on his knees with a scream before half-running, half-crawling for the door of the tent.

The tendrils caught him partway, and his back arched with pain as the energy surged through him. He screamed again.

* * *

Virginia and Rehtse, just on the edge of the meadow, turned as one at the first scream.

"Kieran!" Rehtse said, the wind still blowing her hair back.

Virginia only stared unseeing at the clearing, eyes wide. Another scream. She lurched back toward the camp, and Rehtse grabbed her arm.

"No!" she shouted. "You can't go back there!"

"She'll destroy him!" Virginia said.

She did not know who the boy was who had twice screamed, but she knew the pain in his voice and that he was in Evelyn's grasp, in the Spider's grasp. She strained at Rehtse's grip. She would go back, would trade herself for the child, would . . .

Rehtse released Virginia and pushed her toward the meadow. "Run!" she said. "Run with all your strength for the trees, and Tyrentyllith will give you shelter. I am going back for the boy!"

Virginia opened her mouth to argue, but in that moment they both were silenced by a presence that fell over them with such force that it took their breaths away.

Rehtse looked to the edge of the trees and saw it. A translucent giant, tall as the trees. In the mist and the moonlight, he faded in and out of solidity. His skin was pale and marred like birch bark. His eyes were blue, shining in his face like a sudden splash of wildflowers. Long hair like dark green vines fell around his shoulders. The face itself was beautiful, ancient, and yet, always changing. It seemed to Rehtse that all of the seasons were in this being's features, cycling, changing, dying, and being renewed. Tyrentyllith of the Earth Brethren, Forest Lord, Keeper of the Woods.

The trees pulled themselves away from the ancient being, opening a straight path to the camp so they could see into it. Moonlight poured in. A blue light was shining from a central place near the fire, and a figure in black robes stood by it. Kieran was on his back on the ground, writhing in the grasp of what looked like cords of thick smoke.

"Release my son," Tyrentyllith demanded.

The black figure raised its arms, and the sleeves fell away from the woman's white hands. A sound issued from her, growing in volume and rhythm—a chant, a call. The moonlit air grew darker around the woman, and the forest moaned. Kieran convulsed as the tendrils suddenly vanished from around him.

"As you wish, Earth Brother," the woman said.

The trees on every side of her began to bow, and the moan in the air deepened and increased as their branches grew limp and blackened. Blackness clotted in the woman's hands and broke through in vaporous threads that ascended into the air, drawing life from the surroundings, sucking power from the forest like a parasite sucking blood.

Tyrentyllith's form stood unmoving, but fading like mist. Rehtse realized, suddenly terrified, that the pain shaking the forest had momentarily paralyzed him.

A deep laugh rose from the woman's throat and filled the

air. Memories swirled in the air all around her and impressed themselves upon Rehtse's soul. Seasons. Life. Songs in the stars. The King, walking in the forest in ancient days, calling life up from it in ever more abundant joy. The forest had *lived* for so long, had waited centuries for the dawn that would bring the King back again. And through Evelyn's laughter Rehtse heard them crying, all the orphan ghosts of yesterday. She saw them rising on every side, weeping as they went, the long-silent souls of the forest dragged into the Spider's grasp.

Kieran whimpered. Rehtse ran forward and gathered the lanky boy in her arms, pulling him away from Evelyn, staring at the woman with hatred in her eyes. The witch turned her own eyes on the priestess, eerily blue, shining. She did not move to stop her from taking Kieran. The look on her face was mocking.

Evelyn spoke. Her voice was louder, stronger than it should have been. "Tyrentyllith the Forest Lord," she said. "Learn now who truly rules the woodlands. You were loyal to the King in the Great War, and for that you paid dearly—five hundred years trapped in silence. War is coming again, Spirit of the Forest. Your King does not even play a role in it. The world is mine now, and this time you shall not merely sleep."

The stone near the fire which had been glowing faintly began to ignite with brighter light from somewhere deep below its surface. The light spread across the stone, showing veins of black shot all through it in spidery shapes, and suddenly it burst up and split the night sky, and the light itself was darkness.

Black bands of writhing energy thick as railroad ties pulsed from the light, great black spider legs fraying with a thousand jagged edges. Rehtse had dragged Kieran back as far as Virginia, and now she grabbed hold of each of them to stop them from running toward Evelyn.

"Laird!" Virginia cried.

"No!" Kieran screamed, pulling himself free of Rehtse and running for the blue light.

"Come back!" Rehtse shouted as she made a desperate grab for him. Her voice could hardly be heard over a terrible noise.

The forest, wailing with a sound like nothing she had ever heard.

Kieran had not run six feet before something picked him up and threw him backward, onto the ground at Rehtse's feet. He jumped up to run for Tyrentyllith again, but the force returned and caught all three in a howling gale so strong it lifted them off the ground. Rehtse closed her eyes and concentrated on holding on to Virginia as she lost contact with the earth and felt the trees rushing past and then below them as they lifted higher and higher, flying away like ashes drifting in the wind.

"Llycharath!" Virginia cried, her voice weaker than her words deserved. "Let us down!"

Rehtse screwed her eyes even more tightly shut as she heard the voice that answered from the heart of the wind.

Cannot, little sister. You must not be here.

* * *

The voices that came through Nicolas's drugged awareness were all loud and tangled, pulling him in a thousand directions. They came from everywhere. Pravik. The High Police camps.

From other cities, other villages; from his own hopes and dreams and fears.

When he was not drugged, he could focus on more demanding voices.

The commander's boot caught him in the jaw and snapped his head back, and he tasted blood as he clenched his jaw once more.

"Come on, boy!" the man demanded. "Tell me what I want to know!"

Nicolas spit blood and spoke as best he could with a swollen tongue. "I cannot tell you," he said. "I don't know."

He tensed as the boot swung for his ribs, driving him across the ground. The commander reached down and grabbed him by the scruff of his torn shirt, shoving him up against the thick pole in the middle of the tent. The commander's face, red and sweaty, was inches from his.

"I know there's more going on here than anyone's telling me," the commander growled. "First I don't see the emperor in months, and then he's issuing orders through that swine Cratus to come here and wait and watch that city without attacking. And then it's capture the blind girl, and capture *you,* you with your strange eyes and your answering voices that aren't there. And I swear you know more than you're telling."

He threw Nicolas back to the ground. He coughed and spat blood again, then glared up at the commander. "You've had me drugged," he said. "Of course I hear voices."

"Not on that drug," the commander said. "That root should take you out of this world and every other besides. No, you're like the blind girl was—Gifted is the word. Now you tell me. I'm sick of playing pawn. What are you? And what's going on in Athrom?"

"How should I know if you don't?" Nicolas said. He closed his eyes. A sound was building somewhere, pushing at him, threatening to overcome the walls he'd been building. Between the commander's beating, the voices, and the last vestiges of the drug, he could hardly keep his thoughts together enough to make sense of what the commander was saying.

One thing he did know—something was wrong. The sound was still building—still beating at him—still—

The commander dragged Nicolas off the ground and drew back his fist for another blow, but before he could strike, Nicolas stiffened and screamed.

The commander dropped him. Nicolas curled up on the ground and held his ears. He screamed again.

The sound pulsed through him like a convulsion, like the death throes of a great beast, like black waves pounding against his mind and threatening to shatter it. Mourning, moaning, wailing, dying. Many voices, yet all one voice; voices wooden and leafed and rooted.

The voices of the forest dying.

Nicolas did not know when the commander left him alone —when the guards ducked away from his screaming and shouting for it to stop. The voices tore him apart more surely than the commander could have done in a hundred beatings.

He only knew that when they ceased, fading away in a long, slow wail, he was alone.

And he was not drugged. He could move. Every muscle protesting, he pushed himself to his hands and knees and crawled for a low place in the earth where he could wriggle out from beneath the tent wall. The camp was dark but for a few fires. A wagon stood nearby. Scrambling up as quietly as he could, he darted for it and hid in its shadows. A guard walked past. He did not move. The guard did not see him.

A tent with an open flap stood ten feet away, closer to the edge of the camp. He closed his eyes and listened for voices or breathing within. Nothing. It was empty. Satisfied that no one was near, he crossed the empty ground and disappeared into the tent. He closed his eyes and listened his way through the camp, finding each nearby soldier, listening to their conversations, discovering who was distracted and who was not posted where he should be.

It would not be a quick escape. But it was a sure one.

* * *

In the morning, smoke could be seen rising from the forest in Galce.

An enormous swath of land had been burned out, several square miles of wreckage. Little was left but ash.

High in a tree hundreds of years old, the tallest tree of the forest just beyond the wasteland, Kieran sat on a branch and looked over the carnage with tears running silently down his face.

Behind him, resting in a hollow in the trunk but close enough to the edge to see out, Rehtse and Virginia sat knee to knee. Virginia's eyes were closed; her mind far away. She was pale and weak, her face drawn with recent suffering and still-lingering pain. Rehtse was watching the boy. His grief hurt her, more than the sight of the burned-out woods—his grief, and the fear she had seen in his eyes.

Rehtse started to reach out to him, but she thought better of it and brought her hand back. Virginia's eyes were still closed.

Rehtse sighed. She wanted to feel triumphant. She had found one of the Earth Brethren. She had rescued Virginia. They had escaped Evelyn. Surely the King was helping them. And yet . . .

She looked over at Kieran again. He was still staring out at the green canopy spread out before them and the black expanse beyond that. Behind him, on the other side of the forest, light sparkled off water—the sea.

Smoke was still rising from the ashes.

Slowly, Rehtse unfolded herself from the hollow and moved out on the long branch, telling herself not to look down. She settled into a crook in the branch beside Kieran, laid her hand on his shoulder, and said, "It will be all right."

He looked at her, and his face looked much younger than the fifteen or so years she had assumed were his. "How do you know?" he asked. His voice sounded younger as well.

"Tyrentyllith is a great power," Rehtse said. "The Spider is strong, but it is neither so old nor so good as the Earth Brethren. Tyrenytllith serves the King." Her voice sounded unconvincing in her own ears, but it gathered warmth the more she spoke. "I do not believe he could be vanquished so easily."

Kieran sniffed, keeping his eyes on Rehtse as though he couldn't stand to look back at the waste again. He wiped his nose on his arm and drew his knees to his chest. "My father can go—deep. Somewhere to heal. Perhaps he has gone there. I just wish he was here."

"Kieran," Rehtse said slowly, "is Tyrentyllith really your father?"

The boy looked at her almost in confusion, and then slowly shook his head. "No," he said. "I came here when I was young. I was running away from the Blackness, and Tyrentyllith found me and made me his own."

"But you're not like the rest of us," Rehtse said. "The way the plants respond to you—and the way you fade into the earth so I can't see you . . ."

Kieran shook his head again. "I don't know—I changed. He changed me. I became more like him."

"How old are you now?" Rehtse said.

"I don't know," he said. "I was eleven when I came, before the winter—in the summer."

"Wait," Rehtse said, "last summer?" She looked hard at Kieran again. Of course it was possible that Sunworlders aged differently from those who lived underground, but this much? The boy who sat before her could not possibly be eleven or twelve—and yet, as he sat crying in the tree, he seemed so much younger in spirit than he looked in body.

"Yes," he said. "Last summer. Maybe two—I can't remember. But I've grown older."

"But Kieran," Rehtse said slowly, "you can't have grown *this* much older in such a short time!"

He shrugged. "The forests age differently."

Rehtse frowned. "Yes—trees may take decades to grow. They taught us as much when we trained for the priesthood. But shouldn't that make you age more slowly?"

"They don't all age slowly," Kieran said. "Some things grow very quickly and bloom out all at once."

He fell quiet for a moment and said, "The ones that die early."

He looked up, and his blue eyes sparkled with tears. "I don't know what's going to happen to me," he said. "People aren't supposed to live like I do. I don't know if that makes me stronger or weaker. I just know that I want to be with Tyrentyllith." He swallowed, and Rehtse's heart ached. "I need him."

In a sudden wash of understanding, Rehtse recognized the tone in the boy's voice as belonging to her too—it was the tone she felt when she thought of Caasi. Her heart moved for him. They were both orphans, in their own way. They all were.

Ignoring the vast space beneath her, Rehtse moved closer to Kieran. "Whose were you before?" she asked. "Do you have a family?

Kieran frowned. "It's hard to remember. I think—yes. In the Green Isle. But I don't know what's happened to them. The Blackness came to get us. The others were playing with it—but I was afraid, because I knew if let it, it would change me and make me powerful, and that would be bad for me. For all of us. So I ran to the end of the train, and I felt my father in the woods. And I ran away."

"Does your family know what happened to you?" Rehtse asked.

Kieran shook his head. "Tyrentyllith said they must not know, or the Order would try to find me. He said that in the beginning, when he took me in. I had forgotten until now."

Virginia stirred suddenly, though she didn't move from the trunk of the tree—wisely, Rehtse thought, shuddering a little at the drop beneath them. "Tyrentyllith is alive," she said. "I've seen him. He is wounded and has gone deep, as you said—but the Spider has not conquered him."

Kieran smiled through his tears and looked away.

"And you, Virginia?" Rehtse asked. "You have hardly spoken since last night."

Virginia made an attempt to smile, but it didn't work. Rehtse noticed that she was clutching a small brown pouch, which she tucked away before answering. "Much is wrong in the world, Rehtse. Evelyn intends to conquer Pravik in a few days and hold it against Morning Star when he returns. And she is powerful enough to do it."

Rehtse caught her breath as the words sank in. "But—if— we should go back, then," she said. "Go to Pravik, warn them. Evelyn is a far greater threat than the High Police, and the Gypsies did not know of her, even if they reached Pravik with our message. The Darkworld must know . . ."

"No, Rehtse," Virginia said quietly. "It is too late for warnings. We cannot help them any more than I could help the laird. Huss sent us to go where I last saw the King and seek him out. And that is what we must do. We need him. If the world has any hope now, it must be in the King. We are high— can you see the sea?"

"I can," Rehtse said.

"Angslie is over the sea," Virginia said. "It is there we must go. Kieran, help us down. There is a long walk ahead of us. And we must finish it before Evelyn knows where we are."

10

The Fall of Pravik

Nicolas lay on a sunburned patch of earth where he had fainted. His body ached in every muscle, every bone. Each time his senses returned enough for him to try to move, his head split so badly that it knocked him senseless again.

Hands grabbed beneath his arms and dragged him into shade. He felt moss beneath him, and he was rolled onto his back.

He opened his eyes to a blurred, too-bright world. A face was before him, but it was long in taking on any real form. He could smell something familiar, something mingling with the smells of bark and moss. Smoke.

"Drink this," the face said. Something was put to his lips, and he managed to swallow it. It was cold and sweet. The taste of water mingled with the rust of blood. A damp rag touched his face, washing some of the dirt and blood away from his eyes, nose, and mouth.

"Who—" Nicolas began to croak, but before he could ask, his eyes focused enough. His body relaxed. "Peter."

Peter the Pipe-Smoker, cousin to Marja and lifelong friend,

regarded Nicolas solemnly. "I don't know how you come to be alive," he said. "But I'm heartily glad you are."

Nicolas tried to answer, but words failed him.

"You smell like avis leaf," Peter said. "Beneath all that blood, I mean. They drugged you good. You'll be a few days before you're fully back to normal. But no bones are broken. What was the point of beating you?"

"He wanted—" Nicolas stopped. What had the commander wanted? "To know . . . something."

"Well, I'll tell you something of my own," Peter said. "One of our Gypsies found you in the camp when he was scouting for Marja and betrayed us all."

Nicolas's heart leaped. "Marja?"

"She came for you, but that gutter rat had already tipped the High Police off." Peter knelt in front of Nicolas. His expression was somber, his brows knit together. "She's alive, Nicolas, but a greater miracle than you are. She's badly wounded and not out of danger yet." A crooked smile crossed his face. "If she didn't love you so much, I expect she would be dead now. But she'll not go without knowing you're well."

"How did . . ."

"I found her myself and carried her back to Pravik," Peter said. "She's safe with them for now. Then I came back to look for you. I didn't think they could hold you long. Your children are in Pravik too—have been since the caravan was attacked."

This time Nicolas managed to smile back. He reached out a bloodied hand and laid it on Peter's shoulder. "You're a true friend," he said.

Peter looked away as though the praise made him uncomfortable. "You'll be a day or two more to mend," he said, "and then I'll take you to the city."

Nicolas shook his head. "I don't want to wait."

Peter looked him up and down. "When you can walk," he said. The crooked smile reappeared. "I'm not carrying you."

* * *

A grey, clouded sky bent over the empty streets of Pravik. Libuse had ordered the gates shut and the people hidden in the castle after Peter carried the limp and bloody form of Marja to safety in the city. Not one of the soldiers sent to rescue Nicolas had returned.

Deep in the castle, the Darkworld priests Hazrit and Annan tended to Marja. On the city walls, Libuse had posted armed guards. She spent hours on the highest tower of the castle, looking over the city, its river and bridges, its walls, the forests beyond. Wishing with all her heart for a glimpse of the returning Ploughman. Knowing she would not see it.

Expecting at any moment to see something far less welcome.

She stood there, at the top of the highest tower looking into a storm-gathering sky, feeling a few cold raindrops on her face, her own breath threatening to tear her apart. Somehow she knew the wait was over.

"Help us," she whispered into the storm.

In answer, lightning forked across the sky. The wind was picking up, blowing her hair and skirts wildly. She held onto an empty flagpole as the wind pushed against her. The city below, the green and grey world beyond that, the blackening sky above—none answered her plea. Thunder crashed and lightning forked down again, splitting the sky before her.

It illuminated the faces and weaponry of the High Police who even now marched on the city from every side.

She breathed the words again. "Help us."

She heard feet on the stairs, shouts. "My lady, we are attacked!" She closed her eyes, and tears slipped out. But she steeled her expression and turned to meet her men, the Ploughman's men, the faithful few who might now fight the last battle of their lives.

"Sound the alarm," she said as they burst onto the roof. "Take up arms and gather around the castle. We will fight with our backs to it that they may not get behind us."

"But there is no retreat," the first man said.

"That is our lot," Libuse said.

The man bowed. "My lady."

Libuse turned to look back on the approaching army. They surrounded the city. Behind her, one of the men took a horn from his belt and blew it, long and loud, calling the men to the castle. She watched as the guards at the gate abandoned their posts and ran to rally at the sound of the horn. It was best this way. The gates could not hold the army long. They had not the manpower to make them hold. The tramp of boots grew louder, then the hollow thud as a battering ram hit the doors.

For one fleeting moment Libuse allowed herself to picture the Ploughman, golden in power, strong and tall, the leader they needed, and to wish with all her heart that he was here. For only a moment. She could not afford to dwell on his absence now. Not when her people needed her presence to make up for it.

A flock of birds flew over the tower, undisturbed by all

that transpired below. She watched them go, set her jaw, and left the tower in search of her own leather armour and a sword and spear.

The High Police burst through the gates before she was halfway down the stairs.

*　*　*

The High Police marched through empty streets furrowed by shovels and ploughs. The long-abandoned homes of the city were in disrepair. They marched over the Guardian Bridge, past the carved kings with their empty eyes and hands stretched out—in blessing or beseeching, it was not now easy to say. Houses grew finer as they advanced, showing the care of residents: all around the castle was the city's living core.

At their head the commander rode, a gold, rain-sodden cloak identifying him as leader. He frowned as the castle came closer into view. It seemed that every man in Pravik had gathered in front of it, and they stood now, silently defiant, waiting with weapons in their hands. As his soldiers drew closer, the commander could see the woman who stood before them all, slight, beautiful, and resolute. The last scion of the Eastern kings, Libuse had always been something of a legend in the Seventh World, even more so when she threw in her lot with the rebel called the Ploughman. In his own heart, the commander had admired her. But now she was only so much chaff to be trodden and burned. He had his orders. They were clear enough, straight from the emperor himself.

Take the Seer from her refuge in Pravik. Kill all the rest. Torch the city.

Give no quarter. Not to any.

Libuse stood with sword drawn, her hair tied back for a fight. The commander didn't know if he was relieved or annoyed that she was not asking for mercy.

The march of his men halted. No one moved. Rain fell and puddled at their feet, soaking their armour and their horses' fur, making their torches smoke. The commander cleared his throat.

"Deliver the Seer up to us," he said. "We have been sent to take her."

"She is not here," Libuse answered, her voice strong and calm. "Nor would we give her up if she was."

He narrowed his eyes. "She must be here," he said. "Where else would she take refuge?"

"Nevertheless," Libuse said. "She is not."

A bolt of lightning split the sky behind the castle, illuminating the resolute faces of the men of Pravik. Suddenly the commander knew why they stood here ready to fight, why they did not ask for quarter, why they did not offer to surrender. They knew as well as he did what the High Police's presence here meant. There *was* no quarter. The emperor had lied. They were all meant to die.

And they meant to do it dearly.

Shaking his grizzled head, the commander raised his sword. To his front lines he barked, "Cut them down and find the Seer. Do not harm her. All the rest die!"

Thunder crashed as he lowered his sword, and his men surged forward on every side. Pravik let loose its last battle cry and rushed forward to meet the onslaught. The commander stayed where he was, watching from horseback. He saw the farmer-soldiers of Pravik struggling to reach him, but his men were too many. The rebels were cut down one by one.

Six of his men surrounded Libuse. She killed one of them. The corner of the commander's mouth twitched. She could hold her own. For that he was glad.

Not that she could last.

Not that any of them could. The rain grew heavier, pinging off swords and armour in weird counterpoint to the battle cries, the screams, the groans of dying men. The commander knew his recent history: when the High Police had first fought these people, Golden Warriors had appeared and slaughtered the emperor's men. The streets of Pravik had become a supernatural battleground.

Now it was hardly a battleground at all. This was little more than a massacre.

He sighed. He kicked his heels into his horse and started forward, through the battle that hardly even threatened him, toward the castle. He would head the search for the Seer himself. Her escape from his camp had humiliated him, all the more when word arrived from the emperor that he wanted the woman captured for his own purposes. Where he respected Libuse, he was eager to find and be finished with Virginia Ramsey.

Lightning flashed again, and this time it illuminated a dark figure in his path.

Another woman stood on the steps of the castle. She wore a black cloak. Its long sleeves covered her hands, its hood cast her face into shadow. He recoiled. He knew that uniform: the Order of the Spider, skulkers in the emperor's court, holders of unimaginable power and universally despised. The woman held up her hand, palm forward. A black tattoo in the shape of a spider stained it.

"Stop," she said.

He did not intend to obey, yet his horse froze where it stood. He tried to kick it again, to nudge it forward, but he could not move. He began to panic as he realized the sounds of battle had grown silent.

None could move.

The air around the woman seemed to be shifting and twisting in dark knots, swallowing itself and coming back out again.

"Butchers," the woman said, her tone one of amusement. "How many have you killed? One, two hundred? Your opponents have not done half so well. Shall we even the score?"

Sudden groans and screams split the air. The commander didn't look. He knew what was happening. Somehow, without even stirring from her place on the steps, she was killing his men.

"There," she said. "One, two hundred. And the rest of you? Will you also die where you stand?"

He could not even move his lips to answer. She lowered her hand. "I am releasing you now," she said. "If you are wise, you will come forward and swear allegiance to me. If you are fools, you will die."

The commander felt his limbs loosen, and the flanks of his horse heaved. He was free to move. So were his men. Yet none did.

"Caught in indecision?" Evelyn asked. "How if I tell you that your emperor, to whom you swore allegiance, did not send you here? That he has done nothing for months, for he is a slavering madman and someone else has taken over for him?"

The commander's mouth seemed to move without him. "Our orders came from General Cratus."

"Indeed they did," Evelyn said. "And only from Cratus, for he, a man like yourself, with no greater claims than yours, is ruling in the emperor's seat. I can offer you proof, if you want it. Link!"

A man who had been hiding in the shadows behind her suddenly moved into view. He carried a large, flat stone. Its center swirled with light.

"Sight stolen from the Seer of Pravik," the woman intoned, "serve me once more!"

The commander gasped as sudden visions passed before his eyes. He saw the throne room in Athrom. An empty throne. The emperor, his hair grown long and wild, crawling on all fours like a beast. And Cratus sitting on the throne, giving commands in secret.

"Drop your weapons at my feet," the woman said. "Swear allegiance to me now. Whoever does not will die where he stands. Whoever does has joined a new army and a new rebellion. We will conquer the usurper of Athrom with the same power you have felt restraining your own limbs. Come forward now!"

The commander remained unmoving as his men began to step forward, one by one, then in clusters, and drop their swords at the woman's feet. He felt no emotion as the men he had led abandoned their allegiance and swore fealty to the black-cloaked witch. There were many. Hundreds. Those who had surrendered retreated into the streets, waiting for new orders.

When they had all finished, only a handful still stood unmoving in the street among the bodies that lay growing heavier with the rain.

The commander himself. Libuse, still on her feet. And the hundred or so men who were left to her.

The commander cleared his throat. Slowly, he nudged his horse forward until he stood at the mountain of weaponry that had been left at the woman's feet. He drew his sword and slowly dropped it. He pulled his dagger from his boot, his spear from his saddle, and his axe from his back, and one by one laid them down. Then he bowed his head.

"My service," he said.

The witch's eyes smiled in approval. He moved aside. Her eyes fixed themselves on Libuse. The men of Pravik were gathered around their princess.

"Still resisting?" Evelyn said. "Rebels to the end?"

"Ours is an allegiance of love," Libuse said. "We cannot so easily abandon it."

"Commander," Evelyn said, "have your men arrest all these and take them to the castle dungeons. Bring the princess to me in the throne room."

She turned, and from her dark form laughter began to arise. She clapped her hands, and a whirling pillar of darkness shot up from the blue stone and split the clouds. The rain turned black and heavy for a moment before it disappeared. The darkness still hovered over the city, swirling like a sluggish whirlpool in the air. It was a sign. A challenge.

To whom, the commander could not be sure.

* * *

Nicolas saw the great darkness as it erupted over the city, and he set his jaw and started forward.

Peter threw his arms around him and hauled him back. "No," he grunted.

"Let me go!" Nicolas said, struggling against his friend's grip. His struggles brought both of them to the ground, but Peter refused to release him.

"It's no good, Nicolas!" he said. "That witch is too strong for you, you *know* that. She'll want you for your Gift just like the emperor does. If you put yourself in her hands, what will happen to you? What will happen to Marja, to your children? Think!"

Nicolas stopped struggling. He breathed hard, his nose inches from the dirt. "Let me up," he said. "Let me up; I won't go."

Peter hesitated a moment before releasing him. Nicolas pushed himself up onto his hands and knees. He glared at Peter. "If I had my strength . . ."

"You'd have knocked me flat and gone, I know," Peter said. "But I'm talking sense, Nicolas. Listen to it."

Nicolas nodded. There was blood in his teeth; he spit it out. "You're right, Evelyn's too strong for me. But she's not too strong for us."

"Us?" Peter asked.

"The Gifted," Nicolas said. "All of us. Me, Maggie, Virginia, the Ploughman . . . all of us." He pushed himself back onto his heels. "I learned many things when I went after the River-Daughter, Peter. This was one of them. The Gifted are meant to be woven together. Virginia inspired Pravik to come to the Gypsies' defense. I saw the Ploughman fight in Athrom, and I've heard power in Maggie's songs. We're strong alone—stronger than any of us think we are. But together we're strong enough to stop the witch and win back the city."

Peter's face betrayed his bewilderment. He shook his head. "But you're alone," he said. "And Maggie and the Ploughman are in Athrom."

"Where they've been betrayed," Nicolas said. "It can't have been any other way. They're captives, then."

"Or they're dead," Peter said.

Nicolas shook his head. He knew Peter was wrong—though *how* he knew he could not have said. Perhaps the Gifted were already woven in some way. "They're not dead," he said. "So I'll free them."

"Like you were just now going to free Marja?" Peter said.

Nicolas made a face at him. "No, not like that. Going to free Marja now would be walking into a trap without the strength to get out again. But the emperor won't be looking for me in Athrom. And when I find the others, we'll be strong enough to spring any trap. Believe me."

Peter took his pipe from his pocket and stuck it in his teeth, chewing hard on the end before he pulled it out again. "I'll come with you."

"No, you won't," Nicolas said. "You'll stay here and watch the city. Watch my Marja. My children. Make sure they're all right."

"How am I supposed to do that from out here?" Peter asked.

"You'll find a way," Nicolas said. "Just as I'll find mine.

Promise me, Peter. You won't leave here until I've come back."

Peter nodded. "You and Marja are all the family I have left, Nicolas," he said. "I promise it."

11

Gathering the Gifted

THE IRON SERPENT WAS A WONDROUS THING, with rails stretching from Italya up into the Eastern Mountains. The trains with their dragon-headed engines, only two in all the Seventh World, belched steam and crossed the land like a vision of a future that might have been had the Empire embraced the power of steel and steam—which it had not. Nicolas crept into an empty cattle car and rode to Italya in dirty straw, fighting headaches and making plans. He knew a little of how the trains had come to be, of their invention by a man in the Green Isle and the Empire's futile attempts to buy his brilliance to make weaponry for the High Police. The man had refused, and eventually died. Nicolas knew nothing more about him, but as the train swayed beneath him, he thought of him with admiration.

When Nicolas reached Athrom after several days, he slipped into a tavern, bought enough ale to look like a man about the serious business of drinking—enough, too, to bribe anyone who bothered him to go away—and sat down to listening.

It paid off quickly. Seeking out voices that were disloyal, drunk, or simply diverted, Nicolas soon found a soldier dallying with a mistress in his off hours. Nicolas tracked down the voice, slipped quietly into the house, and lifted the man's uniform. The soldier would not discover it was missing till morning. And even then, he might hesitate to sound an alarm.

Likewise, it didn't take Nicolas long to find two guards at the palace arguing so heatedly that they were hardly likely to hear or notice him slipping past. They didn't.

His body still ached from the commander's beatings, and he found that listening so intensely tired him. He slipped into a garden within the palace walls, found a hidden grotto, and laid down to rest. As he courted sleep, he closed off all but the closest of his hearing—just enough to alert him to anyone coming his way. Even so he could hear the trees and vines and flowers of the garden growing, and the whispering movements of fish and the heartbeats of frogs in the stream that ran through the garden.

Before his encounter with the King and the River-Daughter, Nicolas's hearing had been far less controlled. It came to him at opportune moments, sent him on quests, gave him the edge he needed to stay alive in a world unfriendly to Gypsies and wanderers. But he had never been able to listen with much purpose. That had changed. Recognizing that his Gift had been given to him for some higher reason and that he was part of a greater story than he knew, he had spent hours, days, learning to discipline his Gift.

So it was that he knew the latent power in the other Gifted, and how much they did not yet control it. How much they could control it if they would try. And if the King would touch them.

On that power he was pinning all his hopes.

In the morning, the imperial garden awakened him in glorious waves of colour. Purple and yellow flowers grew in profusion around hanging green trees, and man-made streams flowed throughout them, spanned by tiny bridges and stone walkways. The perfume of oranges and orchids was heady. He rose and staggered to the stream, soaking his head and shaking the water away.

This place was beautiful. Knowing the sins of the Empire that nested here, there was something terribly disturbing about its beauty.

Opening his ears to take in more of his surroundings, Nicolas climbed a stone wall and jumped into an arboured walkway adorned with climbing vines and flowers. He followed it until a gardener's path led off into a private quarter of the palace grounds. Workmen were labouring there. They paid little attention to Nicolas as he strode by with all the confidence of a soldier on patrol. He opened his ears yet more and strained for sounds of distress.

He found them before long. They led him into new lanes and corridors until he had left the beauties of the gardens far behind and found himself looking through a heavy iron gate into a prison yard. He scanned it quickly and almost smiled to himself at what he found. The gate was locked, so he ducked into a tangle of half-burned old wagons and piles of scrap metal to wait. It wasn't long before another guard approached the gate and unlocked it, a heavy whip in his hand. Nicolas slipped in behind him.

The guard strode to a cauldron in the center of the yard

and began to bellow for the prisoners to line up to receive their rations. Nicolas sought out his quarry quickly and strode toward her.

She was a slight, wiry woman. Her dark hair, usually cropped short, had grown long enough to be tied into a knot behind her head. Her clothes were worn, her eyes sharp. She saw Nicolas coming and ducked her head so as not to look him in the eye.

He grabbed her arm and said harshly, "Don't you look away from me, woman."

The other soldiers ignored him. But she did what he had hoped—she looked up in rebellion and met his eyes. Hers widened.

He lowered his voice so no one could overhear. "How strange would it be for me to take you aside?" he asked.

"Not that strange," she muttered back. "The High Police have their fun with prisoners."

He jerked her arm, though not as hard as he hoped it looked. "Good. Come aside then, prisoner."

She put up a decent show of resistance, and with Nicolas half-dragging her, they crossed the yard and ducked into a small hut that stank of birds and ashes. He closed the door behind them.

"Well?" she asked.

"I'm getting you out of here," he said.

"Not alone, I hope."

He smiled. Patricia Black was as doggedly loyal as he remembered. "No, not alone. I've come for the Ploughman and Maggie. I can't get anyone else out—not now, at any rate."

"Good enough," she said. "They matter more than the rest

of us anyway. But you know that."

"Do you know where they are?" Nicolas asked. He scanned the hut for something to prop against the door in case anyone came snooping. It was empty but for piles of ashes and old birds' nests in the crumbling corners of the stone roof. One small opening the size of a fist was all that let in any light.

"They won't bother us," Pat said. "I hid in here for three days once, hoping I could find a way out. But the gates stay locked, and there is no way over the walls. I rejoined the rest of the rabble when I got hungry enough."

"What is this place?" Nicolas asked.

"An oven," Pat answered. "Where they burn anything and anyone they're finished with. But to answer your question, yes, I know where they are. But you'll have a devil of a time getting them out. I've seen them once or twice. They're never released with the rest of us. The Ploughman is hardly conscious—drugged, I think. And if Maggie hasn't gone mad by now, she's got more mettle than even I've credited her for."

"Why?" Nicolas asked. "What are they doing to her?"

To his surprise, he caught a glint of tears in Pat's eyes. "Professor Huss is badly wounded," she said. "Maggie's keeping him alive by her singing. That rat Cratus refuses him medical attention. And she won't give up on Huss. So she sings, day and night, barely even sleeping. It's a miracle she has any strength or voice left at all."

"The emperor is no fool," Nicolas said. "He's keeping their powers under."

"The Ploughman I can understand," Pat said. "He's a warrior, with other warriors at his beck and call. But Maggie's songs?"

"Are powerful too," Nicolas said. "More than any of us know. That's why I've come. I need their help to free Pravik."

Pat started. "To free . . ."

"You were all betrayed," Nicolas said. "The High Police marched on Pravik—but they were not successful either. I watched from a distance. Somehow the Order of the Spider has taken control."

"And you are risking everything to help the city," Pat said. "Why?" Her voice calmed a little. "Be straight with me, Gypsy. I know you have never been all you seemed."

"My wife is there," Nicolas said. "And badly wounded from a failed attempt to free me from the High Police. I escaped on my own, later. But I did not reach the city in time to get her out. My children are there too."

Pat shook her head, incredulous. "And you honestly thought it would be easier to release Maggie and the Ploughman from Athrom than to spirit your family out of Pravik? Well, you've come at the right time. It's not the emperor who keeps us imprisoned—the emperor is mad. He couldn't imprison a mouse. It's Cratus, the general of the High Police. He's not declared himself; most still think the emperor rules. But Cratus is out of his depth. This place is as disordered as I'd guess it's ever been."

Nicolas processed the information quickly. "That's good," he said. "But Evelyn is a very real threat—and we shouldn't discount Cratus or this city. Morning Star will return here one day, perhaps soon. We cannot defeat either enemy until we stand united—we, the Gifted. The King placed us into this world to fulfill a great purpose. We have been fools not to unite ourselves earlier."

Pat nodded. The light filtering through the fist-shaped hole in the roof illuminated ash that drifted through the air. "You have my help, of course," she said. "But how do you plan to work this escape?"

Nicolas was silent a moment. "You say the Ploughman is being drugged?"

"I'm sure of it," Pat said.

"Then I'll stop the drugs from reaching him," Nicolas said. "Long enough to let him gain his strength back. He'll get us all out of here."

"What about me?" Pat asked.

Nicolas looked at her ragged appearance and shook his head. "You'll wait here," he said. "Until I can find you a decent uniform. How closely do the louts who run this prison yard pay attention? They let me walk in easily enough."

"I told you I hid in here for three days," Pat said. "They never knew I was gone. Like I said, there have been a few problems in the chain of command lately. They're preoccupied by rumours and fighting amongst themselves."

"Good," Nicolas said. "Wait here then. Next time there's any movement of prisoners and police in the yard, there'll be an extra soldier walking out."

Pat smiled grimly. "Don't keep me waiting long."

* * *

Two days later, the Ploughman awoke to a warmth in his veins he had not felt in a long time and a voice in his head whispering, *Wake up. We need you.*

He opened his eyes. The surroundings that had been

blurred and confusing were suddenly sharp: a cell. Shackles on his wrists and ankles. Iron bars. A long stone corridor stretching away, lit by a single torch some distance away. And guards, twenty feet down the corridor, grumbling and talking to each other.

Neither of their voices was the one he could hear in his head.

Another voice fell across his consciousness. He turned his head. Two others shared his cell. Jarin Huss lay on the floor. Leaning against the wall by his head was Maggie. Her eyes were bloodshot and dark-rimmed. She was shaking from lack of sleep. And in a whisper, she was singing.

Maggie, said the voice—strangely familiar—in his head. *Maggie, sing another song. Can you hear me? Sing a lullaby. Put the guards to sleep.*

The Ploughman saw confusion cross her features. Her song faltered.

Maggie, you can do this. Put the guards to sleep.

Maggie stopped singing. She looked up, her eyes suddenly more alert, and scanned the corridor. The voices of the guards grew a little louder. The smell of ale drifted over the stones. The Ploughman became aware of a terrible burn in his throat —thirst.

Close your eyes, the voice said. *I know you're exhausted, but try to reach for my strength. For the Ploughman's strength. You're not alone. Weave yourself with us. Sing. We don't want any witnesses when we get you out of here.*

Hope sprang up fiercely in the Ploughman as he realized this was no dream—no drugged illusion. He was awake, the voice was real, and that was real heat and real strength he could feel flowing through him. For a moment the air seemed to turn golden. He murmured, "You can do this, Maggie."

She looked at him, and her eyes widened with joy to see him looking lucidly back. Her mouth formed a word, and slowly she started to sing again. Simple notes. Soft, but loud enough to carry down the corridor. A haunting lullaby. Her voice was scratched, nearly torn to pieces, with no beauty in it. But she sang.

The guards' voices died down, then trailed away completely. At the end of the corridor, two shadows moved into view. They knelt by the guards and got to work tying them tightly, gagging and blindfolding them. Still the men slept on.

One of the shadows ran the length of the corridor and grabbed hold of the iron bars. He wore black and green, but the Ploughman knew him at once, by his familiar face and his fire-coloured eyes.

"Nicolas Fisher."

Nicolas held up a set of keys with a triumphant grin. In a moment he'd unlocked the door. He pulled it open, unlocked the Ploughman's shackles, and rushed to Maggie's side.

"Are you all right?" he asked.

She nodded, wordless. Nicolas looked down at Huss and opened his mouth as though he would tell her to leave him. But she met his eyes and shook her head.

He swallowed and looked down at the ground. Then he slipped his arms beneath Huss's shoulders and knees and lifted him. The old man was terrifyingly light.

The second shadow approached, breathless. Maggie almost fell into her arms. Pat propped Maggie up as the Ploughman stretched himself and looked to Nicolas. "Where to?" he asked.

"The stables," Nicolas answered. "We need to leave fast, and the High Police have plenty of horses."

With Nicolas and the Ploughman leading the way, they raced down the corridor, following Nicolas's unswerving steps. He led them past four more sets of guards—all sleeping. He stopped in a doorway where the sun was shining through and waited until he was sure the courtyard was clear, then ran across it to a low-roofed stable. A soldier was there, just stabling his horse. The Ploughman snatched a tool off the wall and struck the man's head so that he fell, dumbstruck or dead. Pat was already leading out the still-saddled horse. She helped Maggie up and mounted behind her.

The Ploughman took Huss from Nicolas and laid him across another horse before mounting. Finally, Nicolas, still dressed in the black and green of the High Police, swung himself to the back of a grey gelding.

"And what are we?" the Ploughman asked. "Prisoners being escorted out by two of the police?"

"If we're stopped, yes," Nicolas said, gathering his horse's reins. "But until then, we are escapees riding as fast as we can for the city harbour."

"The harbour?" the Ploughman asked. "We're not going overland?"

"It's too easy for them to catch us overland," Nicolas said. "Now let's go."

He urged his horse forward, and together they broke out of the stables, riding for the open gates as fast as they could. A few stragglers in the courtyard saw them and shouted something in question, but they did not stop, and no one stopped them. They had broken clear of the palace altogether before Pat's shout alerted Nicolas to mounted High Police only a dozen yards behind.

Nicolas slapped the reins. "Faster!" he shouted.

They charged down the streets toward the harbour. People, seeing only two sets of High Police riding down on them, cleared the way. Ships were waiting in the sunlight, their sails flashing white. The crowds around the docks were crushing, and fisher wives shrieked as the horses nearly ran them down. Nicolas pulled up sharply and dismounted, charging into the crowd. He knew the others were behind him. The High Police, he hoped, would be slowed by the confused crowds.

A small fishing boat sat at the end of the dock, its sail not yet tied away. Two men were aboard, unloading cargo. Nicolas leaped from the dock onto the ship and shoved the first man overboard. He hit the water with a tremendous splash just as the second man turned to yell in protest. Nicolas caught him in the jaw with an uppercut and sent him reeling. As the man fought for balance, Nicolas kicked the legs out from beneath him and watched him hit the water beside his companion.

Nicolas grabbed an oar and threw a second one to the Ploughman, who had just laid Huss down in the bottom of the boat. Maggie and Pat barely made it in before the men shoved off. "Row hard!" Nicolas said. "We've got to get out of the harbour so the wind can pick us up!"

Twenty feet from the dock, he looked back to see the High Police still struggling through the crowd. For some reason, the people were not moving out of their way as quickly as they had for the escapees.

Nicolas smiled. The wind was starting to blow in the sail. They were away.

* * *

In the palace of Athrom, Harutek thrust open the doors of the throne room and stalked forward, his golden armour—a gift from Cratus—gleaming. He pointed an angry finger at the general who stood bent over a council table beneath the room's glistening chandeliers.

"You have betrayed me!" Harutek declared.

Cratus glanced up at him. "You're one to speak," he said.

"You ordered your army to attack Pravik," Harutek said. "Rumour has reached Athrom—and me." He strode up to the table as though he would grab Cratus by the scruff of the neck, but Cratus withered his approach with a glare.

"So I did," he said. "The Seer had escaped my men and had almost certainly taken up residence there. It was you who told me how important it is to find all six of the Gifted. Was I to let her hole up there forever without any good reason? I sent my army in to take her, and a handful of soldiers to her stinking home village just in case."

"The safety of my people is a good reason," Harutek answered. "We had a bargain, Cratus."

"They were safe," Cratus barked. "Under my men, they would not have been harmed." He looked away, suddenly unable to meet Harutek's eyes.

"What is it?" Harutek asked. "Look at me, curse you!"

Cratus did not look up. Harutek looked wildly down at the dispatches laid across the table under Cratus's hand—they were muddy and torn. News, and unwelcome news from the expression on Cratus's face. The general cleared his throat. "The city has been overtaken by another."

Harutek searched for words to express his disbelief. "Another?"

"The Order of the Spider," Cratus said.

"You said the Order was falling," Harutek said. "To the woman Evelyn."

"Yes," Cratus said. "For the last twelve months it's been disappearing because their leader was killing off her subordinates. Stars know why. But now she's taken Pravik from my men."

"One woman?" Harutek asked.

"No," Cratus snapped. "One woman and all her devilish powers. The same powers I need the Gifted to combat. I see her intent—she means to wrest the Empire from me. I do not mean to let her take it."

"Little enough means you have to stop her. You need the Gifted. You didn't find Virginia in the city, did you?" Harutek asked. "Or in Angslie?"

"Yet," Cratus said. "Not yet. She may still be going to Angslie. We'll have her then."

Once more the doors burst open. Three men strode in, all prison guards. The first stood at attention and bowed.

"Speak," Cratus said.

"There's been a break in the prison, my lord," the man said.

"A what?" Cratus asked.

"Three prisoners have escaped."

Harutek knew the truth as Cratus did, even before the

guard got up the nerve to voice it fully. The Ploughman, Maggie, and Jarin Huss had escaped. Cratus's most valuable prisoners, his hope of overcoming Evelyn, and Harutek's bargain for the safety of his own people.

Cratus's face darkened with anger. He dismissed his men, and Harutek smiled coldly.

"It is justice," he said. "Retribution on you for daring to attack the city as you promised me you would not. Your last means of resisting the Order is gone."

"No," Cratus said. "Not my last means. Nor even my best."

He straightened and looked at Harutek, and the prince was taken aback by the look in the general's eyes. "What I need to defeat the woman is still in my hands. She is not the only one with access to power. I would have used the Gifted—I will still. But there is one way open to me even now. I will not fear to use it."

* * *

Beyond the harbour, Nicolas put his rudimentary sailing skills to work, and with Pat's help, tried to set a course for the northern coast of Galce. Maggie had discovered a few waterproof blankets in the little boat, and she wrapped Huss in them before falling asleep in total exhaustion. Pat watched her with evident concern.

"It will be all right," the Ploughman said. "Just get us back to land."

"The journey will go quickly," Nicolas said. "There is a good wind."

But the wind was not inclined to work in their favour.

They had just sailed out of sight of the coast when it died.

"Now what?" Pat asked.

Nicolas was frowning. "Something's wrong," he said.

"Yes," Pat agreed, "the wind is gone."

"Not that," Nicolas said. "It's something *in* the wind."

As if in answer to his words, the wind suddenly began to blow again, filling the sail and carrying them hard across the water—further out to sea.

"We're going the wrong way!" Pat shouted.

"I know that!" Nicolas replied, wrestling with the sail. "Help me!"

Clouds were gathering on the horizon. The Ploughman jumped up to help Nicolas and Pat, but the motion of the boat nearly threw him off his feet. He was a warrior and a farmer—not, by any stretch of the imagination, a sailor. And his head was still swimming from the effects of drugging. Maggie looked up from her crouch over Huss but only shook her head. Her eyes betrayed her worry as she took in the clouds on the horizon, but she could say nothing.

"Look out!" Pat shouted, and Nicolas ducked as the boom swung over his head, narrowly missing him. The wind was blowing harder, catching the sail and nearly knocking them over into the waves. "Get the sail down!" Nicolas shouted.

He reached for a rope, but even as he did a sickening crack met his ears. The mast was breaking. They were losing control.

And then, sweeping over and around them, they all heard —not a voice, but an impression of a voice. An impression that said, *Not that way.*

The storm ceased as suddenly as it had come. A brisk wind was still blowing, still taking them further out to sea.

"What was that?" Pat asked.

"I don't know," Nicolas answered.

It was Maggie who gathered her voice enough to offer an answer. "It was the wind," she said. "Llycharath."

Nicolas crouched in front of Maggie and looked into her eyes. "The wind is on our side," he said. "Isn't it?"

She smiled weakly and nodded before laying her head down again.

"We can't just let the wind take us," Pat said. "That's foolishness."

Nicolas looked at her wordlessly. She nodded—she understood. They had little other choice. And anyway, everything about this escape was foolish. She huffed and sat down in the prow of the ship, staring out across the water. Clouds continued to gather overhead, and a light rain fell. But no storm threatened them again—just the wind, blowing hard, taking them where it wanted them to go.

Maggie and the Ploughman slept. Pat drifted off shortly after, though not before ceremoniously dumping her High Police uniform in the sea. Nicolas followed suit, and as the others slept, he kept his eyes on the horizon.

He saw it first: an island shrouded in mist, waves crashing off dark rocks. He reached down and shook the Ploughman awake. The warrior scrambled up beside him. "What is it?" he asked.

Pat's voice came from behind them. "I know that coast," she said. "It's the Green Isle. We've blown west of Bryllan."

"But why?" Nicolas said. "What's in the Green Isle?"

"I think we're about to find out," the Ploughman said.

The rocks and waves were formidable, but a sudden wash

of presence came over them once more, and once again they all sensed rather than heard the words.

Be not afraid. I will guide you.

The wind shifted all at once, and they found themselves sailing around the island till they saw a span of calmer water and open shores beyond it. They exchanged glances. They had escaped, perhaps, by their own wits. But something else had taken them into its purposes now.

The boat crossed the calm water until it scraped sand thirty feet from shore. Nicolas jumped out, the water coming nearly to his waist, and the Ploughman handed Maggie down to him. He set her on her feet in the water, and she leaned on Nicolas as they headed for shore. The Ploughman carried Huss behind them, and Pat grabbed a few last supplies out of the bottom of the boat and then splashed in after the others.

It was evening. The island before them was green as an emerald in the calm waters, its sides sweeping up into gentle mountains shrouded with mist. The shore as they reached it was soft and smooth, golden sand stretching some way in both directions. They crossed the sand and found themselves looking up a green sweep of mountain, and below it, equally green fields. A dark, narrow gorge in the mountain appeared to be the only way through. The Ploughman laid Huss gently down on a patch of soft grass. He unwrapped some of the blankets from the old man. Huss's skin was deathly pale. "It looks bad," Nicolas commented.

Fingers lightly touched his arm. "Nicolas," Pat said, her voice unnaturally calm. "Look up at that ridge."

A small ridge lay to the east, lined with short, sprawling trees, their outlines dim in the encroaching dusk. It took

Nicolas a moment to see what Pat was talking about. When he saw it, he tensed and reached for his sword.

Three men stood amidst the trees, weapons in their hands.

For a moment they all stayed frozen, waiting. The Ploughman saw them too and reached for his own sword, a weapon he'd snatched from the sleeping guards in Athrom. But he did not draw it. No sense in provoking a fight.

One of the strangers broke the silence. He stepped forward, coming out of the shadows enough to reveal straw-coloured hair and a teenager's face. He pointed at Huss.

"Is he sick?" he asked.

12

Dark Advent

"THROW DOWN YOUR SWORDS," came an older voice from the ridge. "To show us that you mean no harm. We can help you."

"You ask us to throw down our weapons while you still hold yours?" the Ploughman asked.

The speaker stepped forward. He was a young, strong man, his face handsome and his hair dark red. "You are on our land," he said. "We are defending our home. If you show us that you need no defending against, then we will not harm you." His voice took on a note of urgency. "Your friend needs care quickly—and the girl too, if my eyes are not mistaken. We only ask you to trust us and prove your own good will."

Nicolas threw his sword down suddenly. "The wind led us here," Nicolas said to the Ploughman. "Directly here. I'll trust them."

The Ploughman nodded and dropped his sword. Pat drew a knife from her belt and did likewise. The three strangers sheathed their weapons immediately and ran down the ridge. The red-haired man reached them first. The other two were younger: the straw-haired boy who had first spoken and a freckled, wiry young man of about twenty. The freckled one began to help Maggie up with a reassuring smile. The red-haired man knelt beside Huss, turning his face away at the smell of infection.

"Archer, run ahead," he said. "Tell Miracle to meet us on the way. This man may not last another hour."

He held out a strong hand to the Ploughman. "My name is Michael O'Roarke. I am chieftain of a small clann in these hills. I'm afraid we are wary of strangers. But if you mean us no harm, you are welcome."

The Ploughman shook Michael's hand, and Nicolas stepped in to do the same. He liked Michael—his manner was honest and forthright.

"Have you skill in healing?" the Ploughman asked.

Michael almost smiled. "You might say that," he said. "But come. We must not linger. Archer, be off! Jack and I will lead them."

The teenage boy took off running over the ridge, and Michael began to lift Huss in his arms. He paused and looked first at the Ploughman, then at Nicolas. "If I may," he said. "You are wearier than I, I think."

The Ploughman nodded, and for the first time since their landing, suspicion drained from his face. In its place was gratitude. "I thank you," he said.

Without another word, Michael lifted Huss and started off after Archer, who had already disappeared from sight. Nicolas smiled encouragingly at Pat and Maggie, who was leaning on the freckled young man called Jack. Jack smiled as well. "It is not terribly far," he said. "Are you ill, ma'am?"

"Exhausted," Pat answered for Maggie. "Just exhausted."

Jack nodded, his face showing genuine concern. As the Ploughman had done, Pat found herself relaxing. Nicolas had been right. The wind had brought them here.

These people were friends.

The sky was dusky rose when they caught sight of another little band rushing to meet them across the grassy slopes. Archer was leading the way. As they approached, Nicolas caught his breath.

Archer had a young woman by the hand, and she was without question the most beautiful creature Nicolas had ever seen.

White-gold hair falling over her shoulders, she knelt in the grass as Michael laid Huss down and drew aside the blankets that covered him. She gasped at the sight of the wound and the infection puffing and streaking around it.

"Can you hear me, grandfather?" she whispered. Her voice was accented, but not with the lilting accent of the Green Isle. This woman spoke like a Northerner. Michael leaned over Huss so his forehead nearly touched hers, and the Ploughman swallowed hard at the sight of their oneness and obvious love.

Huss did not respond to the young woman's voice. She laid her slender fingers on his neck and felt his pulse and the heat in his skin. And then, with a hand on each side of his neck, she bowed her head and waited.

Pat started to say something, but Nicolas held out his hand and silenced her. Maggie too was watching intently—she seemed more alert now than she had since they had taken ship.

Nicolas grasped the truth before anyone else did. He looked at the young woman still kneeling with her hands pressed against Huss's face, and he saw with the others the changes being wrought in the old man. His cheeks were filling out, his skin gaining colour. And in the exposed part of Huss's torso, the angry streaks of infection were disappearing as the wound closed.

At last the woman looked up. Her violet eyes smiled. She was breathtaking.

"You are Gifted," Nicolas said.

She smiled as she stood and looked back down at Huss, who was beginning to stir. She held out her hand to Maggie.

Maggie hesitated only a moment before she took the Healer's hand. She breathed in sharply, and Nicolas watched as her eyes focused, her skin gained colour, her whole bearing changed.

The Healer let go of Maggie's hand. She smiled at them all. "I am called Miracle," she said. "I am Gifted, yes. And you are welcome here."

"Maggie?" said Jarin Huss as he sat up slowly. "Maggie, where are we? Who—" He caught sight of Miracle, and his eyes widened. "Oh my," he said.

* * *

Harutek took the torch Cratus handed him as he mounted his horse. His six men waited on horseback behind him. Cratus swung onto the back of his own black stallion and sneered back at the Darkworlders. "Come," he said.

Without fanfare, Cratus led them down the main thoroughfare of Athrom. Not far away, the walls of the great coliseum were dark: cold, abandoned stone looming over the city.

So it was to Harutek's surprise that Cratus took them there. The road before the coliseum gates was still wrecked, torn up by the emergence of Pravik's warriors—and the Darkworld's, led by Caasi—from underground. The earth and stones still showed stains of red blood and streaks of gold where the Ploughman's Golden Warriors had fought. The sight pricked at Harutek's conscience. He had fought on a very different side then.

Beyond the torn ground, the gates were shut. But as they picked their way over the ruins toward the doors, the slow creak of hinges met Harutek's ears. The sound made his skin crawl. A smell met him from within the coliseum—death, disease, starvation. This place had nearly been the sight of a holocaust. Now it was a silent, unnerving memorial of Lucien Morel's last act of madness as a sane man.

Within, Harutek expected to find nothing but an empty stadium floor, with its walls and rows of seating stretching up endlessly all around them.

That was not what opened to his eyes as he entered.

The walls and rows of seats were indeed empty. No spectators had come here since the games before the persecution of the Gypsies. They were shadowed and silent.

But the floor of the coliseum was not empty.

Instead, torches burned in concentric circles, light beckoning them toward something in the center. Harutek approached slowly and relinquished his torch as a robed servant came to take it from him. There were others here as well—silent figures in dark robes, some, like the servant, hovering around the edges of the circle, and others waiting at the center.

"Come," Cratus said again.

This time he led them into the spiraling lights. Harutek followed him, his Darkworld soldiers wide-eyed but silent behind him.

The lights made everything outside the circle disappear into darkness. The robed figures who darted in and out seemed unearthly, creatures of shadow, even though Harutek knew they were simply servants and soldiers. But when Harutek was halfway to the center, they began to chant, and the eerie sound made his skin crawl.

They stepped out of the ring of torches and into the center. A man lay there upon a black bier.

A dead man.

Harutek stepped forward, eyes wide in horror and disgust. The man appeared to have been perfectly preserved. How long he had been dead was anyone's guess. Likewise, his age was unidentifiable. His hair was close-shaven. The face was pale, with dark circles under the eyes, his cheeks sunken and shriveled. He looked as though he had undergone some horror at the end—and yet, underneath that, he had once been handsome.

He wore the black robes of the Order of the Spider.

"This is your power?" Harutek asked, his voice deliberately loud to shake off the atmosphere of the place. "A dead man?"

He heard hisses and murmurs from the cloaked figures who were gathering now among the torches, just out of sight.

"He has been dead two years," Cratus said.

"He is well preserved," Harutek said.

"We have not preserved him," Cratus said.

The words took a moment to sink in. Harutek faced him

with a frown. "What are you telling me?"

"Some other power keeps him," Cratus said. "In life he was called the Nameless One. So completely had he surrendered himself to the Blackness that he had lost his name. Somehow he was killed here in this very coliseum. No one knows how. His appearance is strange, as though he had fallen ill—he was a strong man in life. But since his death he has not even begun to decay. The Blackness keeps him."

Harutek let his eyes flicker from the dead man to the torches and the robed servants. "As do you," he said. "Why this memorial?"

"We thought we might have need of him," Cratus said.

"What use is a corpse?" Harutek kept his voice deliberately steady.

"There are ways to raise the dead," Cratus said. "And to restore them to their former power."

Harutek just stared at him. Then, slowly, he turned to go. "I have seen enough," he said.

"No, my friend," Cratus answered. "You have not seen anything. You wanted to know how I could defeat the witch. Now I tell you. With her own power. With the Blackness."

Harutek turned back, his breath coming faster now with what he recognized as fear. "You cannot use the Blackness!" he said. "You are a soldier, not a sorcerer. This is the time of men, Cratus, not of the powers beyond us. That is what I have been fighting for—freedom from all this—this superstition!"

The chants of the waiting men grew louder. They were closing in. Harutek's soldiers clustered behind him. Their eyes were as wide as their prince's.

"Superstition? You know better than that," Cratus said.

"Do you think the Order existed all these years without teaching us anything? The High Police have always existed in their shadow, called upon to do their bidding time and again. The Nameless One himself led a contingent of my own men into the north to capture a Gifted woman there. Do you think we learned nothing from them? We have secret societies of our own. Knowledge of our own. Knowledge and power far greater than what men alone can possess. You would be a fool to reject it."

Harutek shook his head. Anger and terror were welling in him, but part of him knew it would be foolish to run.

And another part of him did not want to.

All his life the priests had taught him of powers and creatures that shaped the destiny of men. He had believed them, doubted them, hated them, fought them.

Now he found that he wanted to see for himself the power they had painted as the enemy.

He folded his arms and stepped back as the chants took on a new pitch and the robed servants began to form shapes around the bier where the dead man lay. With a word, Harutek directed his men to sheath their swords. Then he met Cratus's eyes and said, "We shall see."

Four candles stood at each corner of the bier. Cratus held up his own torch and uttered several words in a tongue Harutek did not know. The flame turned from natural orange to blue, and Cratus lit each of the candles. He held up his arms, and two of his servants brought a black robe and dressed him in it.

The dark sky above him was beginning to whirl, slowly, the air itself visibly moving like troubled water. Harutek's eyes were drawn up. He watched the strange sky instead of Cratus as the rite continued, as someone cried out, as blood was spilled.

His eyes widened. Two great clawed hands were moving the clouds aside like pieces of a veil, and a face stared down at him.

He heard the words deep inside.

I have come!

The blue light of the candles flared into a great flame that engulfed the bier and the men standing nearest it. Cratus cast himself backward just in time, but the heat burned the skin of his face and hands. He shouted. The robed men were shouting and falling away. This was not what they had expected.

The flame burst skyward in a pillar that looked as if it would split the world in two.

And then it fell, and there was only a burning bier and a few blackened bodies on the ground—and standing before it, the man who had been called the Nameless One.

He was alive, his flesh was filled out and strong again, and his eyes were black—deep black, and gleaming with a look that was not human and never had been.

Harutek knelt, as did his men, as did Cratus, strangled with fear. Harutek recognized the expression on the risen man's face.

He had just seen it looking down from the sky.

The creature who stood before them in the guise of a man laughed. He bent down and took Cratus by the hood of his cloak, drawing him up until the general's terrified eyes met his.

"Greet me," he said.

"Greetings, Nameless One," Cratus stammered.

The creature threw him down. "That is no longer my name," he said. He stretched his long fingers, flexed the arms beneath his black robes. "This was the Nameless One. But I am something different."

Harutek screwed his eyes shut. The words fell on his ears despite his denial. He heard the creature proclaim itself.

Morning Star had returned.

13

The Calling of the Clann

THAT NIGHT, THE NEWCOMERS TO THE GREEN ISLE were welcomed
into the home of the Clann O'Roarke. They gathered around a
bonfire outside a big thatched cottage. In the shadows beyond
the fire, sheep bleated from fenced pens, and rose vines
climbed low-roofed stone barns, their flowers perfuming the
air. Several children laughed and chased each other in the
darkness. The young men and women of the clann sat around
the fire with their guests.

There were several young women, and both Nicolas and
the Ploughman were more than usually focused on the flames.
Thinking of Marja and Libuse, Maggie knew. Her heart went
out to them. Miracle was Michael's wife—Northern, judging
from her accent and striking appearance. The others were his
sister and cousins. Shannon, the sister, was remarkably like
Michael and close to him in age. The other girls were younger
—Lilac, Cali, and Jenna—except for one old woman they all
called Grandmother. Jack, Archer, and a dark-haired fellow
named Stocky finished the male portion of the tiny clann.

Lilac, with dark hair and quick blue eyes, settled by the

fire next to Maggie and wasted little time getting to the point. "Why have you come here?" she asked.

Shannon shot her a disapproving look, but Maggie answered. "I'm not sure," she said. "The wind blew us here from Pravik, where we were prisoners."

"Prisoners of the emperor?" Cali asked, gasping.

"The emperor is no more," the Ploughman said. "He has gone mad and been replaced by his general, Merlyn Cratus. But Cratus wishes no one to know of it quite yet."

"Can it really be true?" Cali asked.

"That one madman has been replaced by another?" Lilac asked. "Of course it can—especially in these dark days. But why were you prisoners there?"

The Ploughman sighed. "It is a long story," he said.

"With one quick answer," Nicolas said. He stood. Maggie knew the tone in his voice: he was getting ready to make a stir. "They were kept prisoner because they are Gifted," he said, "and Cratus wishes to capture the Gifted and turn their power for his own use."

His words had the intended effect. Whispers and looks of concern darted around the circle. Miracle, whose hands Michael held, did not react.

"Nor is he the only one," Nicolas continued. "The Order of the Spider—"

"We know about them," Michael said. He stood. His wife looked up at him questioningly. "It is perhaps best that we do not discuss this," the young chieftain said.

Miracle shook her head, but the look on Michael's face clearly told her to say nothing. She obeyed.

"You ought to hear me out," Nicolas said.

Michael interrupted. "We will hear about the Order when it has to do with us. Then only."

"But this *does* have to do with you," Nicolas said. "At least, it has to do with your wife. And myself, and Maggie, and the Ploughman, and any other Gifted who might exist in this world."

Huss cleared his throat. He was sitting close to the fire, warming his old hands. "The world may be full of the Gifted, but of those you seek, Nicolas, there are only six. You four, Virginia, and one more who is yet unknown to us."

"How do you know that?" Michael asked.

"It is an ancient prophecy," Huss said. "The Darkworld remembers it."

He let his words sink in and then answered the question the clannsmen did not ask. "A race of men who have dwelt beneath the earth for centuries," he said. His eyes were troubled. "One of their princes, Harutek, betrayed us into Cratus's hand—but many of them are believers in the King. The head of their priesthood told me of the Six. And Prince Harutek told Cratus. It is how he convinced him that Maggie and the Ploughman ought to be preserved alive."

"He told me he did it for our sake," Maggie said. "To save our lives."

Huss sighed. "Maybe he did. Or maybe he is simply going the way of his ancestors: betraying what is right for the sake of what seems momentarily advantageous. But Harutek's treachery does not change the prophecy."

His eyes flickered up from the fire and looked at each of the Gifted in turn. "Six there shall be," he recited. "Six to see the seventh free. Six to know the coming day; Six to wake the fire. Warrior, Singer, Seer; Healer, Listener, Voice."

"Who is the seventh?" Nicolas asked.

"The seventh," Huss said, aware that all who gathered around the fire had grown silent, "is the King."

Michael cleared his throat. "Clannsmen, leave us," he said.

"But Michael—" Stocky and Lilac began in unison. Their voices blended as well as their dark hair and blue eyes— brother and sister, Maggie guessed.

"Go, please," Michael said. His expression was more beseeching than commanding. One by one, his family stood. Lilac held out her hand to Moll and Seamus, the smallest of the O'Roarkes, who had come tumbling in from playing in the shadows. "Come," she said. "Uncle Michael will have something to tell us all soon, I think."

She shot her cousin a pointed glance and led the children away. The others followed, one by one, until only Miracle still sat by the fire with Michael and their guests.

Michael looked Huss in the eye with a boldness that made them all nervous. "Now," he said. "Speak of the King."

Huss smiled. "There is another prophecy, one more commonly abroad. Perhaps you also have heard it. 'Take these Gifts of my outstretched hand; weave them together; I shall come.' The prophecy speaks of all the Gifted, yes, but more specifically of the Six. They are here to be woven as one. And when they are, the King will come. That is what the prophecies, the stories, all taken together—that is what they point to. And that is why the wind brought us here. The Gifted are being united."

Michael still held Miracle's hands, and with his thumbs he stroked them. He ducked his head as he spoke. "Professor, this battle is not new to us. My father, Thomas O'Roarke, was Gifted. Perhaps the first of the Gifted. The Order took note of him when he was still a young man and we were a much greater clann. They came here to sway him to their own ways and convince him to join them. He refused."

The flickering fire deepened the shadows in Michael's face, and Maggie saw that he had stopped stroking Miracle's hands and was just clinging to them now. "For some time they continued to try. At last they accepted their final refusal from him, came here, and killed him and my mother. They destroyed our lands and wiped out the entire older generation of the clann—all but Grandmother, who was with us children, hidden away in caves."

Nicolas opened his mouth to speak, but at a warning glance from Huss he stayed silent.

"Years later, our children began to show signs of being Gifted. *All* of them—but most especially Archer, and a lad we have lost." He stopped for a moment, swallowing hard. "The Order began to appear in the Green Isle again. I went north to Fjordland, seeking a safe place for us. I found Miracle."

He released her hands, and she placed one on his shoulder. They met each other's eyes. He continued. "The Order was there in the Northlands as well. One called the Nameless One —"

"But he is dead," Nicolas interrupted. "All the Order is dead but one. Evelyn—"

"I know he is dead," Miracle said, stopping Nicolas short. Her Northern accent sounded especially foreign after Michael's island lilt. "I killed him."

Nicolas was momentarily speechless. "You did?" he asked.

"In Athrom, on the edge of the coliseum as he tried to destroy the Gypsies," Miracle said. "His desire was to tear the Veil between this world and the Blackness. My Gift was not meant to kill, but I had little choice."

Nicolas's mind raced. A memory pulled at him: the sight of the Nameless One wreathed in blue flame, with a woman in his grip—Miracle? The memory shook him. He had thought his own arrival in Athrom with the River-Daughter the final blow that had won the battle in Athrom.

"Well," Huss said. "It seems you have been woven together before, and more than any of you knew."

"But the fight nearly destroyed us," Michael said, his tone growing more intense. "And it nearly destroyed Miracle—not once, but twice. She has fallen into the hands of the Order before; of the Blackness itself. This is no small thing you ask, that she should enter this battle again."

"Michael . . ." Miracle said, but he ignored her.

"Our fathers are dead, and so I am the father here," Michael said. "Of everyone you saw seated by this fire. I am Miracle's husband and a man who has already faced her loss. How can you ask me to give her up and endanger my family again? I have given myself to *protect* them." His eyes bored into Nicolas.

"My wife is in Pravik," Nicolas said, his voice matching Michael's in intensity. "And Pravik has been overtaken by the power of the Order. Do you hear me? My wife is there. Possibly dying of wounds earned while she tried to rescue me from the High Police. And my children—a boy, not two years old, and a newborn girl. I must go back for them. But I will not be strong enough on my own. Together, the Gifted can defeat

Evelyn. We can be woven together as the prophecy says. If we are, power great enough to save us all will be unleashed. As it was, to a lesser degree, in Athrom. To protect the Gifted now is to doom us all. We must go to battle."

"We have had peace since Athrom," Michael said. "That peace is precious to us. It means our lives."

"And this means mine," Nicolas said. "And the Ploughman —his betrothed is in Pravik. And his people—hundreds of them. And perhaps all the world, for the Veil is still at risk of tearing. There is more at stake here than one family."

"Yes," Huss said, his voice rumbling, an interruption that stopped the rising intensity of Michael and Nicolas. "There is a world at stake," he said. "I have told you what the prophecies say."

He fixed his eyes on Miracle. "This choice must be yours, my dear," he said. "You are one of the Six—you are the Healer. And that means you are tied to the King, and you must answer the call to bring him back into the world. Will you turn your back on that calling?"

Miracle's face was full of emotion, but it was unreadable. Tears glistened in her eyes. She turned and looked at Michael. "I will follow my husband's lead," she said.

Michael shook his head. "Pravik is half a continent away from here," he said. "This time it is not our battle."

The sound of twigs popping in the fire filled the otherwise silent darkness. "Remember the mountain, Michael," Miracle said softly. "Remember what else you sought in the Northlands."

She loosed his hand, stood, and smiled down at the newcomers. "I will follow my husband's lead," she repeated. "If he says that I will stay, I will stay. If he says that we will go with you, then that is what we will do. The King will lead him right. I am sure of that."

She left. A moment later Michael stood, nodded a wordless farewell, and stalked away into the darkness toward the hills.

Maggie cleared her throat. Nicolas was still standing, his face stricken.

"It will be all right," she said.

"We need them," Nicolas said.

"We haven't lost them," Huss said. "Maggie is right. Give them time to come around."

"We should talk to the Healer alone," Nicolas said. "While the chieftain is gone. We only need her."

"No, my friend," the Ploughman rumbled. He had remained silent through all that had been said, but it struck Maggie how much he too needed Miracle to agree to come with them. It was his city, his life's work, and his betrothed in danger in Pravik. But his voice did not show the fear he had to feel. He looked up at Nicolas. "You know the bonds between man and wife," he said. "Do not come between them. The chieftain is a good man. Give him time to think it through, and he will choose to help us. But don't ask him to forget who he is. Too many people depend on him."

The Ploughman stood and laid his hand on Nicolas's shoulder. "Don't fear," he said. "We'll go back for them, no matter what happens."

"We won't be enough," Nicolas said.

The Ploughman smiled. "We have never been enough," he said. "But that has never stopped either of us before."

* * *

Michael O'Roarke tramped through the grass and mossy stones in the darkness, heading away from the settlement to the slopes he had known since childhood. Voices followed him; Shannon had returned to the fire and engaged the newcomers in hospitable conversation. Soon strains of music began to play, Jack and Cali with their fiddle and pipes. Platters of lamb and leeks were carried from the house, their scents drifting on the air with the smoke from the fire. Guilt stirred in him for a moment. It was hardly the behaviour of a chieftain, this running from his guests.

But he needed to think.

Michael knew the way well, yet he chose his footsteps carefully. The hills had been friendlier in old days, when his father still lived and he was a boy running through the grass and following the sheep. Now they were crisscrossed by the clann's own handiwork: defenses they had spent more than a year erecting against the attack they had always known would come.

Skirting carefully constructed brush piles like haystacks in the darkness, Michael climbed higher. Moonlight fell more clearly as he drew nearer the top of the gorge, nearer the heavens themselves. The gorge was a dark slash across the landscape, shadowed and dangerous. Nearby, invisible in the night, a mountain river splashed through a shallow, rocky bed down the slopes.

At last, at the highest point of the slope, Michael reached the cascade that was the source of the river, flowing down a last peak from underground. He crossed the river on mossy stepping stones. A small tower was silhouetted in the darkness, one of their more clever constructions, housing machinery he prayed they would never need to use. He leaned against it and let himself sink to the ground, listening to the flow of the water, facing the moonlit sky.

He couldn't hear the voices from below anymore. It was good to be here without the clann, without his sister or his cousins or anyone who was so dependent on him. But he wished he wasn't alone. He wished for the presence of Miracle, or of his old friend Kris of the Mountains, or of Gwyrion, Lord of the Wild Things, who had been their companion for a time. Far away in the Northlands, hidden in a cave, Gwyrion had once spoken to him of the King. Traces of the conversation came to his memory now.

My father saw a great fire in these mountains, Michael had told him. *A light that swept over the whole earth and did not destroy, but purified all that it touched.*

Gwyrion's voice had rumbled in reply. *Your father met with the King.*

It was true. Thomas O'Roarke had never referred to the great Spirit-Lord whose light he had seen on the mountains as "the King," but Michael knew that his father's vision had shown him the same being the Gypsies told stories of, the same being who was remembered in old wives' tales in the islands, the same being Miracle worshiped.

She had not always been open about that. But after their marriage, she had told Michael more and more of what she believed. She had told him that she knew the power that flowed through her was not hers, but belonged to one Northerners called the Great Light. Her grandfather, who raised her, had taught her to revere the Light. And then, when she was thirteen, the Light had come to her in the form of a man and told her that he was the source and the heart of mankind, the great enemy of death, and the healing of the Seventh World.

The Great Light had also shown her that for his sake, she would have to suffer. And she had accepted that.

Michael's jaw clenched as his eyes roved the stars. She had suffered. Her suffering had made her even more beautiful in his eyes, and he had done everything he could to protect her from suffering again. He *would* do everything he could. But now—

We are at war, Gwyrion had said.

The whole world is troubled. Meet evil head on, fight on the right side, and you will overcome it. Your father saw the truth. The Burning Light will come and purify the world again. It has already begun.

"I want to see it too," Michael said aloud. His voice startled him. He let it sink back down, let the words sink into him even as he hoped they carried into the starlit sky. He stood slowly, leaning against the defense tower as he kept his eyes trained on the sky.

"My father saw the Burning Light in the Northern mountains," Michael said. "Like Miracle did. But if you are truly the heart of the world, then surely you are not confined. And if you are truly calling me to war, then I want to see you as they have. I do not have the courage on my own."

Was he surprised as the stars began to move, as they began to shape themselves into a form like a man? He didn't know. But he did know that suddenly the hilltop seemed aflame with white light, and he was looking into eyes that burned with a holy fire, in the face of a man unlike any he had ever seen. He knelt.

"I only want to protect her," he said.

"I know," the man answered. "And you will, Michael O'Roarke. But you must protect her, and the rest of my Gifted, by giving them time. The attack is coming to you, as you knew it would. And you must hold it back."

Michael bowed his head. Tears were pricking at his eyes, but they seemed to him to be tears of light, tears like diamonds. "This will be the end for us," he said.

"Yes," the King said. "As much as anything in this world is an end. But you must believe what I tell you: all ends here are only beginnings. This war has been one of defense too long. Make one last stand here, and I will take the war on the offense forever. Look at me, Chieftain of the Clann O'Roarke."

Michael raised his head and looked.

* * *

Shivering in a cold night wind in a mossy cleft of rock near the Galcic coast, Virginia snapped suddenly awake. Rehtse's hand touched her shoulder.

"Are you all right?" she asked.

She shook her head, desperately trying to clear away the cobwebs of sleep. The lingering pain of Evelyn's attack was still with her, making it harder to focus. What had she seen? What had—

She gasped as she remembered. Her heart was racing as though it would race itself to a finish line and die on the spot, her breath coming faster than she wanted it to. She had seen the return of Morning Star.

And suddenly she felt a pull, drawing her to her feet, drawing her eyes through the trees and the rocky ground in the direction of the coast. For a moment all she could see was shadows behind shadows. Then a brilliant light flashed out of the darkness and flooded the forest with light, flooded Galce, flooded the world. Virginia fell to her knees.

She did not know how much time passed. Only that Rehtse's voice was urgently calling her name. She heard Kieran chime in with an expression of concern. She turned to look at her companions, but her vision had gone black once more.

"Did you see the light?" she asked.

"No," Rehtse answered. "It is still night."

Virginia nodded and curled up against the rock once more. If Rehtse and Kieran had not seen it, then it had been a vision.

And that meant it had been real.

"Hold on," she heard herself whispering, to Pravik and to Maggie and the Ploughman and to everyone in this world who did not know they needed the King. "Help is coming."

Part 2: Advent

14

One Step Ahead of You

ROLAND DREAMED THAT NIGHT. He and Stray were sleeping inside the cave because it looked like rain. Shale crunched under him as he shifted in his sleep. It was uncomfortable, but shelter was shelter—and this cave, with its hard-packed earthen floor and dry walls, had sheltered them well in the months since they'd taken to it.

In his dream, the world had been swallowed by darkness. Every shred of light was gone, and if the sun rose, no one saw it. He wandered in the black world and groaned for light.

A glimmer. Roland thought he was waking up to the sun shining on his face. But no, it wasn't—he was still dreaming, and the world was in darkness. In his dream, he looked up.

Stray was sitting against the opposite wall of the cave. His knees were drawn up to his chest. His blue-green eyes smiled on Roland. They were uncanny eyes, full of light.

Roland pushed himself up and brushed dirt from his clothes. He tried not to look at the boy—he was making him nervous again—but there was no avoiding that gaze. For months the boys had lived together in the cave, fished in the rivers, hunted small animals in the trees. They had climbed old oaks and willows, chased each other, laughed together. Stray told stories and jabbered nonsense. He had not been especially good at anything else. Roland had taught him patiently, teasing him, sometimes frustrated with him. And he had loved him.

And now Stray's eyes were summoning Roland, and their power was unmistakable.

"The sun will rise," Stray said.

Roland heard himself sighing in his dream. He turned his eyes to the cave entrance. A tangle of branches and roots usually cast a greenish light on the inside of the cave, but now, the entrance was nothing more than a black hole in already black surroundings.

"The sun isn't going to rise," Roland said. "Something's awfully wrong out . . ."

His voice trailed off. Soft light was dancing on the cave walls.

Stray had a candle cupped in his hands. The light flickered and bounced, and the boy watched it with delight in every curve of his young face.

"Where did you get that?" Roland asked, aware even in his dream that there were no candles in the cave.

The boy did not answer. He was standing, carefully so as not to jar the candle. He walked to the mouth of the cave and looked back at Roland. His eyes were all the colour of the forests and the seas, his smile a spring morning full of secrets. "Are you coming?" he asked.

Foliage rustled as Stray passed outside the cave. Roland scrambled to his feet and pushed his way through.

The boy was standing in an open place in the darkness

where long grass grew, and the candlelight silvered the bark of slender trees behind him. None of it would have been visible but for the gentle light in the boy's hands. Roland remained crouched at the cave mouth. He could not move. He could not tear his eyes from the boy he had sheltered.

Stray laughed suddenly and threw the light into the air. It remained there, hovering above the boy's open hands—the flame alone. The candle was gone. The light began to grow. The edges of the flame were white, its center golden.

"No more darkness," Stray said.

There was a sound like voices singing, and the light above the boy's hands rose and broke into glittering pieces: they rose higher and higher until suddenly the stars were shining through the darkness and sending silver healing rays down to the earth. The moon appeared and bathed the valley in cool white light. Out of the shadow the silhouettes of mountains took form, tree branches waved gently in a sudden breeze, moonlight sparkled on the river.

Roland took it all in, mouth agape. Moonlight and starlight touched him softly as a mother's kiss. He tore his eyes from the sky and looked at Stray. He was smiling—yes, it was the boy's smile, his eyes, his beautiful face, but the tiny form in rags was no more. A young man stood in the valley with his hands held upward and his face bathed with light.

And the sun began to rise.

Roland woke. Sunlight was warming his face, morning light streaming through the cave mouth. And little-boy Stray was sitting in its rays, watching him with a knowing look in his eyes.

"We have to go to the House of Angslie now," Stray said

when Roland sat up, trying to shake off the effects of the dream and finding that he could not. The blue-green eyes looked into his expectantly.

"All right," Roland said. He wasn't sure why he wasn't protesting. He shook his head a little to clear it. How did Stray even know about the House of Angslie? Why would he want to go there?

What exactly *was* this child?

Roland stood slowly, waiting for something extraordinary to happen. Nothing did. The boy pushed himself up with the usual aplomb of small boys and waited with a tiny smile on his face. Roland exited the cave first, into the morning sun, and blinked. Dew lay on the valley; the sun sparkled off the river on the other side.

Roland pointed. "The laird's house is that way. Across the river."

They ambled over the dew-drenched grass of the valley, silent and companionable. Roland could still see the light bursting forth in his dream, making the sunlight seem magical. *It was only a dream,* he told himself. He was not sure he believed it. They reached the edge of the water, which was deep here, and Roland turned west.

"We can ford downriver," he said. "We'll go by the shallows, since you still can't swim to save your . . ."

Stray didn't answer. Roland turned to look for him.

The boy was standing on the surface of the water, five feet out, one hand held out to Roland. He laughed.

Roland blinked, wondered if he was still dreaming, and stepped out on the surface of the water. It held him. Stray smiled again, and this time there was something serious and approving in his face.

* * *

When Roland and Stray reached the great House of Angslie, Roland felt as though something was haunting his steps. He had not been here since the day he'd run from the village to warn the laird that High Police were coming to take Virginia Ramsey away. What had happened after that was anyone's guess—no one had seen the laird, or Virginia, again. The High Police were found dead on the hillside. For some months more soldiers had come and oppressed the villagers until at last they too stopped hunting for answers and withdrew.

Now the house was a broken mirror of its former self. Windows had been smashed out, gardens and fields destroyed, the house's stores wasted by the soldiers. Weeds were growing through the smashed window panes and running riot over once well-managed lawns. Small animals scattered as the boys approached, but no sign of human life appeared.

Roland felt anger rising in him at the sight of the desecrated ground. Lord Robert Sinclair, Laird of Angslie, had not been a perfect symbol, but his family and his home had symbolized this part of the Highlands. The soldiers had no right to do what they had done.

Just as they'd had no right to take Virginia Ramsey, Roland's hope in the loneliest hours of the night, away.

He had not known her well, but he had never forgotten the day she and her grandfather came into the tavern, and her grandfather haggled with the MacTavish over flour while

Virginia stood in a corner and waited. Roland had approached her, shy and curious and a little fearful of the girl so many of the villagers treated with veiled enmity because she could see into their souls.

She had smiled at his approach and held out her hand so he could touch her and know that she was a friend. And she had said, "Do you want to know what I see in you, Roland MacTavish?"

He said yes.

"I see in you a golden lion," she said. "And a great man." And in a very low voice she had told him, "Someday everything in this world will change, and you will be at the center of things then. Roaring and strong for righteousness."

Every night until Virginia disappeared, Roland had laid awake in his loft bedroom over the tavern, listening to the drunks and the howls of his father in his inebriated idiocy, and he had told himself, *Someday everything in the world will change, and I will be a lion at the center of it.*

The High Police had had no right to take her away, for with her, they had taken away Roland's hope for a future.

"Come," Stray said, tugging at Roland's sleeve. He pointed at a window on the second floor of the rambling house. "It's up there. It's for you."

"What is?" Roland asked.

"You'll see," the boy answered.

"How do you know what's up there? You didn't even know the way here by yourself!"

The boy looked at Roland reproachfully, and he shut his mouth and climbed after the child. They picked their way through the wreck of weeds and walkways in disrepair, and the boy pushed open a door that was already unlatched and hanging slightly open.

The house smelled like dust, mold, and peeling plaster.

Roland coughed in the dust stirred up by the door. Stray walked slowly past him, looking all around with wide eyes. The doors opened into a hall with sweeping staircases and paintings that were a hundred years or more old. As old as this house and the family that had always lived here. The floor was a mess of plaster chips and straw; some animal had been nesting here—or a whole colony of them. Roland could hear mice in the walls.

A memory of the cantankerous old housekeeper returned to him, and he almost laughed at the thought of her seeing this place now. It hadn't been empty more than two years, but it looked like the soul of desolation.

It's lonely, that's why, Roland thought. *This place isn't supposed to be empty, so it's falling apart in protest.*

"It's all right," he said out loud. "We're here now."

Stray's hand tugged at his again. "Come on. Upstairs, remember?"

Roland hesitated another moment and then kicked bits of plaster out of his way as he moved across the floor, up the stairs where everything was brown and sepia, bathed in dusty light from the windows. The hills outside were brown too, beneath patches of green grass and purple thistles. He cast a glance out the dirt-covered window panes, then turned his eyes upstairs.

Halfway up the stairs, his life changed again.

"Roland!" boomed a voice.

Stray was looking knowingly at him when he heard the voice from somewhere in the cobwebs. The voice echoed in the deepest part of his soul and made the stairs shake, though he knew they weren't really shaking—that it was his inward self that was shaking. Stray's eyes shone. His face was joyful as Roland came higher, and he hopped from step to step with glee. "Just a little further," he said.

Roland stopped and looked at him. "Did you hear that?" he asked.

The boy smiled. "Of course."

"Who was it?" Roland asked.

Stray grinned widely. "It was me," he said.

"It wasn't you. You're right here with me. And that voice wasn't yours—it was a man's."

"I left something here for you," Stray said. "A long time ago. A gift. You'll see."

Roland opened his mouth to protest again. Stray was talking gibberish as he loved to do. But an image from his dream came back to him, of the boy throwing light into the sky and becoming more than a boy. And Roland's clothes were still damp from running across the water. He experienced a sudden understanding: that the future Virginia Ramsey had promised him was almost here, and this boy was going to give it to him. He cleared his throat. "You did?" he asked.

"Come *on,*" Stray said. "It's not much further."

Shaking his head, Roland finished climbing the stairs. The voice was still echoing through his head, and as he walked the echoes grew in volume and became a lion's roar.

"Roland!"

This time the voice seemed to pass right into him, to become a part of him. He stopped and held on to a rail as the roar shook the hall where he stood and rattled the paintings on the walls—but no, they were not rattling. It was his insides that were reverberating with the sound.

The roar quieted, and Roland realized he was standing outside a room.

Stray smiled. "Inside," he said.

Roland pushed open the doors.

The room seemed somehow older than the rest of the house, older and more alive beneath the layers of dust that covered it. On a long table that ran the length of it was a book.

It was an old book, bound in red leather, and Roland's hands made their own way to it, felt the smooth cover, sensed the age, the significance, the hauntedness of it. And his hands trembled as they opened the cover.

Writing covered the pages, faded in places, smudged in others, here and there stained with ink or with dark spots that looked like blood. The hand was all the same, long and slanted, an elegant hand but a strong one. The words were in a language Roland did not know.

"I can't read it," he said, his voice small in his own ears.

"Yes, you can," Stray said, his voice sounding at once closer and much farther away that it had been.

And as Stray said it, so it became true. The words did not change, but Roland knew them suddenly; they drew him in and made themselves known to him.

I am Aneryn, the Poet; I am Aneryn, the Prophet; I am Aneryn, the Strong . . .

Roland turned pages and read poetry, prophecy, and the tale of a poet exiled alongside his King in the last days of the

Great War. As he read he felt as though he was there, as though he could remember it all happening. As though he *was* the poet.

Along with the words came the knowledge of his world. He saw, like a story unfolding before him, the way men had driven the King into exile and embraced the reign of death. He saw the founding of the Empire, and he saw the first members of the Order of the Spider reaching through the Veil to take hold of the power of the Blackness, inviting back into the world powers the King had shut away. He saw the way the Empire lied, the way it buried the stories of the King and made the people of the Seventh World think there was no other way to live than to be subject to the Empire's rule, to drink and carouse like the MacTavish, to go bad like the High Police, and eventually to die. They tried to crush every story of the old world and make sure no one remembered the war, no one remembered the King, no one remembered life.

They were liars and thieves, and the people of the Seventh World believed them and allowed them to take whatever they wished.

But their lies would not always triumph.

Tonight I gazed into the fire to shut out the darkness around me. The flames danced in shapes and whispered words. I, the Poet-Prophet, have seen the future. I have seen the signs of his coming again . . .

The Gifted ones whom I have seen will walk the earth and awaken it to the King.

Hear, then, what I have heard.

When they see beyond the sky,
When they know beyond the mind,
When they hear the song of the Burning Light;
Take these Gifts of My Outstretched Hand,
Weave them together.
I shall come.

The tremble that had begun in his hands spread through his body as he turned the page once again, and now he saw a sketch: a lion, tawny-maned and fierce; and standing with a hand in its mane, a child with eyes like the sea. And he read more, about Six who would be Gifted, about the King who would return, about lies and death that nearly strangled the Seventh World, and about Blackness that must have its day . . .

"Roland!"

Once again he heard his name, in a roar, in a voice that broke over him like the ocean's raging. The sound knocked him backward, and he found himself lying on the floor in the house of Angslie with the book clutched to his chest, eyes wide, soul full of what he had heard. The voice was still in him; pounding in him. And the picture.

Stray was gone. But his voice was still lingering in the house, so strongly that Roland could converse with it.

Do you remember the Seer? Stray's voice asked.

Roland nodded.

She needs you. So do the others. They are waiting for you and Virginia in the Green Isle. You don't have much time.

"I don't understand," Roland said.

Maybe you don't, Stray's voice came. *But you need them, and they need you. You have my Gift now—my voice. And it is time for the weaving together. Listen carefully. You must find Virginia and go to the Green Isle. The rest of the Six are there, waiting for you. You do not have much time. Join them, and tell them to come to Pravik. I am going ahead of you there.*

"I . . ." Roland stopped. "I will," he said simply.

You do know me now, don't you?

Roland swallowed hard. The lion's voice was still reverberating in him. And the vision of Stray throwing light into the sky. Stray who was not a stray here after all . . . who was the Heart of the World come home at last. He nodded.

He thought he heard a twinkle in Stray's eye. *Remember,* Stray's voice finished, *no matter what happens, I am always a step ahead of you.*

* * *

It was nearly nightfall again by the time Virginia, Rehtse, and Kieran reached the harbours of Galce—footsore and wearier than any of them could say. Virginia's head plagued her from Lord Robert's blow, and pain from the Spider's draining still ached in every part of her. Only the strength of her visions and conviction kept her going. She leaned on Rehtse, who grew more and more tired but said not a word of complaint.

"There will be no ships leaving at night," Virginia said. "We will have to wait till morning."

Rehtse looked through the trees to the water. The harbour was protected and calm, but she could hear waves crashing off rocks beyond it. Torches cast orange light over the water and into the trees. Men were moving on the docks, their shadows friendly, their voices rough but not menacing.

"I think not," she said, trying to make her voice sound strong. "They are loading a boat now—perhaps they will take us."

"No one takes ship at night," Virginia said. She squeezed Rehtse's arm and laughed wearily. "But then, I am with you. Your luck has not failed us so far."

"It is not luck," Rehtse said. She gently pulled herself free of Virginia. "Wait here," she said.

Virginia frowned. "It's not safe," she said.

Rehtse smiled, though she knew Virginia could not see her expression. "But my leading is not luck. Don't be afraid."

She turned and strode out of the trees toward the docks, where three men were loading a fishing boat with small boxes. Nets and hooks hung from its barnacled sides, casting peculiar shadows in the torchlight. The men were talking amongst themselves, the younger two laughing, the oldest adding crusty retorts. It was he who looked up and saw Rehtse approaching, and his bushy white eyebrows shot up. He said nothing.

I am not trusting to luck, Rehtse reminded herself. *I pray the King I am not trusting to stupidity either.*

"Greetings," she said.

Her voice rang out over the gentle lapping of the waves, startling one of the younger men so badly that he dropped one of his boxes into the water. He swore and dove in after it. The other peered at her through the shadows.

"Who are you?" he called.

"One needing passage," she said. "Are you going to Bryllan?"

"Aye, to the Highlands," the young man who still stood on

the ground said. "Home."

"Have you room for three more?" Rehtse asked. "We are only two women and a boy. We need safe passage—the sooner the better."

"Ye can't get there sooner than we can take you," the young man said. "My wife is due to give me a son any hour now. I want to be home."

Rehtse smiled. "Then you will take us?"

The old man spoke. "Why should we?" he asked.

"Because we need help," Rehtse said. "And here you are. It seems the King's will that you do."

The youngest man crawled out of the water, heaving the box by a rope. He shook water from his long hair and looked, dripping, to the end of the dock where Rehtse stood. "We're taking them?" he asked.

The old man nodded. "Clear space. There's three."

Rehtse turned to get the others. They had already left the shelter of the trees—Kieran and Virginia stood at the edge of the light, arm in arm. Virginia smiled and shook her head as Rehtse took her elbow.

"It is not luck," Virginia said. "But it is uncanny."

Rehtse smiled. "It was not I who brought the wind to our rescue. You also know something of the King's help."

"But I rarely throw myself so boldly upon it," Virginia said.

All three linked arms and stepped onto the floating dock. The men helped them into the ship, where they settled on a pile of nets. Virginia thanked the fishermen softly. The youngest, still dripping, cocked his head.

"Yours is a welcome accent," he said. "Going home too?"

Virginia turned her head so the salty breeze was in her

face. "At long last," she said. "Yes."

Rehtse settled into the nets on the bottom of the boat and let sleep come over her. Kieran leaned his head against her shoulder, seeming again to be younger than he looked. The wind in the channel was strong and steady, and Rehtse drank up the scent of salt air and the sounds of wind and wave. She fixed her eyes on the stars above the boat until she slept, and then the boat was scraping gravel, and they were ashore.

Rehtse stood and helped a sleepy Kieran to his feet. They climbed out of the boat with the help of the sailors, who had already helped Virginia down. The shore rose into low mountains, barren and rocky.

The Highlands.

They were not so dark as the forest had been, for the moon reflected off white and grey rocks and pale grass and flowers. A bird was singing its mournful song somewhere nearby, the strains rising above the pounding of the sea. The air smelled of salt and turf, fish and iron.

"It is dark," Kieran said. "Should we wait for morning?"

"No," Virginia said. "Time is not on our side. Rehtse, can you see a winding path leading up into the hills toward a jutting peak of rock? There should be a great tree bent over the path."

Rehtse searched it out and found it, the path just discernible in the moonlight with a willow casting its sorrowful branches over its entrance. "I see it," she said.

Virginia nodded. "That is the way to Angslie. Lead us on, Rehtse."

One of the men called after them. "Do ye need help?" he asked.

Virginia smiled and shook her head. "We know the way," she said.

* * *

For two hours Virginia, Rehtse, and Kieran followed the path into the nearly barren hills. They crested a ridge, and there, under the moonlight, lay a village with its chimneys smoking. Voices and laughter came from an inn close by, along the road to the village.

"Angslie," Virginia said.

"Might we find room in the inn?" Rehtse asked.

"Best not to," Virginia answered. "I have few friends here, and more enemies than I care to admit."

"But this is your home," Rehtse said.

Virginia shook her head. "I am not sure I have ever had a home other than the hills themselves. Anyway, it is not down toward the village that we want to go. We need to go further into the hills—to the House of Angslie."

She took a step down the path, but faltered, and she winced as she lifted a hand to her head.

"Virginia," Rehtse said quietly, "we have come far, and you are still weak from Evelyn's attack. You need food and drink—we all do. Let me go to the tavern. They do not know me there. I have coin enough for bread. You and Kieran can stay here and rest until I return."

Virginia nodded. "You're right," she said. "I'm sorry. I should have thought more of your needs."

Rehtse just smiled and squeezed Virginia's hand before squaring her shoulders and heading down the hill to the inn. It was well lit, its courtyard full of horses and men. Eyes turned to follow her as she let herself into the yard, but she kept her head high and whispered a prayer for safety.

When she opened the door to the inn, light momentarily blinded her. She blinked to get her bearings, and her heart sank.

The inn was full of soldiers dressed in black and green. High Police. They were drinking, playing cards, grumbling and laughing. But their heads turned almost as one when she entered. She lifted her chin and refused to look at them straight on.

"Well, looky here," one of them said.

Rehtse took a few more steps inside, ignoring the commenter and all the rest of the prying eyes, and approached a man she thought might be the innkeeper. He stood, swaying on his feet.

"I'm looking for food and drink," she said. "Will you sell me some?"

His eyes were unmistakably hostile. "Where do ye come from, foreigner?" he asked.

Behind her, someone said, "Ain't no one in the yard . . . she's alone."

She turned and bolted.

Strong hands grabbed her arms, though she twisted and fought. Voices laughed. "Leaving so soon?" one voice asked. "Are we such bad company?"

The men hauled her back into the inn.

The innkeeper came forward and looked her over coldly. He was unmistakably drunk, but his wits still seemed about him. He took her purse from her hand and shook it, nodding in satisfaction at the clink of coins.

"Those are mine," Rehtse said. "Are you a thief?"

He looked her over again. "Ye came here intending to pay me, I've no doubt. Well now—my roof is over your head, and my patrons will entertain ye for the evening. Neither service is free. This'll just about do."

The soldiers laughed, and one reached out to touch her cheek. Rehtse bit him, and he yelled and shook his hand. Two of them were still holding her arms firmly. A new voice spoke, and a balding man with red hair and an equally red face got up from the corner. He was short but formidable, muscles bulging from his shoulders and arms.

"Leave the girl alone," he said. "What kind of brigand are ye, MacTavish?"

The innkeeper coloured. "Leave the men to their fun, Cameron Blacksmith," he said.

"An innocent girl is not *their* fun," Cameron answered. He drew nearer. "Now, girl," he said. "Who are ye? And what is your business here? These parts are not friendly to strangers."

"I am called Rehtse," Rehtse answered. "I come—from the east. I want only bread. I am just passing through."

"Liar," one of the High Police said. He was a dark-haired man of average height and build, Italyan from his accent, with two day's growth of beard and an unkempt uniform that bore the insignia of an officer. "I have been posted to this forsaken place three times in my career, and the one thing I know is that no one passes through Angslie. You're on an island at the end of the world. There is nowhere to get to from here. If you're here it's because you meant to come and you mean to stay. And you will stay. Till we get the truth out of you."

The blacksmith glared at the cocky officer. "On what grounds do ye think ye can hold the woman?" he asked.

"On the grounds that we are the High Police, and she is lying," the officer said. He moved menacingly close. "And on the grounds that I *want* to keep her here. Now tell me, Blacksmith, what do you intend to do to prevent me?"

"I've a stronger arm than all your men put together," the blacksmith growled. "Come into the yard and fight me, one by one. I'll win the girl from ye."

The officer only laughed. "Get out of here," he said. He turned dismissively from Cam and nodded to the men who held Rehtse's arms in a vice grip. "Take the girl upstairs and lock her up," he said.

The blacksmith hadn't moved, and the soldier glared at him. "You know as well as I do that this woman may lead us to the one we want. I suspect you of protecting her. Watch your step—or you'll land in prison just as sure."

Rehtse's stomach sank as the men pushed her toward the stairs. *The one we want.* They couldn't be looking for Virginia here, not two and a half years after she had disappeared from the village—could they?

Behind her, there was a yell and a crash, and the room seemed to erupt in noise and activity. Her captors let go of her, and she spun around and dashed away from them, snatching up a greasy dinner platter from an empty table and brandishing it as she took in the sight before her. Cameron Blacksmith had picked up his chair and swept the most belligerent of the High Police off their feet in one swift blow. Others had thrown themselves at him in a bewildering fistfight, and now he seemed to be at the bottom of a mass of bodies. But even as

Rehtse watched, the little man cast off the whole mess of them and triumphantly held up the leader of the High Police by the scruff of his neck.

"Back off, the lot of ye!" he shouted. "Or I'll smash the man's head in!"

The soldiers, mumbling and wiping blood from their mouths and noses, backed away.

Rehtse smiled. She wanted to rush to Cameron's side, but too many of the soldiers were still standing in her way.

"Come on now," Cameron bellowed. "Give the woman up. Ye know full well she's not the one you're looking for, and I don't doubt what this rabble'll do to all your hides if ye don't rescue him. I know what *I'll* do to his if ye don't!"

One of the High Police, surly and skulking in a corner, said, "Why do you want her so badly?"

Wee Cam's eyes glinted dangerously. "Because it is a shame and disgrace for men to do what ye're doing. Because I cannot call myself a man if I don't move to help her. Let that be good enough for ye."

One of the soldiers in her way spat on the floor and moved aside. "Take her, then," he said. "And give us our leader back."

Wee Cam waited until Rehtse had crossed the floor and positioned herself behind him, still brandishing the platter, before he threw the leader onto the wooden floor. "Stars know why you want him," Cameron said. "If any of you decide to quit the service of the dragons in Athrom and become real men, seek me out."

He bowed his head. "Good day to ye."

With that, he turned and escorted Rehtse out the door. Her heart was pounding, but no one made a move to stop them.

"Will they not come after us?" she asked.

"They won't," Cam answered.

"But why?" she asked. "After the insults you gave them—"

"They weren't insults; they were truth. They're all afraid, not least their leader. The High Police on the mainland may be valiant, but those who serve in Bryllan are naught but weasels and mice." He surveyed Rehtse seriously as they left the yard. "Are ye all right, lady? They did not hurt you?"

Rehtse smiled. "They did not. The King watches over me."

"I hope he does," Cameron said. "I hope so indeed. And if ye don't mind me saying so, ye can put that platter down now, lassie."

* * *

A rustle in the grass above Virginia's hiding place in the cleft of a rock startled her. It was not Kieran—he had gone in the other direction, down toward the inn because he was worried about Rehtse going in alone. Virginia stayed still and silent, waiting.

The seed pouch Tyrentyllith had given her was in her hand—she had fallen asleep fingering it. In some way the seeds spoke to her. They were a tiny, quiet promise of new life and hope despite all adversity. She tucked it away quickly.

There was a light shower of dirt and pebbles as whoever had been standing above jumped down, suddenly level with Virginia. She heard his voice as though it came from out of the past—a deeper voice now, older than she remembered it.

"It *is* you," the voice said.

"Roland?" she asked.

There was a smile in his answer. "You remember me?"

She smiled in return. "How can I forget the only young lion in the village?"

"I tried to help you," he said. "I ran all the way to the House of Angslie and told the laird about the High Police."

"You did help me," she said, even as his words brought up a rush of tangled emotions. "You did help me. The laird took me away."

"Why have you come back?" Roland asked.

"To seek the King," Virginia told him.

Roland knelt before her. She felt his rough hands touch hers. "He is not here," he whispered.

She frowned. "What do you mean?"

"He has gone ahead of us to Pravik," Roland said. "We are to join him there—but first, he says we must both to go to the Green Isle, where others are waiting for our help. He sent me to you now, Virginia. But he is not here anymore."

She shook her head. His words were too unexpected, too strange. But even so, she grabbed his hands and held them tightly. "We will go wherever the King sends," she said. "Roland, Morning Star has come also. I have seen it."

His voice was reassuring. "The King knows," he said. "I am sure he—"

They heard it together: the click of a crossbow. Virginia waited in her darkness as Roland looked up. He said, quietly, "The High Police have found us."

A voice that Virginia recognized with a sinking feeling as belonging to the village magistrate, said, "That's her. I'd know her anywhere."

Roland released Virginia's hands and slowly stood. "Lower your arrow," he said. "We are neither of us a threat to ye."

The drawl that answered was Southern. This was the soldier speaking. "Strip down, boy. Let's make sure you've no weapons hiding about you."

Virginia's face coloured with anger. Roland did not protest—she heard him unbuckling his belt and dropping a few objects into the grass. But she also heard the sound of the crossbow releasing tension. The immediate threat was, for the moment, gone.

"I see you've not changed, magistrate," she said loudly. "You're still just as much the mouse in man's clothing that I saw you to be years ago."

His anger lashed back. "Hold your tongue! You think I've done this to you? It's your own disrespect for your betters, your own strange ways, that have brought this upon you. And for shame—to drag a boy into it!"

"This may be your last chance, magistrate," Virginia said, her voice still raised. If Kieran or Rehtse heard the trouble, they might be of help. But she was deadly serious all the same. "The world is taking sides. The King will return—the King of ancient days, the one your mother told you of when you were a wee babe and still listened to the truth. And these soldiers are not on the right side. You haven't yet sealed your fate. Help me now."

The magistrate nearly choked on his own anger. "Help *you*, you shameless—"

He was cut off as the soldier yelled and crashed to the ground. Virginia heard the crack as his crossbow hit rock and splintered. Other voices likewise shouted in anger and fear, and she heard the thuds of numerous bodies hitting the earth. Roland's hand grabbed hers and pulled her to her feet, and he positioned himself in front of her as swords clashed for a brief moment. She thought she heard a clang—like a metal platter bouncing off someone's head.

Yet another voice she remembered from the past said, breathing hard, "Good lads!"

"What was that?" Roland asked. "Grabbing them and pulling them down like that?"

"Roots," came Kieran's shy voice.

"Are you all right?" Rehtse asked, throwing aside something that clanged off the rocks.

"What's going on here, Roland?" demanded the other voice —Cameron Blacksmith's, Virginia suddenly remembered.

"It's Virginia, Wee Cam," Roland said. "And I—I don't know where to begin. The child you sent me to the hills with —well, he's not just a child. And he sent me here to find Virginia and go with her to the Green Isle."

Wee Cam snorted. "I told you that boy wasn't canny," he said. "Ye'll be needing to take ship. I'll help you find a worthy vessel. The voyage isn't long. Are those roots secure, lad?"

"Yes, sir," Kieran answered.

"Good," Wee Cam said. "For those fools won't wake with their dispositions any the sweeter. And as ye're all leaving, I'll have to deal with them all myself."

15

The Sacrifice

"Michael," came a voice from the door. It was Stocky, the dark young man, with Lilac at his side. "Are ye ready?"

Michael and Miracle were in the barn along with the Ploughman, Nicolas, Maggie, and Huss—going through supplies and packing what all agreed they needed for the journey over the sea and then overland to Pravik. Pat had gone out with some of the other clannsmen to gather supplies of a different kind—weapons Jack told them were hidden in the mountains.

Michael brushed straw away from his shoulder. "Soon," he said.

"Now may need to be soon enough," Lilac said.

"What do you mean?" Michael asked, his body tensing. If he'd had a sword, Maggie knew he would have reached for it.

"We saw one of them from the hill," Lilac said. "With a whole pack of soldiers. Jack and Archer have gone to watch them. They'll sound the alarm if they come too close."

"Them?" Maggie asked.

"The black-cloaked strangers," Stocky said.

The breathless entry of Archer, the straw-haired teenager, interrupted the conversation. He threw himself through the door, panting and pale.

"They're coming here," he said.

As if animated by his words, Michael turned to his clannsmen in the door. "Lilac, Stocky, tell everyone to head for the mountain. Fire the homestead. You know what to do."

"Truly, Michael?" Lilac asked. There were tears in her eyes. He nodded, but he reached out and touched her cheek. She held his hand against her cheek for a moment, and then resolve came into her face and she turned and ran out the door. Stocky was already gone.

"You're going to burn your home down?" Maggie asked.

"We knew we wouldn't be safe forever," Michael said. "Our plans didn't include protecting all the Gifted—only one, and each other. But we're honoured to help you all. Now listen to me, all of you. Did you see the gorge through the mountains on your way here?"

"We did," the Ploughman answered.

"Head through it," Michael said. "It's the only way to a beach beyond where we have boats waiting."

"They'll catch us," Nicolas said. "There's no way out of there; we'll be slaughtered."

"They won't catch you," Michael said. "Our homestead lies in their path. Its firing will slow them down enough to let you through. Once they're in the pass, we can hold them for several hours at least." He hesitated, as though he knew something he wasn't saying. "We may even do them great damage," he finished.

"You're a handful of men and women," the Ploughman

said.

"Yes," Michael answered, his eyes sparkling, "but we are prepared. My father was a brilliant man, Ploughman, a Gifted man. An inventor. Few know it, but it was he who designed the Iron Serpent that runs across the mainland. He invented other things too, and taught us how to use them. We've built an ambush in these mountains to make him proud. We only need assurance that the enemy will follow you through the path. And they will. For you—all of you—are the most important thing to them."

"Michael," Miracle said, and her voice choked before she could finish. He held her tightly, with so much pain between the two of them that Maggie had to turn away.

"I'll follow you if I can," he said. "We'll all follow you— but you must not turn back. Get yourself out. No arguments, Miracle. You know this is how it must be. For the King."

Miracle looked up at him. He placed his strong hands on either side of her face and kissed her gently before he looked into her eyes, frozen for a moment of good-bye.

Archer appeared back in the doorway. His voice was high-pitched with fear. "They're close!" he said. "And Michael, I saw the leader—it's the Nameless One! He's alive!"

Michael's jaw clenched. "Go, Miracle," he said. "All of you get out now. We'll hold him back as long as we can. The King keep you."

"It can't be the Nameless One," Miracle said. "He's dead."

"It doesn't matter now." Michael pulled a sword from the low rafters and buckled it on. His voice, his whole manner told them they were dismissed. Maggie felt Nicolas's hand at her elbow. "Time to go," he said.

Outside, a strange, foul wind was beginning to blow shadows across the slopes, and unnatural darkness fell over the hut. In the yard, Stocky and Lilac were leading the rest of their clann. They seemed to be digging something up. Maggie saw the remembrance in all their faces. And the fear. The wind was starting to rattle at the windows and doors of the homestead. A smell came with it, and a far-off skittering sound like thousands of insects running over a smooth surface.

Ahead, the gorge was a dark slash through the mountains. The Ploughman lifted his voice. "Follow me!" he shouted.

The smell of smoke came after them as they headed up the slope. The clann was firing their home. Maggie looked back, tears stinging at her eyes. A grey streak of smoke was already rising, and she could see a single tongue of fire licking at the rooftop of the barn where they had just been. Stocky and Lilac were still darting around the yard; the others were scattering to the mountains.

The Ploughman's face was grim. Trees grew thickly around the base of the mountains, and he disappeared in greenery. The strange shadows made it even harder to see than normal, swallowing everything up in gloom. Pat appeared suddenly beside Maggie, breathing hard from following them at a run.

They reached the entrance to the gorge faster than Maggie had thought possible. The Ploughman waited, ushering them in one by one: Miracle, Professor Huss, Pat, Nicolas, Maggie. She hesitated. The Ploughman was looking back toward the little valley.

"Are you coming?" she asked.

"I can't leave them alone," he said. His voice was ragged. Suddenly Maggie realized he had dragged himself to the mountains, every step against his will. But now his will was winning.

"You can't fight," Maggie said. "We have to find Virginia—we have to find the King."

"After." The Ploughman looked down at her. "Follow Miracle; she knows the way. Take the boat and get as far from this island as you can."

"It's no good if you don't come with us," Maggie said. "We need you."

"*They* need me," the Ploughman said. "What good is a warrior who runs away and leaves children behind to defend his back?"

Maggie tried to answer, but no sound came from her mouth. Finally she managed to say, "They're not children. They were prepared for this. Michael is prepared for this."

"There are three of them," the Ploughman said. "Three men and one teenaged boy, and a handful of girls and children—against the Order and a squadron of High Police. It doesn't matter how prepared they are. They're going to die."

He looked away from her again, back to the valley, and she saw his jaw set. The argument was over, she realized with a sinking heart. He was going back.

"Follow my orders," he said. "I'll join you before you know it." His expression softened. "Don't be afraid, Maggie. I'll come back. Don't forget who waits for me in Pravik. I would never abandon that cause."

* * *

The huts, the barns, all that had been home in the little

valley was in flames. Michael shouted to be heard over the roar of the fire. "To the mountains!" he called.

Lilac and Stocky scrambled away from the heat and smoke and followed Michael after the others, all of them armed and surefooted, knowing their way even in the gloom. The young women and children grouped together halfway up, gathering under Shannon's leadership. Moll and Seamus clung to her waist as Michael shouted, "Head for the caves! And stay there!"

When they had gone, the young men split up and headed up the hillside, losing each other in the shadows, battling the wind as they climbed higher.

Michael had nearly reached his destination when a dark-cloaked man jumped down from somewhere and landed in front of him. Michael drew his sword to attack, but the Ploughman's familiar voice halted him. "Hold."

"What are you doing here?" Michael shouted. "Why aren't you protecting them?"

"I am," the Ploughman said. "By fighting alongside you. Where are your fortifications?"

Michael pointed to the top of the mountains on either side of the gorge. "There!" he said. "We've been at work for months —more than a year. We have ways to make the hills fight for us. You needn't be here."

Michael looked behind him as he spoke, and his eyes widened even as he went rigid. The sky beyond the mountains was swirling, and as they watched it seemed to tear, from top to bottom like a curtain opening. What was beyond was black.

The Blackness on the other side of the Veil began to seep through and then take shapes: beasts, warriors, dark figures. And they were gathering and swarming in one place, just beyond the homestead. Gathering around the Nameless One and his High Police.

Somehow the dead man had unleashed the Blackness.

We are at war, said Gwyrion's voice in Michael's ear.

The clann chieftain swallowed back his fear. His face was pale.

"Will your traps keep that horde back?" the Ploughman asked.

"As much as anything can," Michael answered.

"Trigger them, then," the Ploughman said. "Anything that will delay them is a boon—even if only for a moment."

"And what do you mean to do?" Michael asked.

The Ploughman's eyes flashed gold. "I mean to fight." He started forward as though he would go and meet the hordes before the burning homestead, but Michael grasped his arm and stopped him. His eyes were on the valley.

"Wait," he said.

A moment later the valley erupted in fire and smoke as an explosion shook the sides of the hills.

* * *

"He did what?" Nicolas shouted. Wind was shrieking down the narrow gorge, rattling the stones till they were loud as hornets. A sound like a terrific explosion had momentarily thundered through the shriek, silencing it, and Nicolas had turned at the sound to see that the Ploughman was gone.

"He turned back!" Maggie said again. "He went to help them fight!"

"Why didn't you tell us before?" Nicolas shouted.

"He said to keep going," Maggie said. She shook her head, willing out the noise and confusion. She pointed at the light at the far end. It wasn't much further.

"The sea is just beyond there," she said. She looked at Miracle, pleading. "Isn't it?"

Miracle nodded. Her face was stricken, and Maggie's heart hurt to realize how much every step was costing the Healer. She and Michael had told them together that Miracle would go with them, because that was the King's will and they would fight for it. But now—

"Move forward, all of you," Huss said. "This is not the place to remonstrate. We must get out."

With an expression as though he had swallowed something bitter, Nicolas turned and began to push through the gorge again. The others followed, and before long they came out on the side of a bluff, sand tumbling twenty feet below to a beach. The beach was protected, the water fairly calm though the sea beyond was choppy under the shadowy sky.

Miracle began to lead the way down, steadying herself with roots that protruded from the side of the bluff and picking her footsteps carefully. The drop had seemed almost sheer from above, but as the others followed, they recognized the presence of a pathway.

Overhead, clouds were beginning to whirl in dark shapes, ominous and black against a sky that was already much too dark.

* * *

Heat from the explosion burned the Ploughman's face as

he vaulted down the mountainside, closer to the hordes and their shrieks of anger and pain. They had been passing around the homestead when the trap had gone off—how many explosives they had buried under their own homes, the Ploughman could hardly guess.

Enough to wreak terrible damage, even on Morning Star's army. As the Ploughman came closer, he smelled burning flesh and knew, with a sick feeling in his stomach, that many of those who had gone through the valley first had been men. High Police, commanded to be here by whom? Cratus in the guise of a mad emperor? Or by the man who now led them—a man who was supposed to be dead? For an instant the Ploughman thought he could see his own men in the High Police's stead, and his heart ached with a compassion he had never before felt for them.

The fire spread up the hillside, where the Ploughman now saw that the clannsmen had laid a patchwork of dry grass, straw, and wood, haystacks of brush, and bundles of explosives, fuel to ensure that the spreading fire would flare and keep spreading, keep feeding, keep jumping up until the hills were ablaze. Had they planned to burn their whole island? He shook his head, amazed and saddened at once.

The Ploughman stayed behind the leaping walls of flame and smoke, keeping himself out of sight even as he watched the hordes. They had begun to swarm over the mountainside, but a series of small explosions and the almost constant building of the fire pushed them back down—back toward the gorge. He caught his breath for a moment as he saw them hesitating.

Had the clannsmen stopped the Blackness?

Was that even possible?

But something else was happening now. They were gathering in a strange formation, and a rumbling chant began to sound, growing until the flames shivered with the sound of it. The Ploughman remained riveted, his sword in his hand, his eyes glowing golden. The sound was enough to destroy courage, but his held. He had to hold it.

The Blackness began to advance. At first he thought the sound was pushing the fire back; it seemed to bow into itself as they marched forward. Then the tips of the flame changed colour, from orange to blue, down the tongues of fire, until the center of the valley was burning blue. Out of it more creatures came, released upon the world, let through the Veil.

The Ploughman turned his head toward the pass where he knew three men and a boy were waiting. His lips moved in prayer.

King, keep them.

Help us.

Come to us.

And suddenly he knew he was in the wrong place. He should not have come here—he should be leaving the island even now with the others, because what mattered now was not that the Ploughman could fight but that the King could return. That he *had* to return. There was truly no other hope. He thought of Libuse in Pravik, his heart and his hope. Together they had resisted believing fully in the King. But now—now they had no other choice.

The wall of flame before him was burning bright orange and yellow, but as he watched, thin blue veins began to lick up it, and then the smoke turned blacker and the flames turned blue. In the rising heat he saw the air tearing itself open. He tightened his grip on his hilt.

As the first creature brought itself out of the rip in the air, taking shape as massive muscle and sinew, bull's head and lion's teeth, the Ploughman lifted his arm and called, "To me! Golden Riders, to me!"

* * *

Black lightning was cutting through the sky over the water as they reached the beach and raced across the sand to a longboat hidden beneath brush and driftwood. Miracle found it quickly and began pulling the trappings away, her eyes tearing themselves from the sky to focus on the work. The sound of the wind had not ceased; it was not, they were beginning to realize, wind.

Nicolas and Pat tore driftwood and branches away from the ship and began pushing it toward the water almost before Maggie and Huss had reached it. Maggie grabbed Pat's wrist.

"What?" Pat asked.

"Should we leave without him?" Maggie asked.

"The world is coming apart!" Pat shouted. "The sooner we're off this island, the . . ."

Her words were silenced by a crack of thunder that drove them all to their knees, and through a rift in the sky thousands of bat-like creatures poured into the air, all of them flying inland. Maggie turned to follow their trajectory and saw a glow rising above the island—blue and gold mingling in the air.

"What is that?" Pat asked.

"It's the Ploughman," Maggie said.

"He wouldn't have called on the Golden Riders just to fight

men," Pat said.

No one answered that.

Almost as one, they turned back to the sea. Nicolas and Pat laid their shoulders to the boat and pushed it into the water, wading in nearly to the waist before Miracle, Huss, and Maggie pulled them in. There were oars, but for a moment no one took them. Thunder cracked again—over the sea.

From the island, a deep rumble sounded.

* * *

Archer and Jack pumped their fists and cheered as the man-made landslide poured into the pass, crushing all who stood in its way. Boulders and logs rumbled like thunder over the ground and pitched over the edge. Clouds above them were wreathing and intertwining, dark and threatening like eyes glaring down at them, but for the moment victory was theirs. Michael smiled grimly as he watched them, but his eyes quickly went back down to the pass under the rising dust. He could hear the screams of anger and pain, the roar that meant the Blackness was momentarily stopped.

But the moment would be short, he knew.

"Further in!" he shouted, and Jack and Archer responded, climbing up the mountainside to the very top, Stocky going with them, up and over.

Michael O'Roarke stood near the top of this hill his countrymen called a mountain, beneath the writhing sky and over the dust and smoke of battle. He watched as the Blackness was unleashed on his island and on his world. The irony did not escape him—all his life he had dreamed of standing atop a mountain and seeing there what his father had once seen, a vision of a Burning Light, of a terrifying and beautiful King who came to free and to purify. Now, on his mountain he saw only death and dust and approaching ruin. The end of his clann, perhaps. The loss of the woman he loved. But he would give her up willingly, for in her there was still hope of the King's coming again.

Not only a hope, he reminded himself, seeing again the figure in the stars and the white light that had blazed all around him. A promise.

He looked toward the sea. The sky was raging; black lightning and crashes of thunder. There was a good chance Miracle and the others wouldn't escape. But there was a slight chance they would—and it was that chance he fought for, as he had been fighting for his clann and their survival since the day his father had died in their defense.

He started up toward the tortured sky and the crest of the mountain. Behind him was the golden glow of the Ploughman's fight on the mountainside, a fight Michael had only glimpsed and was grateful for. It looked as if the Ploughman was holding back a whole new contingent of the Nameless One's hordes. Rain was beginning to fall, making the ground beneath Michael's feet slick; he slipped and grabbed a sapling to steady himself. Archer, Jack, and Stocky had disappeared into the gloom, though he heard a shout indicating that they were getting into place.

At the top of the mountain, just below the final jutting height where the cascade flowed, was also the pinnacle of the pass: a deep gorge cutting the mountains in half, sheer sides dropping away. A rope bridge leading from one side to the other swayed in the rain, evidence that the others had just crossed it. Below, the gorge was just wide enough to allow marchers through, three abreast on their way to the sea. And just narrow enough to make an attack from above especially deadly.

It was time to unleash the Clann O'Roarke's masterwork. Jack had nicknamed it "fire, flood, and fury." Working together in the heat of the sun, digging trenches and building frameworks, with sweat running down their backs and camaraderie high, even Michael had sometimes forgotten how deadly serious it all was. That this intricate work of defense which would have made his father proud was not a game but a weapon meant to be used on just such a black day as this.

Michael uttered a prayer for Miracle as he followed a muddy trench just a little further, around the top to the last peak where the spring cascaded down. In a normal day it would have been beautiful, a sparkling fountain amidst green grass and white rock, but now the day was dark, and the water darker still. Michael swung himself up onto the rocks alongside the fall, careful to keep his footing, and crossed the little river on a narrow bridge of stepping stones, wet and treacherous.

The rain was falling harder now, and the drops seemed to bring darkness down with them, obscuring the mountain so he could hardly see. He could just make out the shape of the dam in the shallow river, a dam full of open trapdoors that let the river through—until one would come to shut them and force the water down the trenches toward the pass.

The machinery to close the dam was built into the small tower on the far side of the river. Michael reached it and began to climb to the top when pain jolted through him and his fingers released their hold, the strength of his arm gone in blinding pain. He held on with his other arm and twisted his head, barely able to see the arrow sticking out of his shoulder, entirely unable to see the bowman in the darkness.

He dropped to the ground and crouched, scanning through the rain for the edges of the mountain. *There.* He drew his dagger slowly, eyes fixed on the black thing that had moved just enough to give its position away. Pain was throbbing through his shoulder, hot and demanding, his shoulder growing heavy with blood and lost energy. His arm hung limp, and he snarled with frustration, still crouched so the bowman couldn't get a line on him again. He gritted his teeth. The wound was bad—the arrow had nearly gone through his shoulder. But he couldn't afford to be overcome by it now. He had to stay conscious, focused, alert.

And he had to close the dam.

Another arrow shot out of the darkness, and Michael sent his dagger spinning in its direction before the shaft embedded itself in the wood. He heard a howl of pain and drew his sword, leaping up and rushing his attacker. The creature had stationed itself in a cluster of rocks just below the clearing. It was small and spindly, its eyes glowing green in a beetle-like face, and Michael dispatched it quickly. His breath was coming in short gasps. He reached for the arrow but could only just grasp it with his fingertips. He couldn't pull it out.

Groaning, Michael looked around him for help. The tower. He jumped back up to the clearing and ran to it, stumbling as he went. Gritting his teeth anew, he stood with his shoulder to the tower and used it to push the shaft through his flesh until he could grab the end. A cry escaped him as he pulled it out, and he fell to his knees and fought to keep vision and consciousness. The rain drenched him, gathering around his knees in puddles, mixing with blood and stinking much like it. He staggered back to his feet and climbed the tower slowly, using one hand and his feet only. He reached the wooden platform and the small door, locked and chained, which he opened with some effort.

Behind it was a wooden wheel and the whole pulley system that would close off the river and flood the pass.

He grasped the wheel with his good hand and tried to turn it. It didn't move. The pressure against him was too great, and he was losing too much blood. He could see blood splashing the wooden planks beneath his feet, not diluted by the rain. He groaned as he put his shoulder to it and tried again, but still it was no good—still he didn't have the strength. He tried again, crying out with the effort.

And two more hands grasped the wheel on the other side and began to pull as Michael pushed. It turned—just a little. His eyes widened as he looked into green eyes much like his own.

"Push, Michael!" Shannon yelled, and he did as she said.

The chains creaked as the pulley moved. Shannon was moving the wheel with all her strength, and suddenly a small boy appeared at her feet—Seamus, working too, pulling too. He was just enough help. The wheel began to turn on its own, and they all fell away as the trapdoors slammed shut and the river was closed.

The rush of water and the pounding rain made it almost impossible to hear. "Where are the others?" Michael shouted, clasping his shoulder as it jerked in an uncontrollable spasm.

"With the boys!" Shannon answered. She tore strips away from her skirt and began to bind Michael's shoulder, pushing his hand away.

"You were supposed to hide!" Michael shouted again.

Shannon shook her head, and there were tears in her eyes—tears of resolve. "It's the end of the world, Michael," she said. "Let us play our part."

Not far below them, the men and women of Clann O'Roarke readied a new assault.

* * *

Morning Star, in the body of the Nameless One, stood in the valley before the crater that had once been the clann's homestead. With eyes that could see far more than any man's, he watched.

He watched the battle on the mountainside, where the Ploughman and his Golden Riders still held a contingent of late-released creatures back. They had killed—who knew? Hundreds. But there were more. Still pouring out through the flames. Still coming up from Morning Star's ranks. The Ploughman was holding them back as no other man alive had ever done or would ever do, but he would fall.

The chief ranks, led by the men of the High Police, had pushed through the burning wreckage of the homestead and made for the pass. The clann's man-made avalanche had crushed many, men and demon alike. But there were more.

Now he watched as the gorge was flooded from above, the footing suddenly treacherous, the water turning everything to deep mud. That had been their plan too, he realized; the ground of the gorge was soft, without stones and rocks, a manufactured ground meant to become a sinking swamp. It was clever. It would delay his forces.

Worry flickered through the Usurper's eyes. He could see also beyond the gorge. He could see the Gifted, three of his coveted, escaping in a ship—against all odds, for his creatures kept coming, and surely they should be able to overrun every adversary and reach that ship! But the Ploughman and his Golden Riders held the side of the mountain against those who would climb it to reach the clannsmen, and the clannsmen held the pass.

The High Police were getting the worst of it, as they led the hordes through the gorge. But that was a problem in itself. They were in the way.

Morning Star raised his arm and called the creatures to him. Three came in a rush of black wings. The tallest bowed, black wings closing around it, twisted horns glinting.

"Order the hordes forward; trample the men," said Morning Star. "Send them up the sides of the gorge." The creature bowed again and took off, the other two flying after it, short swords in their hands. Morning Star turned to the hillside where the Ploughman and his riders battled in explosions of gold and black. His eyes narrowed.

The fires were dying down.

Morning Star closed his eyes and raised his hands, feeling the power of the covenant flame surge through him. On the mountainside, blue flame shot up again, undampened by the rain.

"Come," Morning Star called. "Come and fight!"

And in the smoke and flame, creatures took shape and

stepped through the Veil.

* * *

Above the pass, Jack O'Roarke shook his sandy head in frustration. "It won't light!" he yelled. Lilac, rain running through her hair and down her neck, every inch of her clothing sodden, threw the fuse down in the mud. "There's no use!" she shouted.

Stocky called back from his position on the other side of the rock. "It has to work!" he cried.

Lilac and Jack looked at each other and mutely shook their heads. There was nothing they could do. They were stationed in a carved-out shelter on the edge of the gorge, a shelter now flooding with the rain. Moments later Stocky appeared above them. "Cut it then," he said.

"Waste the fuse?" Jack said.

"It's no good regardless," Stocky argued. "We can climb down—light the individual fuses. They won't have flooded like this."

Lilac peered wide-eyed over the edge. Far below, she could see the soldiers swimming in the muck of the pass, water still pouring down over their heads. They were pushing logs and wreckage into the pass, making a way through—as the clann had known they would. Strapped to the sides of the pass where the soldiers could not see them were clusters of rockets, fire ready to rain down upon the invaders as soon as they had conquered the flooding.

"It's too treacherous," she said. But Jack had already crawled out of the hollow and was lowering himself over the side, grasping the soaked ropes that formed netted ladders down to the rockets. "Good man!" Stocky said. "Where are the —"

He was cut off when Jack loosed a surprised yell and lost one handhold. He was dangling from the netting. A creature clung to his ankle, raising a dagger. Stocky aimed and threw his own sword into the gorge, piercing the creature through the shoulder. It shrieked and let go, falling back. Jack swung himself back to the netting and grabbed ahold again, but now they could all see them, black creatures swarming up the sides of the pass.

Lilac and Stocky grabbed Jack's arms and hauled him back up, but before he was fully on land again, a slender shape shot past them all and jumped down to the netting. Straw-coloured hair was dark with rain.

Archer.

Nimble and fearless as a mountain goat, the boy leaped from handhold to handhold, lowering himself faster than seemed humanly possible. He held the netting with one hand only; there was a torch in the other hand, light bobbing through the damp as he jumped, and before they could gather their wits the fire had lit a fuse, and three rockets burst from the side of the pass. Two ricocheted off the lower rocks, knocking a handful of shrieking creatures loose to fall back to the bottom. Jack cheered, and they heard an answering whoop from Archer.

Lilac shook her head. "Gifted boy," she said with a smile.

Stocky turned just as Lilac shoved a lit torch into his hand and pushed him lightly in the shoulder. Without a word he dropped over the side, following Archer's example, if more slowly. Jack went next, and then Lilac herself, crossing the rope bridge over the chasm first to let herself down the other side. Archer lit another set of rockets, and they shrieked away from the walls and blasted another contingent of wall-climbers loose.

Jack reached a cluster of rockets, and holding tightly to the netting with his knees, he used his other hand to jerk them free from their previous positions and aim them more advantageously at the enemy climbing the walls. His heart went into his throat when he looked down into huge black eyes so close he could see his reflection in them. He grabbed the netting and swung the torch down, wielding it like a sword. The creature screamed and covered its eyes, falling, but more were beneath it.

Jack scrambled up higher, out of their reach, and lit the fuses as fast as he could. They were almost upon him—and then a volley of rocks showered down, hitting the creatures in the heads, in the shoulders, knocking them back, jarring them loose and sending them hurtling down. Jack looked up. Silhouetted against the sky, Cali and Jenna, his sisters, aimed and threw more rocks.

Across the chasm, Jack could see Lilac struggling to light the fuses on a cluster of rockets that hadn't been shielded as effectively from the rain. She cheered as they caught fire and launched themselves—and then the netting where she clung came loose, tearing away from the chasm wall and dropping her six feet down. She clung to the netting, struggling to pull herself back up, desperate to keep from slipping . . .

And in the next instant the black creatures had reached her. Jack watched in unbelief as they tore her grip loose and she fell to the flooded, fiery chasm below.

He heard himself crying out in grief and rage, felt himself climbing the netting to another rocket cluster, felt the power and the fire that loosed into the army below, bringing death and devastation. And then they were on him too, hands grabbing at his ankles and his legs and then his back and arms and neck, and Jack was torn off the side of the pass and flung into the open air.

At the top of the gorge, Cali screamed. Her hands shook and dropped a rocky missile; she dropped to her knees and scrambled for it in the mud. Jenna was still throwing them, still fighting. Cali's fingers closed around the rock, and she struggled to her feet, just in time to see the black shapes cresting the top of the chasm—many of them now, swarming over the sides, over their last hopes.

* * *

Over the sea, a storm was in full force. Pat, Nicolas, Maggie, and Miracle bailed with all their might, clinging to the boat. They could see nothing but swelling waves and a dark sky. Huss's beard and eyes ran with rain, shadowy rain that seemed to enrage the water. The wind shrieked around them, whipping his wet hair into his face. Black clouds swirled overhead.

"It's no use!" he shouted. "This is no natural storm!"

Pat bailed an armload of water over the side and coughed as another wave poured in, undoing all of her work and knocking her momentarily off her feet. She looked into Huss's face. He had stopped working and was simply standing in the ship.

"Well, then, what do you suggest we do?" she shouted.

For a single moment the storm stilled to a duller roar, and Huss said, "I suggest we pray!"

His eyes widened. Pat whipped her head around just in time to see the wave. It knocked the breath from her lungs even as the ship splintered beneath them, and in the next instant the world had dissolved beneath her feet and she was underwater, bone-cold, black.

She kicked and beat the water with her arms, and a moment later her head was above the waves again, and she whipped dark hair out of her eyes and cried, "Maggie!"

A wave wiped out the world once more, and when she came up again, coughing and spluttering, she could see Maggie only feet away. She struck out toward her. Maggie was bleeding from a cut over her eye, but her eyes were bright, and she was treading water as she looked around frantically.

"Huss! Nicolas!" Maggie called.

Pat grabbed a floating piece of the boat and shoved it in Maggie's direction, reaching for another to buoy herself up.

The storm would kill them.

If the storm didn't kill them, Morning Star was still waiting.

And if the Gifted drowned, all hope of bringing the King back was gone.

"Help us!" Pat screamed. Her eyes to the sky, she swept the black clouds and tried desperately to see beyond them. "Help us! King, power of good, power of right! Help us now! Hear us!"

She heard Maggie's voice under hers, singing, somehow giving Pat's voice greater power and carrying it up to the clouds.

And suddenly, a break came in the clouds and sunlight poured through, striking the water just beyond them where Miracle and Nicolas were, clinging to a single plank and holding Huss by the collar of his robe.

Maggie stopped singing. "There is something . . ." she said.

Something in the water. Something making the sea itself tremble.

The gap in the clouds widened, and the waves shot up in a whirling cone to meet the sunlight, a cyclone of water and light bursting up from below.

Pat and Maggie had drifted just close enough to hear Huss's awed words.

"The Sea-Father!"

And then came the rush of wings and the howling cries of the Blackness, and a swarm was flying toward them from the shore. The cyclone broke apart in the middle to reveal the shape of a great man, aged but strong, bearing a trident in his hand. He lifted it to meet the assault of Morning Star's hordes, but even as he fought, Pat saw one of the winged creatures taking Miracle against her struggles, and another taking Maggie, and another wrestling with Nicolas, and the gap in the clouds closed as bone-shattering thunder sounded. Huss disappeared beneath the waves, and Pat struck out after him.

* * *

The Ploughman stood surrounded on a smoldering mountainside, the fire still battling to hold its own against the rain, smoke rising in pillars all around. The bodies of slain enemies lay at his feet, a hundred or more, heaped and broken, and sand blew around him—all that was left of his Golden Riders. He was wounded and bleeding, but still he stood, swords in both hands, daring one more enemy to come near.

But they were hundreds strong, and they were all around him. He could not see beyond their ranks. Overhead the sky had turned black with clouds; the air was thick with rain; the world had closed in on every side and it was over now.

Much of the blood soaking the ground beneath him was his own.

The hordes broke ranks, and Morning Star stepped forward. The Ploughman lifted one sword. Morning Star lifted his hand as if in greeting. And the warrior collapsed.

16

Woven

The Usurper crossed the battleground and stood over the Ploughman.

Morning Star could hear the victorious shrieking of his hordes as they poured through the pass, bringing the escapees back. Winged creatures flew over and dropped the struggling figures into the midst of the hordes. The creatures of the Blackness formed circles around them, keeping them separated, jabbing and taunting them. The gorge was abandoned; silence, smoke, and the bodies of the dead the only reminders of the clann's last stand.

Morning Star picked each one out with his eyes: the Singer, small and frightened. The Listener, foolish Gypsy with a sword in his hand, trying to fight with creatures that teased and taunted him. The Healer. Beautiful as the Nameless One remembered her.

A cruel smile stretched across his face as memories of Miracle flooded through him, memories linked forever to the Nameless One's body. He marched down into the throng, his creatures parting for him, until he stood across from the Healer. Her face went white at the sight of him, but she held her head high and said nothing.

To the left, Nicolas fell under a blow.

"They are all dead," Morning Star said. "The Clann O'Roarke has fallen, and you are unprotected once again." He drew a crooked knife from beneath his cloak and held its point toward Miracle. She did not flinch.

He smiled. In one swift move he grasped the hilt in the palm of his hand and shoved the knife deep into Miracle's ribs. She gasped and doubled over the blow, struggling for air or voice as her eyes lost focus. He clenched his fist in her hair and held her up for a moment before pulling the knife out and letting go. She fell to her knees in the dirt. All around, the Blackness shrieked with sadistic glee.

Her breath still coming in short gasps, Miracle's eyes refocused. She looked at Morning Star with an expression he could not read. He watched as her breathing slowly grew less laboured, as the blood that soaked her clothes and covered her hands ceased to flow.

"I wonder how many times we can kill you," he said. He lifted his foot, planted it against her shoulder, and shoved her into the dirt. She lay there, still looking up at him, her expression a mixture of triumph and pain. She was healing. She said, with all the breath she could gather, "It is the King's might that heals. And it is not failing."

Beyond them, a song lifted over the ashy wind, into the torn sky. Maggie was singing in the midst of overwhelming darkness, singing like a fool. Morning Star looked away from Miracle toward the Singer.

Behind Maggie, the air wavered. And then he saw them— and realized, with his own eyes widening, what he was seeing.

Four figures coming out of the pass. A woman with the long hair of the Darkworld priests. A boy in whose footsteps plants grew.

And a teenage boy with a dark-haired woman holding his arm.

He knew the last two at once. The Six were gathered.

As they stepped out of the gorge, energy like lightning tore through the valley and over the sides of the mountains, blasting back the Blackness like so many flies. It caught Morning Star in a whirlwind of power and swept him away, and as he fought the blast, he howled with rage. The energy was not lightning, nor was it anything created by the Gifted themselves. It might have been laughter, or hilarious joy, though the survivors in the valley could not feel it. And it said to the Blackness that the Gifted were woven together at last.

17

Following

Maggie's voice carried over the bodies and the wrecked ground, through valley air shifting with dust and smoke. "Virginia," she said.

The hordes had vanished. Morning Star himself had vanished. The sides of the mountains still reverberated with a sense of power, of whatever had happened when the Six drew near each other for the first time. The mountains were still on fire, but even that was dying down.

Virginia picked her way across the wreckage, guided carefully by Roland. Their companions had lingered at the entrance to the pass, two shadowy figures holding back from a scene at once sacred and horrific. Virginia reached Maggie and grasped her hand. Roland looked around the valley with tears in his eyes. He spotted Miracle, and with a sword still in one hand, he jumped over the torn ground and knelt beside her.

"Healer?" he asked.

She smiled up at him. Her hand was slick with blood, shaking as she took the hand he offered, but colour was coming back into her face, and her voice did not waver when she spoke. "Help me up," she said.

Kieran's dark head appeared at Roland's side, and Miracle gasped. "Kieran?"

He hesitated a moment.

"Kieran, do you not know me?" Miracle asked.

"Where—" He stopped. He seemed to be struggling to remember, to put into words memories and questions still too vague for expression. But then, all at once, recognition came over him, and he paled. "Where is Michael?" he asked. "Grandmother? Everyone?"

Tears running down her face, Miracle knelt with Roland's help, and she opened her arms to the boy and embraced him. "We thought we had lost you," she said.

He shook as he clung to her. "Where are they?" he asked. "Are they all dead?"

Miracle pushed him back a little and took his face between her hands. Her own face was streaming with tears, but still her voice was steady. "You are not," she said. "The clann is not dead. You are changed, lost one, but still alive." She whispered, "I don't know about the others. The King knows, Kieran. The King knows."

Slowly, she pushed herself up to her feet, and her eyes fixed on the dark shape of the Ploughman's body. With Kieran's help, she reached him and rolled him onto his back. She seemed to be growing stronger by the moment. The Ploughman was bloodstained and filthy, wounded and torn so it was hard to see exactly where he was hurt. She knelt, rested her hands on his shoulders, and bowed her head.

Great Light, Great King, let your healing flow through me.

He groaned, and in a few minutes put his hand to his head

and sat up, drawing his legs under him slowly as though he wasn't sure he could trust them. He shook his head to clear confusion. Nicolas limped up, and Miracle took his hand and let him draw her back to her feet. When she was standing once again, the wound in Nicolas's leg had closed.

The others gathered around, slowly.

"The Blackness is gone?" Maggie asked.

Virginia shook her head. "It is only temporary. Our coming together drove them back somehow—but they will return, and stronger."

"And yet," Nicolas said, looking around at the devastation, "and yet, how great is our power! It is as we knew it would be. Together, we are incredibly strong."

Miracle looked at him. She was pale, and her face was streaked with blood and dirt. "Strong, but too weak to do what matters most." Her voice broke, and she drew Kieran to her side and wrapped her arm around his shoulders. She rested her chin on his head and looked out toward the hills. "If I have the power to heal, tell me why I cannot raise the dead."

There was silence. Then Roland spoke.

"We will—we will help you bury them," he said.

It was the only thing to be said. The Ploughman and Nicolas nodded, and as one they turned toward the pass and the mountains on either side, where the bodies of the Clann O'Roarke would be found.

Virginia stood alone. She did not tell anyone what she could see—the depth, the magnitude of Miracle's unexpressed grief. Pain so raw and deep it was like the attack of the Spider, threatening to steal life and joy and every hope of a future.

Rehtse came up beside her. "Pray for the Healer, Rehtse,"

Virginia said quietly. "No one else understands."

* * *

Pat awakened on the shore. The sky was still dark, but it was a natural darkness now, though tinged with the residue of Blackness. Light seemed as though it was lingering just beyond the drizzle that still fell. The sea was no longer raging. She picked herself up slowly, her head splitting, sand clinging to every inch of her.

She was alone. She had not been able to find Huss after he disappeared beneath the waves.

The island before her was silent but for the caw of ravens, and Patricia Black, who preferred every emotion to sorrow, found herself walking toward the mountains as through a dream with tears in her eyes.

She turned to survey the sea once more. There was no sign of the boat, no sign of the Earth Brother who had raised his head in the last moments of the fight.

No sign of life.

She firmed her jaw and turned back inland. She could see the dark gash where the pass split through the mountains, and as she neared it she heard the ravens fighting. The mingled smells of blood and smoke, mud and metal, met her nose, and she winced and turned her eyes upward instead.

To climb the mountains would have meant nearly a sheer trek up the cliffs, so she wandered down the beach until she found a narrow ravine running inland, its entrance just above her. She grabbed a handful of roots in the sandy cliff side and climbed up, into the ravine and beyond it, higher till she reached the height of the mountain where the gorge cut through. She smelled blood and smoke before she reached the high battleground.

Her tears ceased simply to sting and began to run down her face in earnest. She passed over the bodies of the young clann members, not pausing, not counting, not wanting to see their faces. Other bodies lay on the ground as well, the grotesque corpses of foul creatures. But they were few.

A tremendous stench met her as she reached the downward slope of the mountain where hundreds of black carcasses lay heaped and strewn. The ground was streaked with gold as though veins of it had been uncovered in the fight. Patches of scorched earth and vegetation varied with deep mud and bloody pools.

Pat bowed her head.

A breeze blew, and in it she heard a human moan.

She whipped her head around and stared back up the hill, her forehead creased. No sound followed, yet she was certain she had heard it, and she sprinted up the hill toward the place from whence it had come. A cascade of water was springing from an outcropping of rock, and it was toward this she headed. She nearly stumbled over another body, a young woman she recognized as Shannon, but beyond, in the mud and the wreckage of what had once been a small wooden tower by the water, she saw life.

She dropped to her knees beside Michael O'Roarke and rolled him onto his back. He groaned again, but his eyes focused on her with recognition. He was covered with mud, and he sucked in a breath as she touched his shoulder. She pulled her fingers back red with blood. A bandage over his arm and shoulder now was soaked not only with rain but with blood also.

His eyes were full of tears. "Did they—"

He gasped and tried to sit up, and instead of pushing him back down as was her first instinct, Pat helped him up. It was slowly sinking in that he could be the only other survivor—her only ally.

"Morning Star came after us," Pat said. "They were taken. I don't know what happened after that."

Michael groaned. His eyes fell on the body beyond Pat and filled with pain that made her recoil.

"They fought bravely," Pat said. "They all did. They did great damage to the enemy."

Michael shook his head. "But all in vain," he said. "We held the gorge in vain."

"No," Pat answered. "It's not in vain while the world remains and Morning Star is not yet in power. The Gifted still live, even if they are in Morning Star's grasp. We can help them."

The clann chieftain, propped up on his good elbow and fighting to stay upright, looked her in the eye and asked, "How?"

Pat opened her mouth, but no words came out. She shook her head, standing slowly, and turned to look at the scene of battle. Words kept catching in her throat.

"We can . . . we can pray," she said at last. She whirled back, eyes alight. "We'll bring the King back ourselves."

"We need the Gifted," Michael said.

"No, we don't," Pat said. "The Gifted need *him*. We need him. The whole world needs him. And he's coming back! Huss said so; everyone believed it, that's why we're here. Even Morning Star believes it, or he wouldn't be trying so hard to capture the Gifted."

She rushed forward and thrust her shoulder under Michael's good arm, pushing him to his feet before he could protest. "I don't know why you're still alive," she said, starting forward with Michael hobbling beside, "but I say we take every favour we can get."

"You'd be better off leaving me behind," Michael said. "I don't know how far I can go."

"I'm not leaving another person behind," Pat said. "You know where another hidden ship is, don't you? You had enough for your whole clann to escape."

"There is another," Michael said. They stopped while he fought for breath, and she saw the way he bent and tensed his whole body against the pain. His skin was pale beneath the mud; he had lost far too much blood. For a moment she wondered if she was being a fool to bring him with her.

But then, she was being a fool in every way, wasn't she? The only thing she could think of doing that wouldn't be foolish would be to lay down and die, and that was the one thing she wasn't willing to do—not while Maggie was in Morning Star's power and Mrs. Cook was trapped in Pravik, not while there was *any* hope.

"Good," she said. "Show me the way."

His eyes focused on something beyond her, and suddenly they filled with hope. She panicked. He was dying; he was reacting to something beyond life. But a shout from over her shoulder made her turn her head, and this time she almost dropped Michael as her own heart leaped.

Nicolas was vaulting up the mountainside toward them.

* * *

As the sun sank, they stood together in the quiet green of a hillside that had been untouched by the hordes. It took the Ploughman, Nicolas, Roland, Kieran, and a healed Michael hours to move the bodies and bury them in shallow graves, but the strange peace on that hillside, which had stayed green and beautiful so near so much destruction and horror, made it the only suitable place for burial.

A cool breeze was blowing as Rehtse walked slowly over the graves, chanting the ancient burial rites of the Darkworld. Michael and Miracle stood together with Kieran before them, each with a hand on his shoulder. Miracle was pale and weak; she had fully recovered from her own wounds, but healing those of others had demanded much from her since the day had begun. Michael was silent, his face betraying a loss too deep for words.

When Rehtse was finished, she returned to the little cluster of mourners, and Maggie stepped forward and sang a lament as the sun slipped the rest of the way over the horizon.

When she fell silent, Roland spoke. "Miracle asked why she could not heal the dead, if the power in her is the King's power," he said. "It is because we have only snatches. Our Gifts show who he is, but not in full measure. Healing is in Miracle, but life is in him—just as song is in Maggie, but all music is in him. The power to hear is in Nicolas, but the power to speak what is heard is in him."

"How do you know?" Nicolas asked after a long pause.

Roland cleared his throat. He was looking at the graves, not at his fellow Gifted—with whom he hardly seemed to belong. "He told me," he said.

"The King?" Maggie asked. "Is he coming back? Did he tell you that?"

"He is already here," Roland said. Somehow his voice was unhappy. "He has been here for months. He has been living with me and I with him."

There was shocked silence. Virginia said, "Roland told us of his life in the last few months as we sailed here—carried by the Wind-Spirit Llycharath and the open arms of the Sea-Father, or we would never have made it to you in time. What he speaks is true, although we may not think ourselves ready to hear it."

"But if the King has been here all this time," Michael said slowly, "why did he not come here? Why would he ask us to take a stand as though he was still absent? Why did he not come and prevent this?"

"Or the overtaking of Pravik?" Nicolas asked. "Why hide in the Highlands all this time? And where is he now? Why did he not come with you?"

"He has gone to Pravik now," Roland said. "He wants us to follow him."

"If you have been with him for months," Nicolas said, "why have you not declared him before this?"

"I did not know," Roland said. He turned and met their eyes, one by one. "He was—he is—a child. I thought I was taking care of him. He talked crazy sometimes, about people and the past and powers beyond the sky, but I thought he was just a child. Just a little boy telling stories. I didn't know until he opened my eyes. I didn't even know that I was Gifted."

"And what is your Gift, son?" the Ploughman asked.

Roland swallowed. "I am a Voice," he said. "Stray—the King—told me things—and gave me a book of prophecy—and I can repeat them. That's all. That, and I can tell you that he wants us to follow him together to Pravik."

"And what will we find there?" Nicolas asked. His tone was bitter. "More death?"

"No," Miracle said. "If we are truly following the King, then we will follow in the path of healing, and it is healing we will find—eventually."

"But . . . a child?" the Ploughman asked.

It was Virginia who put their fears to rest, at least for the moment. "He may look like a child," she said. "But in this world, very little is as it appears. We have all acted against sight before, haven't we? We have all stood when appearances said we should fall. We will do it again."

The others glanced at each other, and some nodded. "That is what it means to be faithful," Rehtse said. "Is it not?"

"Michael, Miracle, I am sorry to tear you away," Virginia said. "But we should not linger here. The Blackness will seek us out again, and next time it will not be as it was today. Something about our coming together struck at Morning Star as though the King himself had struck at him—had laughed at him. But it will not be so again."

"There is another boat hidden on the beach," Michael said. "One big enough for all of us. We will leave tonight—Miracle and Kieran and I too. There is nothing more to hold us here." His eyes filled with tears once more as he spoke, and he lifted them to the mountains as though he beseeched someone there.

"There is one more we should mourn here," Pat said. She had not spoken since Nicolas had discovered her and Michael on the mountainside. The others turned to look at her.

"Professor Huss," she said. "I think he drowned."

Quietly, Rehtse began to pray the rites once more. The others joined in this time, recognizing the phrases from the first time.

And together, the Gifted mourned the man who had believed in them before even one of them had known what it meant to be Gifted.

* * *

That night, under the glow of the moon, they pulled a long white boat out from its hiding place under a low-growing tree, through thick sand, and into the silver waters of the sea. The boat rocked as one by one they climbed in, and the Ploughman and Michael pushed it even farther out. They took up oars and began the journey over the water toward the continent.

Beneath them, the sea blazed with light.

It began with spreading glimmers of colour where the oars dipped into the water. Then fish, fronds, and algae glowed and flashed beneath the waves, pink and blue and green and gold, until the very waters shone. Maggie wove the colours and the spray and the moonlight together into a song of hope and mourning that rose and fell in the soft, flickering glow.

Rehtse watched the lights with her eyes wide, looking up from them only to drink in the bright shining of moon and stars above. She sat next to Virginia, whose eyes looked blankly down toward her hands, and whispered what she could see.

When they caught sight of Galce, at first they thought it was the reflection of the water they saw in the trees. Only as they drew nearer the shore did their quiet gasps announce what they were truly seeing: the trees, like the water, were alight. Moss and leaves glowed soft green and yellow; white and purple flowers shone in the darkness like bright, fragrant stars.

They disembarked quietly, holding their words in wonder. Even Virginia, who could see none of it, seemed to bask in the strange beauty of what surrounded them. As they crossed the sandy shore, she stopped and smiled.

"Do you see something?" the Ploughman asked her.

"Aye," she answered. "Footprints shining in the sand like polished gold." Her voice softened. "The King has indeed been here."

They journeyed deeper into the shining woods. Their path led them between rocky outcrops, and in wonder they watched as a grey wolf pack, the white and silver in their fur glistening, gathered on the rocks and witnessed their passing without threat or fear. And in the light of the trees a tiny brown rock goat, not two weeks old, leaped up to the highest rock in the very midst of the wolves and bleated its greeting.

Miles on, the lights began to dim, and with it, their strength. In a small copse, white lilies emanated a welcome like lamps in the darkness.

"We should rest here," the Ploughman said. "Sleep until morning."

No one argued. One by one, they found soft patches in the moss and flowers and laid down to sleep. And as they did, one by one, the lights of the lilies winked out.

* * *

When morning came, they were awakened by birds singing and sunlight filtering through the branches overhead. Maggie sat up, lilies bending near her head. She smiled and looked around. Some of the others were still sleeping, their cloaks dark in the bright green of morning grass. Nicolas and the Ploughman were gone, their voices drifting back from a nearby brook.

On the far side of the clearing, Michael was sitting against a tree with Miracle tucked into his arms. They were both awake, their faces streaked with dried and new tears. Maggie swallowed. She blinked back tears of her own as the beauty of the forest touched her in a whole new way—not diminished, but deepened by the reality of what had happened. The power underlying the forests—and the mountains, and seas, and stars, and all the created world—was something more real even than the loss of the clann. And it was counteracting the evil that had caused that loss. She wondered if Michael and Miracle could see the beauty, or if they were blinded by pain. And she wondered if they would all see the evil defeated for good when they reached the King.

The Ploughman came into the clearing. His hair was wet with cold stream water and sticking to his face. He took his sword from its place against a tree and buckled it on, then took his cloak from a branch and wrapped it around his shoulders. He looked at Michael and Miracle, his face solemn and grieved.

He nudged Roland, who was asleep in the grass next to Pat, gently with his foot. "It is nearly time we were away," he said.

His words did the rest of the job, and the last of the sleepers stirred and roused themselves. Maggie wandered down to the stream, washing her face and arms in cold, sparkling water that flowed over green and white rocks.

They traveled through Galce all that day. In places they passed through thick woodland, and once through a vast tract of charred forest heavy with a sense of loss and mourning. Rehtse laid her hand on Virginia's arm. "This is where Evelyn attacked Tyrentyllith," she said.

"Yes," Virginia answered slowly. "I can see it."

Kieran's voice was tentative. "Do you see any sign of him?"

Virginia only shook her head.

They skirted villages rather than passing through them. All the time they were aware that something about their journey was not as it they expected it to be. It was Nicolas who stated what they could all feel. "I can't explain it," he said. "But we're moving too fast. It should be taking us days to cover this ground. We're nearing Pravik already."

Rehtse smiled. "We are in the King's footsteps. This should not surprise us."

Virginia, holding Rehtse's arm, cocked her head. "Why?" she asked.

"In the old days, the priests say the King walked the world often," Rehtse said. "He took many forms. One of his favourites was that of a child. But the ground was so glad to see him, and the world so eager to welcome him, that it passed quickly beneath his feet. And if he wished to stop and stay awhile, he had to reprimand the earth for its eagerness."

18

The End of the Order

STRAY NEARED THE VILLAGE OF MORVO a few hours after sunrise. He limped down the rocky slope into the valley, pleasing himself by spotting the sparkles where sunlight hit quartz in the rock. His feet hurt, but he was doing his best to ignore them and stagger on. When the journey began he had skipped. Now he did not skip. The soles of his feet were bloody and raw, and a snakebite in his ankle was festering.

He didn't dwell on that.

A few farm carts rattled past him on the road, the drivers ignoring the small boy straggling through the purple flowering weeds. He kept on, pausing just once to look back up the road as though he was watching for someone. He waited with an expression like a dog with its ears perked, making sure whoever was supposed to be following was in fact doing so, and then smiled, satisfied, and kept going.

Morvo began as a few outlying buildings and fields as the valley flattened out, and then the broad road narrowed and buildings crowded in, houses and shops erected amidst rocky outcroppings on the valley floor. The road had to go around the rocks, so it twisted in unexpected places, and buildings piled up where it seemed odd that they should be. It was easier to build a town in unexpected ways than it would have been to try to dig up the lay of the earth itself. This amused Stray, pleasing him like the flashes of sun in quartz, and he laughed quietly as he wandered into the streets, standing on tiptoe to look into shop windows until he unnerved the various merchants and shopkeepers who caught sight of him and waved him off.

Pravik, he knew, was not much farther up the mountains. And Pravik was calling him, drawing him inexorably in a way that even he did not entirely grasp, because for the moment he was too small to grasp something so powerful and significant.

Stray knew who he was, and he knew that in Pravik significance would break out and nothing would be able to hold it back. But for now, he kept some things at bay so that he could enter more fully into others. He could feel Pravik like a shadow on the road, putting a chill and a silence into the air. He wasn't afraid of the shadow. But for now, he wasn't rushing into it either.

He pushed open the door of the dressmaker's shop and drifted into the smell and vivid colours of cloth and thread and leather, wandering in and out of bolts of fabric and finished pieces of clothing hanging on racks. He let fine cloaks brush his face and breathed them deeply.

"You there!" a sharp voice called. He turned and smiled up at the dressmaker, who returned his smile with a frown. "What do you think you're about?" she asked.

"Just looking, ma'am," Stray said.

"Well, get out," the woman said. "I don't want your kind here."

Stray frowned, his small brow wrinkling appealingly. "What kind?" he asked.

"Strays," the woman snapped. "Vagabonds and thieves." She looked him up and down, and she shook herself as though to rid herself of some unearthly impression. "And not entirely normal, either. Have you come from Pravik, child?"

"No," Stray said. "I'm going there."

Something in her countenance momentarily faltered. Motherly instinct pricked at her, and she lowered her voice. "Where's your mother, boy?"

Stray looked at her for a moment and then said, "You could be my mother."

"Shame," the woman said. "What are you trying to say?"

Stray leaned forward, his face entirely earnest. "If you'll do what's right," he said, "I'll call you mother."

The woman laughed, a laugh that was both mocking and insecure. "What's right," she said.

"Everything is changing," Stray said. "The Blackness is coming here, and so is the King. And if you do what's right, I'll call you mother." He leaned forward and patted her hand. "And then everything will be all right."

She was clearly shaken now, and she looked at him in disbelief. He went on. "Do you remember my Seer?" he asked. "And my Singer? From Pravik?"

A memory of two young women, one red-haired and timid, the other dark-haired and blind, came to the woman's mind. She nodded.

"They're coming here," Stray said. "Take care of them when they get here. They have to go to Pravik too, and they will be hungry. Give them food and something to drink." He looked down and shifted his weight. The floor was smudged red where he had been standing. He looked up apologetically. "And give me something to wrap my feet?" he asked.

* * *

Many hours later, the sun was sinking over the mountains, and Stray shivered in the night air. Pravik was just above, its walls visible from here, black against the fading light. He gathered sticks and twigs and arranged them as Roland had shown him to make a fire, and then, looking around as though feeling guilty, he held his hands over the twigs and waited until a fire flickered in the heart of them.

Satisfied, he sat down and closed his eyes against the aching in his feet. He soaked up the warmth of the fire and listened to it crackling.

Clouds had gathered across the sky, blocking the stars and the moon as they rose to replace the sun, but Stray did not sleep. The fire flickered. The night felt full of menace. Even the usual sounds of the forest had stilled.

Stray did not know how much time had passed when he heard the sound. A rustling, a flapping of wings. He searched the forest around the clearing and was startled to find the source of movement closer to hand—in the clearing with him.

Just beyond the edges of the dim firelight, something was materializing out of the dark. Something glowing amber. He saw two golden lights, burning lamps in the dark.

No, not lamps. Eyes.

It was watching him.

Stray tried to count the minutes as they slipped by, but the night was too full of things that last an eternity. Strangeness. Threat.

And then the night began to lighten to grey as the moon slipped out from the clouds, and the watcher's shape took form. It seemed to be made of black rags—or perhaps feathers—it seemed to crawl on all fours, but then it seemed to be a man, hunched over and spindle-legged.

It ambled over the ground toward the campfire, and Stray looked straight at it. They were not human eyes that looked back at him: they were pupil-less, the colour of liquid amber, and they smoldered. Stray described them to himself as he looked at him—it—because nothing else about it could be described. The creature was a mess of impressions knit together. Man, bird, fire, amber; not human, not animal; too physical to be spirit and too ethereal to be physical.

It made Stray sad.

It crept closer until it was nearly touching him. The creature's face was only inches away.

"Hello, Undred," Stray said.

The creature cocked its head with a jerky, bird-like movement.

"Who art thou?" the creature asked. It reached out a golden hand and smoothed a strand of hair away from Stray's eyes. "I have seen thine eyes before."

"You have to take sides, Undred," Stray said seriously. "There is no more time."

A shiver passed through the creature. The amber in its eyes was swirling with thought. Then another convulsion; all the black feathers of the thing stood on end.

"What are you doing here?" Stray asked.

"Waiting for the Seer," the creature said. It ducked its head. "Dangerous things are tearing through the Veil. I will take care of her." Its voice lowered, and it crooned the words. "I will keep her safe until he comes."

Stray shook his head. "That's not true," he said. "You want her so you can protect yourself. You think you can trade her because the witch wants her and the King loves her." The frown lines on his small face deepened. "You are waiting to kidnap her. It is wrong, Undred. If you do it you are choosing sides, even though you think you're just waiting to see which side will win."

His little-boy voice softened, its childlikeness belying his understanding of this inhuman thing before him—this being frayed and unraveled, a shadow of what it had once been.

"I remember you, Undred," he said. "It was so long ago. When all the armies were forming and fighting, and you just hid around the edges and stole things and waited to see who would win. That's why you're still here, don't you know that? The King didn't take you with him, and the Order of the Spider didn't know about you. So you're still here, waiting to see what side is going to win. But it's not like that. You have to choose sides first, or neither one will take you."

The amber eyes throbbed, and understanding dawned in them—understanding at first accompanied by terror and then by craftiness. The words escaped Undred in a wheeze, as though he had not meant them to: "Art thou . . . ?"

Stray bent his head to one side, looking gently at Undred's indefinable face. He nodded, and then, dismissing Undred without another word, he curled up on the ground next to the campfire and closed his eyes to sleep.

The frayed figure looked down on the child, frozen in indecision.

* * *

On foot, the journey into the Eastern Mountains was frustratingly slow—far slower than the supernatural journey across Galce had been. Nicolas led them, leaping when the others were dragging their feet, matched in energy only by the Ploughman. But while the Ploughman lingered to make sure the others were able to keep up, Nicolas constantly outpaced them, only to double back in silent frustration.

Virginia brought up the rear, leaning on Rehtse's arm. She could not rush who could not see.

Mid-afternoon came, and they found themselves picking their way down a steep slope toward a valley where a village lay. Recognition dawned on Maggie slowly. Morvo—the town which, a lifetime ago, had refused to trade with the Ploughman and thus had increased Pravik's vulnerability to Athrom. She felt cold as they approached, as though the dank air of Athrom's prison was clinging to her.

Though she knew they ought to go around the village and avoid trouble, Maggie found herself scanning the thatched roofs of Morvo and wishing for an inn. It would take the rest of the day before they could reach Pravik on foot—and what good would they be if they reached it only to collapse from exhaustion?

As they neared a low stone wall that skirted the nearest edge of the town, a figure caught Maggie's eye. "Ploughman," she said.

He stopped and looked ahead. It was a woman, walking along the wall as though she was waiting for something. To their surprise, the woman raised her hand and waved at them, then began to trudge in their direction. She carried a large basket on her back.

Maggie nearly gasped in surprise when the figure came close enough to recognize: the dressmaker. She pulled the basket from her back, and the scent of bread and ale drifted out.

"I've food and drink for you," she said. "The lot of you look as though you could use it."

"You knew we were coming," the Ploughman said. "How?"

The woman glared at him. "Is that any way to receive a gift?"

"We thank you," Virginia said hastily, intruding on the conversation. She had only just recognized the woman's voice. "But the question is important, and we mean no rudeness by it. How did you know we were on our way? And needing this?"

"A child told me," the woman said, slowly as though begrudging the information. "He passed through hours ago."

The dressmaker could hardly miss the exchanged glances among the travelers as she handed out loaves and flasks from the basket. She looked shrewdly at each member of the party and pursed her lips. "Best you don't pass through the town," she said. "The people won't be any the friendlier to you now than they were last you came here. Though I wish you well. I hope you'll catch up to that child and take him away from here before he reaches Pravik. What devilry stirs there is nothing any child should see."

"What do you know of Pravik?" the Ploughman asked.

"The witch has overtaken it," the woman said. "High Police too—working together. They come here and take from us, with far less courtesy than you showed. But mostly they keep to themselves. Still, things are brewing there. I can feel it. We can all feel it. The witch does not mean to sit in the city forever. Rumours are she means to make war on the emperor."

"Do you know what has become of those who were there before?" the Ploughman asked.

"Of your lady, you mean?" the dressmaker asked. "Still alive, rumour says. Alive and opposed to the witch. But beyond that I know nothing."

"Thank you," the Ploughman said. "That is enough to give hope."

The dressmaker looked each member of the group over again. "Well," she said. "Seems you could use that. You're a sore and weary bunch." She narrowed her eyes and fixed them on the Ploughman and Virginia. "You two—" she said. "Some say you've come to bring us hope. I don't know. I don't know much of anything anymore. But I hope you can do something against what's in Pravik, if only stay alive in the face of it."

"Oh, we mean to do that," Virginia said, a slight smile playing on her face. "That and more."

Once they'd eaten and drunk, they bade the dressmaker farewell and rounded the town, climbing partway up yet another slope and pushing through thistles and purple weeds. Nicolas was waiting for them on the other side.

Dusk fell as they kept on, resolute and strengthened. The night was dark—clouds hid the moon and stars. Still they stumbled forward. No one suggested they stop for the night. Rehtse took the lead now, her keen eyes searching out the shadows. The others were forced to move as slowly as Virginia.

Pravik was close, and its closeness propelled them on.

A movement in the shadows ahead made Maggie jump. Even recognizing the figure as Nicolas, doubling back once more, wasn't enough to calm her heartbeat quickly.

Throughout the day, Nicolas's sudden appearances had been silent or accompanied by a few questions as to the others' well-being. This time was different. Maggie could feel it in the air. He had something to say and was held back only by hesitation to voice it. The others felt it too, and they slowed in their walk and waited.

"You had best come this way," he said at last. "Something has happened."

The moon had come out by now, and in the silvery light it wasn't too difficult to follow Nicolas's lead. Maggie caught her breath as she recognized a looming shadow ahead as the walls of Pravik. But it wasn't to the city that Nicolas led them. It was to a cold campfire in the shadow of the walls.

They fanned out around it, and Rehtse knelt and touched a place where the weeds were bent around the campfire. "Someone slept here," she said. "Someone small."

"Stray?" Roland asked.

"The child, yes," Nicolas said. "But that is not all. Someone else was here. There are tracks all around the fire—scratches in the dirt, made by claws and something else. Perhaps wings."

Virginia closed her eyes. Rehtse looked at her. "Virginia?"

"The one who was here leaves a mark in the air," Virginia said. "I can see it. I have seen it before. He is unlike any other."

"Who was it?" Nicolas asked.

"He is called Undred the Undecided," Virginia said. "He

came among us once disguised as a man who called himself Asa. I exposed him for what he is—a creature from the old world, very old and very conflicted."

"Is he a threat?" Nicolas asked. "The child is gone. Has this creature hurt him?"

Virginia appeared shaken. "I do not know," she said. "But is he a threat? Yes."

The Ploughman was kneeling. He drew a branch from the fire and stirred it, uncovering a flicker of flame. He lit the end of the branch and lifted it as a torch, inspecting the scratches on the ground. The others watched him, his face deepened by the light and shadows. At last he stood.

"I can see no sign of a struggle," he said. "Yet the tracks lead away, and there are no markings I can see to show where the child has gone. The creature must have taken him."

A new voice spoke. "A creature left here some time ago," the voice said. "I'm not sure if anyone was with him." The speaker stepped into the light of the Ploughman's torch: a brown-haired Gypsy. "Hello, Nicolas," he said.

"Peter!" Nicolas said. "Tell me—"

"Marja is all right," Peter said. "The witch has made sure she's tended to. Your children too." Despite his good news, there was no gladness in Peter's expression. "That is the one good thing the witch has done. You will try to rescue them now?"

"Of course," Nicolas said.

"Be careful," Peter said. His voice shook. "You don't know how evil she is."

* * *

Libuse had not slept all night. It had been a particularly hot night; beneath her, the flagstones of the old throne room felt warm and sticky. Blood had spattered the stone dais and even the base of the throne, and though it had dried, it stank in the heat. Libuse knew it was staining her clothes where she leaned against the base of the throne, held in a cramped position by chains on her ankles and wrists, kept where visitors could see how the balance of power had shifted.

The throne was vacant for the moment. Evelyn had gone to attend to some business outside the throne room, or perhaps just to breathe fresh air after a long night of pacing and muttering while the Highland renegade hovered over the blue stone and watched the witch with piercing blue eyes that shook Libuse to her core.

It had not been an eventful night, as nights went: no killings, no displays of power. But the heat in the air was restless, Evelyn was restless, and Libuse sat tucked up against the throne and let herself feel the depth of the restlessness. She had decided the feeling was good. It meant that something was stirring, *change* was stirring—and while that was true, she could not give up hope.

No matter how many reasons to do so presented themselves.

She was alone in the throne room now, and she jumped when the doors banged open and two lines of six High Police entered and tramped into position along the walls, standing erect with their arms folded against their chests. Evelyn followed, talking to Link, who walked after her with his ever-present burden bound to his arms. Her voice was sharp and agitated, but Libuse found she couldn't catch the gist of the words. She was more tired than she'd thought.

Evelyn ignored her completely as she swept up the steps and took her place on the throne, resting her chin on her hand in brooding. Link began to follow her up the stairs, but she waved him back with an impatient hand.

"Not now!" she said. "Give me room to think, for stars' sake."

Her voice quiet and low, Libuse said, "Having trouble?"

Evelyn glared down at her. "Keep your mouth shut. You do not wish me to tire of you."

Libuse smiled to herself. She knew full well that Evelyn was already tired of her—at least as tired as Libuse was of the witch. But she kept her alive, and kept those with any skill tending Marja in her slow healing, and made sure that Mrs. Cook and a few others were kept well, if not comfortable. Despite all her vaunted power, Evelyn still feared the Gifted. She was keeping her best trading cards alive and useful.

"Think then," Libuse said, even more quietly. "May your thoughts twist in knots and bind you tightly." She could hear Marja's voice in her head—Marja knew a thousand curses and had taught Libuse several that she had since put to use. "How is Marja?" she asked.

Evelyn glared at her again and didn't answer. Libuse fell silent and scanned the twelve High Police. The tapestries over their heads had been torn and defaced, but the scenes of the ancient world where Libuse's ancestors had ruled could still be made out. The soldiers were surly, uncomfortable in the heat and the presence of the increasingly unpredictable woman in black. Link had settled at the table off the dais where the

Ploughman had held council.

Libuse offered up a silent prayer for the Ploughman. She was still uncertain that the King existed, much less that he was listening. But her only two options for action now were to offer remarks that needled Evelyn and to pray. She did both.

The throne room doors, which had been closed behind Link, burst open again to admit Evelyn's recently promoted general—the commander who had led the High Police under Cratus's orders. Evelyn leaped out of her seat, seemingly propelled to her feet by the sound of the doors opening, and with her eyes shot the man full of arrows.

"You dare interrupt my thoughts?"

He was unmoved. "There is a creature to see you," he said. "You'll want to see him."

"I'll tell *you* who I want to see," Evelyn snarled, but her venom dried up in mid-sentence as she looked past the man and saw the shadow lurking in the door. Libuse glimpsed it at the same time.

Creature was the right word, for this thing was not a man. It was twice the size of a man, hunched over and winged. Its eyes glowed amber from a face too shadowed to make out. It seemed to wear ragged clothes, and its feet and hands, as it scraped forward, were clawed.

In its arms it carried a child.

Libuse's heart stopped beating as the creature came forward, into the torchlight, and the light fell on the child's face. He was so young—not more than eight, she thought. His golden hair was sticking to his forehead in wisps. His wrists and ankles were bound. And yet he was sleeping—sleeping as though he trusted this creature.

The boy woke slowly as the creature lowered him to the floor, blinking at the lights and taking in the room bit by bit.

The creature bowed. "Lady," it said in a voice as indescribable as its appearance. "I have brought you a gift."

Evelyn looked at the child and then back up at Undred. "What is it?" she asked.

Libuse kept her eyes on the child, willing him to look at her. He did not. He strained his head back to look at the tapestries and the soldiers, ignoring Evelyn entirely, as though she was part of some grown-up world that had absolutely nothing to do with him. Libuse had never seen anyone so completely free of fear.

The creature looked around, at the lines of soldiers and at Link, who was watching intensely. It hunched itself more, craftiness in every line of its form, and said, "I will tell thee, but only in thine ear."

Evelyn stood and stepped down one step, pausing for a moment to look more closely at the creature and at the child. She nodded shortly. "Very well."

The creature ambled up the steps, leaving the boy trussed up on the floor. It brought its shadowed head close to Evelyn and whispered something.

Libuse heard the whisper, and the words shot through her like a bolt of lightning. She looked back at the child. Something in his demeanor had changed. He was looking up the steps now, at the creature and Evelyn. And slowly, he was sitting up —and the ropes around his ankles and wrists were loosening of their own accord.

Evelyn stepped back up the dais. "What kind of fool do you take me for?" she demanded. "That child is not—not what you say. He can't be."

"He is," the creature insisted, its voice more afraid now. Behind him, the child was on his feet and shaking the ropes off his wrists.

"And who are you to possess such knowledge?" Evelyn snapped. "What are you?"

"I am the last of my kind," the creature said. "I was there. I was there five hundred years ago." Its amber eyes grew larger, glowing fiercely. "I remember it all." It pointed a clawed hand at the child, who was now watching them, still unafraid. "I remember him!"

The child spoke. His voice was pure and clear. "It's true. He is Undred the Undecided," the child said. "He *was* there— in the Great War. But he never took sides. He wanted to see who would win. But he has chosen you now, and that is a terrible mistake."

The child looked at Undred, and his face creased with pity. "You have been a fool, Undred, and a coward, for a long long time. But you are out of time now."

He looked up at the throne, taking in both Evelyn and Libuse with eyes that were not now childlike. They were sea-green and blue, and full of the light on water. He fixed them on Evelyn.

"You are sitting on a throne that does not belong to you," he said. "And you have grave crimes for which to pay."

Evelyn listened as though she could not believe her ears. A half-smile played on her face as she looked from the child to her soldiers and to Link, who stood tensed and ready over the stone.

"And who are you to challenge me?" she asked.

"Undred already told you who I am," said the child. "Why don't you tell these others?"

"You are not the King," Evelyn snapped. "You are only a boy."

"For someone who has practiced deception her whole life," the child said, "you are very quick to believe in appearances." He smiled. "I used to walk as a child. Undred remembers. My priests could have told you." His expression darkened. "Where are my priests, Evelyn? The ones who have been waiting for me?"

The witch did not answer. Libuse spoke into the silence with tears in her eyes. "She killed them," she said. "On these very steps. The Majesty gave them up as the price of alliance with her. It is their blood that spatters the stones."

The boy's face darkened once again. "Step down from that throne, Evelyn Witch," he said. "The time of the Spider is over."

"I disagree," Evelyn said. She stretched out her arm, her hand in a fist. Around it black tendrils like smoke began to play. She smiled. "Whoever and whatever you are, you are about to learn that the time of the Spider has just begun."

She threw her fingers open, and from her hand a dark swarm of tendrils erupted, forming a howling storm that swept through every inch of the room, a hurricane of dark power. It centered around the child, tendrils piercing into and through him, and Link screamed in shock as power surged through him and into the stone. The stone burst with light so bright that it nearly blinded Libuse, and she crouched against the bloody throne in the howl and the light, eyes shut tightly, with tears running down her face.

"No!" she heard herself scream.

* * *

In the streets of the city, Nicolas's eyes widened as words burst into his hearing, words pulsing with importance, echoing from the stone walls and floor of the castle throne room.

"He is the King . . . I was there. I remember him!"

"Where are my priests, Evelyn?"

"The time of the Spider has just begun."

And then a great howl, and a burst of power, and a scream that nearly knocked him to his knees. *"No!"*

The voices propelled him into a run. The others looked at each other and began to run after him, Rehtse helping Virginia as they hurled themselves up the cobblestone streets toward the castle.

"What is it?" the Ploughman shouted.

"He *is* the King!" Nicolas shouted back. "And she's going to destroy him!"

As he ran, everything else lessened in importance. Marja, his children, Pravik, the future—

Somehow this one child meant more than them all.

He was crying as he ran.

* * *

Behind closed eyes, Libuse saw the incredible burst of light that flashed, filled the room for a long moment, and then dimmed. It took her a moment to realize she had heard something else in the midst of the howl: the sound of something shattering.

It was quiet.

Her head had been buried in her arm against the throne. She lifted it now and forced herself to open her eyes. Her gaze was drawn by a bright light—but not now the light of the stone.

The light emanated from a young man in the throne room, a tall, bearded young man with broad shoulders and eyes the colour of the sea. His presence cooled the heat in the room like the presence of a spring rain; power seemed to pulse from him, but it was the power of life, of healing, of new birth.

He took her breath away. And she knew what she had hardly believed a few minutes ago. This young man, who had worn the form of a child only moments before, was the King she had so long withheld full belief in.

Evelyn was still on the throne, but curled up defensively, staring wide-eyed at him. Blue shards, the remains of the shattered stone, were everywhere.

"Woman," he said, his voice booming like a wave through the room. "Come off that throne!"

With every eye in the room on her, Evelyn slowly uncurled herself and slunk down. The King waited patiently as she descended the steps on her hands and knees, coming to rest on the floor before him, tensed like a cornered rat.

"Take this thief away and lock her up," the King said.

The High Police looked at each other. The King sighed impatiently and said, "Yes, I'm talking to you." Two of the soldiers rose from their knees and came forward hastily, taking Evelyn by the arms.

"Don't be afraid—not of her," the King told them. "She has

no power anymore. Everything she took belonged to me, and I have taken it back."

They ushered her out, and the King's eyes rested gently on Libuse. She felt her chains loosen and fall off, and strength came into her cramped legs as she stood. He came forward, took her hand, and bowed.

She fought back the sob that wanted to burst from her chest.

"I heard you, you know," he said softly. "All those prayers." He smiled. "The curses too."

"Marja—Marja taught them to me." She swallowed. It was such a foolish thing to say. With his hand still holding hers, she knelt on the flagstones and bowed her head. "My King," she said.

"I am glad to hear you say those words," he said. "Then I can trust that you will be on my side in what is to come?"

"With all my heart," she said. Words came hard, fighting their way around the lump in her throat. "The Ploughman—"

". . . is here," the King said.

As he finished speaking, the doors burst open once more, and eight bedraggled figures entered. Libuse's knees weakened at the sight of the foremost of them: a man whose face and form she knew better than any other on earth. The Ploughman. He saw her and came forward slowly, wordless, holding out his hands to her. She waited until he had drawn alongside the King, and then she rushed forward and took both his hands.

"Welcome home," she said. "I did all I could to keep the city for you."

His eyes covered her, looking for injury, and finding none,

he drew her close and choked down a sob. She clung to him, letting her own tears soak his sleeve. She drew back, smiling up at him through her tears.

The others were drifting forward, looking at the King in awe and confusion.

Roland spoke first. "Stray?" he asked.

The King laughed. "Yes," he said. "Well done, Roland. You came in good time."

The others still hung back, each one hesitating to believe what they saw. He smiled, a smile that was strangely sad. "You will all know me better soon," he said. "And learn to recognize me no matter how I may appear." Before any could venture an answer, he turned to the Ploughman and Libuse once more. "Warrior," he said.

The Ploughman dropped to one knee and drew his sword, laying it at the King's feet. "You have my service," he said.

"Good," the King answered. "Evelyn was only a beginning, a thief who needed dealing with. The real enemy is still coming. I want all of you here, on my side—my Gifted, united at last. You must all prepare for battle—and for the future. It will not be what you expect."

"Ah! You've all made it!" Another voice burst into the gathering. Maggie turned, her heart pounding.

Professor Huss was standing in the light of the doorway with his arms full of books. He smiled and bowed to the King. "I found them," he said. "Right where you said they would be, buried in this very city! Who would have thought such a treasure could be here? Maggie, do you know what these are? They are chronicles of the Great War, written by secret believers in the King in the Tribal Age! All the truth our world has been missing for so long! This blessed child—though I see he is a man now—told me to look where we had been ploughing, and there they were!"

"But—" Maggie gaped. "How did—how are—"

"The King came by and plucked me out of the water," Professor Huss said. "He said he still needed an old scholar. He sent me on ahead, accompanied by some very companionable old wolves. Now what do you think of that?"

And he laughed for joy.

Part 3: Battle

19

Light

DUST KICKED UP FROM THE HORSES' HOOVES like smoke, carried up in swirls of wind to form plumes of brown and grey over the road. In the Italyan town of Natoli, crowds gathered in the streets to watch the procession of High Police, dressed for battle, that galloped to the town square.

General Merlyn Cratus, his face newly scarred and his battle armour gleaming, climbed the statue of Lucius Morel in the center of the town and raised his hands to quiet the people. Eyes of hostility, fear, and wonder watched him.

"Every man who can bear arms," Cratus shouted, "bear them and join our ranks. We ride to the battle in Pravik."

"Haven't you got enough of our sons already?" one old man was brave enough to call out.

Cratus glared down at their weathered faces. Some of the younger men returned his gaze more eagerly, itching to know what this was all about. "The Empire has fallen," Cratus announced. He raised his hand to silence the gasps and cries that met his announcement. "We are ruled by the one called Morning Star, a great power more terrible than ever the

Empire was. You know me—I was Lucien Morel's general. I tell you the truth now. Morel has gone mad, and Morning Star builds a greater world than we have known. Beginning with *you*. If you wish to be counted among his loyal subjects, prove yourself in Pravik."

His eyes narrowed. "Those who do not come willingly will be brought unwillingly—or left here for Morning Star's hordes to discover."

"Morning Star . . ." one man said. "Morning Star is a myth. That is what we have always been told."

As if in response to his words, a low tramp sounded from beyond the town. Heads turned, eyes seeking the source of the sound. A shadow was gathering on the horizon.

"Yonder comes the Blackness," Cratus said. "The armies of Morning Star following the armies of men. This is no myth. Take up arms!"

A white-haired man stepped out of the crowd. His voice, strong though it trembled with age, was the same as that which had already challenged Cratus earlier. "If Morning Star is here," he said, "then the King is also coming. We have heard the stories the Gypsies tell."

Cratus fixed his eyes on the old man. "The King is not coming," he said. "He has already failed you. The only rebellion is in Pravik. And we are going to crush it."

He drew a crossbow from his back and fitted an arrow into it, aiming it slowly at the old man, who met his eyes and waited.

"So fall the enemies of Morning Star," Cratus said, and loosed the arrow.

There was silence as the old man grunted and collapsed.

Cratus lifted his eyes to the crowd once more. "Every household that sends a man to fight with us will be protected. Your women and children are advised to stay within doors. The rest of you, ready yourselves. We march in three hours."

The High Police scattered into the town by unspoken command, raiding stores and houses for supplies for the march. Some townspeople protested, to be ignored or struck down— Cratus left that up to his men. He waited under the statue of the Empire's first ruler, directing those who came to him into companies.

The shadow on the horizon grew darker and larger. The sound of tramping feet grew until the whole town trembled with it. An ill wind, smoky and sick, blew up the streets ahead of the advancing hordes.

In an hour Cratus's men were on the march again. He sat astride his horse and counted the companies as they rode through the town: ten, twenty, thirty companies of soldiers, due to meet with more at the next crossroads. Trained soldiers mixed with villagers and townsfolk eager to prove their new allegiance.

Morning Star was wise. He would forge loyalty from his new empire by bringing the people of the South Country, of Galce, and of the Eastern Mountains on the way to Pravik together in battle—by giving them a shared enemy and a common victory, by teaching them all fear when they fought among his creatures. There would be time enough after Pravik's destruction to advance his rule into Bryllan and the Green Isle, and from there to sail into the Northern Lands.

The last of the companies left Natoli, and Cratus turned to watch the hordes enter the flagstone streets. The creatures of the Blackness slithered, crawled, and flapped into the town, bringing a creeping darkness with them. The townspeople were locked and shuttered in their homes.

Cratus felt his horse's nervousness, and he patted its neck and urged it toward the advancing creatures softly. It went, every muscle quivering in protest. He reached the foremost of them and stopped, waiting. They parted to reveal the advance of Morning Star, on foot, dressed in gleaming chain mail and a black cloak, the heart of the darkness that swirled through the hordes.

He raised his hand. "Hail, Cratus."

"Hail, Master," Cratus said. "Natoli has given up its men willingly."

"There is blood on the stones behind you," Morning Star said.

"One spoke against us," Cratus said.

"Against me," Morning Star said. "There is no *us* in my world, Merlyn Cratus."

Cratus restrained his own fear and nodded. "My lord."

"And supplies?" Morning Star asked. "Men cannot march on empty stomachs."

"We are collecting enough to take us across Galce and into the mountains," Cratus said. "Our companies will meet at the crossroads, as planned, and divide our resources there. By then I expect some five thousand at our . . . at *your* command."

Morning Star smiled. "After all these years, men come so readily to my banner. Nothing has changed, and that pleases me. Go on; swell your ranks. You do well."

Morning Star lifted his chilling eyes to the horizon. "Pravik and all who huddle there will soon fall."

* * *

High on Pravik's outer wall, a breeze was blowing warmly up from the mountain forests. It carried the scents of summer with it—but mingled with those smells was a faint tinge of ash from the forest Evelyn had attacked. It was just strong enough for Virginia's senses to pick up. It distracted her from the conversation of Roland and Rehtse, who were perched on the wall beside her. She didn't realize their voices had gone silent until another voice called her name.

"Virginia."

Virginia turned slowly, trying to place the voice. It was a man, and her leaping heart told her who it was—yet the reality of this voice, falling on her ears and not only on her spirit, was hard to believe.

Then he took her hand, and unexpected tears sprang to her eyes.

Her visions had come true before. But for the King to step out of vision and into this reality, this reality of bone and sinew and skin, was something she had not been prepared for. She shifted from her place on the wall and slowly, her hand still held in his, knelt.

She could hear the smile in his voice—the serious smile, at once joyous and somber, that she had grown to love in her visions. "Rise, daughter," he said.

Trembling, she did. As the King released her hand, she became aware of other newcomers on the wall with them.

"Cratus is gathering an army against us even now," the King said. "It is time we gather our own. Virginia, long ago I told you what I had for you to do."

She bowed her head. "To awaken the world," she said.

"Roland, you are a voice," the King continued. "I want you to join that voice to Virginia's eyes, and go show the people of the villages the truth. Show them who I am. Show them who they are. And call them to come and join me."

"We cannot have much time," Virginia said.

"You do not—not before this battle," the King said. "But show me, Virginia, what you have been carrying with you since the day you called the Earth Brethren out of sleep."

Surprised, Virginia took a moment to realize what he meant. Then she pulled the little bag of seeds from the inner pocket where she had kept them through all her journeying.

"They don't look like much, do they?" the King asked. "Yet they are life. You and Roland will go and speak to the villagers, and what you speak will be seeds. Trust me to bring them to harvest."

Virginia nodded. The King continued. "Soon, I want you to take those seeds to the forests that Evelyn destroyed and replant them. The trees that grow from them will always be a haven for my faithful ones and a testimony to me."

He turned. "Michael, Miracle, you will train the villagers when they come."

"And I, my lord?" Rehtse asked.

"For you I have quite another task," the King said. His voice grew quieter. "You have been faithful, Rehtse, when so many others turned away. You remember all Divad taught you?"

Virginia could not hear Rehtse's answer—she must have nodded.

"Good," the King said. "None of it must be lost. I want you to work with Professor Huss to write it down. It's time we add to the books the good professor found hidden in the city. Your prayers, too." The smile returned to his voice, and Virginia found herself smiling with pride for Rehtse. "I have heard every one," the King said. "And they have brought me joy."

* * *

The woods of the Eastern Mountains were thick, and the bloodied and battered man who fought his way through them was weak with hunger and the wounds he had sustained resisting the High Police.

When a voice called "Halt!" and a young Gypsy stepped out of the trees with a bow aimed at his neck, Harutek almost felt relief.

"Prince Harutek?" the young Gypsy asked in surprise.

"Darne, isn't it?" Harutek asked, surprised by his own ability to remember. The young Gypsy nodded. He began to lower his spear, but another voice stopped him.

"Hold your weapon!" the voice said. "This man has much to answer for."

This time there was no doubt about the voice's source. Nicolas Fisher stepped out of the trees, wearing light armour and carrying a sword. His golden eyes accosted Harutek with disdain.

"My lord," Harutek said, bowing his head. "I throw myself on your mercy."

"Tell me why I should offer you mercy," Nicolas said. "I took the Ploughman and Maggie Sheffield from a prison to which you betrayed them."

"Because I did not intend to betray them," Harutek said. "I saw what was coming in Athrom. I knew that if I convinced Cratus of their worth, he would keep them alive—and he did. I intended to rescue them myself when the time was right."

"You sold them for a promise of your own people's protection," Nicolas said.

"I sold them into prison only," Harutek said. "I saved them from death, for Cratus would have killed them unless he had believed them more valuable alive. And I had a responsibility to my people, as you do to yours."

Harutek's voice softened. "You have a right to judge me, but not, I hope, to condemn me. I bring word to you now that all Pravik, above and below ground, must hear."

Nicolas regarded Harutek a moment longer. "Turn your weapons over," he said.

Harutek unbuckled his sword and handed it to Darne, who took it more hesitantly than the prince gave it. Harutek drew a knife from his boot and threw it into the trunk of a nearby tree. "That is all I have," he said. "Of greater worth is my news. Morning Star is loosed."

"We know this," Nicolas said.

"And he is coming here," Harutek said. "With a growing army of High Police thousands strong and his own hordes of Blackness. I have seen them. I fought my way free from the High Police and have come to warn you all."

Nicolas gestured with his head, and they slipped back into the trees together, coming quickly to a cluster of Gypsies on patrol. Nicolas called out two of them and assigned Harutek into their care, telling them to take him to Pravik immediately.

"Do not expect a warm welcome," Nicolas said. "Though you may expect a just one. Things have changed here also, Harutek, prince of the Darkworld. Your people sided with the witch Evelyn, who no longer reigns. They slaughtered your priests. Your father and many others are in the custody of the King for their traitorous actions, though they have not yet been judged."

Harutek paled. "Has the Ploughman declared himself king then?" he asked.

Nicolas smiled. "No," he said. He nodded to the Gypsies on either side of Harutek. "Take the prince to the city," he said. "Make sure he delivers his news. Best he sees for himself what has changed there."

* * *

The Gypsies brought Harutek through the thick woods, into the rocky outcroppings under the city walls, and through a small, guarded door in the stone walls. The ploughed streets beyond the door had now been abandoned for some time, and weeds and green shoots were growing sparsely between hunks of rock and debris. The castle rose over the whole scene, a new flag—Libuse's handiwork—flying from its highest tower: a dark blue flag adorned with a silver crown and seven stars.

Harutek's body ached as he followed the young Gypsies, and the ache grew worse as his tension increased. He was still trying to process what Nicolas had said. His father imprisoned—his father a traitor. The priests slain. He swallowed a lump in his throat. In many ways, Divad had been more a father to him than the Majesty; Hazrit more like a mother than the mother

341

Harutek barely remembered. With shame he remembered Rehtse, the priestess Caasi had loved, and the ways he had stood against her and mocked her faith in the days before leaving Pravik. He wondered if she had clung to her faith till the end.

For her sake, he hoped she had.

Harutek shoved down the voice in his heart that told him he was going now to see not just a new king in Pravik, but *the* King in whom Rehtse had so ardently believed, the one from ancient stories Harutek had so strongly called myth and lies. He could not deny the possibility, for he had not believed in Morning Star either, and he had seen Morning Star tear the Veil and enter the body of a man with his own eyes. He had seen the Blackness loosed.

If the King was in Pravik, there would be a battle greater than any foresaw. Perhaps that meant hope for the world. And yet . . .

He pushed his thoughts back down. If the King was in Pravik, he would know it soon enough. The sun was hot, burning down on red cobblestones and on Harutek's already sunburned skin, which was peeling and blistering. He was acutely aware of the Darkworld under his feet, of its damp, cool passages and great carved caverns. Homesickness gripped him, made worse by the knowledge that things were not as they had been—that they would never be the same, and that it was at least partially his fault.

The Gypsies called out to guards as they approached the castle, and the doors were opened to them. They stepped into its shadowed corridors and took the familiar path to the throne room. But when the doors to the throne room opened, it was on a scene entirely unfamiliar and unexpected.

The room was full of children, laughing and playing around the feet of women who were storing food, water, and bundles of other supplies on hastily built shelves and scaffolds all around the room. A group of men were building bunks against the walls, and some of the older children were helping. Mrs. Cook directed the supplies, clapping her hands and calling instructions loudly. A beautiful Gypsy woman was supervising the mending of tapestries that depicted ancient battles and kings—the history of the Eastern Lands. She wore a tiny baby in a sling on her back, and a little boy with a strong resemblance to Nicolas Fisher clung to her skirt. A cluster of young children sat around Professor Huss, who was reading to them from an old book about the far distant past and exploits of the King. And as he read, the children looked up, wide-eyed, across the room at a smiling young man with golden hair, the beginnings of a beard, and sea-coloured eyes.

And Harutek knew as he looked at him that he truly was the King. He had come back into the world just as Morning Star had come back into it.

Through the doors a couple walked: a well-built young man with red hair and the most beautiful woman Harutek had ever seen, her hair white-gold and tied back. Both wore leather armour. The man carried a sword; the woman a bow and quiver of arrows. They approached the king and bowed before him.

"What do you report?" the King asked.

"We are ready to begin training," the young man said. "Roland sends us more villagers every day with his passionate calls to join you. Six came from Morvo an hour ago, along with the dressmaker."

The woman smiled. "They respond well to his lion's roar."

The King nodded, pleased, but his eyes were sorrowful too. "But not all will come," he said. "And Morning Star reaches the Southern Lands first." He shook his head as though dislodging the thoughts. "It matters not," he said, almost to himself. "Begin training with my blessing," he said. "Train them all to fight as courageously and righteously as you do. Tell them about your clann, Michael, and show them why it is so important that they stand against evil."

Michael nodded, and Harutek saw grief mingled with pride in his expression and in the woman's. They turned to go.

Maggie passed them in the door. She knelt quickly before the King, but before she spoke something drew her eyes to the side, and she saw Harutek. She stood silently, staring at him.

Harutek stepped forward, leaving his Gypsy escorts behind, and bowed.

"Rise, Harutek, Seventeenth Son of the Majesty," the King said. His voice was stern, but not angry.

"I—" Harutek began, but he found that words failed him.

"You have done wrong," the King said. "Yet some good has come of it despite yourself. Your father has chosen sides against me. And you?"

Harutek looked into the King's eyes and was shaken by what he found there. "I have no choice," he said. "Reason and right dictate that I join you. I would not be found on the side of the Blackness."

"The Blackness may win," the King said. "As far as you know."

"But I will not fight alongside it," Harutek replied.

The King smiled. "That is a good answer," he said. "Go, follow Michael and Miracle to the training yards. You are a warrior. You can be of help to them. Only take care that you train the arms of my new soldiers only. I want the Clann O'Roarke to train their hearts."

Harutek swallowed and nodded. He turned to go. His eyes fell on a young woman he had not seen with the others, just extricating herself from the tapestry menders. She wore grey, though not her old priestly robes, and her long braids were bound back by a leather tie. She met his eyes calmly. His mouth gaped as he tried to understand how it was that Rehtse was still alive.

"The Majesty dismissed me from his service," Rehtse said. "So I went to seek the King. And I found him."

"You were right to believe," Harutek said. "You and Caasi were right to believe. I am sorry now that I did not side with you."

Rehtse's eyes were full of tears, but they did not fall. He took her hand and kissed it courteously. "I am glad," he said, "that one of the priesthood remains."

With that, he left the throne room to its preparations and repairs and headed for the courtyard where he could already hear Michael O'Roarke shouting orders to new recruits.

* * *

Four days passed. The Blackness crept over the Southern countries, gathered and divided, demanded men and armed them. Shadows moved up through the forests of Galce, led by the hoofbeats and tramping boots of the swollen ranks of High

Police.

In the villages of the Eastern Mountains, a boy and a blind woman from the Highlands stood in market squares and announced that a kingdom had come and a King worthy of love was calling all who would rally to his banner.

Few responded. But each time Roland and Virginia returned to Pravik, they brought another handful with them. More trickled in of their own accord when the message had sunk in—or when the shadows in their nightmares frightened them into Pravik's walls.

The throne room, which was central to the castle and the easiest room to defend, had been transformed into a nursery, kitchen, and bunkhouse for those too young or too feeble for battle. The King still held court in it, happy to let children run around his feet and seeing to it that they helped. The tapestries were mended under the direction of Marja and Libuse, who made sure the old glory was hung on the walls and that new flags flew from the towers.

Night fell on the fourth day. The air was hot and heavy, with the sense of a thunderstorm coming. The horizon was unusually dark before dusk, and the night more shadowed. The Gifted gathered on the high tower and looked out over the city to the forests beyond.

"They are nearly here," Virginia said.

"Can you see them?" Nicolas asked.

"Yes," she answered.

Roland sighed. "I wish I'd had more time."

Virginia turned her head and smiled at him. "You did well, lion-child. More time would not have turned stone hearts. You called every heart of flesh in this province."

"But there is still a world out there," Roland said.

Softly, Maggie began to sing.

They waited.

* * *

That night, the sound of hoofbeats, boots, and wagons trembled up through the ground and echoed off the walls. As the hordes drew nearer, the sounds grew more varied—they could hear hissing, shrieks, roars, dark laughter.

In a cell deep in the castle, Evelyn trembled. In another, locked up at the end of the corridor, the creature called Undred the Undecided went frantic.

"Do we go now?" Michael asked the King, his voice quiet so as not to wake the children in the throne room.

The King shook his head. "They will be here in the morning," he said. "For now we rest. Morning Star will not come by stealth. He means to overpower us in a great show of force and superiority."

He smiled in the faint light of the throne room, as fearless as he had been when Undred had carried him in sleeping in child-form. From above, outside an open window, the sound of singing drifted down. Michael looked up. "She is singing a lament," he said.

"For the world," the King said. "For five hundred years, the song of this world has been a lament." He laid a hand on Michael's shoulder. "We will change that."

The horns of the watchmen sounded as morning dawned. The armies of the Blackness were coming out of the woods.

* * *

It was morning, and the sun was rising. But its light didn't reach the city. The forests and mountains all around were shrouded in grey, in darkness that choked out the light.

The gates of the city had been drawn shut and barred. The Ploughman's watchmen blew their horns, and the companies of the King gathered.

Gypsies gathered on the left wall under Nicolas's command.

Handfuls of villagers gathered on the right under the command of Michael O'Roarke and his wife.

The Ploughman's few remaining faithful farmers and old scholars gathered in the center.

The Gifted stood scattered among the companies.

All together, the defenders of Pravik numbered a few hundred, lining the walls only one or two individuals deep. They carried whatever weapons they owned.

Out of the woods, the Blackness was swarming.

Into the clearing between the city and the trees, companies of High Police, mounted and on foot, arranged themselves by twenties and fifties. There were hundreds in view, packing the clearing; hundreds more still back in the woods. In the air, winged creatures of the Blackness hovered and soared, cackling, calling, crying; the woods seemed to swell and compact with the presence of the shadow creatures. A few of these made their way into the clearing, giants and hideous forms that were not man, not animal, not anything familiar at all: creatures like men and bulls or goats; great hounds and serpents; bat-winged, clawed creatures with eyes that glowed.

As one, the armies of the Blackness let out a battle cry that shook the very stones of Pravik.

"Great stars," Michael O'Roarke breathed.

From the midst of the cry a single figure strode forward, a man but far more than a man. High Police and creatures of the Blackness alike fell back from his approach and bowed on every side. He carried a staff in one hand and a jagged blade in the other. He wore a black cloak with the hood thrown back to reveal a pale, malicious face. Armour glinted beneath his cloak.

Morning Star.

On the wall, in the midst of the Ploughman's rough farmers, the King looked down on the gathered masses.

"Greetings, Usurper," he called.

Morning Star smiled. "Greetings, Ancient Fool. Standing again on the ground of betrayal, in a world that is only a shadow of what it once was. Why have you come back here?"

"To mend my broken heart," the King said. "To rescue those who are lost. And to destroy you."

"With that rabble?" Morning Star said, laughing.

The King smiled grimly. "Indeed," he said.

Then he did what no one expected. He lifted his voice and addressed himself to the High Police.

"Merlyn Cratus," he called, "and all who ride under the banner of Athrom. You are men. You are not thoroughly twisted and deformed as you see these creatures behind you have become. You are not evil through and through—not yet. You have this chance to change sides, even now. To come away from the Blackness that leads you and seek my mercy. I will give it to you. That I promise."

Stunned silence met his words. Then Cratus gathered his

breath and shouted back words that carried to the walls. "Join you? A scrapling, barely more than a boy? And your army—Gypsies, freaks, women. That is the glory to which you call us?"

"No," the King said. He smiled, and his sea-green eyes twinkled. "It is only the beginning of it."

From somewhere—no one could tell where—a horn blew. And as it did, suddenly the woods were alive with something else, something not Blackness. A wind was blowing over the clearing, and in it a voice taunted and exulted, whispering and shouting all at once—Llycharath, Spirit of the Wind. The trees bent over the dark armies in their midst and seemed to swell as a gigantic, translucent form stepped from the western edge of the forest. Around him, wolves, cats, deer, and bears gathered.

Standing on the wall with the new recruits, the boy Kieran whooped with joy. "Tyrentyllith!" he cried. "The Earth Brethren are here!"

In the city, the ravine through which the black waters of the Vltava flowed was humming with another presence. The River-Daughter had come once again.

Morning Star snarled. He raised his jagged sword and shouted, in a voice that shook the mountains, "Attack!"

His armies answered the call with another cry of their own and surged forward, but even as they did, the sound of horns split the sky, and the darkness blazed and danced with light in points and lines, in shining constellations in the clouds. For an instant it seemed as though the stars themselves were sounding battle horns, and then that they were coming down to join the battle.

And then several points of light gathered into the form of a man, and all saw him together: the Huntsman, riding a great white horse, with stars woven into his cloak, a hunting horn in his hands, and the joy of vengeance in his eyes. Behind him more constellations gathered into shapes, forming hunters and hounds, and as the Huntsman sounded his horn once more, they charged down out of the clouds and swept into the Blackness.

The King stood on the wall, shining with the light of the stars, a sword in his hand raised over the battle. The wind blew his hair and his cloak, blurred into visibility around him, and then swept off the wall with such force that it blew back the first line of High Police, knocking them off their feet and hurling them back into their advancing ranks. And the voice of Llycharath laughed.

"To arms, my children!" the King shouted, and the handfuls of fighters and Gypsies on the wall watched in wide-eyed wonder as the constellations still dancing in the clouds above lighted on them, filling them, charging them with light and power. Michael O'Roarke raised his sword and shouted the old battle cry of the clann, and he made ready to lead his villagers off the wall into the battle below. But before he could look for a way down, the wind picked him up, and his fighters as well, and carried them down, leaving only Miracle and her archers on the wall.

On the ground, he could see fear in the eyes of the High Police, and for a moment he felt regret at the thought of killing them, but before he could even reach their ranks, water burst up and carried another hundred of them off their feet, back into the woods under the force of the sudden current. In the spray, the form of the River-Daughter took shape, shimmering like water. Another company of High Police charged forward, and she swept them back with another wave of water from the ground, forming instant ruts and channels in the ground, making it impossible for them to hold their footing. Closer to the forest, Michael could hear the sounds of animals snarling, howling, snapping, and crying. He recognized the giant form of Gywrion, Lord of the Wild Things, leading them.

And overhead, the starry forces of the Huntsman were still riding down into the ranks of the Blackness and slaughtering the creatures of Morning Star.

He laughed incredulously, the sword in his hand suddenly seeming a ridiculous, needless thing. The ground beneath his feet stayed intact, the water carving channels all around him and the villagers but leaving them a place to stand. He looked back at the wall, and it seemed to him that the King was smiling down at them, even laughing.

But then he heard the command, deep in his soul. *Defeat the Blackness.* He turned and looked back at the battle. The River-Daughter had left one clear path, through the struggling High Police into the shadowed tangle in the forest that was the Blackness. Bursts of light could be seen where the Huntsman's forces fought, but the shadow creatures were not easily defeated, and there were more of them—more than Michael's mind could comprehend. For a moment he felt fear.

Then, from another place on the battlefield, he heard the cry of the Gypsies and saw Nicolas leading a charge of his own. He raised his sword. "Onward!" he bellowed. "Take the Blackness!"

He did not wait to see if the villagers were following him, but took his sword hilt in both hands and ran forward, almost flying over the ground. He knew they were filled with the same power that was animating him, and as he ran, he felt that power overcoming fear. A creature half man and half goat, twice the height of any man, horned and hooved, turned and met his advance with a terrifying grin. It lifted a black sword. Michael did not hesitate, but swung his own blade to meet it.

In the instant the blades met, starlight burst from the meeting, and Michael slew the creature in an instant. He was glowing, shining like the Huntsman whose dogs howled in the sky overhead. The villagers were running to meet more of the shadow creatures, and they too shone. With the light of the stars. With the power of the King.

Remember your clann, he heard the King's voice in his heart. *Take my vengeance, Michael O'Roarke.*

With tears in his eyes, Michael fought. With every blow he remembered them: Shannon, Jack, Stocky, Lilac. The children. His father.

Thomas O'Roarke had long ago been changed by the light on a mountain. Michael had sought that light all his life.

And now he was shining with it.

The Blackness fell before the power in Michael, before the power in a handful of hardly trained villagers, before the power in a slender band of Gypsies. They fell before the Ploughman, who fought in golden splendor in the very center of their ranks. They fell before the Huntsman and his starry hosts. They fell under the Healer's arrows.

On the wall, Maggie looked at her hands in wonder as they began to shine, as light burst from her fingers, and she smiled in awe and looked to the young man who still stood with his sword raised on the wall. *He is the Sun-King, and the Moon-*

King, and All-the-Stars King, and he shines like them all together. And we shine, she thought; we shine in him.

We triumph in him.

She could hear a song, singing through the sky, singing over the battle, singing in the wind, singing in the river, singing in the King. A three-fold song, harmony overwhelming in its perfection, melody more bright and pure than anything she had ever heard. Father-Song, Lover-Song, Spirit-Song. She heard it like love and like fire; like life.

She sang what she heard, and tears of joy and wonder flowed down her face as voices joined her. Everything was singing. The sky, the stars, the earth was singing. Beside her, Rehtse, last priestess of the Darkworld, sang the words as though she had known them all her life.

The Blackness shrieked and covered its ears. The High Police, retreating now through the woods, holed themselves up wherever they could as the song welled from the very air. Cratus turned and shook his fist at the city, and he screamed out a curse at the man who presided over it.

But the song drowned out the curse.

The song swept through the castle, and Marja tossed her son onto her back, where he clung to her neck, and cradled her daughter close as she pulled every lock off the doors of the throne room. She burst out onto the wall and looked over the field of battle and the forest beyond.

Light—pillars and rays and points of light—was rising into a sky where pure white clouds met it, embracing the light in mist and piercing rainbows. The High Police were gone. Of the shadow creatures, not one remained. The people of the King were shining like stars, but their light was beginning to fade now. The Earth Brethren were drawing back into the woods and the ground and the air; the Huntsman and his forces were dissolving and withdrawing to the sky.

The battle was ended.

Only one figure still stood on the field, his pale face twisted with hatred, anger, and fear. Nicolas, the Ploughman, and Michael O'Roarke gathered their small forces in a circle around Morning Star, blocking off his escape.

The Ploughman looked up at the King, still standing on the wall. He nodded.

And the Warrior of the Gifted, a man, struck down the ancient Usurper.

Morning Star fell.

It was over.

Marja felt a gentle hand on her elbow. She turned, and as she did, Virginia pressed something into her hand. Smooth, polished, wood. Marja opened her hand to see a whistle in the shape of a bird lying in it. She smiled.

Turning back to face the King, she brought the whistle to her lips and sounded it.

As the King's forces with their fading light began to trudge back to the city and the wall, the birds started to arrive. Great flocks filled the air, migrants and sea birds, geese and ravens, sparrows and starlings, swallows and owls, doves and eagles, northern birds and southern; winging from the Isle of Bryllan and the mountains still to the east. They filled the air with the sound of wings and with their cries.

The King had come.

They had already been on their way.

Nicolas came up behind Marja and put his arms around his

wife and his children, and they watched in wonder as the ancient story Marja had told so many times around campfires came true.

An eagle flew low over them and dipped its wing in acknowledgment. Little Bear waved wildly. Marja and Nicolas looked at each other with a grin. Near them, Virginia was smiling, looking into the sky and seeing things no one else could—things just as wondrous.

The Ploughman climbed the wall and opened his arms to Libuse, who pressed herself close to him, and hand in hand, they knelt on the wall before the King. Others followed suit, Miracle and her archers, Maggie and Pat, and the villagers and Gypsies still climbing back up the wall, as the birds formed a single great flock all around them and swallowed the sky in wings and cries and living flight.

And the King looked on them all and smiled sadly.

His form jerked where he stood. His eyes fixed on them once more and then lost focus. His knees gave out, and he fell. Miracle caught him in her arms, eyes wide with shock at the arrow buried deeply in his back.

The Ploughman had seen it first, had risen, grabbed a bow from one of Miracle's archers, and loosed an arrow in the direction of attack before he had even been able to recognize the attacker. He now looked down the stairs of the wall at the man who lay dead on them, the guilty weapon still in his sunburned hands.

"No!" Rehtse wailed.

Harutek, prince of the Darkworld, was dead.

On the wall above him, the Gifted and their friends crowded around Miracle and the King. She was shaking her head, stroking his neck and forehead, groaning, "No, no, no . . ."

Virginia reached out a trembling hand and touched Miracle's. The Healer looked up at them.

"I can't help him," she said. "He is dead."

Virginia gasped. Rehtse laid a hand on her shoulder. "It is all dark," Virginia said. "Everything has gone dark."

20

A New Kind of Darkness

REHTSE FELL AT THE KING'S FEET, her voice choking out through a throat already nearly closed with tears. "Why?"

Virginia put her arms around Rehtse's shoulders and shook her head, her own tears falling. She wanted to give an answer. But there wasn't one. There just wasn't one. She could hear Rehtse's wailing, Maggie's soft weeping. Grief and fear and anger. More than that, she could hear the silence. Her own silence. The silence of the others. Shock.

And a question.

What now?

Another figure pressed in close, and a boy's Highland voice said, "Stray?" The voice quivered. But in a moment it firmed. "He said—he said things wouldn't be how we expect."

No one responded. Virginia heard the Ploughman lift his voice to the people gathered around them, and she remember-ed that there were others here besides the circle of the Gifted and their faithful lovers and friends. The villagers. The Gypsies. The remaining remnant of Pravik. And they needed leadership now. They needed hope.

"Do not be afraid," the Ploughman said. "The King has fallen, but so have our enemies. All is not lost. Go to your resting places in the city—we will prepare his body for burial. We will honour him as he should be honoured. He has given his life for us. That is not a reason to fear. It is a reason to be grateful. It is a reason to *live.*"

Virginia heard Rehtse's low moan and tightened her arms around the priestess's shoulders.

"What good is life if the King is dead?" Rehtse whispered.

* * *

The death of the King had changed things. They knew that more piercingly with every hour that passed.

The dungeon of Pravik Castle was dank, and Virginia imagined it was also dark. She had carefully descended four flights of stairs to reach it, and now she felt her way along the wall toward the sounds of breathing.

She paused when she knew she was in the presence of others. A torch was flickering on the wall near her hand, kept lit by the few who volunteered to guard down here.

"So your King is dead," Evelyn greeted her. "And now you know your own foolishness."

"He showed you mercy," Virginia answered quietly. Her answer was for Evelyn—but more, for the man imprisoned near her.

"You are better off without him," Evelyn said. "You are all better off without him. No more Morning Star, no more King. You can govern yourselves. That is why Harutek killed him. People will say Harutek was a martyr, you know. The real hero of this story. He has ushered in the age of men."

"Men are traitors," Virginia said. "That is what I have learned."

There was the sound of a man clearing his throat. "Why are you here?" Lord Robert asked.

Virginia hesitated. It was an answer she wasn't entirely certain of. Only, she'd been compelled to come and to speak with him. To make him see.

"Are you still seeking?" she asked.

He was caught off guard; his answer slow in coming. "I have always sought to know the other side of reality."

"As you should now know is not enough," Virginia snapped. "The other side of reality demands allegiance; it forces you to choose a side." She heard Undred shifting in his cell and sighed. "I came to tell you, then, that everything has changed. Reality has changed."

"What are you talking about?" Lord Robert asked.

"Since the King's death no one has seen the Earth Brethren," Virginia said. "Kieran, a child who relied on Tyrentyllith's life to give him life, is dying, and Miracle can do nothing for him. The Gifted are no more. I have seen nothing; Maggie sings nothing; Nicolas hears nothing, and his eyes are beginning to turn brown again."

She smiled sadly. "It was all in the King," she said. "Everything you sought. Even the Blackness was only a perversion of his power. And it's all dying now. The world is a shell. I do not know if it can last much longer."

She turned to go, and paused. "I came to tell you," she said. "Because I hoped that in the last age of this earth—however long it may continue—you would finally acknowledge the truth and honour him. That is all."

She passed out of the corridor, away from the prisoners. Their judgment was coming—the Ploughman could hardly leave them in the dungeon forever. They and the people of the Majesty, their leaders imprisoned on a level below this one, would have to answer for their crimes before the world ended.

Tears pricked at her eyes.

* * *

The throne room, still decked with bunks and shelves and the remnants of children's games, was now a house of the dead. Rehtse had embalmed the body, weeping all the while, and at last had pronounced the work finished and her life over. Virginia, in a panic, had gone after her to make sure she did not intend to kill herself.

"I am not sure what I intend," Rehtse reassured her, "but not that. I will exist. But I cannot live."

Now the Gifted haunted the room where the King's body lay, drawn to it and to each other. The people of the city, joined by others who had come since the battle to acknowledge the Ploughman as the only ruling power left in the Seventh World, came in processions three times a day to see the body, some to weep, some to marvel, and left when the Ploughman shut the doors on all but the inner circle.

Four days had passed. In that time it had become clear that, as Virginia had told Lord Robert, everything had changed. And yet nothing had—nothing visible. The world was a dying patient not yet showing its symptoms.

A cluster of city folk had arrived from Athrom that

morning, bowing and scraping and promising allegiance and restitution to the Ploughman. They brought news: Lucien Morel, the mad emperor, had drowned himself. The High Police had not come back to the city; rumour said Cratus had been killed by his own men. There was no one to take charge, no one to rule. Pravik was all there was left, and the people of the Seventh World, without anyone to reign over them, brought themselves to the Ploughman's feet.

"You know what they say," Pat said, seated on a bit of scaffolding in a corner of the throne room with her knees drawn up to her chin. The Ploughman looked up at her and waited.

"They say we should keep the body here, in this very room," Pat said. "Stories will grow around it. The people will come in yearly pilgrimages to see it. You can unite the Seventh World around the memory of what happened here and the bones of the King."

The Ploughman stared. After a moment he dropped his eyes. "And what will they remember?" he asked. "Power. They won't remember the light. They won't remember that he loved us. They will be afraid. Yes, they will unite, as they did under the Empire. For the same reasons." He shook his head. "I will do all I can to help stitch this world back together," he said. "And we will teach the people the truth about who they are, and about who he was. We will undo the Empire's lies as much as we can. But I cannot dishonour him by making a showpiece of his body."

"That will happen no matter where he is buried," Nicolas said. "Keep him here or bury him in the Hall of Kings, it will make little difference."

"Then we will not bury him in Pravik," the Ploughman said, standing. The answer he had been puzzling over for days was clear to him now. "We will take him away at night and give him to the sea."

They looked at each other. Miracle nodded slowly. "Yes," she said. "That he may belong to us all."

Virginia stared forward and said nothing. They could all see the gathering darkness in her face. The loss of her Gift was doing something to her, plunging her into greater blindness than she had ever known. She was growing distant from the others, and they a little afraid of her.

* * *

That night, Virginia dreamed.

It was not a dream as she'd known before her Gift vanished. It lacked clarity, lacked power, lacked light. It was hazy and confusing and full of grief and a strangled feeling like trying to break free from fear. But in it she saw the King opening doors. Letting prisoners out.

She awoke. The air was hot. It was still night, and the streets were silent.

She rose and wandered up the streets toward the castle, wishing that a breeze would come and cool her face and her tortured mind. Wishing with all her heart that she could hear the wind whispering or feel some presence in it. But no wind stirred. The muggy air was silent and dead.

She didn't know why her feet led her where they did. Perhaps because she had believed so hard in visions and dreams, had acted on them so many times before, that she could not help going to a place like one she had imagined in sleep. She descended to the deepest level of the dungeon, where she could hear the prisoners sleeping, snoring and stirring, the Majesty and all who had led the Darkworld in siding with Evelyn.

She was using the wall to feel her way, and her fingers fell on a ring of keys. They closed around it.

She felt oddly detached from herself as she wandered down the corridor and unlocked the doors one by one, pulling the first few open, listening to them squeal on rusted hinges. She heard the gasps and questions but did not answer them. Her feet took her up a flight of steps, and she stood in the same corridor she had visited before, but this time no torch flickered on the wall. She was alone.

Realization of what she was doing hit her, jolting her awake. She swallowed. She remembered the dream, hazy though it was. *The King opening doors. Letting the prisoners go free.* And suddenly she wondered why it mattered that they be locked up; what more harm they could possibly do. She thought of the King letting the High Police flee into the woods. The way he had unleashed his army to take vengeance on the Blackness but had driven the High Police away. He had spared men—all of them. He had been giving them all a second chance.

She set her jaw, shoved the key into the lock of the nearest cell, and yanked the door open. Silence answered her.

"Come out, laird," she said, her voice jarring in her own ears. "Come out and avail yourself of whatever second chance you can find."

She turned and opened Evelyn's cell as violently, and then

crossed the corridor to the door that barred Undred from freedom, and unlocked it, and pulled it open.

"There are no sides left!" she said. "Go and wander in this world, and when sides form, take one. Change your story, Undred; it's a new world, however long it may last."

She turned, angry tears running down her face now, and knew that Evelyn and Lord Robert were watching her. She held her head high. "I was one of the King's," she said. "Consider this his last gift to you. Now get yourselves gone. If the Ploughman finds you in the city I do not think he will show you mercy a moment longer."

* * *

"You did what?" the Ploughman's voice was shocked, angry. Virginia stood still before his seat on the throne, expressionless, with only her clenched fists to hint at emotion.

"I did as the dream bade me," she said.

"*Your* dream!" the Ploughman said. "Not a vision, not your Gift!"

"Grant me this one last pretending," Virginia said. "I don't know how not to respond to dreams."

Huss's voice was beseeching. "Has any real harm been done?" he asked. "They have fled the city. And the world is already gathering to your banner. Evelyn was hated wherever she went, and she is stripped of power now, nor is there any power left for her to tap into. She is as powerless as . . ."

". . . as we are," the Ploughman finished. He sighed. "No, no real harm has been done, except that some may see this as dissension among the rulers of Pravik."

"Then don't dissent," Huss said. "Declare it as an act of mercy from you. You have set them free just as you are allowing the old High Police to go home unmolested."

The Ploughman nodded. "It is best."

"We should not wait much longer," Maggie said. Her voice sounded ragged from grief. "To take the King's body from here. We need—we need to say good-bye. We all need to."

Virginia imagined that the Ploughman nodded. "I have a few details to take care of, and deputies to place in command. No word has gotten out of our intent. I think it is best that way. We can leave tomorrow night, under cover of darkness."

Virginia almost smiled at the irony. All was darkness to her now.

All would *always* be darkness.

* * *

When the throne room closed up for the evening on the next day, Nicolas and Michael brought a casket in through a back door, and Miracle and Marja helped to maneuver the body into it. Rehtse's embalming had worked to good effect, preserving him well, but the face that had shone with light and life seemed made of wax. It was still a young face, still looking much like the child Roland had called Stray.

The four stood for a long time, looking down on him, before they closed the casket. Michael and Miracle left at last.

"Leave me here?" Marja asked. "Go and see the children; they've been wanting you."

Nicolas kissed her and nodded, shutting her into the throne room with the casket. She drew a knife from her skirt and studied its smooth surface.

The night deepened, hours passing quickly by. A key turned in the lock, and the Ploughman entered, followed by Michael, Roland, and Nicolas. They stopped short and looked down at Marja and her work of art.

She had carved every inch of the casket with scenes of the battle. The style was an ancient one, unique to the Gypsies; the story was vivid and beautiful, from the star bursts and rainbows in the clouds, the Huntsmen and the Earth Brethren, to the shining warriors on the ground. And in the center of it all was a carving of the King, enveloped in light.

She smiled wearily up at them. "I know we are giving him to the sea," she said. "But not without ceremony."

As the men took up the casket, Marja sheathed her carving knife and went down to the courtyard to join the others. They had kept their plans a secret, and it was only the old inner circle that gathered now.

Professor Huss, Maggie, Pat, Mrs. Cook.

Virginia, Roland, Rehtse.

Michael O'Roarke and Miracle with Kieran, his flesh pale and withering.

Nicolas and Marja, and Peter the Pipe-Smoker with them.

The Ploughman and Libuse.

Fifteen, silent in mourning as they met together, remembering others who had once belonged to them. Jerome, the professor's apprentice. The farmers and soldiers of Pravik who had been slain by Evelyn. The Darkworld priests, and Caasi. The Major, Nicolas's uncle. Michael thought of Kris of the Mountains, his old friend from the far north of whose death he'd had word before all this happened, and of Shannon and Jack and Lilac and Stocky and all the others. His clann. His family.

The old members of the Council for Exploration Into Worlds Unseen, so significant still though they had been gone so long: Old Dan, John and Mary Davies, Lucas Barrington.

The Earth Brethren, absent since the moment the King had fallen.

The Shearim, whose voices only Nicolas remembered.

Their ghosts seemed to flicker beyond the edge of seeing, to accompany them silently as the men lifted the casket onto a two-wheeled cart pulled by Roland and Michael and began their procession—the long walk to bury the one who had united them all even before they knew it. Who still united them, the living and the dead, in some way they did not understand.

In the door of the courtyard, a tall shadow stood in their way. They halted. Virginia's heart stopped when he spoke, and she recognized the voice.

"I have no right," Lord Robert Sinclair said. "But tell me I may come with you, and I will be grateful."

"Come," Professor Huss said, not waiting for any of the leaders to speak. "Come. You have as much right to mourn as any of us."

* * *

They traveled east through the night, down the mountains toward the sea, into wild country where few villages were settled and where no eyes would see. They traveled all the next day, and on the seventh day after the King's death, they reached the coast and an abandoned fishing settlement the Ploughman had known as a boy. They found there what they were looking for: a longboat. It needed some patching, but they had come prepared. Michael and Lord Robert did the repairs while the others looked on. At last they pushed it out onto the sands where the water lapped at it.

Roland and the Ploughman carried the ornate coffin from the cart and laid it in the bottom of the boat. They had agreed to give the King to the sea and to the open sky, so they took off the lid of the coffin and sent it into the waves on its own. Roland nearly sobbed with surprise and grief—for an instant, the body in the coffin seemed to be that of the child he had known.

Ankle-deep in the water, Roland covered the body of the King in a cloak that was blood-red against the white planking of the ship and the pale interior of the coffin. The sea beyond was wild and tumultuous and shining with brilliant light.

Michael and Nicolas put their shoulders to the boat to push it out into the waves.

"Wait," Virginia said. The men held, and they all watched as she stumbled forward, into the surf, and found the boat with her hands. She followed its lines until she reached the place where the King lay, and pulling herself over the side, she leaned forward and kissed his forehead.

When she dropped back to the surf, they pushed the ship the rest of the way out until the waves took it and carried it out to sea.

Over the boat, white seabirds circled, calling a mournful cry.

21

In Him

THREE DAYS HAD PASSED. In a little tangle of trees up the beach, smoke blew across the ground from the remains of their campfire, driven by the breeze from off the sea. Fifteen of the mourners sat together, Lord Robert a ways from the others. Only Virginia was missing.

They knew they had to return to Pravik, but none had the heart.

Roland sat closest to the flames with an enormous leather-bound book in his lap. Professor Huss had insisted on bringing the books. Now he insisted that Roland read aloud from them. None protested. The books told old stories of the King, and in a way seemed to bring him back to them. They listened in silence, in tears, and in deep pondering.

"And this is the way Death came into the world," Roland read. "For Death is a stranger, and was not always among us. In the beginning every man was in the King, and in the King is life that does not end. But in the days before the Great War, when Morning Star had begun to lift himself up, he came to men and taught them that a world existed outside the King that was richer and fuller and would reward them with great power and wisdom. And fools that men are, they believed him."

Lord Robert looked away, through the twisting trees at the glistening blue sea beyond.

"And so they gathered together and enacted a rite to cut themselves away from the King," Roland read. "And in the same day two of them came to blows over who would lead them, and one fell and struck his head. On that same day he died, for he had not the King's life to preserve him, having cut himself away from it. So Death came into the Seventh World."

Miracle tightened her grip on Michael's hand. Both looked down at Kieran, who was leaning against Michael's shoulder. His dark hair was sticking to his pale face. His crippled leg had grown so bad that Michael had carried him much of the way from Pravik to the coast. They were not now sure he would ever return to the city. Miracle spent every night bowed over him, silently begging her old power to return. But it did not.

Roland read on. "When the King knew of the rite, he wept. But he swore that one day he would reverse what they had done. One day . . ."

His voice trailed away.

The King had come. But Death had taken him too, and "one day" would never come.

* * *

Virginia walked the shore alone. Waves washed up around her feet. She followed her instincts, not caring much whether she walked too long or too far, or whether she walked the wrong way and found herself in the depths of the sea.

Just ahead, she heard something scraping against the sand—wooden planking?

A hull?

Streaks of light crossed her vision. Grey planks. A single mast without a sail.

The longboat.

Her heart caught in her throat, and her vision grew stronger as she approached it. Something in her urged her to turn, to go back, not to look. Decay could only have set in. The sight could only be more heartrending now.

But something else urged her forward, and she nearly lost her footing in the slipping sand as she picked up her speed, picked up her skirts, ran to the ship. Breathless, she lifted herself above the side. The folds of a cloak lay draped over the side of the coffin.

Empty.

"Virginia."

She gasped and turned her head. Someone was standing on the shore, holding out his hand. For an instant she thought it was Roland—but the hair was golden, not dark; the eyes that smiled into hers were sea-green.

Slowly, she let herself down from the ship. Afraid to believe, Virginia waded out of the surf and walked up the shore.

He was still holding out his hand. Trembling, she reached forward and took it. His fingers tightened around hers. She felt spring in the air.

She dropped to one knee and closed her eyes. "My King," she said.

"Go tell the others," he said, and joy danced in his voice as it had so long ago, when first he had visited her on a hillside in the Highlands of Bryllan, before she had fled with Lord Robert from the High Police and entered a conflict with the Blackness that had lasted until ten days before. "Go tell them I am here; I am alive."

She hesitated, hating to pull herself away. He smiled. "Never fear; you haven't seen the last of me. Go now—they need to know. But be careful. You may have a little trouble finding the way."

She turned to obey, joy welling up so it threatened to cut off the breath from her lungs or burst the heart from her chest. She ran, and she could hear herself laughing and crying as she went.

She did have a little trouble finding the way. Sight was unwieldy here; she had always found her way along the shore by feeling and scent and sound; once or twice sight nearly threw her off. But it wasn't until she had reached the little camp in the woods that it occurred to her to wonder why she could still see.

Her eyes were bright when she stumbled into the camp. Rehtse looked up at her, and her own face lit with wonder and sudden hope.

"You can see?" she asked before Virginia had even caught her breath.

"He is here!" Virginia exclaimed. "He is alive! He waits on the beach—go to him, all of you; go!"

Roland dropped the book in his lap. "Who?" he asked.

"You know who!" Virginia burst out. "He is waiting for you, fools that ye are. Go."

"Virginia . . ." Rehtse said. "Are you sure?"

It was Kieran who stood next, and his eyes were shining like hers. Some colour had come back into his face. "She can *see*. It's a miracle. Who else could have done it?"

Libuse gasped in sudden joy, and all turned to look at her. She was looking at the Ploughman. His skin was glowing golden. His Gift had returned.

Maggie leaped to her feet. "The air is singing!" she shouted. "It's true!"

And she led them in running down the beach toward the place where Virginia had seen him. The figure of a young man stood there indeed, wind blowing in his golden hair, arms folded across his chest, and he laughed as they came running, running and tripping over their own feet until one by one, they reached the sand where he stood and dropped to their knees.

He looked beyond the kneeling crowd to one who hung back.

"Robert Sinclair!" he commanded.

Lord Robert's face convulsed as he tried to answer. Silent, he came closer and dropped slowly to his knees.

The King smiled. "That's better," he said.

Then he looked down at them all, and they lifted their faces in wordless response to the light of his eyes that embraced and filled them and made them whole.

"I told you all would not be as you expected," he said. "Roland reminded you of that when I died. I couldn't finish what I came to do without dying."

"I don't understand," the Ploughman said.

"I went to meet Death," the King said simply. "And I was stronger." He smiled again, and the air around them began to glitter. "I brought some back with me," he said. "I think you know them."

They gasped. Indeed—indeed they did. The forms taking shape in the glittering air were familiar—were beloved. Michael cried out. His clann was there. All he had lost—and his father, and his mother, and the generation the Order had killed. Maggie's eyes filled with tears as she reached out to Jerome, who looked at her as through a veil of light but did not reach back, and Mrs. Cook and Pat joined her in marveling as John and Mary Davies and Old Dan Seaton looked at them, eyes sparkling. Marja and Nicolas looked at each other, beaming with joy, as the Major grinned at them, and Nicolas's father behind him. The priests of the Darkworld were there, and Kris of the Mountains, and many others who had been lost.

Roland found himself facing a golden-haired man he seemed to know.

"Aneryn," he said.

"Yes," the King answered. "The first lion—the prophet whose spirit you share."

Virginia was smiling softly, regarding a figure in the light. "Hello, Grandfather," she said.

Slowly, the figures began to fade. Michael swallowed a lump in his throat, but the deep grief he had lived with every minute since losing his clann was gone, replaced by a healing sadness and joy too deep for words.

"Will we—" Maggie began.

"Yes," the King answered. "You will all be together again. Someday. When your work is finished."

"Our work?" the Ploughman asked.

"The work of turning this world to me," the King said.

"But you are here," Rehtse said. "You are coming to reign

in Pravik; surely there is little left for us to do."

Roland was shaking his head, and the King let him speak. "No," he said. "No, he's not staying. He's going away again. The old books—well, they don't exactly say it. But they hint at it. Even Aneryn's journal hints at it. Don't they?"

"They do," the King said.

"But why?" Rehtse burst out. "Why, when we have waited so long?"

The King pointed, and they turned their heads. His finger was pointed at Lord Robert, whose face reddened beneath his greying hair. "Because of him," the King said. "And all the Darkworlders who turned against me, and all the leaderless people in this world who are coming to Pravik to beg you to rule them. Morning Star and the hordes who became Blackness had their chances long ago. I came back to deal them a final blow. But I have no heart to deal that blow to men—not yet."

His voice softened. "One day I will. Time will run out for them too. But it has not run out yet. The Seventh World has been kept in darkness far too long. You—all of you—are light. And I am sending you back to Pravik to be light, and to spread light, as long as you live. After that you will come to me." He smiled. "You are in me now. Death cannot defeat you any longer."

He was beginning to fade.

"Will you be with us?" Virginia asked. "Even when we cannot see you?"

He smiled. "I have always been with you," he said.

Epilogue

Seventy years have gone by. I am very old.

Some ask who I am. I will never cease to marvel at how quickly men can forget—at how easily stories change, how easily they are twisted by those who would misuse them. But there is always a remnant now, always some who remember and faithfully pass the true tales down. Young men and women sit at my feet and learn of me. They call me the Prophet, though once I was simply called the Voice. Few remember me as Roland MacTavish, the boy whose only real Gift was that he knew the King.

The other Gifted are gone many years, passed into legend. Where once we were Six, only I am left. But those who believe in the King display snatches of the old glory and the Gifts. Some can still sing, can hear the songs, can see beyond the sky.

When I lay down to sleep, I think I can hear them whispering to me. They tell me that all will be well, that my journey is nearly ended. In my dreams, Virginia Ramsey still calls me a lion and tells me to roar all the louder, to roar until my dying breath, so that the Seventh World can't ever completely forget. The Ploughman tells me that it doesn't matter that his kingdom so soon scattered and broke into factions, because the true King will one day rule over it all.

And when I open my eyes, just before the physical world becomes solid before me, I often see the King smiling down on me.

So I wake, and I go and I tell others that he is here. For it is true. He is here, and he is coming. The prayer Rehtse taught us, that the young priests have turned into songs, is both prophecy and petition.

Your kingdom come, we pray.

Come soon.

THE SEVENTH WORLD TRILOGY

Worlds Unseen　　**Burning Light**　　**Coming Day**

For five hundred years the Seventh World has been ruled by a tyrannical empire—and the mysterious Order of the Spider that hides in its shadow. History and truth are deliberately buried, the beauty and treachery of the past remembered only by wandering Gypsies, persecuted scholars, and a few unusual seekers. But the past matters, as Maggie Sheffield soon finds out. It matters because its forces will soon return and claim lordship over her world, for good or evil.

The Seventh World Trilogy is an epic fantasy, beautiful, terrifying, pointing to the realities just beyond the world we see.

"An excellent read, solidly recommended for fantasy readers."

—Midwest Book Review

"A wonderfully realistic fantasy world. Recommended."

—Jill Williamson, Christy-Award-Winning Author of ***By Darkness Hid***

"Epic, beautiful, well-written fantasy that sings of truth."

—Rael, reader

Available everywhere online or special order from your local bookstore.

THE ONENESS CYCLE

Exile   **Hive**   **Attack**   **Renegade**   **Rise**

The supernatural entity called the Oneness holds the world together.
What happens if it falls apart?

In a world where the Oneness exists, nothing looks the same. Dead men walk. Demons prowl the air. Old friends peel back their mundane masks and prove as supernatural as angels. But after centuries of battling demons and the corrupting powers of the world, the Oneness is under a new threat—its greatest threat. Because this time, the threat comes from within.

Fast-paced contemporary fantasy.

*"Plot twists and lots of edge-of-your-seat action,
I had a hard time putting it down!"*

—Alexis

"Finally! The kind of fiction I've been waiting for my whole life!"

—Mercy Hope, FaithTalks.com

*"I sped through this short, fast-paced novel, pleased by the well-drawn characters and the surprising plot. Thomson has done a great job of portraying difficult emotional journeys . . .
Read it!"*

—Phyllis Wheeler, The Christian Fantasy Review

Available everywhere online or special order from your local bookstore.

TAERITH

When he rescues a young woman named Lilia from bandits, Taerith Romany is caught in a web of loyalties: Lilia is the future queen of a spoiled king, and though Taerith is not allowed to love her, neither he can bring himself to leave her without a friend. Their lives soon intertwine with the fiercely proud slave girl, Mirian, whose tragic past and wild beauty make her the target of the king's unscrupulous brother.

The king's rule is only a knife's edge from slipping—and when it does, all three will be put to the ultimate test. In a land of fog and fens, unicorns and wild men, Taerith stands at the crossroads of good and evil, where men are vanquished by their own obsessions or saved by faith in higher things.

"Devastatingly beautiful . . . I am amazed at every chapter how deeply you've caused us to care for these characters."

—Gabi

"Deeply satisfying." —Kapezia

"Rachel Starr Thomson is an artist, and every chapter of Taerith is like a painting . . . beautiful."

—Brittany Simmons

Available everywhere online or special order from your local bookstore.

ANGEL IN THE WOODS

Hawk is a would-be hero in search of a giant to kill or a maiden to save. The trouble is, when he finds them, there are forty-some maidens—and they call their giant "the Angel." Before he knows what's happening, Hawk is swept into the heart of a patchwork family and all of its mysteries, carried away by their camaraderie—and falling quickly in love.

But the outside world cannot be kept at bay forever. Suspecting the Giant of hiding a treasure, the wealthy and influential Widow Brawnlyn sets out to tear the family apart and bring the Giant to destruction any way she can. And her two principle weapons are Hawk—and the truth.

Caught between the terrible truths he discovers about the family's past and the unalterable fact that he has come to love them, Hawk must face his fears and overcome his flaws if he is to rescue the Angel in the woods.

> *"A beautiful tale of finding oneself, honor and heroism; a story I will not soon forget."*
>
> — Szoch

> *"The more I think about it, the more truth and beauty I find in the story."*
>
> —H. A. Titus

Available everywhere online or special order from your local bookstore.

LADY MOON

When Celine meets Tomas, they are in a cavern on the moon where she has been languishing for thirty days after being banished by her evil uncle for throwing a scrub brush at his head. Tomas is a charming and eccentric Immortal, hanging out on the moon because he's procrastinating his destiny—meeting, and defeating, Celine's uncle.

A pair of magic rings send them back to earth, where Celine insists on returning home and is promptly thrown into the dungeon. Her uncle, Ignus Umbria, is up to no good, and his latest caper threatens to devour the whole countryside. He doesn't want Celine getting in the way. More than that, he wants to force Tomas into a confrontation—and Tomas, who has fallen in love with Celine, cannot procrastinate any longer.

Lady Moon is a fast-paced, humorous adventure in a world populated by mad magicians, walking rosebushes, thieving scullery maids, and other improbable things. And of course, the most improbable—and magical—thing of all: true love.

"Celine's sarcastic 'languishing' immediately put me in mind of Patricia C. Wrede's Dealing with Dragons series—a fairy tale that gently makes fun of the usual fairy tale tropes. And once again, Rachel Starr Thomson doesn't disappoint."

— H. A. Titus

"Funny and quirky fantasy."

Available everywhere online.

REAP THE WHIRLWIND

Beren is a city in constant unrest: ruled by a ruthless upper class and harried by a band of rebels who want change. Its one certainty is that the two sides do not, and will not, meet.

But children know little of sides or politics, and Anna and Kyara— a princess and a peasant girl—let their chance meeting grow into a deep friendship. Until the day Kyara's family is slaughtered by Anna's people, and the friendship comes to an abrupt end.

Years later, Kyara is a rebel—bitter, hard, and violent. Anna's efforts to fight the political system she belongs to avail little. Neither is a child anymore—but neither has ever forgotten the power of their long-ago friendship. When a secret plot brings the rebellion to a fiery head, both young women know it is too late to save the land they love.

But is it too late to save each other?

Available everywhere online.